A Lady
in Irons

Sara Powter

Bible Quotes from King James Version

ISBN:9780645110784
(Paperback edition)

Pacific Wanderland Publications
ABN 99 768 734 831

Kincumber NSW 2251

saragpowter@gmail.com
www.sarapowter.com.au

1st edition 2023 printed by Kindle, an Amazon Company;
available on Kindle Unlimited & KDP

Cover Painting by Joseph Lycett
https://www.sl.nsw.gov.au/collection-items/north-view-sydney-new-south-wales-taken-north-shore-1822-j-l-delt

Cover inset
"Reflective mood"
Gustave Jean Jacquet
(French, 1846-1909)
In Public Domain

Front-page inset
Eliza Hunter - the Author's Grandmother

Acknowledgement of Country:
In the spirit of reconciliation, I acknowledge the Traditional Custodians of country throughout Australia and their connections to land, sea and community. We pay our respect to their Elders, past and present, and extend that respect to all Aboriginal and Torres Strait Islander peoples today.

Australian Historical Novels
(All stand-alone books)

A First Fleet Story (1788)
Gentle Annie Soames *(2024)*

The Hunter to Macquarie Collection (1795-1822)
When Upon Life's Billows (2025)
Saddler's Song (2025)
Tuppence to Pass (2025)
His Majesty's Pageboy (2025
Far From the Whispering Sheoaks (2026)
Bound Down in Iron Chains (2026)

Unlikely Convict Ladies Trilogy (1792-1840s)
Dancing to her Own Tune
(co-authored by Sheila Hunter & Sara Powter)
Amelia's Tears
A Lady in Irons

The Lockleys of Parramatta (1800-1900)
Hands Upon the Anvil
Out Where the Brolgas Dance
Diamonds in the Dirt
The Earl's Shadow
Once a Jolly Swagman
Jonty's Journey

The Convict Birthstain Collection (1830s-1840s)
No More, My Love
The Vine Weaver
Scotch at The Rocks
Waiting at the Sliprails
Convict Shadows of the Past
In Defence of Her Honour
I Can't Stop Tomorrow *(2024)*
Madeline's Boy *(2024)*
Jam or Marmalade for Tea *(2025)*

Shelia Hunter's
Australian Colonial Trilogy (1840s-1850s)
Mattie
Ricky
The Heather to the Hawkesbury

Dedication and Thanks

Inspired by the hardships our convict ancestors coped with. Susannah Riley left England pregnant and never saw her husband or son again. She delivered her baby, John, near Rio de Janeiro. Amazingly, John went on to become one of the first policemen in Australia and later married another convict, Catherine Lattimore née Hinds. She had left her husband in England, although he may have been dead by then.

Elizabeth Fry and her twenty thousand followers
did everything they could
for those who found themselves in gaols around the Empire.
Eliza Darling sought her advice before heading to Australia.

Lachlan and Elizabeth Macquarie
Arrived in the country just after the Rum Rebellion.
The country was in turmoil.
Lachlan set out to change the colony of New South Wales and
constructed the bones of the recognisable
country we know and love today.
Many of the hundreds of buildings he ordered built
are those we hold dear.
Macquarie tried to govern justly and
favoured the underdogs and fought for their rights.
He is fondly termed the
'Father of the Nation'

Other Governors followed in his footsteps
and sought to improve the lot of the convict.
Both Lachlan Macquarie and Ralph Darling had to return to London to face
enquiries, both were exonerated.

I say thanks to all those who came before us,
to those who served their time in chains
And to those convicts in our families who did survive.

Thanks also to my husband, Stephen
who faithfully reads all my stories and gives me feedback.
To Roby Aiken who is my punctuation angel.
And to Noreen Robertson, my Beta reader for the final read through.

Table of Contents

*Grammar and language in this book are
Australian English spelling.*

KEY

~ - Time passing in same locality

- Different locality/country

Chapter 1 Before the Anguish

"*I*t was my wedding day, and I felt like a princess. Mother and I had spent weeks making the new gown for the special event. Phil's eyes shone as I walked down the aisle of the small church towards him. Oh, Mary, I was so happy." Katy sniffed back tears.

Her friend Mary knew her sadness all too well. She also had been married briefly. Her husband, George, had been sent off to war only weeks after their wedding and was killed in France. He had intended to sell his commission but was recalled before he had a chance. When on their honeymoon, George was blissfully unaware of anything but Mary. Then, unexpectedly, they receive the news that he had inherited the title from his father, Malcolm. He returned home only to be called up days later. Only months later, he too was dead and would never know they had a son, Malcolm George Miles, to carry on the name. Her eight-month-old son was the 7th Earl of Milesdowne. George would never see the smiling face of the perfect child feeding at her breast. She tickled Colin's cheek to keep him sucking.

Katy sat watching her friend and her babe. Her hands fell to her swollen stomach; her child would arrive soon. She wept as, at least in her womb, the child was safe, as was she. Thoughts of Phillip made her cry again. She had given birth to a son last year, but he had never even taken a breath. He, too, had been perfect. Then, only months ago, Phillip had been killed in a hunting accident when his gun exploded. He would also never see his child. She was an expectant widow, and with both her parents now dead, she was all but alone. Her husband's brother, Eustace, had all but shunned her. If this child was a girl, they would need someplace to live; if it was a boy, he would inherit the title instead of Phil's brother. She would live in fear for her son's life, such was Eustace's hatred of her. If it were a son, he would need protection. At least for the next couple of months, she would have access to money and a roof over their head. She had visited her friend, Mary Miles, as she insisted on being called, when she heard of Mary's husband's death. She had stayed for a month. Now, Katy wanted to be with Mary with Phil away, then when the news came through about Phillip's accident and consequent death, she ended up staying for months as she had not wished to return to the empty Buckland House in the nearby town.

Phil had been hunting with friends and Katy's cousin, Jeramy. They had both died in the explosion. Now Katy was a widow. Tears slid unnoticed down her cheeks as she stared unseeing out the window. Mary reached out and took her hand.

At least Mary had a son and a place to live. Katy knew their house was entailed. All now hung on the child's gender. Fear encased her. "I suppose I will have to go to Uncle Percy if the baby is a girl."

Mary looked stunned, "Oh no, Katy, I want you to come here. You will be company for me, and we can bring up the children together." Mary attempted to engage Katy and lighten the mood. "You were Matron of Honour at our wedding Katy. Do you remember the dreadful pink gown Mother chose for me to wear? You looked so pretty in your pastel blue. It matched your eyes perfectly." Mary was desperate to take Katy's mind off the tragedy, knowing it was already impossible.

Katy nodded; those blue eyes were now swimming with tears.

Mary knew the pain. She knew the emptiness. Over twelve months of being alone had not made it any easier. Katy's grief was raw. She was not even able to go to her husband's funeral. Phil was gone, and she'd not even said goodbye. He'd left on the spur of the moment invitation while she was shopping. He'd left a loving note and had intended only to be gone for a few days with his cousin and Sir Phillip Princhester, another distant relation. They went to his hunting box Mulberry House in Warwickshire. What brought on the accident, they will never understand. When she heard that Jeramy had died in the blast too, Katy crumpled to the ground. Jeramy was the only remaining son of the Duke of Cheatham, Katy's Uncle Percy. His eldest son, Peregrin, had died the same day as her father. A fire had killed them both. Katy had loved Perry from when she was a young girl. When the stables had caught fire, both her father and Perry had rushed in to save the stud horses. They both died. Jeramy, or Jem as she called him, was as close as she had to a brother. When young, she had trailed around after Perry and Jem often.

When word arrived about Phil's death, she had withdrawn, and Mary had refused to let her leave. Prostrated by the grief of the two men Katy held most dear, Mary worried about her. That had been some five months ago. The funeral was over and her husband was buried. She had no reason to return home. So she stayed. While Phil was off enjoying himself, Katy had initially come to share the good news of her interesting condition.

Sir Phillip Princhester had the decency to visit on his way home from the double funeral; however, Katy had not been well enough to see him. Then he too had died soon after leaving Mary's house. His horse had bolted, and now she would never get answers. It was a triple tragedy for the family. Her husband had been named after his older cousin, Sir Phillip. They were good friends and often in each other's company; Jeramy was often in tow. Sir Phillip left a wife, Jane, and their young son, John.

Jeramy had not been married and was the sole heir to his father's Dukedom since the fire. She had hoped to visit them after her child was born, maybe even live with Uncle Percy and Aunt Meg again. If the child was a girl, she knew she would have no choice.

Before returning to Buckland Manor, Katy planned to stop at Phil's cousin's home quickly, Princhester Court in Aylesford, some twenty minutes south of Mary, as one of their boundaries adjoined, so she was nearby. She had always liked Jane, and they could grieve together. Shaking off her blue mood, she again gave her attention to Mary.

After another week with Mary, Katy knew it was time to return home before she became too ungainly to travel at all. Eustace had demanded that the child be born at Harrington Hall in Warwickshire. She would have preferred to stay at their London house. Katy had compromised and said they would travel to the lesser home, Buckland Manor, in Great Buckland, reasonably close to Mary. It had been where she and Phil had spent their honeymoon and where she had been when Phil had left, so it had happy memories. She knew Eustace would be arriving there soon in anticipation of the birth.

Mary begged Katy to allow her to accompany her on the short trip. Mary had family coming to stay, so Katy said no, she would leave.

Katy knew Mary's half-brother, Justin, was coming for a visit. He was a minister in Aylesford, and now and then, he took a night off and came to stay with Mary and Colm. They were the only family close by.

Although she knew him well, Katy still felt she was intruding. She waved her friend farewell. Promising she would visit as soon as she could.

~

A week slid by with no message other than acknowledging her arrival, a month passed, and then another.

Mary had not heard from Katy since she arrived back at Buckland Manor, and she knew the baby should have been born by now. She had her carriage brought around and planned on visiting Katy with Colm. It was soon to be his first birthday, and she had no wish to be alone anyway.

Colm loved the carriage and sat gazing out the window as they sped over the miles.

Mary was quite anxious about her friend; Katy typically wrote weekly. The silence from Katy was not usual.

The carriage pulled into the driveway of the Elizabethan house of

Buckland Manor. She had seen the magnificent building with its vine-covered triple front and circular driveway many times before, but today the place looked different. The topiary-trimmed bushes were all gone, the hedges had been cut back to almost skeletons, and the vines stripped from the building. Mary was shocked as Katy loved the ball bushes that Phil had planted. She had chuckled that she felt like playing boules with them. The carriage pulled up at the door, and a liveried footman hurried to the carriage.

"Good afternoon, Lady Mary," he offered his arm for her to descend.

"Hello, Tom. Is Lady Katy around? Has the child been born?" Mary asked breezily.

A look of fear crossed the young footman's face. He'd come with Katy for her extended visit, and he was a lovely young man. His sister Anne was Katy's maid. His eyes shifted away from her face. "Yes, my Lady, but the Countess of Leatherbrooke has gone." His voice had dropped so only she could hear his reply.

"She had a girl?" Mary whispered in reply.

Tom nodded assent.

"Oh no! Where is she?" Mary questioned.

He was unable to reply as Eustace had arrived.

"Countess Milesdowne, welcome to my ever so humble abode, Buckland Manor; I look forward to welcoming you to Harrington Hall one day." His over-effusive bow was, as always, overdone.

Mary felt dirty even touching his hand. "I have come to visit Lady Catherine, knowing that she will be unable to travel after her confinement." There was no way she would let on what Tom had said to her. She glimpsed relief on Tom's face as he stood behind Eustace.

Tom had blanched, and Mary knew something had occurred, something horrible. Eustace's hand was still clutching Mary's, and she tried to pull her hand away. He held tight, and his hands were clammy. "Oh, my dear Lady Mary, Catherine birthed a girl child and left soon afterwards. I fear she was not well on her departure."

Mary saw a sleazy grin sweep momentarily across his face. So, he'd got the title and banished Katy. It's what her friend had said he'd do. He was so callous and unfeeling. "May I ask her direction?" Colm was wiggling in her arms. It gave her an excuse to pull her hand from Eustace's. His palm was sweaty with lust, yet he'd not even invited her inside. They were still standing on the front steps.

He licked his lips lustfully; he liked Mary and knew her to be a widow. "She left without direction, my Lady." He waved his hand in the air, "Gone in a puff, once the child was delivered. She just said something about going to Percy's." Eustace's snort was almost of glee.

"Ahh, well then, I shall not stay. Pass on my regards if Lady Catherine returns, please." Mary turned on her heel.

Tom was at her side to assist her into the carriage. Tom whispered,

"Stop at the gatehouse. I'll get away as soon as I can, m'lady."

"Okay, Tom." As she sat down, she said loudly, "Thank you, Thomas."

The carriage drove off and was soon out of sight of those watching. As the carriage crossed the stone bridge, Mary rapped on the roof.

The coachman pulled up and opened the sliding communication door to hear instructions. He then drove on until they were hidden behind the gatehouse, he pulled off the road, and they waited.

Mary knew it could take some time for Tom to arrive, so she gave Colm a dry crust for him to chew on.

After thirty minutes or so, Tom appeared from the back of the building. He was puffed. "I'm so sorry Lady Mary, I couldn't get away until my break."

"Tom, thank you for coming anyway. Now, please tell me what has occurred?" Mary was now sitting on a log not far from the carriage.

Tom stood as he spoke. "Oh, m'lady, Sir Eustace stood hovering outside the bedroom door as Lady Katy gave birth. Within minutes of the news that the child was female, he issued orders for her removal. Lord Eustace was now the Earl and insisted on being called Earl Eustace within minutes of the birth. He was determined that all should know his new status." Tom continued, "He did allow Katy one night of rest before he cast her out. And m'lady, I mean cast her out. Having just given birth, she was in a weakened state, as you can imagine. He had my sister, Annie, pack a small valise, and then he had Lady Katy and the babe taken to the side boundary and deposited by the road. Lady Katy was given no money and had no means of paying for a conveyance. As soon as I heard, I sent my father to search the boundary. Sir Eustace's groom refused to say where he'd deposited them." Tom's eyes were swimming with angry tears. "Father couldn't find her. She had just gone. He searched every day for a week, but we found no trace of her. Even Lord Percy came and hunted too. Father had told me Lord Percy stayed with friends down in Maidstone."

Tom blew his nose. "I'm sorry, m'lady, Father would have brought her to you, but she has vanished. No one has seen her. And no one has found a body either." He met Mary's now overflowing eyes with his sad look. "I'm so very sorry, m'lady. It's been weeks, and there has been no word of her."

"The child, it was well?" Mary asked, concerned at what had occurred. There was little she could do that had not already been done.

"She seemed to be. Lady Katy named her Mary after you, but my sister said she was already calling her baby Mia." Tom looked skyward. "I pray for her daily, m'lady, but I don't know if God is listening."

Mary placed a caring hand on his arm. "He is Tom; we just can't see His plan." Mary was desperately fearful for her best friend. Why had she not come to her?

Tom helped her to board the carriage.

Mary turned to him. "Tom, if you or Annie should need a position should things here become untenable, then come to me, please. I shall find you a position at our place. I shall not give up looking for her though, be assured of that."

"Thank you, m'lady, we may appear sooner than you expect," Tom said. He knew Annie had already said she wanted to leave. His father was already in the new Earl's bad books.

~

Ten miles away, in a small, thatched cottage, a young woman lay on a hay-filled mattress. She felt movement at her side and felt gentle hands uncover her breast and place a child at her side. Her eyes slowly opened as she felt the child suckle. She remembered waking earlier to the same feeling but was so weak she'd fallen asleep again. It was just daylight now, and she opened her eyes to see who was tending her so gently. She had vague memories of being held up and drink being held to her lips. She had swallowed greedily. Once her thirst was slaked, she looked around.

She blinked and tried to focus her eyes. The view that met her made her gasp. A man was bending over her. She could not see clearly, but something about him didn't look right. He looked hazy or melted. His face looked blurred, but the rest of the room did not. He saw the action and hurriedly tried to cover his cheek. She frowned; no, her eyes were focusing; it was his cheek that looked odd. Without thinking, she put her hand up to touch his face.

He grabbed it halfway, then let it go. She felt the skin that had looked blurred. "Burns. Oh, how sad!"

Her empathy was for him when it was she who had been so ill. It made him start. "You have been ill. Your child is well, but you have had a fever. You need to drink more." He gently stroked her forehead. His voice was well-modulated and caring and strangely familiar. He also had a slightly familiar accent which she could not place.

She managed to utter, "Thank you," before concentrating on the activity required of her. She tucked the tiny babe closer to her breast. The child continued to feed. "Mia, where are we, do you think?" she asked, addressing the child.

The kindly voice answered from the other side of the tiny cottage. "I found you collapsed by the side of the road. Not knowing who you were, I placed you in the borrowed wagon I had with me and brought you here. You have been very unwell. Ma'am, that was some three weeks ago. The only food I had for the child was from you. You stirred only to drink and when I needed to change your bedding. I'm sorry, but I have no one to assist me, so I have needed to attend to you myself." He was profoundly embarrassed.

"Oh!" She suddenly realised that she was naked and only covered by a sheet. She was sitting on a towel, with another tucked between her legs, and she realised what that was for. She blushed with embarrassment. However, the place was spotlessly clean, and the bedding smelled like soap. She still had not asked his name. Tiredness overwhelmed her, and she again dozed off, the child still feeding.

The next time she woke, the sun was streaming in the window, and the cottage was better lit. She turned her head and saw the man sitting at a table writing. Because of the size of the cabin, she was able to watch him work. He was literate? Her gasp startled him, and he came to her side. In the sunlight, she could see that only half of his face was scarred. The other half looked as it had in her childhood memory.

She frowned; surely, she was dreaming. A face that should not be there turned to her. "Perry?" It could not be so; he was dead. He'd died in a fire some ten years before.

He was stunned. She knew his name. "Who are you?" he asked more abruptly than he intended. Who would know him? And by his family nickname. He wracked his brain, unable to think of who she was.

"I'm Catherine White, your cousin, little Katy. But you're dead; you died the night that father died. I was only young, but I remember that night as if it were yesterday. I lost heart for years that night, as did Mother. We lost two of our loved ones. Mother was never the same. But how are you alive?" Katy sniffed with the emotions that were careering through her.

"Katy? Are you Katy? You were a little girl" The look of horror in his eyes made her weep again. He recoiled in horror.

Rejected again, she nodded on the pillow. "I was fourteen, Perry, you are ten years older than I." She pulled her arm from under the sheet and held it out to him. "Perry, have you no idea how I felt when I heard you had died? Call it a young girl's crush, but I idolised you then. I wanted to die too." A tear slid down her cheek.

His quick movement showed shock; however, he asked, "Only then?" The unburned side of his face smiled. He took the hand she held out to him and came and sat beside her. "Katy, I need to know what happened to you, but first, let me get you a covering so you can sit up. Do you mind wearing one of my old shirts? Your gown is not suitable for being in bed."

"No, of course not. That would be wonderful." She waited until his back was turned, and she struggled to sit up. After lying for so long, she immediately felt dizzy.

He heard her soft groan and was beside her, assisting her to rise. He eased the shirt on and turned his back while she buttoned it up.

"Thank you, Perry," she uttered, exhausted by the small activity.

Now she was covered; he turned back and helped make her comfortable. The mattress was, as she suspected, just straw-filled. She noticed a long hollow in the straw beside her, and it was obviously where he'd been sleeping.

"Do you feel up to talking?" he asked with concern.

She nodded. "And you?"

"Yes, I shall tell you my story, but this…" he ran his hand over his melted cheek, "…makes people fearful."

She reached out and cupped his face in both hands. "You are the same gentle cousin I loved dearly as a child. I wept more for you than for father back then!"

It was his turn to gasp. He'd hidden from everyone for nigh on ten years. His nanny had nursed him back to health, but the scars were deeper than his cheek. Each person who saw him shied away from him. His honey-gold eyes were sad. "My parents did not know if I would live. For the first weeks, I was unresponsive. My nanny treated me with honey and oatmeal poultices and gave me willow bark, thyme, and belladonna for the pain. My hands healed, as did my nose. My cheek had melted, though. When I was well enough, I left. I told Father not to look for me. He was to make Jeramy his heir."

The anxious look on her face surprised him.

"What, Katy? Is Jeramy misbehaving?" Perry thought of his younger spoilt brother.

"Perry, Jem died six months ago in the same gun accident that took my husband. Phil's gun exploded, and they were both killed." She tried to break the news gently, but there was no easy way to do it. "Perry, you are still the heir to the dukedom. Jeramy refused to take the title; now I know why." Her voice was soft, and he held her gaze.

"No, oh no! That is not what I wanted. So father is still alive?" He knew him to be, but Perry had not imagined that this woman he had found could know anything about him, yet she was revealing his private family things. He was in shock at her news about his beloved younger brother's death. He knew his father would be distraught. It could be why Justin was late with the six-monthly money. He should have brought it last week. Maybe it would not come.

"Uncle Percy is alive, Perry, but he is not well. Jeramy's death took a lot out of him. Your mother is strong and holding everything together. I don't know how, but Aunt Meg remained strong for us all. They brought the news of the disaster themselves. Not wanting me to be alone when I heard. When I saw my friend Mary's half-brother was with them, I knew something bad had occurred." She had retaken hold of his hand. "Perry, you need to contact them, and you need to go home."

Perry looked dismayed. "I can't Katy, look at me; they all run from me. If I go out, it's at night when they can't see me. For me to have been out in the daytime when I found you was because I needed food." He swallowed. "You have been unresponsive for so long, and this, in a way, was good. I could minister to your needs and assist you in nursing the child. She is tiny but otherwise well." Perry still had not heard her story; he would wait until she was ready. He'd gleaned that she was now the widow of someone named Phil.

"But for you, I would be dead, Perry. Come close, and I shall tell you of the past ten years." She patted the straw mattress beside her, and he sat near her as she told her story. She'd already told him of Phil's death, but not of Eustace's treatment of her. "Perry, on the day I gave birth to Mia, Eustace, Phil's younger brother, told me he was going to throw me out. I thought I would have some days' or weeks' grace, but the next day I was loaded into a carriage and taken to the estate boundary and literally offloaded in the middle of nowhere with just a valise and the child. I remember little, as I was still bleeding heavily from the birth so, I presume I collapsed." She looked over to her sleeping daughter. "How I did not fall on Mia, I do not know."

Perry filled in the gaps. "Katy, you must have placed her on the bag first. She was safely wrapped in her blanket and asleep. As you guessed, you had collapsed, and so I collected you both and brought you home. It was about to start raining, and there was no one around on that road, and there was unlikely to be any passing traffic." Perry looked over at the sleeping baby. He saw Katy look over at her too. "She's fine Katy." He looked back at the lady sitting in his bed. "Katy, I needed to strip you as you had bled through your gown. I realised that you had recently given birth, but not how recently. I'm sorry, but the only place I had to place you was on my mattress. I lay beside you and held you as you shivered. I had no other way to keep you warm. A few days later, my friend brought a blanket." He could not say that it was known she was with him, but he had confessed he had found someone.

Katy smiled. "If it had been any other man, I would not have trusted them. However Perry, I know of your care for me as a child. You did what you needed to do, do not think more about it." Katy looked somewhat embarrassed too.

"That's easier said than done, Katy. I have compromised you just by keeping you here." Perry was undecided about what he should do about it. He admired the well-rounded figure as he cared for her, but he had not abused her. His need for a woman was strong, and her body, with all its rounded feminine curves was delectable. More than once, he found he had to walk away and leave her wash unfinished. He had not dared to touch her with such desires surging in him. Oh, how he desired her. To find out she was his cousin and that she'd had a youthful passion for him lifted his spirits somewhat. Maybe they could have a future together. He hoped she might at least think about it. One thing he knew and that was he needed to contact his father; he had to go back to him. He had not known she had lived there after the fire.

Over the next week, Katy was able to rise and was soon walking around the cottage. However, that first night Katy was shivering so badly he had joined her on the straw bed. Perry objected when she insisted; they still shared the mattress. He again took her in his arms and held her until she warmed. They had fallen asleep, still entwined.

~

A week passed, then two.

The cousins' relationship blurred one day when Perry walked in just after she finished nursing the baby. Her eyes fell on the sleeping child she had just placed in her straw bed; she felt a tear land on her hand. As she raised her head to him as he entered, his heart lurched. He was by her side in an instant. "Oh, my Katy, what is wrong? How can I help?" Her tear-filled eyes overwhelmed him.

She was now dressed in her clean gown. Her situation had suddenly hit her; she had nowhere to go and no money. She turned to Perry and wept, drawing great comfort in the strength of his arms around her. No explanation was needed.

When her sobs quieted, she lifted her face to his and drew his down to her. "Perry, hold me close; kiss me, please," she whispered.

He did. He kissed her as he'd wished to do for so long. They had lain together each night. The longing to touch her had grown in him with every evening. To kiss her, at her invitation, was beyond his dreams. She knew his story and accepted him, scars and all. He did not mind her touching his face and looking upon his puckered and melted cheek. She even made him a rosehip and geranium oil ointment that eased the tightness of the scars. For once, they did not pain.

She wrapped her arms tightly around his neck. Her responses to his craving need were nearly his undoing. The soft whimper of the child broke through, and he raised his head. "Katy, oh dearest Katy, I'm sorry. I should not have done that." He had tried to release her, but she stood with her arms still holding him.

Her glowing smile gave him comfort. "I did not notice that it was forced upon me, Perry." She once again reached up to kiss him; she said softly, "Call it my girlish dreams come true. I have wanted you to do that for a long, long time."

He bent his head again and accepted the invitation her reddened lips gave. Both stood drinking in the embrace. Perry knew that he should push her away, but to let her go was almost beyond his power. He had seen her naked body and washed her from head to toe. He adored every inch of her well-rounded post-birth body. He was about to take everything she offered when he heard the wheels of a cart arriving. He groaned loudly. He knew it was the minister, as he was the only person who came calling. His father sent Perry a six-monthly allowance to the minister, who then delivered it. He had not told his family where he was but had sent word of how to contact him. Why they had not let him know of Jeramy's death was puzzling.

Perry knew he had but a minute, but he pulled away from Katy, unlocking her arms from his neck. "Katy, will you marry me? I trust you as you trust me. I don't know if I would have stopped, but a minister is about to come in, and I wish to ask him to call Banns."

"Yes, Perry, I'd be honoured." Her heart gave a leap. She had been thrown out of the ancestral heritage she'd lived in with her husband. She had hoped to stay there until they died in their old age. She had married Phil for love and mourned when he died. But now she had nowhere else to go except to Perry's parents. Perry would not only give her a roof over her head but would return the love she had always had for him. Her childhood crush had grown in the last weeks. She had wanted to reach out and touch him as she lay enfolded in his arms each night. She had wished he had shown he cared as much as she did. Now he had. She reinforced her reply, "Yes, Perry, I'd be delighted." She had just answered when there was a knock at the door.

Perry had time to adjust his clothing before ushering in the minister.

Katy gasped as she saw who it was. "Justin, what are you doing here?" she stammered.

The minister gazed from one face to the other. "Katy, what the heck are you doing here with Perry?"

Katy and Justin had become close friends through Mary many years before. The minister was none other than Mary's half-brother. Their titled father had at least acknowledged the son he had fathered with a maid. He had paid for Justin's training as a minister, then had virtually abandoned him.

They were still standing just inside the doorway of the tiny cabin.

Justin had visited frequently over the years. He knew just how small it was. "Mary has been frantic," Justin finally admitted. "Katy, she knows what happened. Your footman, young Tom, told her. They looked everywhere for you, but you had vanished." Perry had told him he had found an unconscious woman and child; Justin knew he was nursing her back to health; he'd even brought Perry an extra blanket. Justin had no idea it was Katy. He thought Perry had meant an older woman. He had not put one and one together. Justin thought Perry would have recognised his own cousin. He hadn't.

Katy was glowing; she met his look with a smile, "And here I was, safe with my cousin Perry all this time." She smiled at both stunned men.

Perry interrupted them. "Katy, you know Justin? How?" Perry looked incredulous. The extremely handsome, young, unmarried minister was enough to make any girl's heart flutter.

Katy smiled at Perry's question. "Yes, Justin's half-sister, Mary, is my best friend. We all but grew up together, didn't we, Justin?" As she looked up at Perry's face, a flash of almost jealousy flared across his face. Wondering how to salve his pride, she just reached out and interlaced her fingers with his. She saw the surprise on Justin's face but no change on Perry's. So she stepped closer and slid her arm around him instead. "Justin, Perry just proposed, and I said yes. So would you do the honours for us?"

Her statement snapped Perry out of his sulks. He looked from one face to the other, realising theirs was just friendship. "Please, Justin? Do you know any bishops? Can we get a Special Licence?"

"Actually, Perry, Bishop James is visiting for services. I have left him asleep, as he's staying for Evensong. If you return with me now, he may even do the service himself this afternoon."

Perry looked down at Katy with his eyebrows raised questioningly.

She nodded. "Can we? Really, that quickly?"

"Why not?" Perry gave her a swift kiss. His heart was singing; he didn't even care that Justin was watching.

"I have a suggestion, Perry. I know Katy will approve, as will Mary, for she is desperately lonely. As I said, she knows what happened. She's rattling around in that big house all alone, and she's missing you so much Katy." He looked around at the minute cabin. "Perry, I know you don't wish to be seen, but if you live with Mary, you will actually be seen by very few people. Her house is not a hub of activity. Will you think about it?"

Katy was clinging to his arm. "Perry? It's not that I don't want to stay here with you, but I have to think of Mia." She turned to him and stroked his cheek. "Once people know the real you, they will see past this. Don't let these scars hide who you are. I love you, the real you that I have known all my life."

Justin watched the turmoil on his friend's face.

Finally, Perry raised his head and looked at his friend. "Justin, can you ask Mary?"

The baby murmured, and Katy went to her.

As Katy attended to the baby and her needs, Perry spoke softly to Justin. In a low voice, Perry said, "We will come and meet the bishop with you. Hopefully, he will marry us today, but if not, Katy must go to Mary tonight; I'll stay with you until we can marry, if that's all right. I've not touched Katy yet, Justin, but I don't trust myself to stay as strong. I only kissed her for the first time today." Perry looked over at her. "As you know, I only have one mattress. I can't have her here any longer if we're not married. I care for her too much to besmirch her that way."

Justin agreed and smiled. Katy had also attracted him for many years, but he knew that she would never look at him that way as he was illegitimate. He had pined for her when much younger, but then she married Phil. Now she was in love with Perry, he wanted her happiness. One day the right woman would be there for him. However, it would not be the Countess of Leatherbrooke.

Chapter 2 Too Good to be True

*J*ustin watched his two friends. Perry's battle with physical emotions was one he knew too well. He had yet to meet a woman who would overlook the unfortunate situation of his birth on the wrong side of the blankets. Now he was grown; he understood the battle his father had; however, he had not succumbed. At least the Earl had not entirely abandoned his mother when he got her with child. His older half-brother, David, was heir to the title, and Justin liked him. The two got along well when boys. They were only six months apart in age; David would make a good Earl. Justin, however, had nothing.

Justin had initially been jealous until one year, when he was twenty, he was summoned for a family meeting.

His jealousy evaporated when he saw the palaver that his brother had to deal with. Not to mention coping with their father's perfidy. Justin realised he was content in the Ministry. His faith had grown since he met a Quaker lady named Elizabeth Fry. What really annoyed him was that he knew his father was still philandering, regardless of what all his family said. He smiled when he thought of his words to his father over the issue. He knew that he was born when his father was in his twenties, but for him to still be chasing the maids at fifty didn't impress him. In fact, it made him angry, so much so that he challenged his father. It was at that family meeting that he discovered that he had three half-sisters, each by other women, and all the mothers had been maids in his father's house. His sisters were not invited to the meeting, but David told him that he was one of six half-brothers that he knew about. He knew his father had been married three times. He had never met either of his elder sisters from the first marriage, Mary from the second marriage and David from the third one. All the boys were underage, so they were still at various schools. When he had also heard there was another child on the way.

Justin was furious. He had challenged his father's morals after that family meeting. But his words slid off his father like water off a duck's back. Earl Weedhame just didn't care. He thought it was hilarious that he had his sons train for the Ministry. Justin had looked after his mother as best he could. She had only been seventeen when he was born. His father had given them a tiny cottage with a yard and an allowance. She had recently married and moved away. He liked his new stepfather, but he was glad that this left him free to move on with his own life.

Justin looked back at his friends. He said, "Katy, feed the baby; then we will leave. I'll wait outside. Perry, pack her valise, will you, just in case. In either situation, Katy won't be staying here again. You had better pack your things while you're at it. I have the cart and can take you both to the rectory with all your possessions." He turned and stepped outside.

Perry waited until the door shut; he walked over to Katy and squatted beside her as she fed the baby. "Are you sure, Katy? You don't wish to back out?"

Her smile was reassuring. "No, Perry, I could imagine nothing nicer. This way, I get to keep the three people I love most together." She leaned over and kissed him. "I can't believe I can do this, Perry."

"You have no idea how much I have wished to touch you, my sweet. Washing you would sometimes take hours as I would need to stop and walk away." The look of delight on his face made her heart race. Seeing her smile, he said, "Oh, Katy, really? Are you sure? I don't wish for you to regret your decision."

Mia was squashed a little between them as he drew Katy close to him.

"I won't, Perry. Ever!" She was over the moon. She returned his kisses, then left him to pack as she fed Mia.

~

Perry packed her bag. He had nothing to put his own clothing into, so when she had finished, he placed his possessions, including the Bible he had been reading, on the bed and folded everything into the blankets they had slept on. He would not need the household goods. He looked around the cottage that had been home for nearly nine years.

During most of those years, Justin had been his only friend. He had found Perry sitting at the back of the church soon after he'd arrived. It had been an Evensong and one of Justin's first services. Perry sat with his head down, waiting for everyone to leave. It was the only time he could go to church. He had not been at the church for long, for it took a year for Perry even to brave a night-time service. Perry liked what he heard in this man's sermons. It was like balm to his hurting soul.

Justin had waited until everyone had left, then went and sat next to the man in the back seat.

Perry always sat on the side with his scarred cheek closest to the wall. Then if someone saw him, he looked almost normal from that side. Justin had sat beside him until he was ready to talk. He only had to turn his face for Justin to understand his reticence to socialise. Words had been unnecessary. Justin's compassion, rather than pity, was what Perry needed.

Over the years, their bond of friendship had grown. Perry knew of a half-sister, Mary. Justin had told him about her reasonably recent loss. Perry didn't realise it was the same Mary that Katy now spoke about. If they could live with her and he could also provide for Katy and Mia, he would do it for them. From what Justin had told him, her house was huge.

Just an hour after Justin arrived, Perry assisted Katy onto the front seat of the cart. He handed Mia up to her, then threw her valise and his bundle onto the back of the vehicle and turned back to lock the door but stopped; he had no need to return. He pulled the door shut, leaving it for some other person if needed. He then jumped up to sit behind them. He was thankful that it was a cool day as he could wrap a scarf around his face and over his head. He pulled his hat down low on that side.

Justin called, "Gee up," to the lazy horse and set off for the rectory.

Katy reached back and took Perry's hand. "Are you all right, Perry?"

"Yes, Katy, from today, my life changes. But am I nervous? You bet!" Perry knew that from today there was no turning back. He had to re-enter life and the world from which he'd fled.

Justin had known of the presence of an ill lady in Perry's cottage as he had come to retrieve his cart shortly after Perry had found her. Neither knew who she was. Justin didn't even look at her. They had discussed the situation and figured she must have been a peasant. Justin asked around, but no one had been reported missing.

Perry knew that merely her presence there had already compromised her reputation. But she couldn't go to Justin as he lived alone too, and there was no hospital nearby. For him to find that she was his third cousin. They shared a great-grandfather along with the previous Duke, Julian. Then to fall in love with her was an unexpected blessing.

He released her hand after they hit a big hole in the road. They all needed to hold on. Hopefully, they would be married in a couple of hours. Then he could kiss her till his heart's content, not to mention that he would be permitted to gaze on her delightful curves once more. Only this time, he would not need to stop when the desire arose in him. Even the thought of that made those few hours torturous. He tried hard to turn his mind from what awaited them.

The trip to the rectory seemed to take forever.

Perry wanted, no, he needed, to be out of the public eye, but he knew he could hide no longer. Katy needed him to overcome his fears. The cream she made him was already helping with the scars pulling. Each application eased the puckered skin.

Perry knew he also needed to contact his father. Jeramy's death would have hit him hard. He released a long sigh; yes, his hiding days were over. At least he would not be alone. With Katy beside him, he could conquer his anxieties.

The rectory finally came into sight, and Justin let them off at the front door. "Go into my office Perry and wait there. It's the second door on the right. I'll take this boy around the back and be right in." Perry had been there before on the night Justin found him. He had offered him a bed and a bath. Justin had known of the cottage and arranged for him to live there. It belonged to a local Viscount, but the land was fallow. Justin waited until they were offloaded. Katy had Mia in her arms, and Perry had their scant luggage under his arm.

The housekeeper opened the door for the couple and ushered them into the office. She was obviously used to strangers at the door. She greeted them as though they were long-lost friends. She didn't even gasp when she saw his face.

Perry carefully placed their luggage on the floor and took Mia in his arms. She was asleep, and he gently lay her on the settee near the window. Once settled, he turned to Katy. "Katy, are you really sure you want to go through with this? I have no reluctance, but I need you to be certain. I know I have said this before, but once we're married, I'll not back out of my vows. They are a lifelong commitment for me."

"Yes, Perry, of course, I'm serious." She lifted her hand again and stroked his cheek. "And pity has nothing to do with it, nor does the fact I have nowhere else to go. I would have gone to Mary anyway. So that's where we're heading now. Only I hope now I will arrive with a husband." She stepped closer to Perry, hoping he would repeat his kiss. She wished he would declare his love for her.

He almost did. "Then, in that case, let's get married for I find that I want you very near me. Very near, my beloved!" He drew her into his arms. Their passionate embrace overwhelmed his resolve not to touch her.

They were oblivious to the door when it opened some minutes later. Catching them still in each other's arms, the Bishop and Justin stood watching. Finally, Justin cleared his throat. That sound finally broke through their actions, and they paused their occupation. Rather than pull apart, Perry kept her clasped in his arms. She hid her face in his shoulder.

Justin met his smiling eyes. "I think we need to get you two married quickly. Follow me, and we'll use the private chapel here. Mia can stay here as we won't be long. Mrs Henderson can keep watch over her while we get ready then join us later." The housekeeper had arrived behind the two clergymen.

Katy's cheeks were flaming with embarrassment. Being caught kissing someone who was not yet her husband was bad enough; when you're caught by two clergymen, one of whom is near the top of the ecclesiastical tree, she felt like shrinking into the floor.

Perry would not let go of her hand. His heart was singing, and he grinned. In the last six weeks, she had become his motivation for living. His life now had a purpose. It had taken nursing her back to health for him to realise how selfish he'd become. His past nine years had been totally self-centred. Caring for a newborn baby and a sick woman had taken him well out of that safe place and peaceful sanctuary, yet, they had already become his responsibility. He wanted to care for them always. For Katy to want him in her life was amazing. He would not let go of her for anything. He had yet to declare his love for her fully, but that could wait until they were private. She was now more precious to him than his own life. He bent and gave her another swift kiss.

Justin saw. Smiling, he said teasingly, "Come on, both of you. Let's get you married. We've already filled out the paperwork, as I know the details for you both."

The Bishop performed the small ceremony with Justin and Mrs Henderson as witnesses. As Mia was still asleep, Mrs Henderson came in just as the short ceremony started.

Now they were married, Perry and Katy were man and wife. Katy was Katy White again.

~

The small group returned to the office. Katy arrived with her new husband just as Mia woke for a napkin change and a feed.

Perry picked up the wet child and changed her rapidly.

Justin was in awe that Perry knew what to do. "How the heck did you learn to do that?"

Perry smiled and continued to prepare the baby for her dinner. "I was thrown in the deep end, Justin. Years ago, I'd seen Nanny do it for my aunt's children but never had to do it myself, and I took note of the one Mia had on when she arrived. The wet ones are easy, but the others... Well, they are not too good on the stomach." His grin twisted the scars on his cheek. For once, he didn't care if someone saw him.

Katy was amazed that he was so comfortable cuddling and bouncing the now-crying child. "I had three weeks when it was 'cope, or she died'. When I realised that, she became my focus." He bent and kissed the top of her head. Her huge blue eyes focused on his face. She nearly let out another cry, her face screwed up, but before she made a sound, he slipped his finger into her mouth. "See, I'm learning all sorts of new tricks." His eyes crossed to Katy, "But Katy, I can't feed her. Justin, is there somewhere my wife can feed the infant?" The grin at saying the words delighted both Katy and Justin.

Justin again called in the housekeeper, and Katy followed her with the softly whinging baby.

Justin's groom had asked the Bishop if he could borrow his carriage. When he explained the reason why, the Bishop suggested that his own coachman take them to Mary's house later that afternoon. He directed that Justin's groom be sent ahead with a message. She would need a warning that she was getting long-term house guests.

Justin did just that. His groom left to ride with a hastily scribbled letter, and he would return with the empty carriage.

~

By five o'clock, they were nearing Mary's house. Inside the carriage, Katy snuggled up to Perry. "I can't believe we are married."

Perry was equally stunned. "I can't believe you wanted to marry me. I'm finding my morale is quite puffed up in consequence," he chuckled and then gave her a deliciously long kiss. Breaking from her grasp, he said somewhat breathlessly, "I look forward to continuing what we were doing when Justin interrupted us if you're still willing."

"I'm more than willing, husband mine." Thankfully, when Justin arrived, she had been dressed in her gown. She had customarily pottered around the cottage in Perry's shirt with the sleeves well rolled up, her legs showing up to her thighs. "Perry, I realise now how hard it must have been for me walking around in just your shirt. I did not realise; I just didn't think."

"Trust me when I say I enjoyed it greatly, my dear. I shall enjoy investigating the rest of you now you are awake. I will be able to touch you guilt-free." He was slowly and evocatively caressing her hand. He was tracing hearts on her palm, then ever so gently stroking the silky skin on the back of her wrist. The action was so sensual he had absolutely no idea how he was making her feel.

Katy would have answered him, but they were pulling up at the front steps of Mary's house on the outskirts of Aylesford. She wished to crawl into his lap and deepen the kisses he occasionally gave her. Instead, she gave him a quick kiss and whispered, "Soon, husband mine, very soon."

His soft groan was reply enough for her.

~

Perry was still fearful of people's reaction to his melted cheek. It had taken wise words from Katy to make him realise that many people carried wounds of one sort or another; only his scars were visible, theirs were not. Both Katy and Mary had experienced broken hearts, and Katy had one of rejection too. She had very nearly died from that experience.

If Justin had not loaned Perry his cart that day, Katy may well have been dead before he'd gone back and collected it. God incidents, he called them. He only ever borrowed it every few months to get to the market.

Since finding her, he had prayed often, especially over those first three weeks. It was the first time Perry had prayed seriously for years. He often had read his Bible as it was all he had to read, but he had seldom prayed more than what he called 'shooting prayers.' He felt God was far away from him. He had felt abandoned and unloved, but he kept shooting God prayers when he had no idea what to do. For years, Perry had no one else to turn to. He had much time to think, pray and worry. The latter, he relegated as not worth doing, so he concentrated on praying and believing.

All the time Katy was with him, Perry had no idea who she was. By the time she woke, he was so in love with her, he could hardly breathe without some thought of her. Washing her while she was so ill had become both a trial and a delight. Holding her while she fed the baby, he could gaze upon her voluptuous form. Her breasts full of life-giving milk were so rounded and curvy. He craved to caress them, but he had not laid a hand upon her unnecessarily. One day he pulled himself up as he realised he was invading her privacy. He covered her up while she fed the child. The babe's head was all that showed.

As a child, he had seen his nanny when she cuddled one of his aunt's children after the wet nurse had finished. She had gently held the child over her shoulder and burped it. It had spat down her back and made him chuckle. How he remembered what to do amazed him. Now, these two people were his delightful responsibility forever. He now had the right to protect them, care for them and love them for all time. With all that going through his head as they drove, he was now willing to let Mary and the staff see his burns. He stood tall. Yes, they would look, but Katy and Mia needed him to be there, to be strong and to be fearless. For them, he would do what he could to be the husband Katy needed. That was what he would now learn to be. He shook away the cobwebs and concentrated.

Mary was waiting for them, and she was almost bouncing from one foot to the other. She had given instructions for the best guest suite to be prepared moments after receiving Justin's note.

Now Katy was introducing him. "Mary, this is my third cousin, Peregrin, but he's known as Perry. Mary dear, he is also my new husband. Bishop James has just married us." Katy greeted her best friend with a kiss and a hug.

Mary's warm welcome was all that Katy could have wished for. Mary embraced Katy with a giant bear hug. "I went to visit you at your home as I'd not heard about the birth. That slime, Eustace, boasted that not only was he now the Earl of Leatherbrooke but said 'you had left in a puff of smoke,' were his exact words. However, your footman, Tom, told me what had occurred and how they had all gone looking for you. They hunted for weeks, but by then, they were looking for your body. Oh, and they are both coming here to work from next week." Mary saw a look of surprise on Katy's face.

Mary had not exclaimed in dismay when she saw Perry's cheek. She turned and greeted Perry. However, he saw empathy in her eyes. Although she saw his scar, she ignored it. She saw him as someone who loved her friend Katy. Soon she was in his arms, and he found he was also being hugged. She looked up and said, "Thank you for saving her and for marrying her too. Now Eustace has no authority over her. Come in, Come in!" She turned and led the way inside.

"See?" Katy said as she walked past her husband.

The look on Perry's face was laughable. "Yes, yes, all right." He knew that her comment was related to the fear of what people would say about his cheek. He had not realised that their marriage was also protecting Katy from Eustace. He smiled when he thought about Mary's lack of horror. Evidently, she had noticed his burns, but he could easily cope with her reaction. He smiled and followed his wife and stepdaughter inside. No, from now on, Mia would just be his daughter. He may not be her blood father, but he had only missed one day of her life. She would be his little girl, someone to love and protect.

They were welcomed to Milesdowne Court by Mary's housekeeper and shown their rooms. Mary left them alone for a while before dinner. Perry managed to keep from stripping all of Katy's clothes from her the moment the door closed. However, he found that very hard to do. Especially when she stepped into his arms and pressed those, oh so delightful curves against him as they kissed.

~

Some hours later, they eventually retired to their room for the night; Katy had little embarrassment in asking Perry to undo her gown. It pooled to the floor before he gathered it up and threw it over a chair. He was unsure of what to do next. He felt like ravishing her, but he dithered.

Katy saw his hesitation and started undoing his buttons. His excitement at what was before him was evident to her, but she realised that his hesitation was more of ignorance than anything else. Soon his clothing pooled into a heap on the floor beside her remaining garments, and he stood admiring her rounded curves he had so lovingly washed. "Oh Katy, my love, you have no idea how hard it has been not to touch you as I have desired. To say I have lusted after your curvaceous body is an understatement."

Katy explained a few things to him. "Perry, even if we had wanted to do anything earlier, I needed to wait at least six weeks after Mia was born. She is now that old, and I'm ready for you." She saw a look of confusion cross his face. "I was still bleeding until last week, my love. However, it has now stopped. We can be together in every way." She reached out for him and drew him close.

He scooped her up and carried her to the sizeable four-post bed. They chuckled when they compared it to the straw mattress on the floor. He was about to say something when she gently put her fingers on his lips, "I love you Perry, and not just for saving me, but for you." Katy slid her hands over his back and pulled him close to her. She ran her hands over his muscular torso, sending thrills through him.

Perry remained silent as his lips were occupied with hers. He was as nervous as all heck. She did not know that this was his first time with a woman. For it to be with his wife was so special. He hoped nature would take over because he had not been taught anything.

His hesitation must have shown as Katy guided him in what to do. She gave loving instructions on how to pleasure her. He would learn and do anything she wanted to, but he would love her until the day he died and he told her so. He discovered that Katy was as willing to sate her desires as he was. He was even more surprised that this occurred as often as he wished, and Katy normally instigated it.

He was fearful that his physical needs occurred more often than he thought she would like. A raised eyebrow or a nod of the head throughout the day was enough to make excuses to retire to their bedroom. In front of Mary, they were the picture of discretion. Neither touching nor embracing lest they make it hard for her.

~

They had been living with Mary for two months when one morning, Katy woke and needed to use the chamber pot. She felt so ill that she had just made it to a basin. As Katy vomited, she smiled. She rinsed her mouth with the delicious lemon water Mary had in each room. She had been through this twice before; she knew she was with-child again. She had wondered when she missed her courses last month, but she was still feeding Mia and thought nothing of it. She turned and looked at her still-sleeping husband. Their enjoyment of their physical union was mutual and frequent, actually far more than just regular. Perry had obviously not been with anyone before, or if so, then not in the years since the fire. She and Phil had enjoyed that side of marriage, and she was not afraid to show Perry that she now also enjoyed her couplings with him. She showed him many ways and positions.

He discovered that her need for him was as frequent as he was for her. They also rarely waited for it to be night-time or even in bed. They had both discovered the joys of the split drawer undergarments she wore and the use of the buttoned flap in his trousers. The chaise lounge in the spacious dressing room was used not just for changing one's clothing. Their attire meant that neither had to disrobe should the desire overtake them, which it often did. For her to now be able to tell him that she was carrying his child was wonderful.

His father, Percy, Duke of Cheatham, had been in contact and even come with his mother for an extended visit some two weeks after they had married. They had all commiserated together with the loss of both Jeramy and Phil. Percy had also apologised to Perry that his allowance had been late that month. In his grief, it had been overlooked. He had wished to write, but he had not known what to say.

Like himself, Justin had presumed that Perry must have been an ill-begotten son of the Duke. He didn't know him to be an Earl. That had only been revealed to him on the cart ride to get married.

Uncle Percy, as Katy knew, had reiterated that Perry would succeed him as Duke.

Perry held his words until they were alone in their room. "I can't, Katy; I can't do it," he said as he drew her into his arms once they had got into bed that night.

"You can, Perry, and I'll be there with you. You were born to this. We don't have to do all the social things, but you will be good. You will understand the hurts people have."

A flash of anger crossed his face. "I wasn't born to it, and you know that well. It was only when dirty old Duke Julian died that Father inherited the title. The dirty old man sired many sons, only one of them legitimate. I don't want to be the Earl of Collingsford, let alone the Duke; I don't want to have a title at all; it's why I'm just simply Perry White, nothing more, nothing less." Perry was anxious, as was to be expected of him.

Katy drew him close, "I promise you, I will be with you, my love. We will do this together." Katy responded to his statement with a kiss.

"You will be beside me?" he asked, eventually needing reassurance like a child.

"I will, with God's help, I will," Katy assured him again. The love she felt for this man sometimes overwhelmed her. She found it hard to believe that she had found two such wonderful men in her life. Phil, she still mourned, but Perry understood her occasional waves of melancholy.

~

Katy was now carrying Perry's child. She sat on the edge of their bed with her hands on her stomach in silent wonderment. They were very unfashionable and slept curled up together each night.

Mia was kept in a cot in their dressing room. She would now need to move to the nursery with Colm, and her own nanny, Nanny Grimes, to care for her soon. Colm had his own nanny, Nanny Barnes. Katy decided she would suggest that today. Mia was now sleeping through the night, so they moved her to the nursery. She was already sitting up at nearly four months old, so the nursery would be better for her as she became more mobile. She would be starting on solids soon too.

Perry had employed a nanny for Mia soon after they arrived. His father had suggested one when he came on that first visit. She was a competent young woman of nearly thirty. She was excited to look after the adorable little girl as the last family had four boys. All the boys were now under their tutor and no longer needed a nanny. She was sad to leave, but the youngest was six and the oldest eleven. When Perry's father had written to his friend, Charles, Duke of Gracemere, and asked if he knew of a suitable person as a nanny for his new granddaughter, Charles suggested Nanny Grimes.

Nanny Barnes was older and was thrilled to have a younger nanny to teach, and she was willing to learn from her.

Katy was still sitting on the side of their bed when she felt Perry's hand slide lovingly around her naked waist. She lay back and rolled into his arms. Her bout of illness had passed.

Perry knew in an instant that something was diverting her attention. The smell emanating from the basin assailed his nostrils. "Katy, are you unwell?"

"Nothing that won't pass, but it will take some time," Katy smiled knowingly.

"How long, love? A day, a week?" Perry was wondering if her flow had returned. He'd seen no sign of it.

"No sweetheart, longer." Her beatific smile was reassuring.

"Weeks?" he asked. He was getting concerned now.

"No darling, longer; I'm thinking about seven months." She fluttered her eyelids, then reached out and took his hand, placing it on her stomach.

"Noooo! Are you carrying my child? But it's so early after Mia," he said in disbelief. They discussed the unlikelihood of her falling with-child while feeding, but it was not impossible.

She nodded, almost giggling. "Well, I thought we'd had enough practise. If it's a boy, you will have your own heir, Perry."

When Nanny Grimes heard there was to be a second child, she asked for a young foundling maid named Lucy to assist her. She had heard she was looking for work and liked her well enough.

Perry was delighted and quickly said yes.

Annie had taken care of Mary and Katy as neither needed a full-time maid as Annie and her brother, Tom, had also joined the household.

~

The happy months turned into happy years.

Jeramy Peregrin arrived; he was also known as Jem after the uncle he would never meet. He had arrived early, just ten months after Mia's birth. He was joined by a sister, Louisa Jane, two years later.

Katy was surprised that Perry had chosen to name their daughter after Mary, as her middle name was Louise rather than Catherine after her. However, he had given her Katy's middle name, Jane. Katy was more than somewhat hurt but remained silent. Hopefully, they will have more children. They now made frequent visits to Uncle Percy's castle, but as Perry hated the palaver at the magnificent Ducal castle in Warwickshire, they never stayed long. A few weeks at a time and then the week-long trip back home.

During one of the first visits, his father had filled Perry in about more discoveries regarding the previous occupant, the odious Duke Julian. They knew he had been a notorious philanderer, but not to the extent he had been. As the current Duke, Percy had spent years assisting as many of the abused female staff as possible. Perry knew most of what had occurred, as did his mother, but they had hidden the extent of the situation from Katy.

~

The companionship of the four grew. This included Justin, a frequent visitor, spending his day off with them as often as he could.

In the afternoons, Perry often sat and read exciting stories from the newspapers. One thing which interested them all was the news from the new colony of New South Wales. There were stories about bushrangers; others were stories about convict issues. Once there was a story about wives being sold in a marketplace.

This article made Justin so angry about those people defiling the sanctity of marriage. Perry read of ships going back and forth and how many convicts were sent. Some papers transcribed letters sent from Sydney Cove, and they described the utter squalor and cruelty of the convicts in irons. Upon reading one paper, Perry announced, "Katy did you know that the legal currency is rum over there, and these has been a military coup over it?"

Another day included a story about marriages again. Reverend Samuel Marsden was doing batch marriages from the gaol. Justin tried to find out more, but there was no further information.

They sat and discussed the various articles covering the annulment of marriages for convicts. This amazed them all. Mary and Justin were quite vocal that it could not be legal, but Perry and Katy were not quite so sure. However, if the government said it was lawful, it must be. There were conditions; the convict had to be sentenced to a term of seven years or more and not be allowed to return to England. A marriage could be considered annulled if this were the case.

Justin said he would investigate and discovered that this was the fact in some cases. All were equally horrified. Justin also had introduced Perry and Katy to a lady and her brother, who were interested in assisting prisoners throughout England. He had met her when she visited the local courthouse.

Elizabeth Fry and Katy had met a few times since doing other charity work. They had become friends. Katy often sorted through the children's clothing and donated old or excess items to her for the gaols. Life was delightfully busy with all the children and great fun.

~

They had been living with Mary for some five years when Katy realised she was expecting their third child. She had not yet told Perry her news and went in search of him one morning. He had risen early as usual, for he had taken to heading out for a long morning walk in the quiet of the day. He could stretch his long legs with few people seeing him. He still hid himself as much as possible and left the town visits to Justin to accompany the ladies. Colm, Mia and Jem would often accompany him on his morning walks.

Katy heard voices coming from the library. As usual, she entered without knocking, only to find Mary weeping in her husband's arms. They were not kissing, but Mary had her arms around his neck and was crying on his shoulder. He was holding her tightly. They were so occupied that they did not hear her entry. She left, closing the door quietly behind her. She made it to her room before the tears came.

Perry had moved into his own room soon after Louisa's birth. He visited regularly but rarely stayed the entire night now. He said it was so she could sleep better. Now, she wondered. She now sat on the side of the bed, considering what she would do.

Perry loved Mary; Katy still loved Perry, and Mary would not wish to hurt Katy.

Reeling in shock, Katy decided that she would leave and not take the children. If her plan worked, they would be better off with Perry than where she intended to go.

Katy sat and wrote a long letter to Perry. Tears smudged the writing, but she did not replace the sheet. Then she set about putting her plan into action. Getting through breakfast would be challenging, but she would do it because of her love for Perry. She knew he could not and would not leave her, but she would do it for him. She loved him that much.

She tugged at the bell pull and waited. She asked Annie for an old carpetbag to be brought to her room as she had some clothing to give to charity. It would be nice to have some clothing, even if only for a few days, not that she would be allowed even to keep that in prison.

They had sat discussing the convicts in New South Wales only days before. All had been horrified when they read about the annulment of marriages in the new colony. This is what she planned. She would disappear and then write to Perry to free him. Once their marriage had been annulled, Perry and Mary could then marry. She didn't think about its legalities; she hurt too much.

Her heart was breaking, but she was determined to free him so he could be happy. She needed to leave before he realised that she was with-child again. Her morning sickness had not yet started in earnest. He would once again become all care and concern once he knew. She would not stand for such hypocrisy.

He had come to her last night, and she had not realised it would be for the last time.

She had fallen asleep in his arms, hoping that he would stay, but when she woke, she was once again alone and the bed cold.

She packed the small bag and tucked it under her bed. Then walked downstairs as though nothing had happened. Her heart was not just broken; it was smashed. She was determined to put on a brave face. She had yet to get through breakfast. Taking a deep breath, she entered the dining room. She would find it hard to look him in the face at breakfast. Both were sitting awaiting her and greeted her as though nothing had occurred. Perry rose and pulled out the chair for her as he always did.

Mary had asked him to sit at the head of the table years ago. So he took his place with Mary on his right and Katy on his left. Breakfast was then served. She was ill with nerves but managed a compote of fruit and some oats. She knew she needed sustenance, even if only for the health of the child she carried. She kept up some banal chatter while they ate. She had no recollection of the conversations they had discussed.

Breakfast was over; they each voiced their plans for the day ahead.

Katy announced that she had arranged to visit some sick parishioners for Justin. She occasionally did this, and they were not surprised at her outing. Perry had some estate books to finish, and Mary wanted to redecorate a hat. Thus sorted, Katy wanted to say goodbye to Perry without realising what she was about to do. So, as they left the breakfast room, she held him back and said, "Darling one, we have not had a chance to say good morning." She turned and walked into his arms.

Their kiss was all she wished.

She pulled from his arms slightly, stroked his burnt cheek and told him of her undying love. She then walked out of his life. Again, she made it to her room before the tears fell.

Chapter 3 Stolen lives

*K*aty asked for the carriage to be brought around. She had sent her bag down with her maid, and it was now in the vehicle tucked under the seat. She told the driver to take her to the church. Once out of sight, she tapped on the roof and changed her destination. Instead of going to Justin in Chatham, she directed him to take her to Maidstone church. From there, she could put her plan into action. She knew the markets were on in the town, but she'd not visited them for many years. The driver was directed to stop at the church gate. She said she was being driven home by another friend and for the carriage to leave. The driver was concerned but followed her orders. She stood watching the departing vehicle. Once it was out of sight, she turned from the church gate and headed for the marketplace. She knew that whatever she stole had to be worth a few shillings but not much more. Only then would she be transported, not killed. With her heart in her mouth, she entered the packed street. The morning rush was over, but many people were still haggling for their produce.

She fingered some fruit and purchased an apple; she bit into it. The red colouring on the outside belied the bitter, unripe fruit. It was representative of her life. It had looked so rosy on the outside until she discovered the betrayal of those she loved. Walking on further, she spied what she sought. A well-dressed lady had a table full of exquisite hand-embroidered handkerchiefs. Katy picked up one and carefully inspected it. Placing it back on the table, she picked up another one and quite obviously placed it in her handbag. The dice were now cast; her arrest was a foregone conclusion. She had seen a constable walking towards her as she tucked the kerchief into her bag. She was duly arrested, and she gave her name as Kate Harrison, but for some reason, it was recorded as Cate Parry. She knew she could not use her name of White, but this was close enough to her previous married name. Her new and unpleasant life was just about to start. She was not wrong.

She was dragged into the courthouse and placed in the lock-up below. Many other women were in the cell, and the stench was overwhelming. The privy was an uncovered bucket that was almost full. She clutched her valise close to her chest, she didn't know why, but she knew that it would not be long before her possessions were rifled and probably purloined. She had a small purse of coins and a locket with paintings of her children in it. She now understood why Perry had chosen not to include himself in the artwork. Mia was on one side, and Jem and Louisa on the other. Katy tucked it down her dress. She did not care for her clothing, but losing her locket would break her heart.

It took a month for her case to be heard in court. She pleaded guilty and hoped that she would be transported. After a month in the squalor of the overcrowded cell, she was now as dirty as the other women. Rather than try to clean herself, she did the opposite. She wished to be incarcerated, and if she were too clean, she might inspire lenience. She did not want that.

She was transported to the Kent Assizes. The judge's gavel fell with the words, "Guilty, sentence seven years in New South Wales." She breathed a sigh of relief. She knew she was not supposed to speak, but she lifted her head, thanked the judge, and even curtsied to him. Her wish was fulfilled. Perry would soon be free to marry Mary, and her children would be safe. She stifled a sob as she was led back to her cell. Now to wait.

It took weeks for her to be transferred to Newgate Prison in London. The Kent cells were luxurious compared to Newgate. All the women were herded together in two large cells and, in full view of the male prisoners. The only way to use the privy out of their prying eyes was to go to the back of the room. She stood back and let the other women fight for the meagre rations their few coins purchased. Before entering prison, she had no idea she had to pay for her own food in gaol. By now, she had made friends with some other women, Amelia and Catherine and a teenage girl named Emily. After so many weeks, her condition was just beginning to show. She had lost much weight already as food was scarce, but a warder ensured the expectant women were given extra slops or gruel.

In Newgate Prison, she was almost discovered on her first day there when her friend Elizabeth Fry came for a visit. It was actually to the charity work that Perry had expected her to head on the morning she had left him. Katy kept her head down and her back to Elizabeth, but she wasn't quick enough. Because they had met through Justin and had become friends. Both had a passion for helping destitute women; for Betsy to be here was a surprise, for she had never spoken of visiting prisons. Katy moved as far away from her as she could, keeping her head down. She had seen Betsy glance at her but looked away.

About an hour later, Betsy Fry returned. She had finally worked out where she knew Katy from and sought her out this time. They were allowed a precious half-hour together before Katy was marched back to her cell. In that time, she had poured her broken heart out to her friend.

Betsy was charged with messages to be delivered to Perry but only after the ship had sailed. "Betsy, promise me you will not tell Perry where I am until it's too late for him to do anything." Katy needed him to know he would soon be free to marry Mary.

Betsy was distraught. "Katy, you can't throw your marriage away like that; you must fight for him. Perry married you for better or worse; you just can't walk out on him."

Katy's eyes could no longer contain the well of tears. "I have to, Betsy, I love him so much; I have to free him."

"That doesn't explain it, Katy. Surely if you talked to him, you could work things out?" Betsy knew this wasn't right.

Katy tried hard to explain how things stood between them. "He would never leave me, Betsy; he would stay and be unhappy. And Mary, I love her so much; I know that she too would never hurt me intentionally, but you can't help falling in love with someone, Betsy."

Betsy rounded on her. "No, you can't help when you fall in love, but that does not mean you do anything about it, does it? Did you speak to him about it? Or to Mary? No, you scamper like a frightened rabbit. Katy, this is just not right." Betsy got up and paced the room. "Ahh! What am I to do with you? You have made me promise I will not tell him of the name you are using, and I will honour that, but Katy, he must at least know you are with-child. Surely you will allow me to tell him that?"

Katy's hand sat on her stomach. She could feel the child fluttering as her anxiety grew. "Absolutely not, Betsy! You promised, remember. You may only tell him I have gone, and he will be soon able to marry Mary."

Betsy knew that it was no use discussing this further. She would write to Perry and tell him what she was allowed; she left to draft the letter. Betsy wished she had not made that promise, but she had; she would honour her word. Katy said to send it care of the Countess of Milesdowne at Milesdowne Court, between Chatham and Aylesford, after she sailed. The letter would be sent the day the ship left.

After another few weeks, word came that some of the female prisoners were to be taken down to the docks. They were chained together, loaded into open wagons, and paraded through the streets; passers-by jeered at them and threw rotten fruit, vegetables, and eggs. They were then unloaded and marched the last two blocks down to the wharf. It was more like a shuffle than a march. There were chains around their waists, wrists, and ankles; they were escorted out in groups of thirty women. All the women were chained in pairs, with side chains connecting them all. They felt so humiliated.

Amelia and Catherine were walking behind Katy, and next to her shuffled Emily. Emily was from Scotland and had also stolen a handkerchief; she had done it to escape an abusive employer. She had run away before and been dragged back.

Katy had seen her arrive, and her protective instincts had kicked in. Her luggage was long since gone. However, she had been able to secrete her small leather Bible, a purse, and her locket down the front of her gown. Her cloak had been stolen while she slept, and all she now owned was the small parcel Betsy had given her. Betsy had thankfully included one of her own woollen stoles for warmth.

On arrival at the wharf, there was no ship in sight. What the women saw was a rotting hulk with no masts.

Gasping in horror at the thought of being kept in the derelict hulk, they huddled together. Sure enough, the side chains were unlocked. Two by two, the women were transferred onto the leaking, dilapidated, decaying, stinking hulk. As she climbed aboard, Katy grabbed the railing, which fell away in her hand. There were holes in the decking, and the stench made her dry retch. Emily clung tightly to her. They were shepherded into a gaping hole with steps leading down into hell. Red-coated soldiers stood guard with rifles pointed towards them. Running was useless. Katy had deliberately got herself into this situation, and now she had to make the best of it. They were in the second group of women to be boarded, and before they were ushered downstairs, their final chains were removed. There was no escape. Katy had no wish to anyway. She had long since confided her story to her three friends; they knew her misery. She had already gained a few small privileges through Betsy.

Betsy had warned Katy to cover one eye before descending into the hold. She explained that it took time for the eyes to acclimatise to the darkness, and covering one eye meant that she could see as soon as they descended below decks. Betsy was right. As soon as Katy reached the deck below, Katy could see with the eye she'd had covered. Leading Emily, who was holding Catherine's hand, led the three girls to the far corner of the hulk. There was a shaft of light coming from above it.

Betsy had told her that the sailors were unlikely to trouble them at night in this back section of the ship. Aghast at this information, Katy shivered.

They settled in as best as they could. A shaft of sunlight meant that Katy could read her Bible when the sun was shining.

~

Days had blurred into weeks in the hulks. Then into what felt like months. The rain dribbled in through the cracks above, but they moved, so they didn't get wet. Rats were frequent visitors, and the stench was overwhelming. The smells from the filthy river invaded the rotting ship hulk.

Betsy visited again and told Katy that it had only been a month since her arrival on the hulk and three months since her conviction.

Katy was now showing with the child she carried. More from the fact she'd lost so much weight than the months along.

One day, there was a bump and voices from above. A ship pulled alongside and tied up to the hulk. The women were loaded onto a vessel called *The Wanstead*.

Betsy visited for the final time. She would have come earlier, but she had recently given birth herself to a little girl named Louisa, after Katy's daughter. Betsy told Katy that it was August.

Katy knew her child was due in four months. In her previous confinements, she was much bigger by this stage. Betsy had brought a baby bundle for each of the nine expectant women and five spare bundles for those who fell with-child on board. She knew that the sailors and soldiers would have their way with some of the women. She did what she could to help. She had come to see the prisoners settled on board and make sure they were humanely treated. She couldn't stay long as she had to get home to feed Louisa.

The Wanstead was reasonably new; it was only two years old and didn't leak. Amelia was surprised to see that they were confined in cages, thirty to a cell. Catherine, Emily, and Amelia clung together. This time, they had no choice where they were sleeping. The bunks were again planks of wood, and they were barely wide enough for two bodies to share. With only sixteen of these beds and thirty women, conditions would be harsh. At least on the hulk, they could walk around the entire area below decks; here, they could not.

~

On August 24, the ship finally left the Thames River.

The soldier who brought them food had mentioned the date as he filled Katy's bowl with the sloppy meal. He sloshed it down her gown and boasted that it was a date she should know. The meal was horrible and swam with fat.

Katy looked at the soldier and heard his snigger of joy at her situation. Katy refused to be drawn and retired to her bunk to eat the meal.

The movement of the ship broke Katy's last resolve. She wept. She curled up on her wooden bunk in tears.

The other women knew why and left her alone in her grief. They too had broken lives, but she had a broken heart.

Katy could feel her child moving, and it brought her comfort. This child would be the only thing she had left of Perry's. Her hands sat on her stomach, and she prayed for their safety on the journey.

They were not yet under sail, but the tugs were towing them down the Thames River. Betsy had explained that they would travel out on the tide and anchor when it changed. The words she had used were to *go with the flow*. Katy had asked what she meant, and Betsy had explained that the ships sat in the tidal flow and were carried out to sea.

Three days later, they reached the open sea by nightfall. They all felt the jump of the ship as the wind filled the sails. It leaned into the wind, and the deck below became unsteady.

The first week the weather was kind. Now they were at sea, the hatches above were opened, and daily exercise was allowed for each group. When a squall arrived, they were kept confined below decks for at least three days. The stench of the hulks became sweet compared to the mixture of unemptied or spilled buckets of faeces and the ammonia of urine mixed with vomit. There was no crack in the decking like on the hulk that had allowed in light. This ship was an eerie black hole below the stairs. When the hatches were closed, it was claustrophobic. There was no air and no light; however, this also meant no seawater seeped in. The hull was watertight, and rats were few.

Once the squall passed, the hatches were thrown open, and the cells were cleansed. In groups of ten, the women were allowed on deck to bathe. This consisted of being stripped naked in front of the sailors and frigid seawater thrown over them. Some also took the opportunity to wash their gowns in the salty water.

Katy refused to remove her drawers and chemise. The bulge of her condition was now more pronounced, but she had heard from other women that once stripped, they were raped violently by several of the sailors. One had been abused by so many she was returned bleeding to her cell cage. Others freely offered their services to the men on board, enough to satisfy their lusts so thankfully, Katy and her friends were left alone. They usually asked to wash last, so the sailor's lusts had been well sated when their turn came.

The ship sailed on, taking her further away from Perry and Mary. They restocked at Cape Town and set sail across the Indian Ocean. A ferocious storm hit, and again they were confined to below deck. At one stage, a sailor snuck down and unlocked their cell doors. "Just in case," he had said to her. He realised her condition and snuck her extra bread and sometimes even an apple.

This storm took over ten days to pass. It had caused damage to the rigging, and the women were kept confined below decks all that time with the hatches battened. Two had died from another cell block and were wrapped in torn sails and thrown overboard with a few words spoken over them. Katy prayed for them, but she could do little else.

Months before, in England, Perry had stood pacing in the foyer of the big house; Katy had not returned with the carriage. He was frantic as she had not given instructions to the driver with whom she would be returning. She had gone to Maidstone instead of Chatham, which worried him as she knew no one there. He sent for both Justin and the constabulary when she had not returned by nightfall. He had not yet gone to her room. The children were now asking for their mother, and Perry had no answers. She was gone. But why?

Perry was up all-night pacing. She had still failed to return. Finally, when dawn approached, he went to her room. The first thing he saw was a letter propped up on her dressing table with his name on it. A cold chill descended on him; he tore open the seal and read the long screed. His heart sank. "Oh, Katy! Katy, my only love, why did you not trust me?" He had to find her. She had poured out everything. She had seen them embracing and was leaving so they could be together. Believing that marriages could be voided if she was sent to New South Wales as a convict, that's what she planned to do. He yelled, groaning. "Darling Katy, I don't want to marry Mary; I want you, only you." He knew she could not hear him. He would find her. He took the letter and searched for Justin, who had stayed the night. He pounded on his door, then marched in. "Justin, she's gone. She thinks I want to be with Mary, so she left."

Justin had been asleep and groggily sat up. "What do you mean she's left you?"

Perry shoved the missive at him. He paced the room while Justin read the sheets. Perry was running his fingers through his hair with anguish.

Justin, now fully awake, said, "Perry, what the heck happened? What did she see?" Justin knew that Katy would not have left without reason.

"Justin, I don't know, well I do, but she got it all wrong. Mary was upset about being alone. It's eating at her. She sees us so happy, and I found her weeping in the library yesterday morning. Somehow, she ended up in my arms. Justin, I was just comforting her. No more than that, seriously! I love Katy, and only Katy, and Mary knows that. Now Katy has left me. I need to find her. I have to go and look for her." Perry walked to the window in the bedroom. He stood unseeing just like Katy had done the morning before, only from her own window. He let out a howl of grief. "Oh, Katy, my only love, what have you done?"

Justin dressed quickly, and they both went to tell Mary what had happened.

Mary sank into a chair and cried in despair, "No! She saw me in your arms, but why did she not say anything?"

Perry was still pacing around the room. "Mary, she misread a lot of things, and it's all my fault. Even naming our daughter after you, rather than her, moving from our joint room after Louisa was born. It was all done innocently, and she has read it all wrong. Now she's gone. I am going to find her and bring her back. If it takes me all my life, I will find her."

Perry left for Maidstone mid-morning; the coachman was to take him to where he left her. The children were to stay with Mary and the staff. Justin needed to return to his Parish duties. Perry headed off alone with just the coachman who had dropped her off. His anxiety about his face was forgotten in his anguish over his wife. He would find her. He needed to find her. Perry arrived at the church in Maidstone; he sent the coachman home via his father's friend. He would stay at Gracemere Castle while he hunted. Perry then sought out the minister, Reverend Hector James. He had not seen her or heard of her in the area. Perry walked the streets and spoke to every person he saw. No one had seen a thing. The only possible lead was a stranger arrested for theft the day before. However, the name did not match. He was informed that the man thought that the name of the thief was Cate Parry. He didn't follow that lead. From Maidstone, Perry went to Coxheath and every other surrounding town. Days of searching and living at Gracemere Castle turned into weeks. He became oblivious to the stares of the people when they saw his face.

While he was living with his friend, Charles, Duke of Gracemere and his family, he searched. The Duke's sons, even though teenagers, also helped look. They checked through Aylesford, Coxheath, and an assortment of other hamlets. Nothing!

Perry returned to the children for a week. He packed up his family, took them to his father, then slept, prayed, ate and then left again. Still no word. He was now moving from town to town, expanding the search for her. She had gone without a trace.

After three months, he returned home again to find a letter waiting from Elizabeth Fry. It was addressed using his title and redirected from Mary, so he knew she'd spoken to Katy. The details the letter contained could only have come from Katy, so the letter was genuine. Finally, he had confirmation that she was still alive, and he gave a sigh of relief.

Elizabeth gave few details other than to say that she would be on a convict ship called *The Wanstead* bound for the far shores by the time he received this missive. He now knew Katy had been convicted of theft and convicted for seven years. She was using a false name, so he could not find her. The letter had waited for him for two weeks. It was now mid-September. Determined to continue his search, he now knew it must move offshore. He tucked the missive into his Bible.

Perry wrote to his father for advice. Jem was to stay with the Duke in case something happened to Perry while he was hunting for Katy. His son was now six and ready to start his education. Louisa was four, and Mia was nearly seven. He could cope with both girls as Nanny and Lucy were to accompany him. He had wanted to take Jem, too but knew that he would be in safe hands with his father. If something happened to him, they were safe with him, plus they had already formed a bond. Jem would often have a week or so with his grandfather. He needed to settle his son before he went looking for Katy. Justin would care for his sister; Perry knew that his priority needed to be his own family. Katy was foremost in his mind.

Chapter 4 On Katy's Trail

*J*n October, Perry and the two girls set sail on the ship, *The General Hewitt*, with a maid, Lucy, and their Nanny Grimes. His farewells to Jem had been sad, but when Perry explained that he would bring Mummy home, Jem seemed to understand; however, telling him that they could be gone some years was much harder. "Jem, when I find her, if I can't bring her home, I'll send for you, and you can come to us. Will you look after Grandfather for me?"

The six-year-old boy nodded. Tears flooded his eyes, but he tried to stay strong for his father. He missed his mother so much. "Yeth, Papa, I will. You find her for me, won't you?" he asked through his loose front teeth.

"I will, Jemmy! I'll find her, that I promise." Perry hugged his son. He so wished he could take him too, but his father was right. Jem must stay. Sailing so far on a possibly endless quest was dangerous. The heir must stay.

The journey to New South Wales would take months, and it would be perilous. Perry had letters of introduction to Governor Macquarie; his father had met him in London before the Governor took up the role in 1808. He'd been staying with his friend Charles Lockley, Duke of Gracemere. On his return home, he stopped in London and met the new Governor. Charles had invited Lachlan to dinner, and Percy had heard of the country that ran on rum. If anyone could help, it would be him. It was the first time Perry was pleased his father was a Duke. This time Perry intended to use his title. He would use any and all means to find her. Perry White would once more become the Earl of Collingsford.

Now Perry wished the wind would blow and the miles pass more quickly. However, the sea remained calm and the winds light. Day after day, Perry stood at the bow and watched the rolling waves. His mind was trying not to dwell on what Katy's trip would be like. He heard little of the convicts in the holds below but knew that the becalmed status of the vessel meant that rations needed to be cut. Rather than interact with others, he remained aloof. He was not interested in conversing with any of the other passengers. The 46th Regiment was on board, guarding the convicts in the hatches below. For the first few nights, he had to sit across the dinner table with Captain Earle and Major Ogilvie, the commander of the 46th. His daughters were unsettled in the cabin, and it was not long before the two girls joined him in the dining room. He was given a small table with just the girls, Nanny Grimes and Lucy. They enjoyed the solace from the rowdy soldiers. Eventually, they started eating before any others arrived for their meals.

Their arrival in Cape Town was to restock supplies.

Two days later, they were on their way again; every mile was closing the distance between Katy and her family.

The Wanstead was nearing the shores of the west coast of Australia. Conditions were easing in the cells as the hatches had been opened most of the trip. Katy was now large with child, as were some of the other women. More women were now expecting after frequent nocturnal visits from a myriad of sailors. Emily had escaped abuse, but sadly, both Amelia and Catherine had been victims of these night visits. As the cell doors were now left unlocked, they were free to wander around below decks. However, it also meant that there were no sounds from the sailors or soldiers as they crept in to molest the women. The first the women knew was a hand clamped over their mouths and a trouser-less sailor lifting what remained of their clothing and soon raping them.

Calling out was useless; no one came to their aid. It was often over quickly. Catherine had been married and had left a child with her husband. She knew she would never return home. Katy knew that feeling, and they often sat discussing their families. Amelia was not much older than Emily. She had stolen some food for her family and been caught. Both Catherine and Amelia had conceived, but thankfully, both lost the babies early. Neither knew who the father was. The cells had been dark, and they had no way of identifying their attackers. As their abuse had not been confined to a single night, there may well have been more than one potential father. They would never know. The sailors thought it funny to see how many women they could abuse and get in the family way, as they termed it.

Soon after leaving the freshwater creek on the country's western coast, where they stopped to replenish the water and supplies, Katy knew her time to deliver her precious bundle was near. Her back ached, and she was uncomfortable. She'd had three children already, so knew the signs.

Catherine sent word to the ship's doctor. He had taken pity on Katy and given her some extra rations. Katy was taken from the holding cells and moved upstairs to a small room next to the doctor's sick bay. It was in this tiny room that Jacob James White entered the world. Catherine had been allowed to assist the doctor.

Katy decided to give the baby his real surname so that his parentage could be acknowledged should Perry ever wish to. His registration in the ship's surgeon's log would be able to be confirmed. It was Christmas Day 1813. She lay cuddling her newborn son. Jacob meant sorrowful or supplanted, and James meant supplanter, as that was what she had felt; she had been betrayed by the two closest to her. Jacob was so much like Jem when he was born that she wept. She missed her children so much, but at least she now had this little cherub. She clutched the locket at her neck. She'd never taken it off and never intended to. This little mite was the last thing of Perry's she could keep. She would give her life to keep him safe. However, her melancholy was so pronounced that the doctor feared for her well-being. Her weeping over the small child as she fed the baby worried him.

The doctor was able to keep her in the small cabin for some days before he allowed her to return to the cell block. In that time, she poured out her story to him. Her love for her husband was so deep that it almost crushed her. So, Katy wept.

He was dismayed. He was stunned that Katy's love was so great that she gave her husband up to another for his own happiness. "Katy dear, you have told me you believe in our Lord. Have faith, for I know of nothing else to encourage you. I will, however, give you a Bible verse. It's from 'John 15:13. Greater love hath no man than this, that a man lay down his life for his friends.' For you to have done this for your husband and friend, well, Katy, I am stunned, and quite honestly, I'm not so sure it was the correct thing to have done. Mayhap you should have stayed and fought for him." He rubbed the side of his nose. "We'll see!" He was determined to see her well settled.

She shook her head; how to explain to the nice doctor? Lifting her tear-filled eyes to his kind face, she replied, "I would have won without a fight, Doctor; I almost forced him to marry me. It's a long story, but I had no right to force him to stay with me. You see, I love him too well for him to be unhappy." Her melancholy was concerning the doctor more each time he spoke to her.

The doctor finally said, "Then you must live for his child, Katy."

Unable to reply, she just nodded. She fully intended to.

~

The day she was released from sickbay, they arrived in Port Phillip Bay for a water replenishment stop. The babe was swaddled in a flannel shawl that Betsy Fry had given her in a baby bundle. Her milk had come in, and she was able to feed him. Katy returned to the squalor of the other women prisoners. Catherine had cleared out a bunk so she would not have to share. One of the women who had died was from their cell group. Two other women had a single bunk each, and by Amelia and Catherine forfeiting their midday meal ration, they had agreed to share for the last leg of the journey.

They only had a short stay locked below decks, as they were not released from the cells while inshore. Even with no settlement nearby, it was too risky for the women to be left unchained. The water was quickly replenished before continuing their journey. The doctor had visited and let them know that once underway, they would only have about a week, possibly less, until they reached their destination.

It was now early January, and the cell was stiflingly hot. The stench was overpowering, and the women's tempers were all on edge.

Perry's ship had just sighted land on the West Coast. He was standing in his usual spot at the bow, only today, he had both girls with him. Mia stood between his feet and Lou in his arms. His impatience was building. He knew it to be Christmas Day, but his soul was disquieted. He felt that something momentous was occurring, yet he did not know what it was.

They had travelled further north than he'd expected because the currents and winds had blown them some distance off course to the north.

The captain had informed his illustrious guest that the land ahead was only an island; the mainland was still days away.

Perry's identity had been discovered after leaving Cape Town when a note had been sent to him from Government House.

When the captain received the message, he saw it was addressed to the Earl of Collingsford. Being the only person who could possibly hold such a title, he asked Perry if he knew who it was. Perry merely sighed, nodded and put his hand out for the note. He had never used his title and had no idea how the information had been discovered. He knew the other letter in his pocket was addressed to the Governor of New South Wales, introducing him with his full title, but there had been no whisper of it in any other written form. Nanny and Lucy had been sworn to secrecy. It was a puzzle to which he would never discover the answer. However, his cover was blown.

The weather was fine and the seas calm. The tailwind was now propelling them forward without tacking. The strong winds had blown out one sail which needed repair. Hopefully, it would not delay his trip.

Dolphins were regular visitors, and the girls adored them, Mia especially. Gulls landed on the rigging and brought coos of delight from the girls. They noticed an albatross come to investigate the billowing sails above the ship. Masked gannets and other sea birds were occasionally seen, but it had been weeks since they had seen a seagull and even longer since they had sighted land.

~

Ten days later, the ship arrived in Hobart.

Sadly, the captain delayed departure until the sail was either replaced or repaired. He chose the latter, which delayed their journey another two days. It was frustrating, but Perry had no choice but to await the repair.

It was the end of January by the time they left Hobart. He had discovered that *The Wanstead* was only a month ahead of them. They were now due in Sydney Cove in early February.

Perry found his temper short and often released a shout of exasperation at the delays. The heat was sapping his energy, and the girls were also moody. He'd learned to wear a hat as he'd been sunburned badly once or twice. It was February and should be cold, not the searing heat that scorched his skin through a light shirt. Although a heavy rain shower eased the constant heat, it didn't ease his mood.

The children grew restless. Louisa had suddenly thrown a tantrum. She missed her mother and plonked herself on the cabin floor, rolled over and with hands, fists and feet flailing, she let fly. Perry let her wail for a time before gathering her to him; Mia now sat under his other arm, and the three wept together. "We'll find her, girls; we'll look all over the world for her. I'll bring her back, I promise. I promised Jem the same thing. I'll find her for us all." Both girls were stunned to see their father cry. He'd kept his emotions hidden, but now they realised he also missed her. They clung to him, all too drained to speak. Nanny found them like this when she walked in to collect the children. Perry shook his head, and she left them alone.

~

Two more days of inactivity ticked by. They walked around and around the deck. The wind had dropped, and they were almost becalmed. Then overnight, on the second day, a squall rolled in. The wind howled, and for once, he felt at one with the ocean. It was too dangerous for the girls to move from the safety of their bunks. Nanny Grimes sat reading them stories and playing games. They were stuck in the cabin for two days. Seeing they were safe and settled, he once again headed outside. He was about to open the door to the deck when a large wave broke over the railing and sent him reeling.

The scuppers on deck had a hard time draining the volume of water on the ship. Seeing the danger outside and knowing how close he was to seeing Katy, he returned to their cabin. Perry had chased her halfway across the world, but he'd still not thought about what he'd say. How could he deny he'd taken Mary willingly into his arms? Katy had seen their embrace. If she had stayed watching a moment longer, she would have seen them push away from each other. But how to make her believe that? Still, he should not have hugged Mary. He knew that now. He should have brought Justin over and let him comfort her. He was so angry with himself. And, in a way, frustrated that Katy had doubted him. Having read her letter through many times, he could see her point. After Louisa was born, Katy was exhausted. He had moved out of her bed to let her sleep. He should have moved back in, but he did it for Katy. He hated leaving her alone each night rather than taking his fill of her as he wished to do. He had done it for her, but it had been so hard.

After seven months without her, a thought suddenly occurred to him. Why had she come down that morning? She was rarely out of the nursery before breakfast. She obviously needed to discuss something with him to be up and dressed so early. He'd failed her dismally. He stood contemplating his own question. Unable to find an answer, he shrugged. His heart was in his mouth. He had no idea what to expect once they arrived. He knew his first call would be to Government House. Surely the Governor could find her. He surely had access to all the files of the convicts. At least Perry knew what ship she had been on. He had Elizabeth Fry to thank for that bit of knowledge.

The Wanstead sailed into Sydney Cove on January 9th. They had barely stepped off the ship when they were herded into eight wagons and taken to a gaol some hours travel westward and in a place called Parramatta.

Katy was given little chance to look around, but what she saw filled her with horror. If this was the main town, what was the place they were heading to like?

The baby lay asleep in her arms, seemingly not minding the bumpy road. She had just changed him, so hopefully, he would sleep for some time. He was now two weeks old. He had Perry's eyes and a dimple in his chin. Jem had not inherited that, but he had Perry's dark curls, but Jem had been born with dark curls like Perry. Lou and Mia were like her, light brown hair with blue eyes. Both boys would probably have Perry's honey-gold eyes and dark curls, as the baby's eyes were darkening already. The wagons trundled down the dusty road heading westward in the bright January sunshine. None knew what was in front of them, but it was hot, so very hot, and there was nothing to drink and no shade.

The doctor had kindly asked if Katy could be watched as he feared for her well-being. Little did he know what he was condemning her to. It was more that she had just given birth alone than that she'd do anything to herself. She loved her child too much for that to occur.

On arrival at the gaol, the wagons pulled up to the gates and waited for them to swing open. One by one, the wagons trundled in, unloaded, and moved off for the next one to take its place. Katy and her friends were in the third wagon. The building didn't look big enough to house them all. The jangle of irons sounded as all the women, but Katy, were leg shackled and hustled off the wagons to stand in a line outside.

Katy was spared that indignity. She was carrying a baby, and a soldier grabbed her arm, she dropped everything but the child, and he marched her into the building first. She was forced into a small room and stumbled as she was pushed inside the dark doorway. The sound of a key turning in the lock sent shivers through her.

Surely this place could not be as bad as the hulks. Compared to that, this would almost be a luxury. Katy looked around her; even the roof looked solid. At least compared to the heat outside this room was cooler. Hopefully, in wintertime, it would also be warm. She had no idea how long she would have to stay incarcerated.

As she had been marched in first, she knew all the others were still lined up in the scorching sun in the courtyard. Their only head covering was the mob caps they wore. Her own cap had fallen off as she was dragged off the wagon. It lay somewhere in the quadrangle outside. It was January; it should be cold. This heat was soul-sapping. Even sitting still, the perspiration was dripping from her, and her clothing was damp with it. Oh, for some cool water or a glass of chilled wine. Her throat was parched.

As her eyes adjusted, she saw there was a stone bench seat which she sank onto. The baby was thankfully asleep again, but he was wet through. She had nothing to change him into. She had fed him as they travelled and had used the last of the clean flannels. The old carpetbag she had placed his things into had been left outside. Sitting in the small room, she wondered how long she would be left there. She was thirsty and knew she needed to drink to keep her milk production up. There was a small, barred window in the door, and she walked over to it, but she was too short to see outside. Her only option was to stand on the bench seat built onto the far wall. From there, she might be able to catch a glimpse of the world outside.

Carefully moving the baby onto the floor, just in case she fell over and landed on him, then she climbed onto the bench seat.

She saw a procession of mob-capped heads. She called out, forgetting that the babe would wake. "Catherine, Amelia, Emily, can you hear me?"

Her voice carried to Catherine, who was within earshot. "Katy? Where are you?"

"I'm in here, behind the door with the grill, Catherine; pray for me as I will for you." She didn't know what else to say.

"I will," was all she heard as the voices and shackled marching feet faded away.

Katy heard an angry woman's voice shout, "Hey you, no talking unless spoken to, or you'll get flogged."

Katy gasped. She sank back onto the bench seat, hoping she'd not get her friends into trouble. Movement on the floor caused a glance down at her son. The baby was now awake and screwing up his face. She knew what that meant, a dirty napkin.

Katy really didn't like the name Jacob nor James, "I shall call him JJ," she said to herself. Both names reminded her of betrayal, but that was not his fault. "Yes, I shall call him JJ." Soon he'd be screaming that would hopefully bring someone to their assistance. She sat watching him as he squirmed. Rather than pick him up, she sank onto the floor next to him. The temperature in the room was rising. It was now far too hot to hold him. She unwrapped the swaddling shawl letting him have some space to kick. He was hot, and his face was flushed. She wiped off his filth and covered it. Unwrapping him meant that he would stay happy only for a short while. But at least he was a bit cooler. She sat watching him. His cooing gurgles made her smile. He clutched her finger as she stroked his hand.

It seemed like an eternity since she'd been locked in the tiny airless room. Her eyes had quickly adjusted to the lack of light. She thought that surely she wouldn't be here long. She could do nothing but pray, so that's what she did. She bowed her head in prayer as she moved, and something dug into her chest. Her hand flew to her corset. A slow smile spread over her face. She also still had her Bible and her locket. Her purse had been stolen while she was delivering the baby.

JJ cried on and off for over an hour. He was nearly hoarse by the time they released her from the tiny room. She had fed him but not being able to change him worried her. His poor little bottom was red-raw and sore from sitting in a dirty flannel for so long.

A woman finally unlocked the cell door. "Come and bring the little'en." She held the door open to Katy and expected her to follow.

Rather than be taken to the other women, she was taken to another tiny cell. This cell at least had a window, but it only looked into another room, which was a barred opening with an office of sorts. The new cell had a slat bunk, bucket of water and another empty bucket for use as a privy. She was pushed inside and looked around her.

"At least this room has a few more facilities," the woman said.

Katy saw a bundle of flannel napkins for JJ and set about changing his dirty napkin. She had not needed to use the privy, and knew her fluid levels were low. She had found a tin mug in the bucket of water, so risked the danger and had a long drink, then another. An hour passed, then two. No one came, and no one spoke to her. Why had she been singled out? Was it because of the child? She had eaten nothing all day. She was tired and hungry. JJ was sleeping; she thought she might as well too.

She had no idea how long she had been asleep, but she was woken by the jangle of the keys in the lock of her door. She was awake in an instant; she sat up and waited.

"Up now, grub's on." A filthy woman handed her a large bowl of ambiguous tepid vegetable stew and a big chunk of dry bread. "You get extra as you'se got a kiddie." The woman gave the food to Katy, and she took it willingly. "Water is in the bucket; you drink it and wash in it too, so careful not to foul it. The little tike had better not use too many of them flannels; you will only get six a day, so use them sparing like. You'll be allowed out to wash 'em each morning. From tonight you'll be watched through there." She pointed to the barred window.

"What do you mean watched? Why me? What have I done?" Katy pleaded for an answer.

The woman looked surprised at her comment. "Doc on the ship says you want to knock yourself orf, so you're gonna be watched." The curt voice spoke abruptly.

Katy finally understood. "I don't want to kill myself. I have my baby to live for. I stupidly said I wished I was dead when I was in labour, but it was from the pain. I would do anything to stay alive for him." Katy turned and looked at the sleeping baby. "I love him so much; I would do anything at all."

"Good, 'cause I got nuff to do than watch a lunatic lady." The lady slammed the door shut but spoke through the grill. "Eat, I'll talk to Matron, I may come back for you soon."

Katy heard her footsteps receding. She held the tepid bowl of stew-like food. There was no spoon, so she sipped it. She broke the big chunk of bread in half. The woman had given her almost half a cob loaf; Katy shoved most of it in the pocket of her gown. She hungrily ate the watery meal, mopping up the last of the food with the stale bread. She placed the empty bowl near the door and waited. JJ's dirty napkins sat in a pile. She thought she may as well try to wash them in the currently empty toilet bucket. She scooped out some water with the mug and managed to sort of wash the fouled cloths. If she hid these, she might be able to get more than just the six. She hid the remaining dry ones up her skirt.

She sat and waited while JJ slept again.

A different lady returned some half an hour later. "Hello, I'm Janey; come with me, dearie." This woman was friendly. She walked to JJ and stroked his cheek. She also was clean and well-spoken. "Cute little fellow you have, dearie." She held the door open, waited for Katy to collect the baby, and then asked her to follow.

Katy was led along a corridor and up a set of stone steps. She could hear the voices of many women seeping through the grill in the door. The murmur of men's voices from the ground floor faded as they climbed the stairs.

The lady pulled out her keys and unlocked a door. "I'm sorry, but you must go in there with the others, dearie. The room should only fit sixty, but you'll have to make do as best you can. It is hot, and I'm sorry about that. You'll all get assigned soon enough, so don't make yourselves too comfy." She slammed the door shut, and the bang awoke JJ.

The child's cry brought her friends to her side through the stinking throng and the cacophony of noisy women.

"Where have you been?" Emily asked as she clung to her.

Katy told them of the doctor's report and that they had her in a cell so she couldn't hurt herself.

Emily and Catherine escorted her to the corner they had claimed. Amelia grabbed a large handful of flannel napkins for her and followed.

The night fell.

The temperature dropped a little. With so many women jammed in one room, there was no spare space. There were only thirty pallets; those already had two women sharing. The four friends lay on the stone floor. At least it was cooler. They realised the floor was actually better than sleeping on the pallets.

JJ woke everyone at dawn when the rattle of keys was heard again. Katy had changed and fed him twice through the night. She was so tired.

The nice lady was followed by a short fat man in clergy robes. "You, you, you, and you, wait outside." The four sleepy women he pointed to moved towards the door; many others soon followed.

Within half an hour, half of the one hundred and twenty women from the ship had been taken from the overcrowded room. They were to be sent for assignment.

"I'll send instructions for more tomorrow." With that, the fat little man left after inspecting the faces of the remaining women. He took notice of Katy's clean face with a raise of his eyebrows. He saw the child asleep in her arms and walked past her.

The four friends stayed huddled together at the back, not daring to move. The rest of the women reshuffled themselves, spreading out so they were less cramped. They again spent the day confined in the still overcrowded hot room. Katy realised there were only thirty bunks in the room and sixty women, so it was still stuffy. They all lay back and relaxed as best they could. There was absolutely nothing else to do.

JJ drank, slept, and needed his napkins changed. Each took turns in walking around the room with the hot grizzly babe. They made Katy sleep as Catherine knew she needed it to keep up her strength.

There was little water, and food came only once a day, but they made the best of what they had. Katy still had her Bible, so she read it aloud to those who wished to listen.

For their evening meal was gruel to eat again. The meal was thin and flavourless, but it was something. Katy still had the bread in her pocket. It wasn't much, but she secretly shared it with her friends. Hopefully, tomorrow they would be assigned to somewhere with better food.

With half the women gone, the air was slightly less heated, but the difference was hardly noticeable. They settled down again for an early night. Tomorrow most of them would probably be leaving.

Chapter 5 Assignment

*T*he following day brought a flurry of activity outside at dawn. The rattle of keys signalled the start of the day for the women.

JJ had been restless, and Katy wished she could sleep longer. That was not going to happen.

The water buckets were empty, so they had no way to wash hands, bowls, or clean flannels for the baby, let alone drink. The dirty lady brought in a bucket of porridge-like slop and ladled it into the unwashed bowls used for the scant meal the day before. Again, they had no eating utensils, so using their filthy fingers was the only way to consume the food.

The water buckets were collected and returned half an hour later. One was soon emptied as everyone was so thirsty. Again, the only means of drinking was to use the same bowls they had eaten from. Katy was cranky that she'd not thought to grab the mug from the last cell. They were so parched that no one seemed to mind. JJ was crying because he was thirsty too. Her breasts were flat, and her milk was low as she had not had enough to drink.

The keys rattled in the door lock again.

The kind lady named Janey came in again. "This is for you, love; get this into you. The bub needs his tucker."

Katy was handed a large tumbler full of warm frothy milk, obviously fresh. She met the eyes of the lady with surprise and thanked her profusely.

"The matron has little'ns herself, so drink up. They don't give you enough to drink as it is. I'm to stay until it's gone; no sharing. Please, drink it, dearie," Janey said with a smile.

Katy downed the milk. She noted that it was not even watered down; she badly needed the fluid. Her breasts were almost flat, and JJ's napkins were hardly damp; no wonder he was crying; he wasn't getting enough to drink.

Katy looked apologetically at the other women, but they all understood.

Catherine had a child she had left at home; they had talked about the children, worried about how her family would survive. Her husband was out of work; at least they could go to a workhouse if things got any worse. He was a good man, and she knew he would do the best he could for them. She was only here for three more years. She had spent time in prison in England. Hopefully, she would be allowed to go home at the end of her time. Long ago, Katy told her of the new ruling that married convicts could get their marriages annulled, allowing the remaining spouse to remarry. Although surprised, Catherine hoped her husband would do that if she could not return.

~

Two hours later, all the remaining women were lined up outside with their few possessions. The fat minister returned with others and then vanished inside.

It was already getting hot; their mob caps did little to guard against the sun. Katy didn't even have that. They had been told they had to wait for at least an hour. They were all dehydrated already.

Katy knew her baby was thirsty and needed a feed. However, she dared not move, and she could not feed him in such a public place. She felt dizzy, and rather than drop her son, she sat down on the hot pavement with him, resting on her lap.

Booted feet appeared in front of her. "Who said you could sit down? Git up!" A hand reached down and grabbed a handful of her hair, tugging her back on her feet.

Katy struggled to get up. As she did so, the baby cried.

The shock on the man's face was almost laughable, "Cor, you got a kiddy? Sorry lady, I thought you got a bundle of clothes. You go sit over there, lady." He pointed off to the side; thankfully, it was in the shade.

The soldier's attitude now changed, as he pointed to a bench seat under a tree.

With his assistance, Katy stumbled over to the rough timber bench. Her head was pounding; her tongue was swollen with thirst. Her baby was now screaming with hunger and heat, and he now needed a change.

The temperature was now overpowering. The light shimmered on the pavement, and the reflection from the pale stone courtyard was blinding. It wasn't even mid-morning. How long would they all need to wait?

Katy felt so sorry for her friends. She could now sit with her back to the group and feed her hungry child, not that she had much milk. The baby was wet but not dirty, as it was so hot, she left him naked on the damp flannel napkin. As she was now sitting in the shade, Katy had unwrapped him and let him lay on the seat beside her. He could kick his legs but would not get sunburned. She sat with her hand on his little tummy, making sure he didn't move too much.

His cooing noises belied the dire situation they were in.

Katy had been watching her son when she noticed a door into the quadrangle open. The little fat minister walked towards them, this time followed by a few reasonably well-dressed gentlemen and another eclectic group of slovenly-dressed men. An older lady in a smock followed them; she heard someone address her as Matron.

Katy thought, so that's who she was. It was the voice she had previously heard; she watched as Matron seated herself at a table that now sat in the quadrangle. The table's arrival must have been the noises she heard while feeding the babe. She hadn't looked. Katy figured the first lot of women had undergone much the same treatment the day before.

The rotund minister walked over to the shade near her and stood watching the other women. He barely glanced at her. She had covered herself just before he arrived.

One by one, the other men walked up the line of women as if inspecting cattle. Katy sat observing the insulting activity in the courtyard. Some men even checked their teeth.

There was one man who stood out from the rest. He was clean and a little better dressed than many of the others. He walked along the line asking each a question, to which each woman shook her head. Then he walked into the shade near Katy.

Other men had made their choices and went to the desk, filled out their documentation and taken their new possessions home to do with them what they wished.

Katy's heart bled for them, knowing that many would be violated. Some would be consenting, but many others not. They would have no say in what those men did to them and nowhere to turn for help, assistance or compassion. If they fell with-child, they would be discarded, returned to prison, and replaced with another innocent young girl who would then be abused until she too fell with-child. The vicious cycle continued.

Katy wondered what her lot in life would be. Would the man who claimed her be kind? Would she also be abused? She kept watching.

The clean man, who had asked the questions, finally saw her off to the side. He had asked every female available but her. Meandering over to her, he stood looking at her and asked, "I don't suppose you can read or write either?"

"Yes, sir, I can both read and write." She didn't elaborate.

He looked stunned but turned on his heel and walked to the table. "Is she available?" he pointed to Katy.

"Yes, but she's got a kiddy, and he is free-born." Matron went back to writing who was assigned to whom.

He uttered an oath, "Damn!" Then he returned to Katy, "Hey you, I don't suppose you can add numbers too?"

"I am good at bookkeeping, sir, I used to do work for my husband

and friend on the estate where we lived." She sat looking at the man. This man was not only well dressed; he was clean. Hopefully, if he claimed her, she would be well treated.

"You can? Good, well then, you can have your kiddy with you but keep it out of my wife's way; we don't have any, and I don't want trouble." He stood watching her expression. "And I don't want no funny business at my inn." The man looked at the tiny infant. "Is he your husband's kiddy?"

"Yes, sir, only he doesn't know about him. I was arrested before I was able to tell him I was expecting." The naked baby had fallen asleep again.

The man looked relieved. "Good, as I said, no funny business from you, and you can keep him with you. One step wrong, and he goes to the orphanage. Understand?"

Katy nodded. At least she could keep her baby.

He waited until the other women had been signed out. Another man at Windsor had taken Catherine. She would be all but next door to Amelia; hopefully, they would help each other out. Amelia was assigned to a settler at Windsor who lived in town, and Emily was taken by one of the well-dressed gentlemen in a uniform. She would be heading to Government House in Sydney as a laundry maid. Emily waved and gave Katy a double thumbs-up sign to her friends as she left for her new life.

The man next to Katy was telling her who the others were. He had introduced himself, "I'm James Albert, the publican at the Freemason's Inn." Then he sat beside her. He breezily chatted while they waited. "I drop the 'Free' though. We just call it the Mason's Inn."

Katy sat listening. He didn't sound as though he intended to mistreat her. She sighed with relief and thanked the Lord.

By the time it was their turn to fill in the assignment book, JJ now needed another feed and change. This was done quickly, and she followed Mr Albert to the assignment desk. She filled in her details as Kate Harrison in her lovely flowing calligraphy and turned to leave the scorching quadrangle with the man. She had smiled when the man in England wrote her name as Cate Parry, she didn't correct him, but noted that it was listed as an alias, but she knew her conviction was under the name of Harrison. Hopefully, she would be able to do her work, keep her head down, and keep her baby quiet. Katy knew that the first months would be achievable, but once he grew older, it would get tough.

She was just getting ready to leave the compound when the lady named Janey called to her. "Hey, Kate Harrison, I have something for you; it was in the storeroom." She was carrying a baby basket, which looked full. "We have nobody else here who needs it, and you have nothing. You may as well have it." She was struggling to carry the ungainly load.

Katy asked her new owner if she could collect the gift.

Mr Albert nodded, "Give me the kiddy if you want."

"He's wet," she said, expecting the man to refuse.

"I'll cope, get your gift and hurry up." Mr Albert gingerly took and cradled the now sleeping tiny baby in his arms. He wished for one of his own, but his wife seemed unable to fall with-child. He stroked the downy cheek of the sleeping child with his crooked finger. The babe was adorable.

Katy walked quickly to the lady and collected the basket. She whispered, "Thank you so much." Katy was close to tears.

Janey whispered, "I filled it with other things you can use. Just don't look till you are out of here. There are some clothes for you too. And a new blanket. Shh!" Katy met the smiling face of the lady. "My name's Janey Brien; I'm a 'lifer.' Just look after the little kiddy, dear. Oh, and pretend the basket isn't heavy, please."

"Thank you so much, Janey." Katy did tear up this time. She wanted to hug her but knew she couldn't. Other than her friends, it was the first kindness another had shown her.

Janey said, "I love children. You just take care of yourselves and cuddle the little one for me." Janey squeezed Katy's arm and walked back inside.

Katy lifted the basket and was surprised to feel how heavy it was. She wondered what was under the blankets. She dared not look. As she walked across the hot pavement, she tried to make it look like the basket was empty.

Mr Albert assisted Katy into his dray and handed her the baby. He stowed the basket at their feet and made sure she was seated with the baby safe before he took off.

She was surprised at his consideration.

They didn't have far to go; he had been to Government Stores before coming to collect some help from the gaol. He didn't expect to find a literate woman, but he had asked all the men available, and none could read or write. This woman would have to live in the small storeroom off his office, which he would now have to give her for use. She couldn't share with his other male staff, especially with a child. Cook and the two maids were already cramped in their tiny room. He knew his wife, Maybel, wouldn't like it, but she couldn't complain as she couldn't do the bookwork. She couldn't even read. He needed a competent person. Hopefully, this woman would be as good as her word.

~

Katy's new life started with a room to herself, and Janey had packed a treasure trove of items. She had not been abused, and it looked as though she would be safe from that indignity. The basket from Janey had an assortment of clean dresses; three mob caps, one with lace edging, a dozen clean and almost new flannel napkins for JJ and a selection of wraps for him as well. At the very bottom, there were also four books, a pair of lace-up boots and a hooded cloak with a burn hole in it. Knowing what her luxurious wardrobe at home contained, she was over the moon at the fabulous and thoughtful gifts. As Katy was still wearing the clothes she had left home in some seven months before, she was looking forward to a change of attire. Hopefully, there would be washing facilities she could use. She had not had a chance to look at what the books were.

On further investigation later that day, she found three volumes of poetry, George Crabbe's The Borough; Mary Mitford's, poetry collection and Walter Scott's The Lady of the Lake. The fourth book was the first edition of Debrett's Peerage; she had heard about this but had not seen a copy. It had only been produced seven years before. Katy picked this up and flicked through the pages. She wondered if Uncle Percy was in there, let alone Phil and even herself as well as Mary's husband. She flicked through the back, presuming the titles would be under the family name; she found Uncle Percy as expected, listed under White but also listed as Duke of Cheatham. Perry was in there too, as she was, as his wife. They were listed as Earl and Countess of Collingsford and little Jem as Viscount Jeramy White. Perry's brother, Jeramy, was an entry as just The Honourable Jeramy White and the year of his death. Phil's name was there too, as Earl of Leatherbrooke. Each time she found the name of one of her loved ones, she ran her fingers over it as though touching them. She smiled at Eustace's listing, thinking of his principal seat at Harrington Hall.

Eustace had been livid when he found out she had remarried her cousin and was again a Countess and would one day be a Duchess. Even now, her precedence was higher than his as Perry's title of Earl was older than Eustace's. Even in the tragedy of Phil's death, something good had come from that. She smiled, God at work again.

Then she thought of Cheatham Castle in Warwickshire. She grinned, thinking of the enormous palace-like building, like Stowe House and Meldon Hall in Billingshurst, and then she compared them to the small room she now lived in with JJ. She sat looking at the sleeping babe in the basket; one thing she had not yet done was to find out if she needed to register his birth. She didn't need to do that at home, only his Baptism. She would ask about getting that done sometime too.

Katy turned back to the book on her lap.

Phillip and George both were listed as deceased, as was Sir Phillip Princhester. Mary and Colm as still listed as living at Milesdowne Court in Aylesford. Colm was even in there as the 7th Earl of Milesdowne. She ran her fingers over their names. As much as she was hurting from their betrayal, she still loved both Perry and Mary. They couldn't help falling in love with each other. She was just sad and in pain. She ran her fingers lovingly over both their names as though she was caressing them. Yes, she still loved them both. That emotion surprised her. With that thought still in her mind, she carefully closed the book and tidied their tiny new room.

~

Life at the Mason's Inn fell into a routine. JJ was happy. Katy had food to eat and lots of milk and ale to drink.

Mr Albert had recommended that she drink at least one glass of black stout a day while feeding the little one. Overwhelmed at his generosity, she undertook to drink the potent black, frothy brew he would send her at lunchtime. If Maybel were not around, he would send another large tankard full with her dinner.

She had learned to move silently around the tiny room when Mrs Albert was nearby. It was hatred at first sight from her. She had heard the Albert's fighting over her. It was loud enough for Katy to hear every word. He'd gone for a male convict and come back with a woman and baby. There had been a screaming match between her new owner and his wife the afternoon she had arrived. The woman was a pretty face with the manners of an alley cat. Maybel Albert was not a woman to cross, so Katy just stayed out of sight as much as possible. There were months of back receipts to sort and arrange into their proper order, then record.

Katy was allowed to walk outside after luncheon, which meant JJ could get some sun on him. However, she was careful not to let him kick in the direct sunlight, but the overwhelming summer heat usually sent them back inside after about ten minutes. After the first few days, she asked if she could go in the mornings rather than at noon. Mr Albert gave her permission as long as she kept out of everyone's way.

~

At the end of the first week, Katy asked the maid who brought her meals if she could see Mr Albert. She needed a new ledger to continue the work. She had worked out a Daybook, Incoming costs and Expenditure book with the ledgers she had found in the office, but she required another one for stock on hand. Salaries were not paid as they were all convict staff, so she didn't need that.

Mr Albert had not come near her for two days, and she decided as JJ was asleep, she'd go in search of him. She heard his voice in the taproom. It was the one area he had forbidden her from entering. So, she stood out of sight, hoping he would need to leave the bar to go to the cellar.

Sure enough, the door swung open after about half an hour. "What do you want?" he asked, grabbing her arm. "You'll be the death of me if you're seen down here. Maybel will have both our necks."

"I need another ledger, sir. I thought that next time you are somewhere near stores, you could get one, please." Katy was surprised at his brusqueness. He hurt her when he grabbed her arm and marched her back upstairs to the office. He sounded short with her, which was unusual.

"I'll see what I can do, now go back to the office and don't leave until I say." He waited for her to enter, but he wasn't quick enough.

Maybel saw him watching her walk away. "What are you doing with that slut? If she's making eyes at you or you with her, I'll scratch them all out, and you'll both be blind if I have anything to do with it. You're mine, and I'll thank you to remember that." She gave him an almighty full-hand slap on the cheek.

Katy heard the sound and turned and gasped.

Mr Albert grabbed Maybel's hand and twisted it behind her back but did not hurt her. In a deep guttural voice, she heard him say, "You touch me again, and you'll regret it. Do you hear me? She merely came to ask for a ledger. Unlike you, she was doing her job; you can't even beget a child. You may be a pretty face, but you have much work to do on your temper, my dear. You're just jealous of her. If you would learn to read and write, I could get rid of her." He was now holding her so close and grabbed her chin with his free hand. He dropped a light kiss on her lips, then forced her back into their section of the inn. Katy saw him push her inside gently and shut the door.

He turned to head back down to the taproom. He knew that Katy had seen the entire episode. He shrugged with his hands held up and walked back downstairs to the bar without a word. Other than forcing her into the room, he had not retaliated at all.

Katy had seen Maybel slap many of the convict maids in the last weeks. So far, she had escaped this, receiving only tongue lashings, but presumed that she would soon be on the receiving end of Maybel's hand. Katy got on with her work.

~

Three days later, a new leather-bound ledger was brought to her by the laundry maid, Milly. "Mr Albert says you needed this, Missus." The poor lass looked around; she feared being found somewhere she should not be by Maybel. She dumped the package on the desk and scurried out.

Katy saw how all the staff were treated and knew that Maybel Albert was worse with all of them than she was with Katy. Mr Albert was quite nice in comparison. Yet they were all treated like dirt. Little consideration was given to the comfort of any of them. Katy refused to complain about anything as she knew what she had was far better than any of the other convicts at the inn. She was getting almost claustrophobic in the small hot office with the door shut; the heat was suffocating, opening the window made it worse as it was even hotter outside, so she opened the door. At least the sandstone walls of the room gave some protection from the scorching sun. It was so hot outside now that Katy had started taking her break in the gardens soon after dawn instead of mid-morning.

No matter what she had to put up with, she would stay silent because JJ was thriving. He was now five weeks old, and she was beginning to feel more herself. She had no post-baby weight to lose as she was lighter now than before she conceived. For exercise she spent half an hour in the cool morning light walking in the back garden of the inn. There was a side gate, but she never even looked through it. She did not dare to. Only the laundry maid and kitchen staff were up at this hour, so Maybel was unlikely to see her.

~

She had been at the inn for three weeks; she normally sat enjoying the garden and the freshness of the morning. However, this morning when she took her usual deep breaths, the air smelled different. This morning it was not the usual clean, sweet smell, of gum leaves, but she realised the scent was quite different. She smelled smoke. It was an unusual scent, unlike the coal or peat fires at home, but more acrid. It was the smell of gum leaves burning, and it almost seared her nostrils.

JJ was now coughing, and his tiny face screwed up with the unpleasant air. She knew that she had to go back inside quickly. She realised that she could see the mountains to the west from her small upstairs office window. They usually looked almost blue. It had been dark when she had risen, so she had not looked outside. On her way in, she had to pass through the kitchen. Mr Albert met her there.

She curtsied and greeted him with, "Good morning sir, there is a funny smell outside, but it has a strange scent to it, like smoke. Could it be a fire? It's been hot enough."

The word fire caught his attention. "Did you say smoke, outside? Quick, up to your office; it looks westwards." He almost ran to her room.

She followed more sedately, carrying the child.

Maybel heard the hurrying footsteps and recognised her husband's tread. "You, slut, what's happened?"

The woman had not used Katy's name since the morning of the slap.

"Good morning, mistress; I think there may be a fire somewhere. Please come and view the hills if you wish." She curtsied again and strolled toward her rooms, not wanting to be in there with Mr Albert. Maybel was hard on her heels. JJ was still coughing occasionally, and Katy was concerned. Hopefully, the smoke would not permeate inside. She would need to keep her window shut. She had opened it wide to flush the stale air as she left for her walk.

As Katy was ambling and caring for the baby, she was slow.

Maybel wanted to pass, and she pushed her out of the way. "Move, slut," she said as she pushed past her.

The office door was closed again, and Maybel swung it open. Seeing her husband standing at the open window in another woman's quarters sent Maybel into an angry frenzy. "What are you doing in the slut's rooms? I told you what would happen!" She flew at him, scratching and clawing at him.

He went to grab at her as Maybel ran towards him with her arms flailing. She stood pummelling his chest.

Katy heard the ruckus and stood at the door watching, then turned her back to them, covering JJ's ears from the noise.

Maybel turned on her. "I told you, slut, leave him alone." Maybel was screeching at the top of her voice. She landed a few punches on Katy's back but missed JJ. The jolt from each blow made her stagger.

Mr Albert grabbed Maybel from behind and held her with her arms now imprisoned. He was fearful she would hurt the baby. "Maybel, leave well alone, will you? I was checking the fire. Mrs Harrison was not even here. This is my office, remember, not hers. She works for me." He still had his arms around his wife, and they were like steel bands. "Now go to our rooms, and we shall talk further."

She was fighting for him to release her, so he did. He had hardly even raised his voice.

By now, many of the other staff had heard the noises and were in the corridor watching the mistress screeching at her husband and Katy.

What happened next was witnessed by all the staff but Katy.

Maybel turned and continued to attack him, punching, screaming and kicking at him.

Katy still had her back to Maybel, and JJ was now crying at the shouting. Katy completely missed the next action as she was now watching the staff draw closer.

The loud ranting from Maybel continued at the top of her voice, with her screaming non-stop, and then there was silence.

Katy thought he must have covered Maybel's mouth until she noticed Milly's appearance.

It was the silence, as well as the look on the cook's face, which made Katy turn. Cook's face was one of stunned surprise, then horror; her eyes wide open, as was her mouth.

Katy turned; the room was empty but for Mr Albert.

Maybel had vanished.

Katy realised that she must have fallen through the large opening. She walked to the open window; although there was the verandah roof under her window, she could see Maybel's body had not only hit that but must have rolled off the roof, and the inertia made her be flung some distance from the hotel. Katy could see she was lying on the ground with blood beginning to pool around her head. Pulling herself inside, only then did Katy look at her boss.

Mr Albert blanched, and he was shaking. "She came at me; I just stepped backwards." He sank onto the desk in horror at what had happened. "I didn't touch her! I didn't."

Cook came in, her bulk now filling the small office door as she passed through it. She was followed by two of the barmaids and the timid maid. The cook said, "I see'd it, Missus, he stepped away from her. Backwards like, and she careered into him as though she were gonna push 'im out. She fell, Missus, she felled all on her own." Cook was weeping. "Mr Albert, he didn'ta touch her at all; he didn't. Not a single hand on her when she fell."

Milly was nodding her head in agreement of Cook's words.

Katy wasn't sure if it were of relief, or shock, possibly both. She was surprised at her own reaction. Her first thoughts were that it was a pity that Maybel had not known who she really was.

For some moments, Katy stood still in shock, shaking her head in disbelief at what had occurred. She knew someone needed to take control.

Katy turned to Mr Albert. "Sir, then we need to call the constable or at least the Major from the Barracks." She had met the man, and he seemed reasonable. As he remained silent, she said, "Milly, run down and fetch him. Esme, go with her and tell him there's a fire out near the mountains too. Cook, go and start preparing food for the firefighters," and to the well-endowed barmaid Biddy who had only started that week, Katy said, "Go and clear out the taproom and shut up the inn for the day, then go help Cook."

All the girls nodded and took off.

Katy then rounded on Mr Albert. "Sir, you need to get out of here. But could you shut the window again, please? We're all witnesses to what occurred. Sir, we'll speak for you; make sure you tell them that. We all offer to be interviewed." After he shut the window, she ushered him out of the office and into his private sitting room. She watched as he collapsed into an armchair. She knew no work would get done that day.

~

The following hours were horrendous.

Maybel's smashed and battered body was removed that afternoon after the authorities had interviewed everyone.

After the Major had given permission, Milly, Esme, and Biddy scrubbed away the dried blood. All chatted happily as they did so. Katy could even hear them giggling.

Katy's office was sealed off until it had been thoroughly investigated. She had been able to grab a handful of clean flannel napkins, but that was all; thankfully, she had taken some clothes down to be washed as she left for her morning stroll. They were now hanging outside on the line. She shared Milly's tiny room that night.

Along with all the eyewitnesses to the accident, Mr Albert was released at the end of the day.

The inn, however, remained closed.

Most of the soldiers from the barracks had been sent to fight the fires; a small detachment stood guard at the inn. Mr Albert had to stay with them until an official interviewed them. None of the staff was allowed outside, not that they wished to leave. They were now huddled together in the kitchen. JJ needed a feed and change, and there was no way she would do that with any soldier watching her. The babe was restless.

Cook could see what was worrying her. She came to her aid. "Use the larder, dear; it's cool in there too." She said to the soldier, "Eh, Mister soldier, you go check it first. There ain't no door out, so she can't runs away. She's gotta feeds the babe. The poor mite is so thirsty he can't cry no more." To keep busy, Cook cooked.

The soldier stuck his head around the larder door. And nodded for her to use it. "No tricks, mind you, lady."

"No sir, thank you, sir," Katy said, curtsying; she took her baby into the cool larder. She half shut the door behind her and then heaved a sigh of relief. She wished she could go down to the cellar, where it was delightfully cool, but it had a back door.

The bushfire blazed through the day until an intense storm developed and doused the flames at twilight. Cook had kept busy, and when night fell, there was plenty of food, but now no one to eat it. The soldiers had all gone, and with the inn closed, there was no one to serve meals to. The food would keep.

The following morning the Governor came and interviewed everyone. The inn reopened after he left, and things returned to normal.

A few days later, Katy realised it had been a month since she landed.

Chapter 6 Perry Gets a Clue

*P*erry remained anxious as the ship docked in Sydney. Nanny and Lucy had packed everything and were waiting with the children. Perry sighed, knowing his impatience would not help anyone. He would work out accommodation after he had spoken to Governor Macquarie. He had his father's letter of introduction, and it felt like it was burning a hole in his pocket. His priority was to see the Governor and then play things from there by ear. He would then seek accommodation, if not stay on the ship, before beginning the search for Katy.

With the gangplank down, Perry carried Louisa while Nanny, Mia, and Lucy followed. A somewhat tattered carriage waited for anyone looking for transport. Perry walked over to it and loaded his family in, giving directions first for Government House. The coachman could return for their luggage later, but Perry didn't want to wait for that to be unloaded.

When Perry gave his direction, the coachman looked up in surprise. He drove off once his passengers were seated. These people were obviously important. The tattered cabby headed up the hill from the docks into town. It wasn't often he was asked to take a cove to Government House, let alone kiddies too. The coachman smiled as he drove; the destination was not far away. The somewhat aged and leaky building was on the edge of the growing town. He drove carefully as he always did when he had two kiddies on board, let alone two staff ladies. He would return with their luggage as soon as he deposited them. The mountain of luggage would easily fit on the back. The coachman knew that there was no way the posh gentleman could walk there with the kiddies in this heat. "I wonder if the Governor is expecting this cove. I bet he isn't." The coachman was correct.

Perry's arrival at the lime-washed two-storied building surprised the occupants of the sitting room.

Governor Macquarie turned to his wife, Elizabeth. Calling her by his pet name, he asked, "Elspeth dear, have you arranged any visitors, my love?"

"Why no Lachlan, has someone arrived?" she asked.

"Yes, and it's a man with two children and staff in that shabby cab from the dockland. I wonder who he is?" Governor Lachlan Macquarie had a rare day at home with his wife. Typical that they would be interrupted on his day off. He shrugged in a resigned way.

Elizabeth Macquarie was also looking forward to a day at home with her husband. She was nearly seven months gone with-child but in good health. She had retired from society until the birth of their baby. If she had done this earlier the last seven times, she might not have lost them. She was normally so busy that she was as occupied as Lachlan. Consequently, she rarely saw her husband alone, and a day off together was a delight. No, these visitors were not something she had planned. The pace of Lachlan's work had been constant, and they had been looking forward to some peace and time together. They waited to see who it was.

The butler soon knocked. He had a silver salver with a crumpled letter on it. "The Earl of Collingsford, The Lady Mary Harrington and The Lady Louisa White to see you, sir, if he may. He has just arrived in the colony on a personal matter."

The Governor turned and looked at his wife. "Do you know him?"

She shook her head but did not reply.

The Governor took the crumpled letter and noticed a Ducal crest. He flicked open the red wax seal and read the letter from Perry's father. His eyes opened wide as he read. "Elspeth dear, the letter is from this man's father, the Duke of Cheatham. I met him in London at another Duke's place. Nice chaps." His startled look made him turn back to his butler. "You'd better show him in, James. Did he give no reason?"

"No, sir, none, sir." He bowed and walked out backwards.

Moments later, he was back. In a deep sonorous voice, he announced them. "The Right Honourable, the Earl of Collingsford, The Honourable Mary Harrington and The Honourable Louisa White; Lord Collingsford, may I present His Excellency, Major General Lachlan Macquarie, Governor of New South Wales, and Lady Elizabeth Macquarie." The butler bowed and waited to be dismissed. He was surprised to find that when he was, he had two little girls attached to his hands that he needed to return to their Nanny.

They stayed silent and waited until their father permitted them to accompany the esteemed servant. They curtseyed perfectly, and then Mia and Lou trotted alongside the butler and joined their nanny in a private room.

One glance at the tall, debonair gentleman drew compassion from both Lachlan and Elizabeth. Lachlan asked, "Sir, how may we be of assistance?" The Governor waved to his wife to include her in his offer.

Perry was used to pomp and ceremony, but he was nearly ready to bust. The months wasted looking for her in Kent, followed by months of inactivity on board, had been harrowing. Blow this, he thought; I'm just going to tell him everything. So, he did. Perry sank down into the armchair offered and said, "I've lost my wife." With that one line, his head sank into his hands. He felt the moisture on his cheeks and felt like sobbing, but he knew that he yet had to explain everything.

Elizabeth was by his side in an instant. "Oh, sir, how did she die? Was it on the trip out here?" She met her husband's eyes and pleaded for help. It was not forthcoming.

Lachlan shrugged again and while Perry wasn't watching, he lifted his hands in resignation.

Somewhat surprised, Perry said. "No, no, she's not dead; I have lost her." His comments made no sense. He looked from the first lady to her husband and back again.

Elizabeth motioned to Lachlan to ring for tea. "A good cup of tea will help." She seated herself again, then waited. After a while, she asked, "Where are you staying, sir?"

Perry was already emotionally drained. His glassy eyes and blank look showed he had nowhere to go. He was borderline to breaking point. He had made no arrangements; he shrugged this time. "I'll find somewhere later, ma'am. I've just arrived; we'll possibly stay on board." He had waited eight months, and now he had arrived in Sydney; he had yet to find Katy. But where to start looking?

The tea tray was brought in, and the butler oversaw the maids to place it correctly, and then they left again.

Perry lifted his head in surprise when he heard Elizabeth say, "Please, make-up rooms as our guests will be staying."

Once the door closed, he said, "That is not necessary ma'am; I shall find somewhere; I can even stay on board for some time. I just don't know where to start looking for Katy." With that, Perry poured out the entire saga. "All I know is that she came as a convict on *The Wanstead* under an assumed name. I must find some way to track down all the women and find her. A friend of hers told me the ship's name but not the name she was using."

Finally, Lachlan understood. "Ahh, well, I think you have actually come to the right place."

Once Perry had explained his situation, they spent the next hour mulling over their action plan.

The Governor's heart had gone out to this grieving man even before he opened his mouth. The hideous scars on his cheek were enough to make any grown man hide from the world; this man had met the world head-on. He seemed oblivious to the many stares. Lachlan's compassion was now stirred, and he said, "First call will be the barracks office in town. They have the ship indents and, if filled in correctly, have a physical description in them. The second stop will be the barracks in Parramatta. The women from *The Wanstead* should have been assigned by now as there is little room at the Female gaol. We can eliminate many from the descriptions they keep in the ledger. We are returning to Parramatta tomorrow, and you will all come with us. We are only here for His Majesty's birthday ball last week. The main Government House in the colony is in Parramatta. My dream is to build a new one here, but there are far more needy things to achieve before building a comfortable place for myself. My wife's condition and the possibility of a bushfire out in the West made us delay our departure last night. You can make your headquarters with us out there and start searching."

Perry looked up. There was a spark of excitement on his face. It was not about the free accommodation but his quest, "You'll help me find her? Really?"

The First Lady replied, "Yes, My Lord, I shall answer on behalf of my husband. We shall turn over every clue we can. We'll find her, I promise," Elizabeth said, feeling great compassion at his anguish.

Perry jerked his head up at the reference to his title. "May I ask another favour? I have never used my title before today; I'm known simply as Peregrin White and just Perry to my friends and to Katy. She does not like using her title either. She is a Countess twice over; her first husband, Mia's father, was the Earl of Leatherbrooke. He died, with my brother, in a hunting accident six years ago, just before Mia was born. Katy is my third cousin. We share a paternal great-grandfather." Perry told them his story.

Elizabeth mouthed, "Oh!"

Perry looked at them. "As cousins, we knew each other well, um, before this." He put his hand to his cheek. "I tried to save her father and couldn't; I nearly died, but he did. I hid myself for ten years until the day I found her crumpled in a heap on the roadside with a newborn babe beside her. I did not recognise her as she was a child of just fourteen when I had last seen her. I nursed Katy day and night, also taking care of baby Mia, and I fell in love, deeply so. We were so happy for over five years." He ran his fingers through his hair, stood and paced the room, thinking back to the horrible confusion of the situation that caused this mess. He returned to his seat and continued, "We were living with Katy's best friend, Mary, Countess of Milesdowne, a widow as well. One day I found that lady in deep distress and weeping. It was hard for her to see us with everything she had lost. I comforted her with a hug, that's all, I swear! But sadly, Katy apparently entered and saw us. We did not hear her, and that day Katy left me. She explained her reasons in a long letter, but she was wrong. I left the three children…" He paused as he saw the puzzled expressions on the faces of his audience. "Oh, we have a son, Jem, whom I have left with my father, as he is my heir." He said as though that explained everything. "Anyway, I left the children with Mary and went looking for Katy. First, for a month, then I returned, moved the children to Father's place and kept searching. Nearly five months later, Katy's friend, the philanthropist Elizabeth Fry, sent me a letter telling me Katy was on her way here as a convict on *The Wanstead,* but she was not using her own name." He once again put his head in his hands. "Oh, dear God, help me. What have I done? It was just an innocent comforting hug for a friend who was hurting." His shoulders shook with released emotion. Moments later, he lifted his tear-stained face to them and said, "I love my Katy so very much."

Elizabeth could see the grief etched on his face. She turned to her husband and said quietly, "Lachlan, what can we do?"

Governor Lachlan Macquarie knew that if Katy had been on the convict ship, the passenger list would have been filed at the officers' quarters near Hyde Park by now. He walked to a small desk, scribbled a note, then called in a footman and asked him to deliver a message.

Then they waited.

~

Major Thomas Turner arrived within half an hour with a large ledger tucked under his arm.

The butler had told the Major who was in with the Governor.

As he entered, a waddling Elizabeth made her excuses and left to check on the little girls. The three men sat discussing the situation.

Perry looked down the list of names. None rang a bell until he paused, Kate Harrison and child. His face lit up, but then he frowned. "I think this could be her, but it says she has a child."

The Major knew the situation. "Err, My Lord, the child was born en-route shortly before arrival. A boy, I believe. I saw them disembark; he was certainly a newborn."

Perry counted on his fingers. He smiled broadly. Musing aloud, he said, "So that was why she came down early that morning. It was to tell me she was expecting." Finally, the last bit of his puzzle fell into place. "Now I'm sure it's her. How do I now find her?" The bedevilled look on his face was now gone, his face glowing in anticipation of seeing his wife again.

"Are you sure, My Lord?" the Major enquired.

"As sure as I can be without a description. So, what's the next step? And Major, 'sir' will suffice, please." Perry's pleading look made Tom smile. "Her friend told me she was not using her real name."

Perry was hoping there was something the Governor could do.

Lachlan looked at the Major enquiringly. "I am sorry, sirs, I don't have the assignment book here. This is just the passenger list. We will need to go to Parramatta for that." The Major looked at the Governor, somewhat concerned. "Your Excellency, if she has been assigned already, then only you can change that."

Lachlan lifted his eyebrows in acknowledgement of the comment. He replies a little tersely, "I am well aware of how the system works, Major; I am in two minds to wonder if she has been assigned or if she's still incarcerated in that hell hole of a room they call a gaol, as she has a child!"

The Governor was slowly pacing the room as he spoke. "Wherever she is, we will find her. My Lord, I mean Perry even if we must visit every single woman on the ship. Reverend Marsden should know. I doubt she was taken without the proper credentials being filled in. I have cracked down on that."

"Thank you, Your Excellency," Perry said. His hopes of a short while ago were somewhat dashed. It now depended on someone else's bookkeeping skills.

Lachlan smiled. "We're heading out there tomorrow, so as you are staying here tonight, we can leave early before the heat sets in. The Major will dig a little deeper, and we'll go hunting tomorrow. Major, we're trying to keep their identities as quiet as possible. I shall introduce Lord Peregrin as a personal friend, and he will use no title whilst here. Do you understand? He is merely Mister White."

The Major's eyes twinkled, "Yes, Your Excellency, I shall stay mum, sir." Major Tom gave a shy grin. If only he could tell this Earl that he wasn't the only title in the colony. Another, a gentry gentleman anyway, was hiding his light under a bush. He knew his friend Sam Corbett's secret but had not even let on even to him that he knew his real identity as the second son of the Earl of Meldon. Maybe one day he could introduce them. They looked about the same age; they even had similar accents. You can't grow up in the shadow of Sam's enormous house and not know who lived there. Sam had befriended Tom because of his West Sussex accent, or vice versa if the truth were to be told, but Tom was being paid to watch over Sam's wife, Annie. Tom had known or at least suspected who Sam was, as his own mother had been a nursemaid at his big house. Tom had grown up hearing the rumours about Sam's suspected and possibly dubious parenthood. But that was another story. He thought maybe that introduction needed to be done sooner rather than later. After a few minutes of more discussion, Tom folded the ledger and left. What he heard next surprised him.

The Governor's voice carried across the room. "Turner, we'll collect you on the way out tomorrow, nine sharp, so be ready," the Governor said.

"Yes, Sir," Tom saluted, then bowed to both gentlemen and left. Good, he wasn't going to miss this adventure for anything. Tom had learned that by keeping his mouth shut, he not only learned things but became a trusted soldier. He was thrilled he would get to know more of this saga.

As the door shut, Lachlan turned to Perry, "My Lord, no, Perry, let's get you settled. Come and introduce me to these two daughters of yours. Sadly, we lost our little girl just before we came here five years ago, so I have no doubts Elspeth will be occupying herself with them. Nearly eight and four, I believe you said?" His innocuous chatter kept Perry's mind off the delay. At least they had somewhere to stay and now even had more than a clue of Katy's identity. He had the name she was travelling under. He was now sure it was Katy. No other name on the list had ties to her. Also, the timing was right for the child. He wished he could hasten things along.

The butler let Perry know his luggage had arrived as they passed through the foyer.

Perry nodded his thanks.

The Governor walked beside Perry and led him through the rooms of the Government House in town. It was about the size of his father's gatehouse at Cheatham Castle. The rooms were well appointed and the decorations tasteful, not that he noticed them; it was more that he didn't. They were not garish. He had lived so many years as simply Perry in a minute cottage that having to appeal for help using his title galled him somewhat. At least it had worked. Hopefully, tomorrow he will find his Katy.

After settling in for the afternoon, Perry and the girls went for a long walk. He let them romp on the grassy headland. The town was far less developed than expected.

The following morning their two staff were ready by the prescribed time. The girls would travel with Nanny and Lucy in the second carriage with the Macquarie's aide, valet and maid. The first carriage would stop and collect Major Tom; then the convoy would proceed to Government House.

The Governor had duties back in Parramatta and invited Perry and his entourage to stay in the guest rooms for as long as required. There were no other guests expected for some time. "Perry, I do have to warn you, though, I will be unable to absolve her conviction. I looked into the case while you were chatting with the Major. She pleaded guilty," Lachlan paused, swallowed and said, "Perry, she can't leave the colony, at least not yet. I will certainly arrange a Ticket of Leave for her when I can, and I can even reassign her to you, but until I clear it, she must stay here in the colony. After that, I will arrange an Absolute Pardon for her to return home."

The look on Perry's face was one of horror. "Stay, we can't leave? For how long?"

The Governor looked over at both men sitting opposite him. "Until her term is up, Perry. I can't make an exception just because she has a title and is a friend's wife. Once she has served her time, I can issue a release for her to travel. I'm just reworking the categories and system. Under the new procedure, there are four categories, including Ticket of Leave, which she will gain soon if she hasn't already. They are supposed to have served a minimum of three years, but I can change that. Then Certificate of Freedom when she completes her sentence. Then there is a Conditional Pardon and an Absolute Pardon. This last one is what I will arrange for her so you can take her home. She will need an Absolute Pardon to return to England, but it's not something I can exactly pull out of my hat. Well, I can, but I won't. I won't break the rules." The Governor sat thinking, "Perry, if you stay, which I think you will have to do, then I may use you both to help me with some changes to the system, and it will give you something to occupy your time."

Perry nodded, unsure what he'd agreed to, but it would give him something to do. Six years! At least he'd be with her.

They had a privy stop and a drink en route to Parramatta. Lou joined her father in the front carriage as she was somewhat anxious.

Tom looked over to the man sitting next to him. Perry would need friends. Sam Corbett could be one of them if he'd allow it. Time would tell; there was little hurry. He folded his arms and was puzzled about how to introduce them.

Perry had spent much of the time watching the green-grey scrubby bushland pass him. There was little to interest him. Then he saw some bounding animals. Sitting bolt upright, he exclaimed, "What the heck? Oh, I'm so sorry, ma'am, but what was that bouncing animal?"

Elizabeth chuckled; she had seen the kangaroos and watched them bound away. Knowing what she had thought the first time she saw them, she expected a similar response. She replied, "That, sir, is your first kangaroo. There are smaller ones they call wallabies, and there are animals like cuddly bear-like creatures called koalas, and raucous birds that will wake you in the mornings. They are locally called kookaburras." Elizabeth observed his face as he watched the strange furry animals bound away.

"Are they common? Will they attack?" Perry enquired.

Tom was beginning to like the big man with the horrific scars. Speaking quietly, so as to not wake the now sleeping child, he explained, "The big male kangaroos can sometimes cause some concern, but on the whole, they are gentle beasts. The koalas have long claws, but they are timid creatures that live high up in the gum trees. It's not them you have to be aware of, but the insidious invaders in this place kill. There are snakes and shiny black spiders, the like of which I have never seen before. Both will kill."

"Kill? They are that bad?" Perry asked, not liking the sound of either of these.

Lachlan elaborated. "Yes, and sadly the snakes are about now due to the heat. There are a few kinds to watch out for. The worst ones are the browns, but just to confuse things, they are not always brown but an assortment of colours, as are tiger snakes; they are usually marked with subtle bands. There is also a short, squat one which I have heard some call a death adder, but the most common is a black snake. A child nearly died from a bite recently, but they can make an adult terribly ill too. As the Major says, the spiders are the nasty and, yes, insidious critters. They crawl into things, especially in spring and after rain. A few deaths are reported most years. Sometimes they are found in beds, often in boots left outdoors. So, check the beds before putting the children down." He did not wish to scare the Earl, but he knew that knowledge of the dangers was best.

Tom continued to expand the risks in the area. "Bush fires are also a hazard in summer. Last week, we had a fire that worried me, but a storm put-paid to it quite quickly. Over winter, the local aborigines regularly burn the scrub, which is good, as when summer comes, there are large sections already burned that protect the towns. When the winters are wet, they can't burn much. That happened a few years ago, and the fires that year were bad." Tom waited for a reaction.

"Cor, fires, snakes, spiders, hopping animals, ones with claws. Is there anything else I should know about? Next, you'll tell me about dragons." Perry looked worried.

"No dragons Perry, but there are big sharks in the tidal rivers, so if you are wishing to swim, be aware of them too. Best to swim above the weir in town. Keep clear of all tidal waters. The water above the weir is fresh, so it should be safe enough. I should mention as the weir is new, we may well have trapped a shark on its top. There are the usual leeches and ticks, but they go with freshwater even at home." The Governor saw they were drawing close to town.

~

The journey to Parramatta had taken much of the day. They had a few quick stops along the route and a picnic by a waterway. Although Lou wanted to travel with her father, no sooner did they set off after luncheon, she fell asleep in his arms. Perry's adoration for his daughter was written all over his face. Even at three, she was so like Katy, with her colouring and attitude to life, vibrant and bombastic.

Elizabeth had stayed out of the earlier conversation, but the compassion she saw had brought tears to her eyes. Having lost her daughter, seeing him cuddle the sleeping child was difficult. She placed a hand on her distended belly. Lachlan had tried hard to get her to stay in Sydney, but she had a couple of months before the baby was born. She did not wish to be alone at any time. For this trip, she knew he would need to stay in Sydney for a week and insisted she would come. She was thrilled she had as she would not have missed this meeting for anything. If she and the Earl's wife, Katy, could become friends, that would even be nicer. She had little knowledge of children, and it seemed that Katy had four. A slow smile spread across her face; she was a convict who would stir up society.

The afternoon saw the carriage pull into a lovely building set on the top of a hill. It was a little bigger than the Sydney house but was vastly superior to the majority of residences they had passed. It was about the size of his father's hunting lodge. The first two carriages pulled up to the porticoed entrance, and they all alighted.

Elizabeth needed the assistance of both her husband and Major Tom to get down. Lou had awakened and was still groggy from her nap. She sat, awaiting her turn to alight. She had hardly spoken all trip.

Perry gathered her into his arms and, with Mia in the other hand, followed the Macquaries into the house. The housekeeper met them and offered to take the small child and show Nanny to their room. They were unexpected guests, but the woman did not seem surprised to see them. All was in readiness, and Perry was soon settled in guest bedrooms to the side of the house. The children and staff were out the back in the nursery. Perry knew that if they were to stay in the colony, he needed to find accommodation for his family quickly.

Perry was eager to find Katy; he found the waiting intolerable. The official wheels moved slowly, he knew that, but he'd spent so much time looking for her that he wanted the wait to be over.

Chapter 7 Reunited Again

On the westward journey, the governor said, "Perry, you outrank me in so many ways that I insist that you call me Lachlan. It will also infer that we are friends of long-standing and no questions will be asked. Major, not a word, please."

The Major stifled a huge grin, "I promise, sir."

Perry had agreed. It was nice to have a male friend, two actually, for he liked Tom as well. He'd been surrounded by only females to talk to for so long that he did not realise he missed the male companionship. "Thank you, Lachlan, I shall." Their friendship was now sealed; they had relaxed for the remainder of the trip.

On arrival, the governor summonsed the Senior Officer from the local barracks. He instructed him to bring such paperwork regarding the assignment of convicts from *The Wanstead*.

They poured over the large ledger. Page after page of names until the last one, Kate Parry and son, Freemason's Inn, alias Harrison. Not spelled Cate Parry as he'd seen in Kent but similar enough. It was not a name on the passenger list but the only one with a child. He read the name of James Albert as the person to whom she had been assigned. When he saw her signature, he knew for certain it was her. Most other entries were just marked with an x. But Katy had signed for herself, but as Kate Harrison, not Parry. Her elegant script almost jumped off the page. How typical that she had changed her name again. He shook his head and smiled. "Yes, it's her, Governor! I'd know that penmanship anywhere," Perry leapt up and shouted with glee. "Where is this Freemason's Inn? How do I get there?"

"We will go tomorrow, Perry; one night won't matter. Trust me on this." Lachlan watched Perry pace the room. "Perry, give me a bit of time to sort things. You don't want her to run if she finds you here in Parramatta and chasing after her, you could scare her off."

"No, Lachlan, I need to see her now. Tell me where this place is, and I'll go and see her. Please, I need to do this. One more night would nearly kill me." Perry felt his eyes water. "Please, Lachlan, please," Perry pleaded.

"Damn it, all right, but I'll come with you. It's within walking distance, but I won't say where, as I know you will hare off and go looking for yourself. Just give me five minutes, will you? Major, you'll come too, please, and bring a guard."

Lachlan went and told Elizabeth where they were going. One block from the front gate, they had passed the inn on the way into town. Perry had even remarked on the size of the building compared to others in the area. Lachlan said a quick farewell to Elizabeth with a kiss and asked her to pray. He assured her that Major Tom would accompany them, and also, he'd have the security detail a short distance behind should trouble arise.

Elizabeth stayed in her room praying for them. The three men made their way down the driveway up which they had driven just a short time ago. A security detail followed at a discreet distance. Perry would have run if he'd known where they were heading. They walked out the front gates, the guards there saluting the Governor. Tom and Lachlan led him across the street and walked down the next block.

The building he'd admired earlier was on the corner in front of them. It was a solid-looking two-story sandstone building with a verandah running along the top floor. They watched the goings-on from across the street; they stood talking with Tom to one side. Their security detail caught them up and stood to either side of the three men.

Outside the inn was a drunken group of debauched-looking males. Some were currently jeering at the buxom barmaid carrying a tray load of ales. One drunken lout was pawing at her breasts, untying the cord holding the gown closed. She was laughing and flaunting her well-endowed chest. Her breasts were soon exposed, and the drunken young man bent to kiss them.

Perry was disgusted at the now indecently clad maid. She actively encouraged the drunken man's hands to continue wandering over her body. She had a booted foot up on the bench seat, and another man had his hand cupping her buttocks, a third had his hand up her skirts, and she wasn't pushing any of them away. Perry tore his eyes from the public obscenities flaunted in front of them. "My gosh, my wife is in here, Lachlan? Are you serious? I have to get her out." Perry was horrified.

Lachlan was too but held his tongue. He'd heard of this behaviour but not seen it for himself; it reminded him of his life in India.

Perry was disgusted that his beloved Katy was living in a Public House that was almost a brothel. "Lachlan, I thought you said it was an inn, not a drinking hell hole. This is a debauched whore-house!"

"They are the same thing here, Perry; beggars can't be choosers. It's why I would not let you come by yourself. We don't have many options. This is one of five inns in this town; many more are throughout the colony. Most are as bad; often they are worse. One or two are only for accommodation, but they are few and far between. They nearly all have a taproom of sorts, and many brew their own liquor. Drinking here is a big problem. Until a few years ago, rum was the currency of choice in the colony. I don't believe there will ever be another country in the world where that will happen. I've worked hard for four years, but little has changed. On the one hand, I have the free settlers against me wanting power for themselves, and the convicts undermine all the good I try to do for them, on the other, by their rebellious behaviour. I'm stuck between a rock and a hard place." Lachlan listed the other inns in town. None sounded much good.

Perry felt himself clenching his fists. "If anything has happened to her. Oh, Lachlan, I'll never forgive myself."

Lachlan put his hand on his new friend's arm. "She's assigned, Perry, but James Albert is known as a fair man. Mr Larra owns the lease, but he has Albert running the day-to-day business. Mr Albert's wife died in a tragic accident last week, so I was here to see the site myself. She fell out of an office window. I may have even seen your wife and not known it. I was not introduced to the convict staff, but I did question them." They crossed the dirt road at the front of the inn.

Tom and the security detail cleared the path for the Governor to enter. Two waited at the door to stop anyone else from entering. The security detail placed themselves to protect them.

A man came hurrying to see the trio. He bowed low and greeted them. "Good evening, Your Excellency; this is a great honour." He was clean and well-presented.

Lachlan waved away other listeners. "Take us somewhere quiet. We need to speak to you." The man led the Governor and the two men through a side door into a sitting room.

"This was my wife's room, Your Excellency; we will not be disturbed here." Mr Albert ushered them in and shut the door. He wondered if this was about his wife's death again. He showed little grief at her loss.

Tom stood on guard outside the room.

Minutes later, Perry flung open the door and was racing towards the stairs to the upper level. He called his wife's name as he ran. "Katy, Katy love, where are you? Katy, sweetheart, I need you."

~

Katy had not long fed JJ and had put him down for a short nap. At six weeks old, he was so cute. He had taken to clutching her locket as he fed. He had broken the chain only the day before. Today he was feeling around for it. She had worn it every day and kissed it each night just before she slept. The baby was becoming more and more like his father every day. She missed Perry so much. She stood looking down at her son in the fading evening light.

It was as though she could hear Perry calling for her. No! Someone was actually calling for her, and it sounded so much like him. She caught her breath, turning slowly; she walked to the office door. Clinging to the doorpost, she could not believe her eyes or ears.

Perry stood on the threshold, puffing.

Their gazes locked.

Katy would have fallen if Perry had not grabbed her and pulled her into his arms. Tears were cascading down both their cheeks. She was crushed in his strong, loving arms, her forehead on his shoulder as she sobbed. He had come for her. He was kissing her neck, then her forehead, and finally her lips. He loved her, after all. After some while, she murmured, "Perry, why are you here? You should be with Mary; I left so you could be free."

"My darling love, how can I be free when you took my heart with you? It's not Mary that I love, but you, my darling goose. It has always been only you. If you had waited, we could have explained all. My dearest darling love, Mary found that living with us and we were so happy made life hard for her. She had a melancholy moment and needed a hug, but that is all." He paused to kiss her again. Something he had wished to do for a long time. His passion almost overwhelmed him; such was his sheer happiness to have her in his arms. He had worried about what to say, but the truth was always best. He knew she needed to hear everything from him before starting their future anew. After some moments gazing down at her, he continued, "My darling one, I was heading out for my morning walk when I came across her weeping and in great distress. I was merely comforting her. We had no idea you had entered and seen us. If we had, we would not have broken away guiltily; I would have brought you in to aid with her comfort. My love, there was nothing for us to be guilty about. Mary loves you, and I adore you; I find I cannot live without you. When we realised you were not coming back that evening, your trail had already grown cold. She willingly looked after the children when I searched for you to bring you home to us both. It took a month before I returned. I stayed with my father's friend Charles, Duke of Gracemere, in Kent. On my return, I packed our things and sent the children with Nanny and Lucy to Father. Then I left again and checked every town and gaol. It never occurred to me you would have used a different name. Then after three months, I returned to let Mary know of my failure. It was only then that I received a letter from Elizabeth Fry. By then, I had long ago completed the move to Father's place and left Mary and Colm at their house." He kissed her tears away as a look of horror crossed her face.

"Oh, Perry, what have I done? I thought you only married me for pity and then fell for Mary. You moved out of our room, and… and… I heard you laughing with her often. I was so jealous of my best friend and my beloved husband wanting to be with her. You no longer spent the nights cradling me. Oh, Perry, I'm so sorry." Her voice broke. She once more was sobbing in his arms.

He could hear the distress in her voice. He cradled her again as she wept, stroking her head. After some time, he threaded his fingers in her lovely long hair and lifted her chin. She responded to him with a deep and satisfying kiss. "Don't ever leave me, Katy; I find that I cannot breathe when you are not beside me. I have been forced to journey half the world, and I have born the horrified looks of people, but I would do it all again to get you back. I have found the stares bearable only because I knew that every mile I traversed would bring me one step closer to you. Don't ever leave me again, my Katy. I could not bear it."

They stood locked together for some time. A small cry broke them apart. "Katy, I think I know why you came down early that morning. Am I correct?"

Katy nodded. "Come and meet your son, Perry; he is the image of Jem." Katy led him through the office and into their tiny room. The baby was in his basket and stirring. Perry would not let go of Katy, so she bent down with his arm still on her waist, picked up the swaddled child, and then showed him to Perry. "I called him Jacob James, JJ for short."

Perry frowned, "I know why, both names mean betrayed or supplanted, but darling, you are so wrong, so we shall rename him, um…" he thought for a moment, "I believe David, it means 'beloved'. What do you think?"

Beaming, Katy replied, "I think that's perfect. He doesn't suit either name I had chosen for him. He's not Baptised yet so we can add it easily, but he's listed as Jacob James White on the surgeon's log. Maybe we can just add David to the front. He need never know the meaning of the other two names." They stood cooing over their son David. They were concentrated on the small child that neither heard footsteps approaching.

A cultured voice with a Scottish accent spoke. "It seems, Mr Albert, that your bookkeeper may be leaving your premises. She can work from her residence until I sort out a replacement. Can you please have her things packed and ready to leave in fifteen minutes and send for assistance to carry her things to Government House?"

Katy had met the Governor only last week. So, she recognised his Scottish lilt. She turned and sank into a deep curtsy as she had done at their meeting the previous week. She may well outrank him, but he did not know that… or did he? She glanced from her husband to the Governor, then back again. What was he doing here anyway? Why were they together?

The Governor walked to them and lifted her from her curtsy, then motioned with his finger on his lips for her to say nothing until they were alone. He watched, waiting for James Albert to leave, then said, "Countess, we are pleased you are safe. We will discuss the situation more at home, but please make yourself ready for a short walk. I knew we should have brought a carriage Perry," he said, almost to himself.

"Your Excellency, I am assigned to him," Katy exclaimed.

"Oh, I know, but please remember, I am the Governor. We'll sort that tomorrow; in the meantime, your daughters await you at Government House." Lachlan looked at the couple in front of him. He saw the stunned look on her face. The Governor looked to his new friend, dressed in the height and tasteful elegance that fashion could buy, and his wife in the brown drill gown of a convict. Yet she was still standing proud and holding her head high. She was strong and stunningly beautiful with the bearing of a queen rather than either a countess or convict. Her bright blue eyes shone with merriment. What she had been through, he couldn't bear to imagine. He knew all too well the filthy conditions of the gaols. He was keen to find a way to improve them. Lachlan looked at Perry and hoped he would be caring towards Katy. He was sure he would be even after knowing him for a day.

Her heart was thumping with excitement. "The girls are here?" Katy asked Perry.

Grinning, Perry nodded. "They are waiting for you, my beloved." Perry could not wipe the smile from his scarred face. Katy, too, was now grinning from ear to ear, although her face was now tear-stained. Tears started to flow again, but they were ones of happiness.

Lachlan, too, smiled with relief, knowing things had worked out well. "Now to get you out of the inn with minimal fuss."

"I know a way out the back," she volunteered.

Perry removed his son from her arms. His baby was so innocent and, thankfully, unaware of his sordid beginning. He could not hold back his own smile at his youngest son. Katy quickly placed the pile of his clothing into the baby basket. They had very little in the way of possessions. Perry realised she was going to pack her dresses. "You won't need those, love; I brought two cases of your clothes, sweetheart, as I knew you would not have much. Leave them. You won't need them; although your London gowns may need some adjustment, as you have lost too much weight."

Katy nodded, still grinning, and she ran to him. "Did I tell you I love you too, Perry dearest?"

Perry nodded, still smiling, unable to wrest his eyes from her for a moment lest she vanished again.

She went back to collect the last of her things. She would certainly keep the four books and her Bible, which she once more tucked down her bodice. The broken chain and locket she still had in her pocket, but she checked it was still in there. She would get Perry to buy her a new chain. Only yesterday, she read the passage in Isaiah 12 verse 2, where she was comforted about being under God's care. *Behold, God is my salvation; I will trust, and not be afraid: for the Lord, Jehovah is my strength and my song; he also is become my salvation.* Katy just had not expected her salvation in the from of to be her husband appearing with the Governor by his side. By the time she had placed everything in the basket, one of the outdoor male convicts, Gilbert, was waiting at the door with Mr Albert. She wrapped Elizabeth Fry's shawl around her shoulders and waited to leave.

The Governor said quietly, "Until tomorrow at nine, Albert, my office, and don't be late." Lachlan instructed that the basket be taken to Government House after they had left. They now needed to get her out without being seen.

Katy asked permission from Mr Albert to use the garden entrance, and she would take the four of them out the back way.

As the Governor was with her, Mr Albert was not prepared to say no to the group. They left via the kitchen door.

Tom scouted in front of them. He ushered them through the shadows until they reached the side gate at the bottom of the driveway. From there, they walked towards Government House. The soldiers on duty stood to attention as they walked past. Once past the sentries, they would be safe.

Tom returned to the inn and dismissed the protective detail. He allowed them to stay for a drink before returning to duty. He smiled. Life may just get a little more interesting. He escorted the manservant back up the hill with the baby's basket. They each carried a handle.

The enormity of the situation of her release hit Katy as they walked up the hill. After eight months of holding back her sorrow, it was like a dam burst. Her passive tears turned into rivers, causing her to stumble; now unable to see clearly, she tripped. She could not even catch her breath, and she found it impossible to walk any further. She fell to her knees, sobbing, now totally unaware of her surroundings.

Perry handed their sleeping son to Lachlan and scooped Katy up in his arms. She clung to him as though she would never let him go. Her hacking sobs were now so violent that they rocked him. He cradled her to him; he could feel her bones through her thin gown. He wondered what she had been through over the past months. He realised that she had been starved. Time would unfold her story, but he would not probe for that tonight. It was enough he had found her. In the meantime, he would be there for her. He had nursed her before; he would do so again. Only this time, it was the mental scars she had rather than a grave illness.

On arrival at Government House, they were met with surprise by the guards on duty at the front door. The Governor had certainly not left with a baby nor a collapsed and weeping lady. She was in the arms of his guest. The butler flung wide the door to enter the spacious foyer. The Governor said, "Guest wing, Francis."

The butler led the way to the guest rooms, throwing doors open as they walked to the side of the main building. Katy's weeping had eased, now with just an occasional hiccough. Perry laid her carefully on their bed; her reddened eyes and swollen cheeks nearly broke his heart.

Lachlan said, "Tomorrow will be time enough to talk. Sleep, I will have food sent in. I shall take David to Nanny." He left. They were now alone.

Perry gave his undivided attention to her. He didn't want the girls to see their mother in such a distraught and bedraggled state. He would get her bathed and put to bed; then tomorrow, she could dress in one of her own gowns. She had lost so much weight that they would hang on her, but it was the best he could do. Considering she had birthed a child only six weeks ago, she was vastly underweight. His concern for her had mounted when he carried her. She was as light as a feather. At home, her delightful curves had been his joy. When nursing Katy after the birth of Mia, he knew how rounded she had been. She was now skin and bone. He was amazed that their son was so well. He knew Katy would have sacrificed herself to see he had enough nourishment.

The maids had already unpacked the cases of clothing that Perry had brought her from England. A nightgown was laid out on the bed. Little else would now fit her. Perry rang and ordered a bath or some form of warm water to be obtained to wash her. He had no idea what facilities they had here, but he would bathe her.

A large hip bath was soon brought in with many buckets of hot water, and he assisted her in purging herself of the horrors she had experienced. He was right; she was skin and bone. He chose a gown for tomorrow and sent it away with the last maid to see if someone could take it in for her. Lucy was good at sewing; maybe someone could help her. Katy's skin hung wrinkled on her stomach, and it no longer glowed with health and vitality as it had once done. Perry rubbed her back and washed her long lank hair as they talked of happy things. She sat willingly, accepting his loving ministrations. He soon wrapped her in a luxurious towel and carried her out of the bath. Their talk had cleared up many things. He dressed her in the nightgown, which now hung loosely on her figure, and then he helped her to bed. He lay beside her, just holding her in his arms. She dozed on his chest while he stroked her wet hair. He gazed at her beloved face and drank in her presence and her sweet scent as she slept. She awoke when they heard a tap on the door.

Easing from her embrace, Perry answered it.

Nanny had brought little David for a feed. "I'm so pleased you found her, sir. Is she well?"

Perry greeted her with a smile. "Yes, Nanny, but she will need lots of feeding up. Can you please bring a mug of tea, some egg custard, she likes that, or something else nourishing? Whatever you find will suffice." As soon as Perry heard that Katy had had a baby, he told Nanny about the child. The Governor mentioned the baby's new name when he took him to her.

There were no secrets from Nanny as she already knew what had occurred and why Katy had run. So Nanny had prepared a place for the baby as soon as they arrived. Elizabeth Macquarie had a cot ready for her own child. She suggested they use that until they could get their own. Nanny said both girls were already delighted with their baby brother. Nanny would not have bothered them had it not been necessary.

Katy heard her son's hungry cry. When she saw Nanny carrying him, she wept afresh. "Oh, Nanny, thank you for looking after my family." Katy held out her arms for the baby but took Nanny's hand too.

Nanny Grimes reassured her. "All is well, m'lady. The little girls are safe and well and itching to see you. You just get well, ma'am." She then set to cleaning up the bathing area.

No one had mentioned their other son. Katy looked at her husband anxiously. "Perry, where's Jem? Has something happened to him?"

Perry shook his head. "He is fine, sweetheart. He's at home with Father as he needed to start schooling, and I couldn't bring a tutor for him and Nanny and the girls, so I thought it safer to leave him at home. I promised him I'd bring you back."

She nodded her understanding. She knew the bond between her eldest son and her father-in-law was warm and loving. Jem would be both safe and happy there. "Can I see the girls once I've fed this little man?" She gazed at the baby on her breast. "Perry, what about Davy as a pet name for him?"

His twinkling eyes caught hers. "Yes, I like it, sweetheart, and yes, I think we could arrange for the girls to come." He sat and watched her feed their son. For a while Davy's tiny hand sat flat on her breast while he drank; then he seemed to be looking for something, his hand stilled as Katy caught it in her own.

Katy explained. "He pulled and broke my locket chain yesterday."

"Then I shall buy you a new one." Perry watched her face, now visible in the lamplight. He wondered how he'd break the news to her. Lachlan had again told him on the way down to the inn that they had to stay. As he had done before only the day before, he thought the direct approach would be best. "Katy, we can't leave; we must stay until your term is up. You pled guilty, darling, and therefore Lachlan's hands are tied." It was best she knew what was ahead of them. "Katy, I've had little time to think, but Lachlan will get you reassigned to me. We will find our own place and make our lives here for a while. Jem can join us for a few years, then return to school when he's old enough. His tutor can bring him out as soon as we are settled."

Nanny tidied the room and heard his comment; she had caught his eye and nodded her approval to Perry. Smiling, she then left them alone.

Katy drew a deep breath and released a sigh. "If only I had trusted you. I am so sorry, Perry. Put it down to baby brain."

Perry was still in awe of his wife. "For you to love me enough to leave me for Mary. Oh my, Katy!" He just could not find the words. He wiped away a tear as it rolled down his scarred cheek. He choked up when he thought about her, thinking he no longer loved her. He found he could not express the emotions of both love and desire he felt for her. She was back in his life, and for the moment, that was all that mattered. His heart finally reunited with his body. He would never let her leave him again.

An hour later, the nearly complete family sat on the big feather bed in the guest room at Government House in Parramatta. Perry held their son, and the girls were cuddled up to either side of their mother. There was much laughter from the girls as they gave a minute-by-minute description of everything they had seen since they arrived in Sydney. Mia understood that her mother was happy to be back with them but could not understand why she was crying if she was so happy.

Katy chuckled, then said, "They are called happy, sad tears, poppet. I'm just glad we're together again. I miss Jem, but hopefully, he will join us soon too." Katy thought they might as well know what was happening sooner rather than later. "We will stay for a few years, then hopefully, we will all go home together. Jemmy may have to return to school, but we'll see what happens."

Nanny collected the three children for their dinner and bed. Katy kissed them and promised that she'd see them all in the morning. Dinner trays were brought for Katy and Perry to eat alone in their room.

Perry had ducked out to speak to Lachlan and to thank him as Nanny brought in Davy for his late evening feed and waited while chatting with Katy about things. At six weeks old, the baby had settled. Katy told Nanny his routine and then handed him over to her care.

Perry returned, and at long last, they were alone again and not likely to be interrupted for some hours. He watched her for a while, then changed into his nightshirt. He snuffed the lamp and slid into bed beside her.

Her soft voice said, "Hold me, Perry, and never let me go." She ran her hand over his cheek. "I told you never to be afraid of the scars. For you to be here, you have overcome your fear of people. I find that I now fully understand what you meant. Physically I am unscathed; no one touched me as I was obviously with-child, not like some other girls. I feel our Lord protected me that way. But I have seen things and heard things that will take a long time to forget." Katy found it hard to believe that Perry loved her and had come for her no matter what happened.

"We will be each other's support, my love, as we always have been." Perry leaned over and kissed her, easing her nightgown off one shoulder so he could kiss her neck.

"I need you closer than that, Perry; I have missed our being together. I need you, as close as you can be. It is six weeks after his birth, and I want you," She slipped off her nightgown. "Touch me, Perry, love me."

His nightshirt joined hers in a heap on the floor. There was no more talking for some time. Each was relishing the closeness of their beloved partner. They were obeying the physical needs they desired and had missed. Still entwined, they fell asleep. Whatever the morrow would bring, they would be together. Their healing could now start. He would not leave her alone at night ever again.

Katy awoke in the middle of the night. It seemed she had just gone to sleep. Nanny was bringing in Davy for a two o'clock feed. They just had time to put on their night attire before she entered. Katy fed the child, and Nanny departed.

Perry waited until the door closed and reached for Katy again. "Are you tired, sweetheart?" he asked hopefully. They did not immediately return to sleep but enjoyed another coupling before curling up in each other's arms for the remainder of the night.

Katy woke again soon after dawn, desire raging through her once more. Nanny was due back in about half an hour. Katy turned her head on the pillow to see Perry's eyes wide open and watching her, grinning.

It seemed he had the same ideas. He was smiling at her somewhat lustfully. "Good morning, wife; sleep well?" His morning kiss fanning the desire in her.

Katy stretched luxuriously, drawing him close to her. "Yes, but waking this morning seems so much nicer than yesterday and the many lonely months before that."

His hand slid over what remained of her post-birth stomach. She felt it almost do somersaults with desire. After Nanny had taken Davy away at two o'clock, Perry had reached for her again. Last night had been the fulfilment of both their dreams and lusts. This morning, she reached for him. She needed to show how much she wanted him in her life and in her. She knew that their baby would need a feed soon, and she also had to go to work until things were sorted out. In the soft morning light, her thin frame was easily visible through the delicate lawn nightgown. He was right in thinking about how much weight she had lost. The curves were now gone; her ribs were visible. Her breasts should have been filled with milk, but they sagged, yet how beautiful she still was. He would spoil her and care for her, as he'd done before. He would nurse her back to health once more.

Their physical yearnings were once again satisfied; they had just adjusted their night attire and had added their dressing gowns by the time Nanny brought Davy to their door.

Katy could see how tired she was. "Nanny, Lucy can do the night-time run, or better still, Davy can sleep in here with us until he's sleeping through. Can you arrange for his basket to be in here at night? You can't be on your feet all day then nights too."

"No, m'lady, it's just that it was a strange bed. I'm not used to feathers and softness like this." Her eyes twinkled. "I'm ever so glad to have you back, though, m'lady."

"Nanny, shh! Here I'm just Kate Harrison or Katy White now, I suppose. Above all things, do not let on about titles." Katy looked somewhat concerned.

"Oh, ma'am, yes, Mr Perry said that. I told Lucy to call you Mrs Katy as we do at home. I hope that is suitable?" Nanny knew this couple and how much she loved them. Most Earls and Countesses lauded it over everyone and never considered others' needs. Miss Mia may not be Mr Perry's child, but she had a special place in Nanny's heart. The young girl was unspoilt and adorable. She had looked after the child from a month old. She had been at a loose end in her previous post, as her four charges had already started school, but they had not wished her to leave. Mr Perry's father had met her some years before and knew she needed a new position. Nanny had come directly to them. She had no other family as she'd been a foundling. She had never married, as she'd been employed all her life. She had cared for children from her very first job in Kent, but the four boys were all grown now. Mia was her favourite charge. She had an adorable nature and would often be found helping the staff with their chores. "No, she was not a usual Earl's daughter," Nanny smiled.

Perry thought it was as good a time as any to ask her if she'd stay for the years they needed to be here. "Nanny, while you are here. I need to ask you something. You know the situation with Mrs Katy; it seems we may be unable to leave for some six years. Would you be willing to stay that long? Can you discuss it with Lucy and let me know?"

Nanny grinned. "Mr Perry, I do not need to ask her. You are our family. Neither of us have anyone else at home; we were both foundlings. We are like Ruth from the Bible, sir, '*Wither thou goest*' and all that. Sorry, sir, but we're staying with you both; no, sir, we're staying with you all." Her grin spoke volumes.

Perry was delighted. Now he needed accommodation for his family. Once Katy's placement was arranged later today, that would be the next thing on his agenda. He must decide where they would live.

They were ready for the nine-clock meeting. The children were taken out for a walk around the gardens before it got too hot. Davy was not due for a feed until ten.

Chapter 8 A Plan of Action

Mister Albert promptly appeared at Government House's front door at nine o'clock. He stood under the covered portico staring at the solid timber door with the arched glass window over the top. He was brought inside, shown into the Governor's office, and asked to wait. He hardly dared move. He was so nervous.

The foyer of the grand house was awe-inspiring enough. The official office made his knees shake. He barely had time to think since his wife's death last week and now this. Being summoned to Government House was not what he expected this week, and he could have done without it. Meeting the exalted Scottish gentleman last week had been fearful enough. His interview and the corroboration of his staff had seen him released without further enquiry.

Now he sat quaking, literally on the edge of his seat. He should have realised there was something fishy about that lady. He knew it was too much to expect her to stay, for she was so good at her job. He sighed. At least without his shrew of a wife, he supposed he could do the books himself. He knew this lady was married; he just had not expected her husband to turn up with the Governor. He wondered who she was. A frown sat on his brow as he waited for his summons.

~

When James Albert was escorted out just over an hour later, he was over the moon. His main concern was the bookwork. He was content for Mrs

White, as she was now to be known, to be reassigned to her husband's care, but she would still do the books for him, only at their residence, wherever that was to be. For him, this was a win, win. She would do his work, but he no longer had to supply her keep, and he would get his office back. As he walked outside, he punched the air in glee. "Yes!" he said to himself. His only regret was that Katy was not to visit the inn at all, ever.

The soldiers at either side of the doorway glanced at him, quite surprised that he was leaving in such a good mood. When anyone was summoned to the Governor's office, they were not usually there for a good reason. Rarely did they leave happy.

Perry, too, now had some direction; however, the Governor's decision meant they had to stay locally. If they were there for six years, he wanted to purchase or, better still, build a house for his family as there was nothing in town that he would wish to live in. In the short term, he had to find a rental somewhere. Katy was only partially reassigned as Lachlan did not want to show favouritism, and Perry would not permit him to break any rules.

Lachlan had said there was land aplenty, and he could arrange free labour. After James Albert left, they perused the last few news sheets while Katy went to feed Davy.

Perry read the advertisements. "We passed Phillip Street as we drove in. There's a rental in Phillip Street, near Hyde Park, Lachlan; where's that?" Perry asked.

"Oh no, that's in Sydney; you will need something nearby; you may have to take rooms at an Inn, even Mr Albert's one, until you can find somewhere. It's one of the better inns in town." Lachlan watched the horror cross Perry's face. "I wish there were somewhere better, but that is also on the 'to do' list. I want a better Inn in town but have not found the right couple yet."

Perry nearly burst. "I don't want my family living in an inn. Is there nothing else for rent?" Perry pleaded.

"I'll ask my secretary, John Campbell if he knows of anything. He's due here this afternoon. I left him with some work to be finished before joining me. Are you sure you won't take a grant of land straight away? There's no immediate hurry for you to leave here. We won't have visitors until...." Lachlan consulted his diary, "...April Perry, that gives you eight weeks. With our baby due, I tried to clear the schedule somewhat. In that time, you can select some land and get a building started. I can allocate a building gang or even two. It will be quicker to build in brick, but the stone is cooler. If you choose land down near the river, it gets some breezes, but admittedly, some of that area can flood." Lachlan was looking somewhat anxious. "Perry, there is something I want to ask you. It would actually suit us if you could stay until after my Elspeth has delivered our child. I would really appreciate this. I feel you are a godsend to us at this time. We are so alone, and to have someone near, I now consider a friend. We have the Campbells and my nephew, but

Perry, to put it bluntly, I'm fearful. Even though we have known each other for so little time, I feel I can trust you. A big plus is that you are not here to feather your own nest like other free settlers. I'm not sure if you know, but we have already lost one child and had numerous miscarriages; Katy obviously knows about parenting, as does your Nanny. Elspeth has a friend here in Elizabeth Macarthur, but she will be unable to assist for various reasons. If you stayed here at least for a month after Elspeth has delivered, that would be wonderful. Oh, Perry, I am so worried about both her and the bairn." Lachlan looked pleadingly towards Perry.

Perry was both surprised and delighted. "Lachlan, of course, we'll stay if you wish us to. I feel we are already imposing on your kindness. But I must ask, though, what's the hospital like here? It would be better to be in Sydney at the newer place, wouldn't it? Just in case something goes wrong, I remember you said something about a new hospital there. Having said that, our children were all born at home. However, we always had a doctor standing by just in case." Perry thought back to the amazement he felt when helping Katy deliver Jem.

Lachlan nodded. "The hospital there still needs completion, but it is certainly better than here. I have a man chosen as the chief surgeon, but he can't start yet. You will learn his name soon enough; it's D'Arcy Wentworth." Lachlan fell silent, weighing up the pros and cons of where she should give birth.

Perry watched him pace the room.

Lachlan finally said, "Yes, I suppose you are right. We'll stay here for a week or so, and we'll have a hunt around for a place to rent or buy, then some land for you and get a building started. I shall then ask around for someone who can design and build you a house if you so wish. I heard there were some skilled labourers on the ship you arrived on. Some were convicted for forgery. You will need a good sturdy design with a verandah for shade. This is not something we consider at home, but here it's vital. In the meantime, I know of some cottages being built in Phillip Street. I shall ask if they are for rent. If so, one should be completed in months, if not weeks. They will do until you find or build a place for yourself and your entourage."

Perry frowned, then said, "Lachlan, what about Katy and her work? She can't be in both Sydney and Parramatta," Perry asked.

Lachlan had been thinking about that. "I have a suggestion. Her work is not something she has to be on-site for. For the duration of when we are all in Sydney Town, I could set up a series of couriers to bring in the paperwork each afternoon, and she could do the work over the next day and return the ledger pages with the returning courier. We could all come back here once our child is born when my Elspeth can travel. We both prefer it here as Elspeth loves the parkland. We'll go for a walk later and see what she has already done to the gardens in the domain. We open it up to the public frequently."

Perry smiled in agreement. "Lachlan, I have learned never to underestimate the strength of a woman. I have been with Katy during the birth of our first two children. Her forbearance was incredible." Perry knew what he had seen Katy go through. "She has now gone through this willingly five times. If it were me, once would have been more than sufficient."

Lachlan frowned. "Five?"

Perry nodded. "Her first son was stillborn. He would have been the Earl of Leatherbrooke had he lived."

Lachlan gave a nod and then said, "You were with her as she gave birth? Seriously? Were you not made to wait outside?" Lachlan was incredulous. "I have absolutely no intention of having anything to do with pain, blood or births. Just not going to happen."

Perry gave a chuckle. "Oh, trust me, I wished to do just that, but Jem wasn't moving. She was exhausted, and I needed to support her as she walked around the room. The midwife was late, and Mary, Nanny, and I were the only ones at hand. Lachlan, I would not have missed that experience for the world. I insisted on being with her throughout Louisa's birth. She had to squat for her delivery, and I needed to support her again." Perry sat thinking back to that fantastic day. "Lachlan, for her to go through that alone in a convict ship horrifies me. She told me they had a kind doctor on board, and she was taken with one of her friends to a small cabin and gave birth in reasonable cleanliness. Davy survived, but even more importantly, so did Katy."

Lachlan shook his head. "I'm still not intending to stay for the birth. I know I need a boot up the nether end, but I would rather host a bunch of arguing politicians than attend a birth. That, by the way, is the only function I have booked in the next few months. I bet the child will come on that very day." Lachlan shuffled with uncertainty. "Perry, we need you with us even more than I thought. Please say you will come," Lachlan was now pleading. "I find I also need a friend, one who is impartial. I feel like you are both a gift to us from our Maker."

Perry smiled. "Of course, we'll come." He too, thanked the good Lord for how things had worked out. He may well be an Earl by title, but the fact the Governor had befriended him to this extent was somewhat surprising to him.

Towards the end of February, the White family moved back to Sydney with the Macquaries. The trip would be slow, and they would space it out for the women's comfort; Elizabeth, in particular, was getting very ungainly.

Lachlan had not realised that the sixteen miles of road were in such need of an upgrade. When travelling with a heavily expectant woman and one's wife at that, Lachlan noticed every jolt and bump. It was so bad that they were at a walking pace for some of the route. He decided to set a team to work immediately on repairing the surface and improving the thoroughfare so it could be traversed at some speed and comfort.

His mind had been active all the time they had been in Parramatta.

Conversations with Katy had already given him an incredible insight into the conditions of the women at the gaol. He knew the situation was dire, but not how bad it actually was. Katy had told him about her time in solitary confinement with no explanation and barely more than an empty bucket. The more he spoke to this vibrant lady, the more he admired her.

The room they had been kept in had sleeping facilities for only thirty women. Over a hundred and twenty had to bunk down that first night. Thankfully half were moved out quickly. Although she had been there for a minimal amount of time, she saw much. He had increased food and water immediately. He also knew he needed to improve sanitation further on his return.

Katy found it very hard to explain that the only privy was a shared bucket. She was so embarrassed to have to discuss bodily functions with the Governor. Then she had to explain that there was no place to empty it or wash it after using it. More often than not, the room was so overcrowded that the women just squatted where they could as there was barely space to move in the overstuffed room. They had no facilities even to wash their hands afterwards, nor any way to bathe. The stench and filth turned her stomach, even thinking back to that time. Katy went on to tell them of the lack of facilities for her with a baby. She had been allocated only six napkins and again had no washing facilities for her child. She mentioned that one of the staff was helpful and even supplied her with a glass of milk.

Both Lachlan and Elizabeth had been horrified.

"Only one glass?" gasped Elizabeth. She was aghast and said, "Katy, were you really given only one glass of milk in two days? And you had little water, am I right?" Her face blanched when she heard this.

Katy nodded. "I felt guilty drinking it too, Elizabeth. The gruel was thin and not very filling, and the morning porridge was cold and gluey, but at least it was filling. The others were just as thirsty. I have no idea what the men get, but I'm sure it's not much better. And they have to work all day on that in chain gangs."

Lachlan was horrified. That too would be addressed immediately and he could do that from Sydney.

Katy thought of what was needed, and she said as much. Water needed to be taken in at least three times a day and food increased to something nourishing morning and evening, with at least bread and ale for mid-day meals, even on the chain gangs.

Lachlan knew her words would give him some ammunition to improve all the convicts. He would send instructions back as soon as he arrived. Before they left Parramatta, the Colonial Secretary, John Campbell, found Perry a large block of land, and Lachlan had the transfer expedited. A convict-building gang was assigned to the project.

Perry oversaw the initial planning but soon had to leave the overseer in charge. He discovered that some of the convicts on site had arrived on *The*

General Hewitt as he had and were skilled draughtsmen. These men had been convicted for forgery and were clever with their hands. Three, Francis Greenway, and Henry Kitchen, were architects, and the last, Joseph Lycett, was an artist. They were obviously acquainted. John Watts was a soldier with draughtsman skills. All were now working with the building gang assigned to construct three small cottages next to each other in Phillip Street. Perry had found out their names by chance. He saw Joseph sketching on the back of the plan. He had visualised what the finished cottage would look like for Perry. Francis pointed out a design flaw to the overseer while Perry was there one day. Perry overheard the conversation and walked over to see what the problem was. The overseer, John Watts, pointed out the issue, and Perry agreed with the convict. The changes were made, and Perry instructed that these two convicts be brought to him. After discussing their talents, he decided to see if he could find them both some drawing materials and a pad of sorts.

When Perry looked at the size of the cottages planned, he paced out the area of the rooms and the orientation of the buildings. He agreed with Katy that they did not need a big mansion to live in, even though it would be only a short-term stay. He asked for the western end one to be completed first. It was slightly larger than the other two and would give them three good-sized rooms to live in, while the next one was built for Nanny and Lucy. While it also had three rooms, they were slightly smaller due to a large rock on the ground where it was to be built, the third cottage was the same size as the top one, but the deck at the back would be smaller as its garden flooded.

Lachlan had an extra contingent of convict workers allocated to speed the construction. They were to move bricks onto the site from the brick pits. When they returned in about eight to ten weeks, Perry hoped that the first cottage would be completed and the second nearly ready.

Mr Albert was not that keen on this new arrangement, but as it still meant he was getting the required bookwork done for free, he was willing to let the Governor to make whatever arrangements he liked. It also meant that he had the government and the inn's owner, James Larra, off his back. With Maybel now gone, life at the inn was once more peaceful, at least from domestic tension. The patrons often still were rowdy, but he could cope with them. He did not realise how much Maybel had screeched at him. He would be more careful with his choice if he married again. She was a pretty face, but her nature did not match. He would instead marry an ugly woman with a loving heart. It was a pity that Katy's husband had turned up; she was the woman he'd like. She had obviously married for love. The man's face was almost melted on one side, yet she seemed to adore him. What a woman! Yes, he'd look for one like her. He so wanted a son. He might even look around for a convict wife; at least, she'd be appreciative.

On March 28, 1814, Lachlan Macquarie junior entered the world on the afternoon of the official dinner party.

Perry had been in the colony for some six weeks.

Katy and Nanny had Elizabeth up and walking around the room, much to the horror of the antiquated midwife. The doctor wished to bleed her before lying her down to deliver. Elizabeth turned to Katy. The desperate appeal on her face made Katy chuckle. "We'll walk, and you need to breathe through the contractions. When you are too tired, you can have a hot bath. Lachlan can support you, although he's determined not to be with you through this birth. Nanny has delivered more children than your midwife. Her technique may sound strange, but it works. Trust me about this."

Elizabeth nodded her agreement.

Lachlan joined her for a while after they had prepared her for the birth. She was in a nightgown, and she had a significant contraction as he walked in. She clung to him as Nanny talked to her, breathing through the pain of the spasm.

Hours later, she was so tired. Lachlan stayed until she had a bath. He had to go and change for the function. Elizabeth had just emerged from the hot water; it had eased the pain, and she had three contractions while in there. Lachlan had returned while she was dressing and was with her for two more contractions, then he said, "I will go and check on the proceedings downstairs." He was called downstairs to do his duty and promised to return as soon as possible. However, he had no intention of doing so.

Ten minutes after she had dried off, she needed a basin and then vomited. Then gave a blood-curdling scream.

"Ahh, good, action stations, everyone; I believe we're about to welcome and new little Macquarie," Nanny said.

The doctor walked over and inspected Elizabeth. "Yes, she's fully dilated and ready to deliver."

Nanny handed him a bottle of rum. "We've washed up already, doctor." She expected him to wash his hands, but he took a swig rather than wash in it.

Katy and Elizabeth saw his reluctance to cleanse himself, and Elizabeth asked Nanny to deliver the child.

The doctor was livid. "Why am I here then?"

Katy left to find Lachlan to let him know of the situation.

Although she was having another contraction, Elizabeth said in a pained voice, "In case you are needed, Dr Langford, and only then. They should be able to handle this," Elizabeth muttered. "It's my call. Where's Lachlan?"

"Him be back shortly, dearie, he's been got called away," the midwife said in her imperfect English. She stuck her head out the door and asked for him to be called.

Katy came in as she opened the door. "He's on the way, Elizabeth. Now you have to push this child out."

Elizabeth nodded, then took a few deep breaths and pushed. On the third push, the head was out.

Lachlan came in dressed in his official dinner finery and nearly passed out at what he saw. A substantial lump the size of a small melon was protruding from his wife's nether regions.

Katy quickly ushered him to Elizabeth's side. "From here, you don't see as much of the gory things, but you get to see the good bits. Hold her and comfort her, encourage her too. Just listen to Nanny." Katy stood back and watched the miracle of birth unfold. She may have had five herself, but she'd never witnessed a new life being born.

The baby was out, and Nanny held him up so they could see him. The baby was moving, but he was slightly blue. Nanny turned him over and gave him a swift smack.

Taking a deep breath, the baby wailed, his lungs filled, and he turned a healthy pink.

Nanny held the long cord in her bloody hands. "See, the cord is still full? Watch it pump and then go flat." They all stood watching. Even the doctor observed quietly. He was leaning on the mantelpiece. Then the midwife handed Nanny some string, and Nanny tied the cord twice. She asked the Governor if he wished to cut it.

He shook his head, unable to speak. His eyes were unbelieving at what he'd witnessed. For him, the entire thing had taken less than ten minutes. He ignored the hours of labour his poor wife had just endured.

Nanny had Katy cut it while she held it firm.

Lachlan was in awe. Thinking, "How did my Elspeth lay a baby like that? She is so small, and the child was not."

Elizabeth was exhausted. He sat kissing her face. "We have a son Elspeth, and he's a wee bonnie little lad. And he's got healthy lungs too. Listen to his bellow."

Nanny suggested that he go and share the good news downstairs. She knew the afterbirth coming would cause much pain. If the Governor passed out, she didn't want a bevy of soldiers in the birthing room.

Lachlan bent and kissed her forehead. "Thank you, Elspeth, from the bottom of my heart. Thank you." He stroked her forehead again and left.

As he closed the door, she asked, "Has he gone yet? It's coming." She let out another blood-curdling scream and delivered the afterbirth.

Lachlan heard her and raced back inside. All he saw was so much blood. He stood frozen to the spot. "What's happening? Is she all right?"

Nanny was as calm as usual. She quietly answered, "This is the afterbirth, Sir. As 'Howdie' or your midwife, would you like me to bury it for you?"

He nodded, amazed that she knew of that Scottish tradition, and he returned to Elizabeth's side. "Elspeth, darling love, I didn't know the pains of what you go through to bear a child; it is not worth it, my beloved." He thought to himself he would manage to avoid any contact with the birthing room altogether if there was a next time. His gaze took in the activity in the room, but his eyes fell on his exhausted and pale wife.

"But look what we have now, Lachie. A beautiful bairn, and I want him to be named after you." She struggled to sit up.

Lachlan assisted her.

Katy handed the swaddled baby to Elizabeth, and they were cooing lovingly over him. He was beautiful. His small round face had been wiped clean, and he was swathed in linen and lay wrapped in his mother's arms.

Nanny and the doctor were deep in conversation about the cleanliness of one's hands when birthing. She was scrubbing the blood from hers, and he was nit-picking over her attitude.

The midwife had taken over cleaning up Elizabeth. "Ye needs to feed the little tacker, ma'am. T'will help yer flow slow down."

Lachlan took the hint and left them alone, returning to the official dinner party below to deliver the good news.

Doctor Langford had just gone, having not been needed. He had returned to the hospital.

~

A month in Sydney flew by quickly.

Katy had caught up with her friend Emily. She loved her work and told Katy that one of the grooms had asked if she could walk out with her. They had been given permission.

Elizabeth was up and about only days after the birth. Little Lachie was thriving. Katy and Elizabeth's bond grew while they spent time nursing their baby boys. Katy had been spoiled with every possible treat that Perry could source. Eggs, custard, fresh clotted cream, and he had even found some delicious fresh fruit. She had put on some of her lost weight and was looking healthier.

Lachlan and Perry had also become firm friends from the strangers who had met in very unusual circumstances.

Soon they had all moved back to Parramatta, and the two men went for long walks through the expansive gardens. There they discussed many of the areas that needed improvement, including a desperate need for decent accommodation in Parramatta.

Perry's impartial eyes saw things that Lachlan missed. He'd been able to walk around the streets of Sydney Town in old clothes and talk to many of the town's men. His scarred cheek let him mingle with the convicts, many of whom also bore similar wounds. Some were visible, and many others had their backs scourged. He could easily have been a visiting sailor. He listened to conversations and discussions about grievances that the Governor would typically never hear about.

After Perry's first sojourn, he had learned to dress down for such walks, and he purchased some serviceable work clothes, as he called them.

~

In the two months, they had been absent from Parramatta, the first cottage was complete, although it had to be fitted out. The foundation of the second cottage was already started, and the ground was being cleared for the third one. This one would be for friends or rental; they had not decided on its use but had taken the lease on all three. Perry had ample funds, as his father had given him a wad of hundred-pound notes before his departure. He also had a few purses of coins. Perry had asked for the bulk of his money to be kept safe in Lachlan's office. He would have liked to place it in a bank, but there was none in town. Perry suggested that Lachlan open one in the colony.

It was another building Lachlan added to his list to construct.

Once back at Government House in Parramatta, Perry and Katy kept away from the prying eyes of society. They never appeared at any dinner where other guests were invited. They made their life as simple as they could.

Katy had kept up the bookwork, and Mr Albert was happy. He'd not yet discovered her entire identity but knew her husband to be a friend of the Governor. For him, that was enough. He knew her now as Mrs Katy White. He had been asked to keep her activities quiet, and he had. Katy was thankful things had been able to be arranged so skilfully. Even at church, he gave her a slight nod of acknowledgement but never overstepped the bounds of propriety. He was indeed holding up his part of their bargain.

Chapter 9 Moving Forward

*L*ife settled into a routine, and soon it was time for them to move forward.

The first cottage now complete and furnished. The second one was finished enough for Lucy and Nanny to move into after Easter. The cottages were minute compared to life at Government House either in Sydney or Parramatta.

Lachlan had arranged a convict cook for them, and Lucy and Nanny did everything else. They planned that the cook and Lucy share one room, and Nanny was to have a room to herself. However, they found that the cook was married, and her husband only lived a street away in his own cottage. She was allowed to live at home and come in daily. She was a convict but she had fourteen years to serve and had to work, like Katy. So in Perry and Katy's cottage, there was enough room for the three children in the second bedroom of the main cottage. The third room, which was on the street front, they used as a sitting room. These cottages would do until Perry built them a proper house.

On return to Parramatta, the building began on the vacant block on the corner of George and Church Streets. The backyard was large enough for both stables and an orchard.

Lachlan said, "If you build towards the front, you can have a large garden in the backyard, you can have lots of privacy too. It's also out of the flood area, so you can add a huge cellar. I find that having a cellar or basement is a delight in the heat of summer. Arriving in February, you only felt a few hot days this year, but the heat is so intense that the candles melt in their sconces some years. Trust me in this; you really need a good cellar and wide verandahs, both top and bottom. A big deck out the back will also be delightful as you can eat outdoors occasionally."

Considering Perry was used to being cold over Christmas, eating outdoors and a hot summer took some getting used to. The orientation of north-south also was something he needed to take into consideration

With Lachlan's assistance, a large two-story stone house was planned. It was, of course, to have a large cellar, an enormous storeroom, a pantry, and wide verandahs all around but even wider at the back. As well as the two storeys, there was to be a large stable at the back, with not just a hayloft but rooms for male staff. There was also an area under the house that could be converted into an apartment if required. Perry smiled when he saw this room as it was more significant than the cottage they were currently living in.

Perry needed some time to grasp the sun's north-south change. When the building was designed and the orientation sorted out, they were getting excited about their first home. Perry had only rented the tiny cottage in England. It was just a single room with no privacy at all. He and Katy had lived there in complete happiness until they had moved to Mary's house. They had cuddled to stay warm under the blanket Justin had brought them. This new house would be their first real home.

The planning and building were a huge learning curve for Perry, but he enjoyed every moment of it. He enquired around and was given the name of the architect he had met earlier while building the cottages. As Francis Greenway had arrived as a forger with three others and was a convict, his services were free if he proved himself. This could be a possible path for the felon to pave a new life in the colony. So, with this build, Francis threw everything he could into the plans he drew for Perry. With Lachlan's assistance, they put the design into being. It would be the best and strongest house in the street.

~

By the time the cellar and first floor were completed, Katy was expecting another child. Davy was now eight months old. She had put on some of the previous weight she'd lost and looked much healthier.

Neither Nanny nor Lucy were coping very well with the independent living, for Nanny wished to be on hand twenty-four hours a day for her charges. Mia and Lou adored their little brother. Both girls would entertain him until he fell asleep, often laughing. His deep-throated chuckles and gurgles of delight brought joy to them all. He was such a happy baby. His hair had grown, and his luxurious dark curls bounced as he frequently threw his head back and gave his adorable baby chuckle. His belly laugh would set them all off, and he would often fall backwards from laughing so much.

Perry had finally written to his father requesting that Jem, his tutor, and whomever else he wished to send come for an extended period of about five years. He had written home as soon as he had found her. When Katy's conviction was served, they would all return to England. That would be towards the end of 1821. He wasn't exactly sure when they counted the date from her arrest or her conviction. Until then, they would do what they could to help this infant town and colony grow.

In the tiny cottage, Perry and Katy would sleep wrapped in each other's arms. They could never get close enough. Throughout the day, they would often pass, just needing to touch each other. A hand on the shoulder or Perry's hand on the small of her back. They were just loving touches of utter contentment. Over their meals, he insisted that she sit opposite him at the small kitchen table so he could gaze on her at will. He loved watching her mobile mouth as she spoke. His love for her deepened daily. However, they never talked about Mary.

Perry and Lachlan had already sat down and as Lachlan put it, written a campaign plan. A list of buildings he would love to see constructed. Perry was the silent partner in his building campaign. He insisted that his name and his family be kept out of documentation of any sort. He became Lachlan's eyes and ears, and they would pore over the next improvement to tackle at their weekly meetings. Being Governor had both its benefits and drawbacks; Lachlan had many different projects going at once; however, he was now constantly adding more.

One evening over a joint dinner, Lachlan had explained his first months as Governor, "Bligh was still here, and the deposed Governor did not take kindly to my arrival. The colony was in turmoil after the Rum Rebellion. Macarthur, even in his absence, was still stirring up trouble. Do you know Bligh was supposedly found under his bed hiding? I have some doubt about those rumours." Lachlan chuckled. "I shouldn't laugh, but the retelling to me was, shall I say, interesting. Macarthur and I passed as I was *en route* here, which was a blessing. His estimable wife is an admirable farmer. I should confess my Elspeth, and Elizabeth Macarthur had met in England before we married. She is having trouble with trespassers at Elizabeth Farm like we are on our domain. She even inserted a notice in the paper asking people not to traverse her farm in town here; now we have the same problem." He told them of his plans. "I opened a new marketplace in Sydney in my first year and brought a semblance of order to the rabble. I'm still working on coping with the glut of food, followed by famine and only last year did we obtain enough coinage to supply our needs. We are still short of funds, but things are slowly sorting themselves out." Lachlan had left his conversation there as Elizabeth said she needed to feed Lachie and Katy needed to get Davy ready for bed. Rather than go home, the ladies retired to the nursery and left the men with their port.

Now that the ladies had gone, Lachlan had continued where he had left off with their conversation about children. He sat staring into the depths of the port in his hand. "Perry, I never told you I did something I should not have done. Did you know I was married before Elspeth?"

Perry gave a non-committal shrug. He had heard rumours of this, but his friend's words were a confirmation of the words.

Lachlan's voice almost broke. "My beloved Jane died, and I was heartbroken. I was stupid and took my comfort with, shall I just say, unwise decisions; the drink was the least of them. Hence the pox marks. Perry, I became ill, very ill; I contracted a disease of which I am ashamed. Sometimes I still find myself melancholy from Jane's demise. Even when I met Elspeth, I was still mourning for my wife. I poured out my grief to her when I came home. Although she knew all about that, Elspeth secretly agreed to marry me; she is also my cousin, much like you and Katy, by the way. Then I went to India again as I needed to be healed before becoming man and wife. She waited three years before we married. I married Elspeth; I do love her, you know, but she knows me well. Well, she was expecting our daughter, and I was overjoyed. When the baby was born, I named her after my first wife. Elspeth was understanding; however, she knew that Jane was the love of my life; I adored her. I wore a mourning band around my arm for many, many months after her death. Far longer than required. Sometimes I wish I still had it on, but that's not fair to Elspeth. As I said, my dear wife agreed, but then our daughter died too, so I have lost Jane twice. Then Elspeth and I lost more babies to miscarriage. When little Lachlan was born, I braced myself for his death as well, but Perry, he's such a bonny babe." He finally looked across at Perry. "You are so blessed, Perry, Katy has bounced back to good health after Davy's birth, and she seems to carry children easily."

The two men continued to discuss children and their small achievements for some time. Eventually, Perry and Katy were taken back to their cottage in their small unmarked carriage. Lachlan often used this in Parramatta to move around the town in relative secrecy. Both the carriage and horses were just standard vehicles like many others used. Also, Perry was often seen driving it, so few realised the Governor privately owned it.

Perry liked this incognito idea and decided to hunt around for one himself. He perused the weekly newspaper and also started looking for furnishings for the new house. He found an advertisement that caught his eye. A man was leaving the colony and selling his house's entire contents. This included books, furniture and, best of all, vehicles and horses. He took note of the information, contacted the agent, and purchased the lot.

~

Only a week later, Perry thought back to that conversation with Lachlan. Katy fell in the back garden, and she lost the child she carried. He had heard Katy scream and was by her side mere moments later. She had severely twisted her ankle and had fallen face first. He had carried his weeping wife inside. She was bleeding by the time he reached their bedroom; her skirts were now soaked with blood.

Nanny tended to her and came from their room to say she had lost the baby. Perry went to her and gathered her to him. They wept together. Nanny buried the tiny babe in their back garden.

Katy took weeks to recover from this. It emotionally drained more from her than her time in irons. When Perry revealed that Elizabeth had lost babies in the same way, Katy asked if they could visit her as she was still bedridden because of her ankle.

The Vice-Regal couple had arrived at the tiny cottage in the unmarked carriage; it would return for them in an hour. Both Perry and Katy now understood Elizabeth and Lachlan's grief.

Elizabeth went to Katy, and they could talk and weep together. For the next hour, they talked and cried and talked some more. Each gained strength from the understanding and caring friends they had become.

For Katy, it was what she needed. She did not know about the excruciatingly powerful waves of emotion she would suffer at this early stage. She had certainly experienced them after the loss of her first son but was unprepared, considering she was but three months along.

Elizabeth called in both men, and the four discussed the loss and grief experienced after losing a child or a miscarriage. Both men had no idea that the loss of an infant at this early stage caused a woman so much anguish and emotional turmoil. Elizabeth told her that this was normal. She had experienced this each time she lost a baby.

Lachlan had been so busy each time Elizabeth miscarried that he'd not been around much. Finding comfort in a friendship with others who had experienced the same thing brought solace to both women and understanding to Lachlan and Perry.

Soon, Katy could stand on her injured ankle and slowly return to her duties. She even wanted to go and collect her daily work, but Perry had put his foot down about her ever returning to the inn again. All the receipts were brought to the cottage, and the ledger was completed there.

James Albert noticed that the handwriting was often different, but he'd not quibble if the work was done. While Katy was ill, Perry had completed the books or even worked with her if she'd been busy. It was usually only an hour's work if they did it together. The ledgers had to be presented weekly to the Freemason's Inn's owner, Mr Larra. He insisted they must be done perfectly, or he'd could lose his licence from the Government.

While Katy was partially bedridden, Lachlan, Elizabeth, and an entourage of others attended the road's official opening across the Blue Mountains. Members of the official party included: John Campbell, Dr William Redfern, William Cox; Sir John Jamison; John Oxley; George Evans, James Meehan, and a few surveyors. Others were Major Henry Antill, and Lieutenant John Watts, the military officer and architect. John Lewin, who was the official artist for the event, collected many insects for his natural history collection, and finally, Joseph Bigge, their coachman.

The trip took the best part of a month. It was April when they left; it had been hot, and by the time they spent the first night on the mountains, the frosts had arrived, and it was bitterly cold. Sleeping quarters were virtually non-existent. If it were not raining, a tent, although sometimes they slept in the carriage.

Lachlan and Elizabeth huddled together to keep warm. They may well be Scottish and used to the penetrating cold, but they lived in thick-walled houses over there. But here, there was no protection from it at all. At least it wasn't raining; however, it was so cold that it would have turned to sleet or snow had it done so.

On their return, Elizabeth was delighted to be reunited with her son. She was also delighted to find Katy healthy again. Elizabeth sat talking with her friend while Perry's meetings with Lachlan resumed, but in Perry's sitting room rather than Government House.

Perry was surprised that Lachlan often travelled around the colony with Elizabeth and had pumped his friend for information about the trips they had already done. Lachlan had also admitted that they had become so disoriented on one early trip that they had classed themselves lost. It had been on that trip that he named Windsor, then Richmond. They also visited further areas to the south to Castlereagh, Pitt-Town, Wilberforce, and Liverpool. He had existing roads improved and new ones built.

That same year, he had recently seen off three explorers on a trip westward to find a passage across the Blue Mountains and beyond, hopefully. Blaxland, D'Arcy Wentworth's son, William, and Lawson, were told to report on anything they found of use, farming land, water, minerals, terrain, everything. He was desperate to find more farming land. He hoped there would be fertile plains over the mountain range.

Lachlan frequently picked Katy's brains about the treatment of the convicts in the hulks and transports, the local gaols, and the female ones in particular. Katy may have only been incarcerated for a short time, but it was more than they had. He added more ideas to his list.

The new Hyde Park Barracks in Sydney had been completed four years before and were a thing of beauty if one could call an army and convict barracks such. It sat proudly on a hill near the parkland on Macquarie Street. The first stage of the hospital was recently completed, with the chief surgeon, D'Arcy Wentworth, now in charge. Expansion plans for that were already underway. Also, the turnpike road to Parramatta was repaired once more, and the road was extended westward.

Lachlan and Perry listed a swathe of other buildings that needed attention and others yet to be built. Perry still wanted Lachlan to open a bank and a decent accommodation Inn in Parramatta.

Perry had been so impressed with the work of his convict architect that he brought him to Lachlan's attention. Perry lost count of the ideas now on Lachlan's list. Francis Greenway was now conscripted to design some other government and public buildings.

Katy laughed, saying that Lachlan would need to retire and concentrate on building if he didn't take a rest. He was tireless.

Perry agreed but said, "Katy, he's utilising the convict labour. He could put them in chain gangs as they used to be, but they are all learning a skill while they work, so few are now just labourers. Many have become so good that they are beginning to be paid for their skill."

~

A few months later, Perry and Katy were both on hand for the Macquaries when a major catastrophe occurred. It was early October, and this day became seared in their memories.

Elizabeth was being driven to Sydney when her coachman hit and killed a small child. To make matters worse, it was the little boy's third birthday, and he was well-known and much loved by them all.

Charlie Thomas had been waiting for his father to come home for his special day. He knew his father was a bodyguard to the Governor; he'd be riding with the official coach, which was due past his house. Sadly, as the coach rounded the bend too fast, the child was standing on the roadway waiting for his papa, and tragically, he was run over. The coach pulled up almost instantly.

Charlie was the youngest son of Private William Thomas, a Light Horseman in Governor Macquarie's personal bodyguard. The Private William saw it all happen, almost in slow motion, and could do nothing to stop it.

Although Elizabeth had not seen the accident, she had felt it. She was shattered when she discovered that a child had died, and she both knew and loved the little boy. Although the front horse had knocked him over, the two side carriage wheels had passed over his tiny body. An angry mob of neighbours soon surrounded the carriage, and the horses were released. The now-empty carriage was pushed to Government House; Elizabeth had alighted before this occurred. The crowd parted and allowed her to go to the child's body. Elizabeth had picked up the dead boy and carried his little body in to his mother.

Mrs Thomas collapsed when she saw whom Elizabeth was carrying. There was little blood, but the child was obviously dead. Private William Thomas was distraught, as was expected, and yet he was desperately trying to protect the staggering drunken driver from a lynch mob that was forming.

The growing crowd was now trying to kill the driver. To make matters worse, Private William's eldest son, also named William, had seen the entire incident unfold. Private William eventually spoke to the crowd and asked them to leave, as he had to attend to his family; only then did they all realise he was the child's father. They went as quickly as they appeared. Private William collected his eldest son and went into his wife.

Elizabeth waited for what seemed an eternity before the doctor came. He said the death was instantaneous. By the time she had made it to Government House, Elizabeth suffered a nervous collapse; the incident prostrated her for some weeks. Even with a seven-month-old baby to care for, she didn't move from her bed for over a month. To know it had been her carriage that was responsible shattered Elizabeth.

Katy and Perry came from Parramatta as soon as they heard, and

Katy sat with her, just holding her hand. There was little more she could do. Elizabeth would be drifting off to sleep when she would jerk awake. She kept feeling the bump as the carriage passed over the child. When she did sleep, she'd jolt awake or have a nightmare.

The funeral was held a few days after the accident. Elizabeth was not permitted to go. Perry later told her that the mother also had not attended. Private William and his eldest son stood hand in hand and watched the small coffin being lowered into the ground as young Charlie was buried.

Lachlan had come to her side as soon as he could, but he'd been away on government business. Mary Campbell, the Colonial Secretary's wife, and Katy alternated their time at her bedside. Even Elizabeth Macquarie came and sat near her friend for a while. No one wished to leave her alone.

It took weeks, but little Lachie's needs eventually drew Elizabeth out of her melancholy. They all returned to Parramatta; Elizabeth didn't want to be in Sydney.

Perry made sure that the driver had not been drinking before they departed. From that day, both men made sure their coachman never drank and drove again.

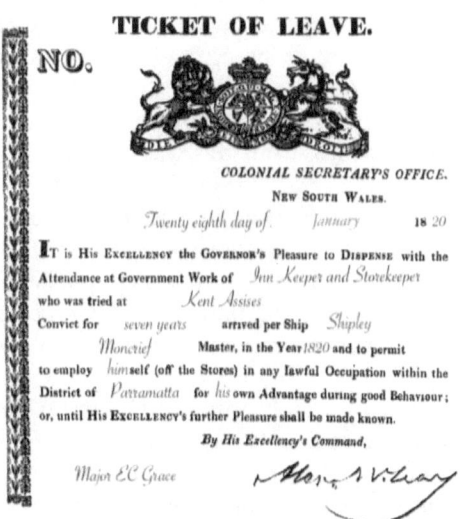

TICKET OF LEAVE.

NO.

COLONIAL SECRETARY'S OFFICE.
NEW SOUTH WALES.

Twenty eighth day of January 18 20

IT is His EXCELLENCY the GOVERNOR's Pleasure to DISPENSE with the
Attendance at Government Work of *Inn Keeper and Storekeeper*
who was tried at *Kent Assises*
Convict for *seven years* arrived per Ship *Shipley*
Moncrief Master, in the Year 1820 and to permit
to employ *himself* (off the Stores) in any lawful Occupation within the
District of *Parramatta* for *his* own Advantage during good Behaviour;
or, until His EXCELLENCY's further Pleasure shall be made known.

By His Excellency's Command,

Major E C Grace

Chapter 10 Future Developments

*L*achlan acted on many of his ideas, and one, in particular, was at Katy's

suggestion. This included that the special women's prison have a large workplace that Governor King had initially suggested. Some of these reforms were his ideas, but nothing had previously come from them.

Lachlan had already decided to overhaul the ticketing system for convict indenture. With so many more convicts arriving, the ability to house them became dire. He could not place them fast enough, particularly the women arriving with children. No one wanted them. So, he revised a new Ticket of Leave system, allowing the convicts to work and live off-site with those assigned. He now made the convicts work for half their term before considering their release onto the ticketing system. With his revisions, the better-behaved ones could gain almost instant release as a seven-year term was normally partially served in England and on the voyage out to the colony. Government stores still supported them, and food was still rationed. He was thrilled to see the new permanent barracks completed in Parramatta, Windsor, and temporary ones elsewhere. Emu Plains farm was redeveloped, and fresh produce was now being shipped to Government stores for distribution. Halfway between Parramatta and Emu Plains, a government pig farm was expanded, as the stench they made was best kept well away from the settlement. They called the farm Rooty Hill. Other livestock were also housed there, and the productivity of this farm exceeded expectations.

Churches were also built-in many areas, and wherever possible, all Government convicts were to attend divine service. This caused ire amongst many, but the crime rates were dropping, and so was drunkenness. Drunken debauchery was often the source of many crimes. Lachlan knew this needed immediate attention, reining in the immorality that had grown out of all proportions. He knew how disastrous this was not only to the health of the body but also to the soul.

The night Perry found Katy at the Freemason's Inn, they both had an eyeful of the loose behaviour of convicts, emancipists, and free settlers. Lachlan had already closed numerous inns and public houses in Sydney, reducing them from seventy-fire to only twenty. Crimes figures in Sydney Town were easing, but immorality was still out of control. He had to think of something else.

As a chief surgeon at the hospital, D'Arcy Wentworth was made superintendent of a police force. He saw both sides of the story and gave Lachlan his advice.

Ten months after Perry's arrival, their house was nearly complete. The speed at which Lachlan had made things occur was astounding. However, Perry sat with his head in his hands one evening.

Katy was watching him, unsure if he was praying or worried; she was concerned. It was a cold winter evening. After the children had been put to bed, she sat knitting. Nanny and Lucy had already returned to their cottage for the night. She hoped they would soon move into their new house. "My love, something is disturbing your peace."

He nodded and looked up at her. "It's Lachlan, sweetheart. I'm worried about him. He is presenting his new idea tonight, and I've been praying for him. In a way, we are responsible for them." Perry again ran his fingers through his hair.

"Oh, how?" Katy enquired.

"We were talking last week, and rank came up, you know, me and having a title. One thing led to another, and soon he was telling me about the King's proclamation to Governor Phillip when the colony was started. I'm not sure how well it will go down, but I foresee much resistance from certain sectors." He lay back in his chair. "Katy, as a reward for good behaviour, Lachlan wants convicts to be able to resume their rank from which they came before their convictions. Governor Phillip wrote to him, and Lachlan showed me his letter. His actual words were to encourage *the benign Spirit of the original establishment of the colony, and His Majesty's paternal instructions as to the mode of its government.* Apparently, Captain Phillip is encouraging him in this endeavour," Perry continued.

Katy was still listening intently.

Perry knew that Katy loved hearing of the growth in the colony. Both of them had thrown their ideas thick and fast to Lachlan, and he had listened to most of them. Perry continued, "Sweetheart, he wants to see emancipists as equals once they have served their terms, and we have seen that he certainly treats you as no different to me, and you are still doing your time. Where would we have been without his assistance? I have no idea, Katy. Did you know that both Justices, Simeon Lord and Andrew Thompson, were emancipists? For I did not. Reverend Marsden refuses to sit down at the table with them, let alone serve with either of them in court. So much for Christian forgiveness, eh? He calls them immoral!"

Katy nodded in agreement. "True, I have my own issues with Reverend Marsden, for he knows who I am. At least he knows I was if not still am, for I am still a convict. He will not speak to me unless you, Lachlan, or Elizabeth are present. Imagine if he knew I, no we, had titles; he would be crawling all over us both, I'm sure. He makes my skin creep, Perry. I feel it will all come to a head shortly. Thankfully he does not know of our exalted connections. I'm sure he would somehow use that tit-bit of knowledge to his advantage." Katy kept knitting but was deep in thought. She didn't hear him when he next spoke.

"Sweetheart, we can move next week," Perry repeated it, and she still didn't answer. He had been preparing for the imminent move by purchasing furniture and household items for them. He could see she was now thinking deeply about something. "Katy, love, did you know that Marsden Street was named after Reverend Marsden as a sop to appease his ego? I think it may fail."

Katy nodded but didn't stop knitting but replied, "I guessed that was how it got its name; he has influence and power in his pocket, but he associates with the wrong sort of people. I can see how he reacts if someone crosses him. Did you know he shipped the first wool back to England?" Her brow creased. Something was worrying her.

Perry spoke to her again.

And again, she didn't reply.

A frown crossed his brow. "Katy? What is concerning you? Twice now, you've not heard what I said, and that's not like you."

Katy looked up and frowned as though deep in thought. "Hmm? Oh, sorry, love, it's Janey Brien who has been on my mind, Perry. I told you about her, she is working at the gaol, and I know we will need some staff. She's a 'lifer'; I didn't know what that was until recently. She will never be released, as she is doing a life sentence. Perry, could we see if she would be able to come to us? She was the one who gave me the books and things for Davy. If she were with us, I would at least know she would be well treated. I thought that when Lachlan moved the women out of gaol, she would need a placement. It won't be permanent, but it will be for five years and by then, who knows what else Lachlan will have built?"

Her concern for people who had shown her kindness never ceased to astound him. "There's more, though, isn't there?" he asked.

"Yes, I thought that these cottages will be vacant when we move. If we extend the rentals on all three, we could use them as accommodation for expectant women and abused prisoners rather than stay in whatever conditions they are placed into in gaol like I was. What do you think? It would be a start. Janey could even oversee the welfare of the women in the cottages."

Perry was surprised, he had not thought of them being quite so hands-on with helping the convicts, but he liked the idea. "I'll certainly ask, love. Lachlan has registered me, so I can get what convict labour I wish now. I suppose they could come under our care. If we give them some light work to do here, like sewing, they could work from home. I don't like the thought of 'owning' people. I feel it goes against what the Bible teaches. I pay Lucy and Nanny, and they are with us by choice. They are as good as family to us both. To some extent, our cook Betty, too, as her husband is a free settler. She would have been sent to Windsor if she were not with us. With her husband now just up around the corner, it's convenient for us all." He tipped his head to the side. "You know, with the barracks just down the street, the soldiers could oversee them." Perry fell to thinking about their move. After some time, he asked, "Katy, have you started packing yet?"

Somewhat surprised, she replied, "No, dear, are we nearly ready to move to the new house?" Katy asked rather absentmindedly.

Perry chuckled. "I didn't think you were listening. I said we can move in next week."

"Oh really? That is good news. And thank you for your offer to ask for Janey."

"Did I offer?" He chuckled again. "I thought you had asked me if we could? Katy, this is not like you. Something is on your mind."

Katy nodded; she was now concentrating fully on his words. She put her knitting away. "Perry, we need to do more for them. Elizabeth and Lachlan need more ideas, and I would like to be able to help. I have this need deep down inside of me." Her fist punched her chest. "Perry, I just need to do more. I am in a position to help. Of course, I want you beside me, but I know what they are going through."

"Really? Lachlan has asked me much the same thing. Have you any ideas?" Perry looked over at his wife anxiously.

"Oh yes, Perry." Her face was now radiating joy. She was delighted that her input was wanted. "Elizabeth has asked us tomorrow afternoon to meet with a gentleman doing great things in Sydney. I wondered if we could come under his banner and work with his new group. He calls the group 'The Benevolent Society of New South Wales'. It sounds just like what we would be able to help with."

Her pleading look made him chuckle again. He was already planning to be part of this group but had not heard about the luncheon. He and Lachlan had discussed the benefit of such works in the town. He lay back in the chair and stretched his legs toward the fire with his arms behind his head.

"Katy love, the founder's name is Edward Smith Hall. Lachlan was telling me of him at our last meeting. Edward is in contact with Sir Robert Peel and William Wilberforce in London, and they are looking for supporters for their planned works. Lachlan told me that he already has one taker, and it will set the cat amongst the pigeons when his name is released. Katy, it's Simeon Lord. When Lachlan made him a Magistrate, it got many noses out of joint; well, he is on the board of the Benevolent Society."

Katy was intrigued. Giggling, she said, "Simeon approves of this new society? Oh, Reverend Marsden will not like that! He won't even stay in a room with him if he and Simeon are invited to the same function." She chuckled again. "I know whom Lachlan will support. I don't know how they all work together as Magistrates. Some others are also stirring things up again. Elizabeth told me that the goal of this group was, in her words, "For promoting Christian knowledge and benevolence." I think it's quite hypocritical that the main spokesman against them is a minister. Not because of their principles, but because of the emancipists involved." She picked up her knitting again and clicked away before saying, "Perry, if we get involved with this here, then when we get home, we can assist Sir Robert and William Wilberforce too. It's also one way of healing some of what the previous Duke did to all the young girls."

Perry had been listening to her and agreed. "You'd be happy to do that?" He saw her nod. "Father had the devil of a time cleaning up after Duke Julian." He still found it hard to believe they had the same great-grandfather. Perry said, "Lady Mari's maid, Sarah, accidentally revealed that she had been one of his victims, as had her mistress. That discovery had come about when the young girl came in looking for her mother. The girl's name was Betsy. Sarah revealed that Betsy was her daughter by Duke Julian. Oh, my love, I had no idea that a man could be so debauched that he would abuse his own daughter as well as her maid. When Father and I went and stayed with Lady Mari Broome-Hall just before the fire, I was sitting in the library reading, curled up in a winged armchair, when she and Father came in. I should have made my presence known, but I was deep into my book. By the time I realised they were in an extensively personal discussion, it was too late to reveal that I was there. Katy, when Father inherited the title of Duke of Cheatham from Lady Mari's father, he had no idea what he was assuming. Father's first years as a Duke were spent placating and paying off many parents of the children the previous Duke had sired. Considering how old the man was when he died, I was stunned."

"You mean Lady Mari was abused by her father?" Katy sat up astounded; she was alarmed at what Perry had revealed.

"Yes, I thought that's what you meant." He was horrified that he had let that cat out of the bag. He realised that she now needed to know the rest of the story. "Yes, sadly, from when she was thirteen. Then he had at her maid and sired Betsy. Sixteen years later, he also abused their own daughter,

Betsy. But they were just three of the myriads of others that Father found. The minister in the local parish certainly had his hands full. Being the Duke's only legitimate child, Lady Mari refused even to allow the Duke to have a funeral. He was placed in the family crypt and forgotten. Father said that they threw a party on the village green when the village heard he was dead."

Katy gasped. "I heard about that, but I didn't know the reason. Oh, Perry, I wish I'd known. I would have been able to have done something for some of the girls and their families, let alone Aunt Mari. Not that she's my aunt, she's just a cousin, but that's what I call her out of respect for her age." Katy was so sad. "I didn't know Perry. Why didn't I know? I thought he was just beating them. I had no idea he raped anyone."

Perry tried to ease her pain. "Sweetheart, you were only about fourteen when he died, and that was when I found out. It's not something that you can even mention to a married lady, let alone to a child. Darling, the fire happened soon after we returned from that trip. Your father died, as you know. Then I was so sick with the burns that I nearly died a few times from infection. It took years, but I survived; however, after that, my melted face brought horror to so many that I left."

He sat looking at them. "Katy, we had so little time to think back then; we just got on with helping where we could. Father is still coping with the repercussions. When I went home just before coming out here, he had recently heard of another woman trying to cope with the child she bore to the previous Duke." Perry thought back to finding the poor girl and her sick mother, who had been a maid in the kitchens. They were living in squalor, and his father had loaded them into his carriage and taken them back to the castle.

"Seriously, Perry? How is he helping them?" Katy had once again put her knitting aside.

Perry explained what his father had achieved in the years past. "As he had the estate to restaff, he's been re-employing many of the abused girls and their children if they were old enough. Father has found about thirty of those poor mites so far. He built a school to educate all the little ones. The school was also for the village children. I had known it was being built before the fire but had not realised why."

Katy sat wide-eyed listening to Perry's words. "I know about the school, but it's for Duke Julian's illegitimate children?" Her mind was wandering; she sat thinking. "You know, we could do that here, sweetheart. Teach other children to read and write. We're already teaching our own; why not take in some more?"

Perry loved watching her think. He could see the micro frowns and small smiles whip across her face. "You would like to do that? I'll ask Lachlan when I see him tomorrow."

She nodded. "Perry, I've also been thinking about Lachlan's idea of the Female Gaol. He asked me to think about what they needed, so I thought of what they could use there. It needs to have cooking facilities, preferably a good kitchen, a bathing room, dormitories, of course, to have some room around them. But they also need some work to do if they stay any length of time. If occupied, there is less likelihood of trouble happening, at least it's so with staff. I wonder what they could do to occupy themselves?"

Over the next few days, Katy kept a small notepad on her person. For if she thought of an idea, and by the time she found something to write it down, the children had distracted her, and she would have forgotten her thoughts. So she now carried a pad and special graphite pencil Perry had found for her in the stationery box. Perry was busy with Lachlan, so she had gone for her morning walk alone; he joined her when he could. While Lachlan was around, they always had their heads together over some project or other. Her morning walks along the riverbank were a good time for thinking. Nanny and Lucy would have the children, so she was free for a while. She usually relished the time they spent together now, but she didn't mind being alone. She would have a few hours between feeds for Davy and used the time to stretch her legs before she had to start on the bookwork.

~

One morning she left the cottage and walked down to the river's edge. It was so peaceful in the morning light. On a previous visit, she had found a fallen tree that was some twenty feet from the edge of the mangroves. It had a lovely view of the river. She often sat on this log, writing notes and ideas on her little pad. Other residents were constantly walking in the cool of the morning along this area, and they would wave to her or sometimes stop and chat. However, this morning, Katy was alone. She usually sat listening to the sounds of the town, the mill creaking as the wind turned the sail, the calls of soldiers chastising the convicts, lowing of the cattle and the intermittent whinny of the soldiers' horses, not to mention all the delightful bird sounds. Occasionally she would hear the crack of a whip.

Katy would jump at that, hoping and praying that it would be for a beast, not a man, not that she liked seeing beasts whipped, either. This morning, however, there were far more noise than usual. She could not figure out the ruckus, but the soldiers were looking for something or someone. She shivered but felt sorry for them, the escapees. If she'd known what being a convict entailed, she never would have embarked on her ridiculous idea. It was too late for regrets, so she would use her position to assist others. She put her head down and kept writing. There were shouts and an odd shot. She glanced up but saw nothing; she could not see anyone close. Maybe one of the convicts had escaped. She knew she should head back to the safety of the cottage, but she was across the river from the commotion.

Katy was deep in thought and did not hear the fall of footsteps behind her. She had no time to scream before a hand was clasped over her mouth and nose. Flinging the pencil and dropping the notepad, she tried to claw away the stinking fingers and uncover her mouth to scream. She had no chance. She was lifted off the log backwards by the person she now realised was probably the escaped convict.

He wrapped his other arm around her and dragged her towards the nearby thick mangroves.

Katy was kicking and flailing with every muscle she had; a slipper came off and lay unnoticed on the path. She tried to kick backwards but was hampered by her skirts. She managed to kick his shins once, but he just laughed at her efforts. The manner he held her, she could not make a sound. She tried biting the fingers on the hand, but she was held so tight she couldn't even do that. Her nose was squashed, and his fingers were digging into her cheek, and they hurt. The man's stench was overwhelming; it took her back to the smell of the gaol. The way he held her, she also was now finding it hard to draw a breath.

Her struggle became one for her life. She needed to breathe. Her fight to pull his hand off her nose became her primary battle. She gave it all her concentration, but she knew she was fighting a losing battle. She prayed Perry would come, screaming to herself of her love for him.

While she struggled, they reached the mangroves. The filthy man said, "Shut up and stop wiggling."

So, Katy wiggled harder, and her other shoe came off. A thought flew through her mind; if she freed herself, she would find it hard to run on the rough surface.

It was all to no avail. The effort used up the last of her air, and the world blacked out. By the time he arrived at the path into the mangroves, Katy was limp in his arms.

He released the hold over her mouth and dragged the now unresisting Katy deep into the bushes. His thoughts were of the delectable woman and what he intended to do to her. Blood was already pumping to his nether regions. He could barely wait to get her to an area where he could have his way with her. He'd been dreaming of a woman, any woman, for months. His own manual gratification did not slake his lust for this beauty. For her to almost fall into his lap was a dream come true. He had been hiding in a flattened-out area in the mangroves for over an hour. He saw her walking along the riverbank and couldn't believe his good luck and that no one else was around. When she sat down only twenty feet from him, he felt like cheering. Now she was out cold; he could take his time. He not so gently lay her down and untied the string holding up his filthy trousers. He slid them off entirely so they would not hinder his activities. His buttock was covered with dried filth, and his genitals were covered with sores. He was so engorged that he knew his actions would not take long.

Katy was still lying on her back, totally unresponsive. Thankfully he'd not killed her. He ensured that she was breathing; he'd tried it with a corpse before and had not enjoyed it. It had been dead too long and was swelling. He decided he liked them warm, breathing, and preferably responsive; fighting was fun too. But beggars or convicts, he laughed to himself, could not be choosers. He lifted her skirt, and rather than undress her; he needed to use her first, then he could have fun afterwards. He presumed she would wear the split drawers like other women of her day. He would plunge in and plunder her private parts, sating his desires. The sight of her pretty petticoats halted him; her lacy drawers and neat ankles were enough for him to be unable to hold back any longer. He did not even get to view her private parts, let alone use her before he released his seed. It went all over her thighs. He groaned with anger. However, he knew it wouldn't take long for him to be ready again. It had been so long since he had a woman he wouldn't miss this opportunity. He battled to undo her drawers. "Oh, gad, she's beautiful!" he muttered not so quietly. It was such a pity she wasn't wearing split nickers; he would have dived straight into her. The beautiful lace-edged, fine lawn drawers were almost see-through, and they were so pretty. He fingered them and stroked her pretty ankles too. He liked ankles. His wife had been like this when he married her, but she had become fat. She was still in London, so he couldn't even get relief from her. To get at Katy's underclothes, he had to undo her gown and then her petticoats. He groaned with desire, his bulge beginning to swell again already. She was starting to stir, and he started to panic. He didn't want his fun cut short, and yet he didn't want to hurt her either. She was too pretty, and he only wanted a woman; he didn't care who. He tried just tugging her drawers down. He was still struggling to remove them from her when his own world went black.

Like Katy a short time before, he didn't hear the footsteps behind him until it was too late.

Perry had returned because word reached him that a convict had escaped. He knew Katy had gone for her morning walk. He arrived at her log to see the pencil and pad on the ground; he picked them up and stuffed them in his pocket. With his heart in his mouth, he looked around and saw some drag marks behind the log heading down to the mangroves a short distance away, then just heavy-pressed footprints from there. Nearby was one of Katy's shoes; he pocketed that too.

"Oh dear Lord, help me find her," he prayed. Knowing he had no backup, he quietly moved to an opening where he could see into the trees.

He regularly fished in this area, so knew his way to the river's edge. There were a few pathways, and he just hoped the convict would have used the closest one. Before entering the passage, he picked up a broken branch the size of his arm. He had no other weapon. "God help me; I have to save her," he prayed silently. He crept through the trees and knew he was on the right path when he heard, 'Oh gad, she's beautiful!' Perry's heart was in his mouth as there were no words or screaming from Katy. Was she alive? Was she all right? He had only taken a few steps when he saw her other shoe. He added it to his pocket. Perry chose his footsteps, being careful not to step on a branch. His going was slow, but he had to be. He arrived to see the man with his naked faeces-smeared buttocks battling with Katy's clothing. Anger seethed in

Perry, and he swung the branch with all his might.

The convict was sent sideways and didn't move.

Perry gave him a cursory glance to ensure he was out cold before seeing to Katy. She was stirring and, thankfully, still fully clad. There was a wet patch on the leg of her drawers; however, they had not been removed. He released a great sigh; she had not been violated. He pulled down her skirt and drew her into his lap.

She stirred in his arms. Waking to see his loving face, she tried to take a deep breath. It was jagged and hoarse. "Perry, oh Perry!" Sobbing, she looked over to the unconscious man.

The stench now emanating from the convict was stomach-turning. The man had opened his bowels, and a circle of foul-smelling black excrement pooled on the ground where he fell.

Perry gently ran his fingers over Katy to check her for injury; nothing, and no blood. Relieved, Perry said, "Oh, my Katy, I came to find you to tell you a convict had escaped and to go indoors. I found your pad and pencil and knew I was too late," Perry kissed her.

"Oh no!" she sobbed, her eyes open in horror. "He... he used me?"

"No, no, my love, I was not too late for that, but too late to stop him taking you. He was battling with your clothing when I arrived. You have not been violated. Wrap your arms around my neck, and I'll carry you home."

She saw he had her shoes in his front pockets, so she struggled to sit up. "No, I can walk, but get me away from here. Perry, we must let the soldiers know where he is before he comes around." She quickly slipped on her shoes.

As they emerged from the mangroves, soldiers arrived from the barracks searching for the missing convict.

Perry called them over and told them where to find him. He explained that he saw a half-naked man dragging his wife into the bushes but not that Katy had been attacked. She didn't need that stigma; she would be saved from the innuendo of violation. He still needed to get her home and safe. Once the soldiers were out of sight, he scooped her up and carried her home. She clung tightly to him but held back her tears until they were safe inside.

As Nanny opened the door to them. Perry briefly outlined what had occurred as he walked by her. Perry carried Katy straight into their bedroom; only then did she release her tears. Great hacking sobs shook her body, much as they had after they left the inn in February. She clung to Perry and would not let him leave her, even for a moment.

Perry lay with her on the bed and held her close. He knew there would be questions, now was not the time for those. He held her while she sobbed. Katy knew she was safe. Perry had arrived, and she had been unscathed. Eventually, her tears eased. Perry helped her change. The clothes she was wearing would be burned. As pretty as the new gown was, it would go into the kitchen fire. Perry had told Nanny that she had not been violated but was in shock from the attack. She didn't need this with everything else she had been through; no one did. He just hoped he had not killed the man. He didn't want that on his conscience.

Within an hour, Katy was sitting in a new gown on the side of the bed. Perry had also washed her and removed everything that could carry the man's vile scent. He had bathed her legs before redressing her. She sat mute, watching Perry gather her discarded clothing and take it into the kitchen to burn. She had not yet said anything; she was just sitting with a glazed look on her face. She was numb.

He had been through shock himself after the fire. He knew what would follow; once the initial distress was over, she would show some confusion; he certainly had. Then he had to cope with the permanent side effects. Thankfully she had not been raped; he had no idea what that would have done to her. He also remembered that he went through a state of exhaustion, so he expected that. It was again what happened to him. He had not been able to accept what had occurred. His once handsome face had melted, he was no longer the person he had once been. It was the feeling of being almost someone else that had made him leave home. He no longer felt he was himself. It was like living in a nightmare world, consistently alone. He had reached the stage of feeling that there had been little point to life when he had found Katy. From that day onwards, his life changed. So Perry knew she would take time to recover from this, but she was strong. He hoped Jem would soon arrive and give her something to look forward to. The best thing for her now would be to move into the new house as soon as he could. She needed a complete change of surroundings. He checked his watch; he still had two hours before Davy needed another feed.

After putting her gown in the firebox in the kitchen, he would tell Nanny and Lucy to prepare immediately to move into the new house today. Lachlan said he could use a flat wagon from the barracks and some soldiers. The entire house full of furniture he had purchased was already in place and waiting for them. Lucy had already set the fires, and they had planned to move in two days, so all was in readiness. Perry also scratched an apology note to Elizabeth Macquarie; they were expected up at Government House for afternoon tea. He asked Nanny to take it up with one of the soldiers to escort her. Neither of the ladies was to be alone at any time. He permitted her to tell Elizabeth what had occurred in private, but he would not put it in writing. He half expected that she would call in rather than write a reply.

When he returned to Katy, he found she had not moved. She was staring at a spot on the floor and didn't even look up when he entered. He sat next to her and gently drew her to him.

She snuggled close. "I should have moved, Perry; I should have come home. It's my fault, isn't it?" She lifted tear-filled eyes to his.

Perry had forgotten the blame stage. "Oh gosh, no, Katy! Yes, you should have come home, but it's not your fault. Absolutely no way is there anything you could have done. Thankfully I got there in time. It is now just shock, sweetheart." He was somewhat puzzled about why she had not called out. "I can't find an injury anywhere." Perry had checked her all over, and the only bruises were finger marks on her cheek.

"No, he held his hand over my mouth and nose. I couldn't breathe and passed out." She lifted a hand to her bruised cheek as it still hurt. "I struggled as hard as I could, but I didn't have the strength to pull his hand away. I prayed that you'd come; I prayed as hard as possible, then I blacked out."

Perry hugged her tightly, "I came, sweetheart; I will always come to you. I chased you halfway around the world, didn't I? I love you, my Katy." His heart hurt. If only he'd been a few minutes earlier... but he'd made it in time. It would take a while, but she would be all right.

Chapter 11 New House, New Start

𝒯he move to Glenmere was achieved with little fuss. The distraction of the new house and the family and friends packing around Katy eased her shock. They stayed there the night of Katy's attack. She slept fitfully in Perry's arms; Katy wept a lot for the remainder of that first day.

~

Earlier, on the day of the move, Elizabeth came and collected Katy and the children and took them back to Government House.

Meanwhile, Perry moved the rest of their things. A wagon arrived after luncheon, and the final items were placed in situ with the assistance of an entire detachment of soldiers.

Lachlan had been horrified when he heard that the woman who had been attacked had been Katy. He had been with Elizabeth when Nanny had arrived with the news that morning. They had come down immediately and collected Katy and the children for the afternoon. Lachlan then instructed some of the 46th Battalion soldiers to complete the move. They had been responsible for guarding the escaped prisoner. It was one small way they could recompense for their lax guarding abilities.

The prisoner was now in ankle shackles and locked into the stocks in the street. His trousers had been left in the bushes. His state of undress made all who saw him laugh at his predicament. He was still covered in his own filth, although it had now crusted down his legs.

He had roused some ten minutes after Perry had removed Katy. Thankfully Perry had done him no lasting injury. As he came-too, he noticed many booted feet standing around him. His head ached, and he knew his brief moment of freedom had come to an end. He had failed in his lustful endeavour; he had failed in his life. He knew he would not get another chance to escape. He was an utter failure. He knew that every breath he drew would soon be one of his last. He realised there would be punishment, probably flogging. In his weakened state, he doubted if he would survive that.

The memory of the lacy drawers and see-through fabric sustained him. That memory alone was enough to stir his body. The desire for her once again flooded through him. As he stood bent over in the stocks, his private parts stood erect at the mere thought of the beautiful woman who had so nearly received his attention. He could not relieve his physical pains, but he smiled to himself. They couldn't steal his memories. He shut his eyes and relived those precious moments when fingering her lacy drawers.

~

Over in Phillip Street, the move was well underway. Perry oversaw the loading of the wagon. Lucy watched the packing of personal items, and Nanny was responsible for overseeing the unloading the furnishings into the new house.

Within a few hours, the cottages were all but empty. The old beds, settees, table, and kitchen chairs were staying, as the new house was already outfitted with beautiful furniture purchased from Mr Robert Jenkins at auction. Perry purchased almost everything Mr Jenkins had for sale and more. Not only was there furniture, books, and household goods, but Mr Jenkins had included his stable too, including a carriage and buggy. The books included were listed as history, voyages, travels, law, novels, and plays; however, the first large box Perry had opened contained a large quantity of stationery, paints and pencils. It was one of these new graphite pencils Perry had given Katy. Not needing much stationery, Perry gave the box to Lachlan.

Lachlan was thrilled about that, as stationary was in drastically short supply in the colony.

Perry didn't need much writing material, so he kept enough for his personal use and disposed of the rest. He filled a drawer in his desk and sent the remainder of the box to Government House. For the last week, Perry had spent a few hours a day unpacking other items he'd purchased.

Lachlan had said that as Perry had room for staff, he could now get a convict allocated to help in the stables and to their establish gardens. In the meantime, as punishment, Lachlan sent the soldier who had overseen the escaped convict. He had to do everything, including mucking out the stables. Perry wasn't initially told who it was, just that a soldier had been sent on detail. He just knew the work was being done while he had his hands full. The entire back garden had soon been fenced off, de-grassed and dug over. A chicken coop had been quickly erected and stocked from the government farm at Rooty Hill. Perry didn't really want a cow as they could buy milk from the Government Dairy behind Government House.

~

Katy was in the sitting room, staring at the window. Since they moved, she had not been outside onto the back verandah or down into the garden. The bruises on her cheek were fading, but she still jumped at every new noise or footfall. Perry had been doing Katy's bookwork as she still could not concentrate.

About ten days after the kidnapping incident, Lachlan called into the new house to see Perry and Katy. "I thought you should know that the convict didn't die that day, Perry. He was given fifty lashes and collapsed at forty-five. However, I have just had word he died this morning." Lachlan heard Katy gasp.

Katy had not given her full attention to Lachlan until he said the man had died. She had never even asked the man's name, and none wished to tell her.

Perry had noticed her attentiveness and also that she remained silent, "Who was the magistrate, Lachlan? Was it Marsden? I've heard him called the flogging parson," Perry asked as he had heard that the minister often gave an excessive number of lashes.

Lachlan replied to his question, "No, Perry, actually, it was Simeon. Marsden would have given him a hundred lashes; either way, he would not have made it. Katy, the man is dead. He's gone. Do you understand?" Lachlan gently took her hand. "Katy, you are safe."

Her ghostly white, haunted face turned to him. "It was my fault Lachlan; I was in the wrong place at the wrong time. I should have gone home. Now, I no longer feel safe outdoors." A single tear rolled slowly over the bruises on her cheek.

Perry was beside her in an instant. "Darling Katy, I said before you were not responsible. He was a bad man, sweetheart."

Lachlan sat watching the care Perry showed for his wife. This wonderful couple had become dear friends, and he knew of Perry's adoration for his wife. He felt the same for his Elspeth; only he could not show it in public. It took years for him to realise how blessed he was to find a second wife he cared for so well.

While still cradling Katy to him, Perry wanted to change the topic from something so traumatic for his beloved. "Lachlan, you have never asked about the name of our house, '*Glenmere*'. The *Glen* is in homage of you. Your Scottish background and all, and the *mere* is after a place belonging to friends where I stayed to hunt for Katy, Gracemere Castle. They are friends of my father's." Katy snuggled into the safety of Perry's embrace.

Lachlan thanked Perry for the honour; they sat drinking tea and chatting. Katy was still quiet, although she had gently extracted herself from Perry's encircling arms.

After a few minutes, Lachlan cleared his throat, "Perry, Katy, I have some news for you. The *HMS Kangaroo* has just arrived from Ceylon. It brought a letter for me that I know will interest you. Permission has been given for a young lad and his tutor to come on a troop ship. Jem will be arriving in about March on the *Hebe*, Katy." Lachlan hoped this bit of news would be just what she needed.

Instantly she was alert. "Really? He's coming?" She spun around to Perry. "Perry, he's coming. He must be on the way already; we must pray for him, my love." Her face was no longer the dismal and wan one of just minutes ago. It glowed. "Oh, Lachlan, I needed this. I really needed it." She broke protocol and jumped up, and gave Lachlan a big hug.

Perry sat with a smile and mouthed "Thank you" to Lachlan. He was astounded by the change in her attitude. Perry thought it was an excellent time to show Lachlan what Katy had in her notepad. He had been so preoccupied with her well-being he had shelved his discussions. "Lachlan, Katy has been jotting and doodling of late, but what she had been noting down is astounding." He handed Lachlan the small pad he had picked up on the day of the attack.

Lachlan flicked over each page. It was a detailed drawing of what she wanted to see built for female convicts. The notebook contained details of each floor and even a draft internal design. After some minutes, he lifted his eyes. "Katy, these are fabulous. These details are exactly what I need. I shall get the architects working on these plans immediately. May I take this?" He held up the small book.

She nodded. "Yes, Lachlan, I have finished my ideas for that building. I do have other thoughts about other things, though." She had snapped back to her old self.

Perry gazed lovingly at her; the news of Jem coming in only a few weeks had given her a new lease on life. Katy herself had done that for him years before.

~

Christmas was celebrated the week after the move into the new house. Perry, Katy, and the children had been invited to Christmas luncheon with Lachlan. Nanny and Lucy were to celebrate with their staff. There would only be the Colonial Secretary, John Campbell and his wife, Mary, to dine with them.

As John was someone whom Lachlan trusted and was Elizabeth's cousin. All had become friends. Mary was Irish; Elizabeth Scottish; and Katy English. These differences brought totally different aspects to the conversations and their ideas of how to point the colony forward.

Lachlan trusted them all absolutely.

As a Christmas surprise for Katy, Perry had asked Janey Brien to be assigned to them if possible.

Janey arrived the day after Christmas, and a new man for the stables was with her. Abel Jones was also a life-sentence convict.

Lachlan knew of Janey's work at the gaol but signed the transfer papers somewhat reluctantly as she had been one who had never caused trouble. Far from it, she usually stopped it.

It was Janey's first time out of gaol in five years. When she arrived at the beautiful new two-storey house, she couldn't believe what she saw. Her eyes were as big as cartwheels as she drank in the beautiful edifice. Hopefully, no longer would she be sleeping on a wooden pallet or looking after the needs of convicts, but she would almost have a real life. Her only sadness was that as a life-term convict, she would never be free. Considering that her life had been one of servitude anyway in London, there was little difference, except the climate was nicer. Only now, she wasn't being paid.

Perry escorted Abel through the house and into the stables while Katy and Nanny greeted Janey.

Abel Jones was also a trusted worker from the gaol. He had been convicted of horse theft, but Lachlan knew his family as he had served with his father in India. The man would look after the family well.

Abel couldn't believe his good fortune when he saw his quarters. A room to himself over the new stables. It had a bed, and a brazier with a small hob stove where he could even cook snacks for himself. All food would be provided; he would eat with the other staff. A smile of joy spread across his face. Life here would be good, it wasn't a farm, but it would be good. His new boss said he could plant a vegetable garden, and Perry said he would also buy a milking cow as the dairy on the hill had occasionally run short of milk.

Janey had grabbed her tiny bundle of possessions from the wagon. She didn't even own a change of clothing. She expected to be taken to the back door and sent to work in the laundry. To be dropped off at the front door and now welcomed by a well-dressed lady with a hug was not what she expected. She was overwhelmed when she realised that the lady was the young mother she had assisted ten months before.

"Kate Harrison?" was all she managed to say.

"Yes, Janey, come inside, and I'll explain." Katy pulled her in through the doorway and down the corridor to a small room with a real bed, a mattress, a chest of drawers, a wardrobe, and pretty lacy curtains. "This is your room, Janey. I do hope you'll be happy with us."

Janey was astounded, "My room, Katy? You mean I don't have to share?"

Katy laughed, "No, Janey, this is all for yourself. Your duties will be to assist Lucy and Nanny Grimes with the children and household chores; you did say you liked children. Perry has all sorts of new things built into the house, so life is quite pleasant for us all."

"Perry, ma'am?" Janey was wondering who Katy really was.

"Perry is Peregrin White, and he is my husband, so I'm now known as Katy White again. He came and rescued me a month after I was sent to the Freemason's Inn. He has brought our two daughters with him, and we're staying here until my term expires." Katy knew she would eventually know about their friendship with Lachlan, but for the moment, she would just get her settled. "Our eldest son, Jeramy, known as Jem, is coming in March, so with Davy, our family will be complete."

"Davy, ma'am? I thought the babe was named JJ?" Janey was confused.

Katy explained the name change.

Janey just shook her head. Somehow, she had fallen on her feet by her simple act of kindness.

Katy grinned; she knew there were more surprises to be revealed. "Dear friend, look in the wardrobe; these are for you. I had to estimate your size, so I hope they fit."

Katy threw wide the wardrobe door. In the wardrobe hung six new gowns, each of a different colour. Five were simple but serviceable dresses, and one was a Sunday best. It even had lace around the hem. There were two bonnets, a straw one for shopping day use and one for Sunday. On the top shelf are some new pretty mob caps. There was also a shelf for undergarments. Katy smiled at Janey. "Janey, you gave me my dignity back with the clothes you gave me; this is the least I can do."

"Oh, ma'am, oh really, these are for me? I've never had a new gown before nor beautiful things like these, ma'am." With that, Janey sank onto the bed and wept. "Why me, ma'am? Why do I deserve such kindness?" Janey was astounded.

Katy smiled and quoted a Bible verse, "Because of this Janey, '*And the King shall answer and say unto them, Verily I say unto you, inasmuch as ye have done it unto one of the least of these my brethren, ye have done it unto me*'. Janey, in the Bible, this verse is found in Matthew, chapter 25, verse 40, so that is why. Jesus gave us His instruction. You assisted me, and this is how I can repay you. We will help others, and I hope you will help us with that. You were the first kind person in months. This way, I can help you. Janey, you will see and hear things that you must keep confidential. You are not to tell anyone. If you do, you will not be allowed any freedom lest word gets out."

"Oh, Katy, sorry, ma'am, I'll promise anything you want. Please let me stay, ma'am," Janey begged.

"Okay, firstly, I'm 'Mrs Katy', and my husband is 'Mr Perry'. Secondly, we have some close friends here often at their place. Yes, I'm still a convict, and yes, I still have work to do for the Freemason's Inn, but my status is somewhat ambiguous." Katy saw the confusion on her face and thought she might as well tell her everything now. "Janey, Perry's best friend here is the Governor."

"What? I'll meet the Governor?" Janey was astounded. She was too stunned to comment further.

"Um, yes, but not only that, we are both working with him to assist with improving the lot of the convicts here. So we might ask you for some input too." Katy waited for that to register.

"You want my help? Really? I'm a nothing, Mrs Katy, just an

unwanted nothing." Janey now wept in earnest. She was soon gathered into Katy's arms and given a big loving hug.

The scent of her clothing made Katy realise that she really needed a bath. "Janey, I'm going to leave you now, as you will have a bath and wash your hair. Lucy will assist you and show you where the bathing room is. As I said, Perry had everything built into this house, and a bathing room is one luxury I love. The bath is set up permanently and has a bath plug, which waters the trees in the garden. Also, it's near the kitchen, so there is no lugging hot water upstairs. All staff are expected to wash and be clean, including a daily scrub, if not a bath. We must save water, so there is a bathing schedule; Abel will be last. So normally we all use the same water, after the children and I, but today Lucy has a bath prepared for you now. Abel will follow you, so leave the water in. Choose a dress and follow me. I have even made you some rose-scented soap, Janey."

Janey's face nearly exploded with excitement, "The blue one, ma'am, sorry, Mrs Katy. I love blue!" Janey wiped her eyes with the back of her hands.

The action left smudges on her cheeks. Yes, she needed a good scrub.

~

Janey settled into life at Glenmere. In her first week, she had been let into the secret of precisely who Katy and Perry were. However, this had occurred by accident one morning.

Janey was cleaning Perry's office, and she was tidying his desk. Perry had been called away early that morning and didn't have time to pack up his desk as usual. He'd left his Bible open, and Janey carefully moved it so she could clean and tidy. A letter addressed to Lord Peregrin, Earl of Collingsford, was underneath the book. It was the letter from Elizabeth Fry and used Perry's title. "He's an Earl?" she said to herself, her eyes wide with astonishment.

Katy was just passing the door and heard her comment. "Yes, Janey, he is. I said you would hear things you are not to tell; this is the most important. Our friendship with Lachlan and Elizabeth is another, and the relationship between Kate Harrison and Lady Catherine White, or the Countess of Collingsford, is the last one. I didn't even know you could read." Katy looked at Janey, intrigued.

Janey was still in shock. "Yes, m'lady, I can. I was the one who owned the books I gave you. I see you still have them. They were a gift to me. I wanted the Debrett's to see if my father was in there. He is, or was, as he's dead." She turned and pointed to the books she'd given Katy months before.

"Will you keep our secret, Janey? Will you do this for us, please? When we return home to England, I must forget all this if possible." Katy had already told Janey the story of her conviction and how she had intentionally stolen something to be arrested.

"Yes, m'lady, of course, I will stay mum." Janey would do anything for Katy now. Her life in Glenmere was wonderful. She was treated as equal to both Nanny and Lucy.

Janey had not revealed her story; and Katy didn't press her; she would tell if and when, she was ready. Lachlan had already said he had checked her conviction to see what she was in for. He had said she was not a danger to the family. He had not revealed what she had done.

Katy thanked her and said, "Then enough of the 'm'lady' Janey." Katy chuckled. "You'll give the game away in a moment."

"Sorry, Mrs Katy, I'll try to remember." Janey smiled and went on to explain, "I was taught to read by my mother, and then the Countess allowed me to read books where I worked. That was before… well, before my conviction, Mrs Katy." She turned away quickly, but not fast enough for Katy. She saw tears fall.

Katy went to her side. "Did that Earl attack you, Janey? Is that what happened?"

Janey nodded, shaking slightly. "I pushed him away, and he fell. He hit his head on the hearth and died. It wasn't my fault. He'd done it before; often, he used to sneak into my room after I was asleep. It was over before I could scream. I had no say, Mrs Katy; he used me and then held it over me to keep me quiet. Mama told me she had the same thing happen to her." She was shaking in earnest now with her eyes glassy. "All I did was push him away, Mrs Katy, honest that's all, but because he was an Earl, I got life." Her eyes could no longer hold the tears, and they oozed down her cheeks. By now, Janey was sitting in Perry's chair.

"I had just realised I was with-child, his child, and I didn't want him to touch me again. I knew what he'd want. He rarely did it during the day, but sometimes I'd be summoned to his office if her Ladyship was out. He'd take me in the office, usually on the settee, but sometimes on the floor or the desk." Janey sniffed and wiped her tears away with the back of her hands. "I'd not been with a man before him and I was only eighteen when his attention started. It went on for some years, and I was surprised I'd not fallen with-child before. I told my mother, but she wouldn't let me leave a good job. I worked as an under-governess, Mrs Katy." She paused the retelling for a few minutes and dropped her head onto the desk. She sniffed, then said, "My own father was a Duke; I didn't want history to repeat itself. Mother said the same had happened to her, but the Duke liked to be violent. I suppose I should be thankful, but I lost the baby in gaol." Janey fell silent.

Katy stood looking at Janey; her accent was similar to hers. Cultured and relatively well-educated, the dialect was familiar to her as her own family. "Janey, may I ask, who was the Duke?"

"It was Cheatham; why Mrs Katy?" Janey looked at Katy with a puzzled look on her face. Janey wondered why Katy had asked about the Duke and not the Earl.

Katy almost collapsed; she leaned on the desk, gasping. "He was your father? Really? Janey, stay there."

Katy left her in the office and returned moments later with Perry who had just returned. Katy shut the door as they entered. Neither looked angry, just sad and stunned.

Perry motioned for Janey to stay seated at his desk. "Janey, I need to hear from your own lips; who was your father?" He was white and anxious.

"Mother worked at the Cheatham Castle in Warwickshire; Mr Perry, Julien, Duke of Cheatham, was my father; when mother found she was with-child, she never told him, as other girls had gone missing when they found themselves in the same condition. The minister got her away, and I was born. We lived in Lincolnshire with the minister's family. When I was two, my mother returned home, and I was brought up under the name of Brien. Why, sir?" She looked from one to the other face.

Katy said to Perry, "She can read Perry, and you left Elizabeth Fry's letter on your desk."

Perry nodded, then turned to Janey. "So you know that my title is Earl of Collingsford; what you won't know is that my father inherited the title from a distant cousin, Janey...." Perry paused, wondering how she would take this information, "... My father is the current Duke of Cheatham."

"Oh cor, sir! Then we are cousins? And you too, Mrs Katy?" That meant they were third cousins. Janey was certainly astounded.

"Um, yes, I suppose we are. The old Duke Julian was our third cousin, wasn't he, Perry?" Katy had not grasped that fact herself. My father kept me away from him. I don't even remember meeting him, but I certainly heard stories. One of his friends certainly sent shivers down my spine, and that is Sir Francis Dashwood."

Perry looked stunned. "Dashwood was a friend of his? I had no idea. I heard some of the rumours about him and his cronies. Things like girls going missing and even Black Masses. But surely they were just rumours?" Perry was now sitting on his desk, astounded by where this conversation had led.

Janey said, "No sir, they weren't rumours; they were real. Have you heard of the Hell Fire Club? That was them."

"Yes, I have, but, you're kidding, aren't you? I had no idea. Why didn't Father tell me?" Perry was stupefied that he had not been informed.

Katy said, "Perry didn't you know that Julian and Francis did the grand tour together in 1729? I remember Papa told me that a small group travelled together. After Papa died, Mother told me there were stories of their debauched activities and rumours of girls being killed, but no one could ever prove anything, so nothing came of it."

"I had no idea! None at all." Perry was shaking his head. "I just knew Father had a hell of a time cleaning up after Duke Julian and his many illegitimate children around the Estate."

"Nooo, really?" It was Janey's turn to be astounded. "So I'm not the only one?"

Perry looked somewhat sad, "If only you were, Janey. Sadly Duke Julian was a terror where young women were concerned. The more innocent, the better. Father has his hands full looking after the poor women he abused. When my he inherited the title, he started a school for them. After so many years, even some of the younger children are now starting their own families. Father is encouraging all of them to apply for jobs on the Estate. If you give me your mother's contact details, I shall get him to write to her and offer what assistance he can. Would she accept it?"

"Oh yes, Mr Perry, she's having a tough time making ends meet and would love to return home. She had to go back out to work when I was arrested. She was working as a governess in the castle to Miss Mari."

Katy sat thinking. "She's Lady Marianna Broome-Hall now and has a few children herself. She lives down in West Sussex. She'd be... let me see, um, sixty-threeish now. The old Duke died in 1798, and Perry, you grew up somewhere near the Broome-Hall's, didn't you?"

He nodded. "Sort of, Blackberry House was closer to Aylesford, but we rarely saw them. I know Lady Mari met her future husband up near our castle, as they had a hunting box next door to ours. Mari married when she was seventeen. I met her only once, just before the fire." He touched his cheek. "She married when I was little." He wouldn't mention that to Janey.

Katy explained his scarring, though. "Janey, Perry tried to save my father from a fire but was severely burnt in the process. We had all thought he died, too as he disappeared. I was only fourteen and had just lost my father. It was 1798, and I remember it as if it were yesterday." Katy sat thinking back to that time.

Janey gasped. "Oh, sir, truly, how heroic," she stated.

Perry pulled a face. "I wish that were true, but in a way, it was stupid. I don't remember much after the fire for some months. But I was so ill; anyway, the old Duke had died not long before it happened. Father was trying to cope with the Estate issues. He had no desire to inherit and did not like his status change, believe me!" Perry sighed. "When he found out about the mess he'd been left, he was aghast. Oh, there was money but little else. Most of the staff at the castle were old. No young ones would work there, and it didn't take long to find out why. After his wife died, he set about employing numerous young girls, the old Duke got into as many of their beds as he could, and that was the beginning of the troubles for the estate. Once the news spread that Father had inherited, one thing led to another, and soon the staff were queueing to come back. They could see Father was not like the old Duke. Then I had gone from being a strong farm worker to an invalid. I horrified anyone who looked at me. The scars have healed a lot now, but they were red and weeping. They were not a pretty sight. I actually found it easier to live when the face was totally bandaged."

Perry was swinging his legs under the desk. He was deep in thought for a while. The two women sat looking at each other, unsure what to say.

Janey broke the silence. "I think I must have known some connection you know, Mrs Katy. Something in me reached out to want to help you. You were certainly not the first to arrive with a small child and nothing else." She shrugged. "I have no idea why, but I just wanted to help you."

"I was the same, Janey, and I think we'll drop the Missus and Mister, eh? We're all cousins. Nanny and Lucy will have to know, but if it's all right with you, we'll keep things as they are in the house for the moment. We'll work out something, though."

"Oh no, Mrs, I mean Katy. No, I'll stay in my position, but it would be nice if I could borrow some of the books occasionally. That would be a real treat for me. I could brush up on my reading." Her impish grin was a surprise as a dimple popped on her cheek.

Perry glanced for Katy to their new cousin. "If you can read, then we may even have a new job for you. Read to your heart's desire. Janey, how would you feel if you helped us start a convict children's school?" Perry thought this was as good a time to ask her as any. He was looking for teachers for a new project he and Lachlan had, it is an orphan's school, but he needs literate teachers.

"You mean it, Mr Perry? I mean Perry, sorry sir, I'll have to stay with Mr Perry for you, sir, I can't do it. It's too familiar. I'd love that, but could I still stay here? Please?" Her eyes flittered from Katy to Perry and back to Katy. "Please, don't make me leave. Please!"

"Oh no, Janey, you don't have to leave, not at all. But if you want to go and live in one of the small cottages, you can, but I'd love to have you stay with me." Katy was thrilled.

"Oh yes, please, I'll stay, but can I stay here, not go to the cottage? Mr Perry, I'd love to teach the little ones if you think I can. I can at least teach them their A, B, C's."

"Then I'd say that's settled. Lachlan said I could hire whom I wished, convict or free. Hopefully, I can find more educated convicts and get them into good work. I know you will never be free, but if we can make the path a little easier for you, life will be quite good. Leave it with me, Janey. Maybe you might even want to teach some older women to read?" He turned to Katy, "Sweetheart, I have to go, I'm late for a meeting with Lachlan, but I will talk to him about the school." He bent and kissed her before turning to Janey. He bowed, then said, "Welcome to the family, Janey." Then he left.

Perry had much on his mind as he walked up to Government House. He would tell Lachlan about Duke Julian and Janey being a cousin. Before saying anything to Janey, he would double-check her story with Lachlan's records again. If they matched, he'd do what he could to see if Lachlan could adjust her sentence. He may not be able to give her a Pardon, but he might arrange an official Ticket of Leave for her, if not a Certificate of Freedom. Maybe she could even be indentured to them on their return. He would not ask Lachlan just yet, but see what, or if, he would offer anything. He was sure something would occur.

Chapter 12 Together Again

*T*wo weeks passed, and on this day, Perry was returning from his meeting with Lachlan, and he held an invitation for Janey, Katy, and himself to come for afternoon tea. Lachlan had arranged for Janey to have a Ticket of Leave, and although normally, she would never be able to leave the colony, she would now be paid for her work. She would be, in essence, free. It was beyond her wildest dreams.

Janey had been with them only weeks, but she had shown her worth. Perry now understood Katy's bond with the woman she had met and befriended. He had noticed certain similarities between the two ladies. He nearly encircled her waist only last week before realising it was Janey and not Katy. They looked similar from behind. Katy often wore work clothing, and Lucy did their hair the same way, and he was just in time to stop himself. With Janey's history and Perry's relationship with Duke Julian, as well as what Katy thought had occurred between himself and Mary, it would've been a disaster. He had double-checked every time since. Now he sighed with relief. He knew they were all cousins. He chuckled. "Won't they both get a surprise?" He whistled as he walked home with the document in his hand. Not every day you get to tell a life convict that they are virtually free.

Nanny, Lucy, and Janey fell into a happy routine. At Janey's request, only those who needed to know would discover their relationship. She was content just to know she could stay with the family. With her new status of holding a Ticket of Leave, Janey was even willingly accept a few coins as payment. Nanny and Janey had become firm friends. Janey was thirty-nine, Nanny four years younger, and Lucy was only twenty-five. The three ladies worked together to make the household happy.

Weeks passed, and the family prepared for Jem's arrival. Perry had arranged to go to Government House in Sydney to wait for the ship. All they knew was that the *Hebe* was due in early March. Perry would not miss Jem's arrival. Katy was safe, as Janey was sleeping in the sitting room on the settee while he was absent. Lachlan had also assigned a guard to keep watch from across the road subtly.

Katy had wished to go too, but Lachlan expected other guests to arrive on the ship. If she went, then the others would want to go too, so she stayed home, as there would not be room for them all. Katy still smiled when she thought about the one hundred and fifty-odd rooms at Cheatham Castle. Here, Government House had about ten, and most were not bedrooms. She would stay home and prepare for her son's arrival. Perry would return as soon as he had collected Jem and whatever staff were accompanying him. She hoped there were not too many, as they would need to double up. Beds were even prepared in the room next to Abel.

Lachlan asked Major Tom Turner to show Perry around town. He willingly agreed as he wanted a chance to introduce Perry to his friend Sam. As Perry now had his own carriage, and the day after he arrived, Tom took him on a town tour. Much building was going on, and one project interested Perry.

Tom had hoped it would, as Sam was the designer. His son Danny was the chief builder, and his business partner, Josh Comfrey, owned the building company. Sam was forty-two, and Perry was a year older. Tom could not wait until they met. It was not the meeting he expected. Tom knew the huge rock outside their tiny cottage was in the process of being removed. However, the reaction of both his friends was of delight. For unbeknownst to Tom, the two had met long, long ago. Perry had been at school with Sam at Christ's Hospital in England.

The looks Sam gave both Tom and Perry were of puzzlement. As soon as Tom gave Perry's name, Sam finally recollected where he knew him; however, he waited for Perry to see if he remembered him. The conversation that followed revealed that he certainly did. Perry was a year older than Sam. They had played in the same sports teams and occasionally holidayed at Phillip Princhester's Estate and also next door at Pittsfords Estate. Neither voiced where they had become friends. That could wait, but both had a twinkle in their eye when Tom asked how they had become friends. Eventually, Perry had just answered Tom; they had known each other from school years before. A knowing smile followed and then silence. For Sam to have an old friend close by was a delight.

After chatting for a few hours, Perry said he'd return tomorrow if the ship were not sighted. Tom knew where he would be and was instructed to come and get him should the ship arrive.

Perry returned the next day, and the two men again reminisced about the choir they belonged to. They had first met aged eight and nine and were both chosen to join the choir. Both had been boy sopranos and, as such, stood next to each other in the choir. Sam had forgotten about those happy days. Perry was one of the only people who had seen through Sam's sadness. Perry knew Sam's mother had died when he was little and befriended him. Perry had learned early to stay quiet about his happy but poor family life. He knew his father was heir to a Dukedom, but they had no allowance and few luxuries. They lived in a small cottage but were happy. The Duke paid his school fees as he was the oldest son of the heir. Therefore he realised Perry would need a good education when he took over as Duke. For Perry to be in the colony now was wonderful for Sam.

Life was tough for Annie and Sam as he had no way to assist Annie other than in the market garden and to sell the excess vegetables he grew. He had just started doing some drawings for Josh, and this was beginning to pay a few pounds.

Perry wondered if Government House could buy produce directly from him and ease his burden financially. He decided to say nothing to Sam but would certainly ask Lachlan. He knew Sam would not take money, but he would appreciate the sales. Perry fully understood solitude and poverty. He promised he'd return whenever he was in Sydney. He'd told Sam what had occurred and how they had ended up in the colony.

Sam reciprocated with some of his own story.

~

Two days later, word came that the ship was in sight of South Head. Within the hour, Perry headed down to the dock to wait.

"Papaaaa," a joyous cry came from the deck of the *Hebe* as the ropes were thrown to tie it to the wharf. Beside Jem stood Terrence Buckridge, the tall, well-dressed tutor Perry had employed. He was in his mid-twenties and was the son of the Duke of Cheatham's estate manager. Buck, as he was known to Perry, had been looking for work, and although he wanted to travel, he had no money; before he departed England, Perry had asked him to tutor Jem. Buck jumped at the chance. He wouldn't even have to leave home to work. Even then, Perry asked him if he would care to bring Jem out to meet up with the family at some stage. Considering this was his dream, he willingly agreed. Now he stood with a caring hand on Jem's shoulder. The lad was jumping with joy. Buck was worried Jem would try to climb over the railing, so he kept him close. Perry waved as hard as Jem.

As soon as the gangplank was down, Jem ran down the ramp. He was swung up into his father's arms and hugged. Buck caught up to his young charge. "I'm sorry, sir; he was too quick for me." Buck apologised to Perry as he joined them on the dock.

Perry laughed with Jem tightly wrapped in his arms and legs around his waist. "Buck, if he weren't keen to see me, then I would have worried. Over a year without your parents is hard." He mussed up Jem's neat curly hair.

"I've missed my elder son so much, tiger."

Jem drew back a little and asked, "Eldest son, Papa?" The gap in his teeth made him lisp a little.

"Yes, my eldest son, you have a little brother named Davy. He's sixteen months old and a young version of you. Your sisters adore him, as I'm sure you will too." Perry was wondering how to bring up the addition to their family. Jem had been quick to pick up the information.

Perry had brought his carriage to the dock, and they were soon loaded and on the way to Government House to collect Perry's things.

Perry had brought Jem up to speak when spoken to, but the young boy was just too excited. He introduced Jem to Lachlan.

Jem bowed appropriately, and then his words spilt over his lips with the enthusiasm of youth. "You're the Governor? If you are important, I thought you would live in a big house?" He knew how big his grandfather's castle was. The one-hundred-plus-room mansion made the small building used as a Government House look like a cottage.

Lachlan smiled. One day his son would be as cheeky as this little boy. Perry had told him of the Ducal Castle. Even his own family estate in Scotland was larger than Government House. "Yes, sadly, we don't have castles like your grandfather's one here. This is the best we can manage, although I have another one planned up on the hill over there. This is warm and dry, and really that's all we need." Lachlan looked up and caught a glint in Perry's eye. "You see, Jem, here it's so nice outside we aren't cooped up indoors all the time."

Jem's eyes grew large with excitement. "No snow?" He swivelled to look at both his father and tutor. "Can I learn to swim?"

His father smiled. "No snow, but we do get an occasional frost. And I don't see why you can't learn, but we will use the river; here, they have sharks in the bay. So don't sneak off by yourself, eh?" Perry didn't want to lose his son, considering he'd just got him back.

"Sharks? Wiff sharp teeth?" Jem said with joy. "I want to see one, Papa." He was now bouncing with glee.

"Yes, and they will eat you, so no swimming in the sea or river. Okay?" Perry waited until he gave a vigorous nod of his head.

"Okay, Papa." He was again clinging to his father's side.

Perry was just about to leave when he remembered his thought about Sam's vegetables. "Lachlan, I want to have a chat with you about sourcing some locally grown vegetables for your table here. An old school friend has a market garden with some excellent produce. I thought you might be interested."

"Absolutely, Perry; I'll catch you in Parramatta later in the week." Lachlan's visitors had yet to arrive as although they were on the same ship, their luggage was extensive.

Perry checked that his own bags had been brought from the room he'd stayed in; he took his farewells from Lachlan and joined Buck in the carriage. They waved until they were out of sight.

~

Four days after Perry left Parramatta, he was back again with Jem. Now seven, he was no longer a small boy, as he had grown so tall. Jem was frustrated that he lisped as both his front teeth were missing, but he was itching to see his mother and show her they were gone.

Perry later told Katy that Jem was the image of what he'd looked like at that age. Katy had not been born when he was seven.

As soon as the ship was sighted, Lachlan sent a rider to Katy, telling her they would return that afternoon. So, Katy was waiting for their return in a cane chair on the verandah of the house. Perry had the carriage pause at the front gate, and within moments, Jem was in his mother's arms. His small legs were wrapped around her waist, and his arms were locked around her neck. This time there were tears, joyous welcoming tears from both. They clung to each other as if they would never let go. Her son had grown so much in eighteen months.

"Oh, Jem, oh, my Jemmy," was all Katy could say as she hugged her son tightly.

He pulled back from her hug and said, "Look, Mummy, no teeff," he grinned, showing the gaps and his half-grown front teeth. "But I can whistle," and proceeded to demonstrate by whistling as they walked upstairs to his room. His sisters came running at the unusual sound, and soon Mia and Lou were bounding around him, welcoming him home. The three chatted non-stop.

Once Jem made it into the room prepared for him, he got to meet his little brother.

Davy was toddling beside Lucy. "Me too, me too, meet brover."

Jem shook off his sisters and greeted his brother.

Davy momentarily stood looking at the older version of himself, then catapulted into his arms. "Hug me, hug me, brover."

Jem did.

It didn't take long for the family to settle down into the new routine. Buck was quick to be warmly welcomed to Parramatta by everyone.

Lucy especially liked the handsome tutor. She found she was only a year older than him. She also discovered that in the colony, most servants were encouraged to marry, especially the women. None of the convicts had taken her eye. No man had until she saw Buck. He had been at college when they stayed at the castle, so they had not met, although she knew about him.

Buck wanted to settle in before entangling himself in any relationship, but he was not averse to her; quite the reverse. She was pretty, and she worked for the same family. This could be very convenient. So even at home, it would make life easier. He would think seriously about her.

Perry loved having another male in the house. He had liked Buck when he met him, and now he was living with them; he proved his worth.

Buck quickly realised that in Parramatta, lines of work were blurred. As his tutoring only took up five hours a day, he pulled his weight in the house the rest of the time as everyone else did. Buck pitched in and assisted the ladies with any heavy work. He often listened for Lucy's dainty footsteps and was always free on washing day when she had to carry the heavy cane baskets of wet washing to the clothesline.

Buck was officially free to do as he pleased when not teaching the two older children. Nanny and Janey would often walk the four children along the riverbank. Buck would look for something useful to do. Sometimes he would go for a walk by himself, but more often than not, his wishes were to now assist Lucy in her chores. Occasionally he helped Abel in grooming the horses. He now also insisted that he accompanied Lucy when she visited the market. The week after he arrived, she had been accosted by a stall-keeper and came home in tears. Buck was the only one home when she returned from the markets.

Lucy was so distraught that she was enfolded in Buck's caring arms and sobbed on his shoulder. He comforted her by stroking her long hair. It had come loose from her mob cap and cascaded down her back. Her long wavy brown tresses were like silk and smelled of lemon. He breathed in the delicious scent. His resolution not to entangle himself was fast dissolving. He discovered he quite liked the feeling of holding this lovely lady so close. And lovely she certainly was. How she had made it to twenty-five unwed, he didn't know, but this one hug made him decide to ask Mr Perry if he could court her.

She had wrapped her arms around his waist and held tightly to him.

He found himself rubbing her back in such a way that he surprised himself. He ran his hand up and down her back in long, caring strokes. He hated seeing her upset, and it did strange things to his heart.

She had seemed to enjoy being held and comforted as much as he delighted in holding her. Her soft curves that were pressed hard against him were very pleasurable. After some minutes, her sobbing eased; she hiccoughed a few times, then reluctantly pulled away a little.

Buck looked down into her tear-stained face. "Lucy, what happened?"

Lucy lifted her eyes to meet his. Her tear-stained face made his heart skip a beat. "I was pushed by a fellow shopper, then fell onto a stand of apples. A few were sent rolling off the table, and the lady who owned the stall then accosted me. One thing led to another, and soon I was the centre of a melee which ended in her slapping my face."

He had seen the red mark on her cheek but had presumed it was from the crying. He could now see the red finger marks on her cheek. His ire was raised. "How dare she? Lucy, you must not go alone again. Will you promise me that, please?"

Lucy realised that she should not be in his arms; she pulled back and said, "Buck, that is not necessary; I have been shopping alone since we arrived. It's just today that feelings in town were uneasy."

Buck released her reluctantly. "Lucy, I don't like you walking unescorted. Anything could happen. Will you let me accompany you?" He was worried about her to the point that he made her promise that she would allow him to accompany her on future visits. "You must promise me you are not to go alone again." He drew her to him again into a comforting hug. His hand was now caressing her neck. She nodded on his chest. She didn't want to move from his arms this time. She had dreamed of being held this way by Buck since he arrived. When he finally released her, they went into the kitchen to have a mug of tea. Buck carried the shopping in as Lucy led the way. Since then, Buck had noticed her willingness for him to assist her in various chores and her chatty nature made her a joy to be with.

Over the following weeks, Buck accompanied Lucy shopping and anywhere else she needed to go. She planned her visits to the markets when she knew Buck would be free.

Soon, any free time Lucy had was spent close to Buck. That included casual walks along the river edge, walking to church or just sitting in the backyard drinking a mug of tea.

Both Katy and Perry noticed the sly glances and knowing smiles that Lucy and Buck gave each other.

~

Lachlan called to see Perry one afternoon in April.

Perry wanted tea, but knowing that most of the staff were out, he went into the kitchen himself to put on the kettle.

Lachlan was so stressed he was pacing back and forwards across Perry's office. When Perry finally joined him, Lachlan thrust a document at Perry. "Read this!"

Perry held a report about a horrific massacre of native locals from Appin. Perry read the official-looking document and sank into a chair. "Oh no, why did they do that?"

"I didn't mean that when I gave the order, they were supposed to apprehend one or two, and then drive the rest over the mountains. One or two have been attacking indiscriminately, and I wanted it to stop. I ordered Captain Wallis and his men south towards Appin in southwest Sydney." Lachlan read from the report he'd taken back from Perry. "How can he write this? It's horrific. He almost sounds proud of what he's done. *In the early hours on 17th April 1816, the cry of an Aboriginal child broke the silence of the night and alerted Wallis to the whereabouts of a group of sleeping men, women and children near the Cataract River.*"

Lachlan read aloud about the annihilation of an entire tribe of aboriginals, including women and children. He sank into a chair, horrified at the report. Unable to even process the murder of so many innocent humans. He failed to stop, his eyes watering up. Lachlan almost shouted, "Damn it,

Perry, Wallis has contravened my clear instructions to seek their surrender as 'Prisoners of War' and to 'save the lives of the Native Women and Children.' I can't believe Wallis engaged in a night raid killing indiscriminately, driving people off the gorge, and shooting them. I bet the official death toll of fourteen is likely much greater, but he'd not dare to tell me knowing my instruction. Here, read this...." He shoved his diary at Perry, "Read my exact order. Yes, all right, I instructed for the troublemakers to be hung, but I specifically said only the troublemakers and to free women and children."

Perry took and read the diary entry for the beginning of April. *"I have this day ordered three Separate Military Detachments to march into the Interior and remote parts of the colony for the purpose of Punishing the Hostile Natives by clearing the country of them entirely and driving them across the mountains; as well as, if possible, to apprehend the Natives who have committed the late murders and outrages, with the view of their being made dreadful and severe examples of if taken alive. I have directed as many Natives as possible to be made Prisoners, with the view of keeping them as Hostages until the real guilty ones have surrendered themselves or have been given up by their Tribes to summary Justice. In the event of the Natives making the smallest show of resistance or refusing to surrender when called upon so to do, the officers Commanding the Military Parties have been authorised to fire on them to compel them to surrender; hanging up on Trees the Bodies of such Natives as may be killed on such occasions, in order to strike the greater terror into the Survivors."*

Lachlan explained to Perry, "We've had trouble with just one or two of them indiscriminately killing stock. I suppose they see them as free food, but they were breeding stock. There have been incidents of settlers being killed too. I needed that stopped. For this to occur is not what I intended." The situation caused much anguish for both the Macquaries and Whites. They knew this would haunt them for a long, long time.

~

Some six months after his arrival, Buck's emotions came to a head one laundry day. It was a hot September day, and the convict groom, Abel, had taken Perry to see the Governor; the mistress was busy with the books. Buck had carried the heavy basket of wet washing outside for her, and he was walking back to the house when he heard her bloodcurdling scream. He had just made it up onto the verandah and was back down the stairs and running into the backyard to her assistance.

Lucy was holding her skirts up high and was frozen still. "Stop, Buck, don't come closer. I need you to stomp your feet on the ground." Lucy told him how the brown snakes hate vibrations and move away. She just had to stay very still. They were attracted by movement. Buck could see up to her knees; at her feet was a snake curled up, and its head was coiled back as though ready to strike. Lucy sounded calm, but he could tell from her voice that she was far from it. "Trust me, Buck. I need you to stomp on the ground. But do not come closer." She was sheet white.

Buck did as she requested. He stomped as hard as he could on the ground. Within moments the snake flattened itself on the ground and slithered off. Only then did Lucy drop her skirts and run to him. She was shaking like a leaf. The tears of shock overflowed from her fear-filled eyes. Buck went to her side and gathered her to him. She slid her arms around him, appreciating his quick actions and support. Buck found he was shaking himself, "Cor, Luce, don't scare me like that. I thought it had bitten you." He rested his cheek on her hair.

This was how Perry found them some minutes later.

Neither had moved, and both were unaware that they were being observed. They had stood hugging for so long; each needed the companionship and physical closeness they didn't even realise they wanted. Buck finally pulled back a little. "Lucy, may I ask Mr Perry if I can court you? I'd like that."

She nodded. "I'd like that very much. Can I call you Terry instead of Buck?" she said shyly. She was still loosely held in the arms of a man whom she was not courting.

Buck grinned, "Yes, of course, you can. I'd like that. And about us, I shall ask him at the first chance I get."

"Um, I think that's now, Terry; he's watching us." Lucy giggled.

Again reluctantly, Buck released her. "Now is as good as any. Are you sure?" He waited for her nod then they walked to join Perry on the verandah.

Perry waited for them with a smile, his arms folded in mock anger.

"Good morning, sir. May we have a word?" Buck tried to sound confident, but he was far from that.

"Um, it would seem appropriate," Perry said with a chuckle.

"Yes, sir, it was a snake this time, sir," Lucy said with a quick glance to Buck, and then her honest face met Perry's eyes. "Truly, sir." She gave Buck's arm a gentle squeeze. Both Katy and Perry had been told about the market incident, as the smack mark on Lucy's face had been impossible to hide. Knowing how convicts peopled the colony and what Katy herself had been through, Perry encouraged Buck to go with Lucy the on all of her outings. He also escorted Nanny or Janey if they were to go anywhere alone. Abel was usually with Perry if he was out, so it was nice that the ladies were not alone at home anymore.

Perry looked from one to the other. Both people were dear to the family. "Well, I could say that this is a surprise, but you have both been mooning around each other for weeks."

Buck was stunned. "You don't mind, sir? Really?"

"Why would we mind? We're delighted. This way, we get to keep you both. You have our absolute blessing, but the one problem will be, Buck, you should not be staying here. However, we have no choice about that, and the only other option is you move into the empty room next to Abel." Perry held the door open for them, "Let's talk inside. The sitting room, I think."

Buck escorted Lucy into the front sitting room with Perry following.

As Perry passed the office, he asked Katy to join them. As Buck and Lucy were out of sight, Perry bent and kissed Katy quickly. "Our suspicions were correct; he wants to court her. Come into the sitting room, and we will sort out where he's to stay."

Chapter 13 More Growth

By 1817 Francis Greenway was becoming well-known in the colony. Perry thought Lycett had vanished, but Lachlan informed Perry that he was in Newcastle serving time. He'd been caught forging again and been sentenced to two years in Newcastle. Governor Macquarie had initially arranged a Ticket of Leave for him and Francis Greenway. Lycett didn't last long, but Greenway had set up his own business. Having said that, the Governor kept Francis fully occupied. Perry and Lachlan would consult with Francis and discuss the possibilities of various designs for the planned buildings. Thanks to Perry, Francis was not the only one to benefit from the Governor's patronage. The other two architects were also given things to build. However, their works did not inspire Lachlan.

Joseph Lycett served his second term and was again granted freedom to record the colony in paints. Lachlan wanted a pictorial record of the developments that Francis was making. Joseph would find a perch from a distance and draw the skyline of the new buildings.

~

Only weeks after Buck had asked permission from Perry to court Lucy, he asked her to marry him. He had found her carrying two buckets full of coal and was struggling under their weight. Buck had relieved her of the load. However, instead of carrying them for her, he put them down next to her, dropped to one knee and proposed.

Lucy willingly agreed to his delightful suggestion, and as they were now engaged, he overcame his shyness and kissed her. He had wanted to for some time but would not overstep the bounds of propriety. Now that they were engaged, he felt he could. She had wrapped her arms around his neck, and both were so occupied that neither heard the approaching footsteps.

Again, Perry found them in each other's arms. He waited for a few moments before clearing his throat and saying, "I do realise that this occupation is enjoyable, but is it entirely appropriate, Buck?"

Instead of releasing her, Buck lifted his head. "In this case, sir, it is, for Lucy has just agreed to become my wife." He still had his arm slung around her shoulder, and she was snuggled to his side. Her look of absolute adoration for Buck told Perry her feelings.

"Terry just proposed over a couple of buckets of coal," she giggled. "I never thought coal was romantic before."

"Then congratulations to you both," Perry was thrilled. "Terry, eh? And a kiss, well, this is serious. I think she likes you, you know, Buck." He chuckled again. "Are the quarters out the back that bad, Buck?" Perry teased him.

Buck knew he was poking fun at him; their relationship had blurred from tutor and employer to friends. Yet Buck was still respectful. He knew Perry's actual status as an Earl, as did Lucy. However, even that status was blurred to the degree that there were only convict and free in this town. He laughed. "No sir, they are actually very comfortable. We might both move in there once we are married as they are larger than either room here." He saw Perry's eyebrows raise. "No sir, I have not been in her room but know it to be much the same as mine. She used to clean mine and remarked on how similar they were."

Perry gave a nod; he was thankful that Buck had respected Lucy and the moral rules required of his staff. He asked, "I don't suppose you have had any time to discuss dates yet. There's no Bishop in town, so it will have to be done by Banns."

"No, sir, we haven't. Can we have a quick chat and see you in a few minutes? I'd like it to be soon, but Luce might want some time to get ready." Buck looked down at Lucy; she was shaking her head.

"As soon as possible is fine by me, Terry." Lucy was still glowing with happiness. Unable to believe her dreams were coming true.

"Looks like we won't need time to discuss it, sir; as soon as possible it is. All we have to do now is see Reverend Marsden." Lucy was nodding. She had a smear of coal dust on her cheek.

Buck didn't care. He thought she was the most beautiful girl he'd seen. Her honey gold-brown hair and dancing grey eyes delighted him. "We might have to wash up before we go, Luce. You have a smut of coal on your cheek." Perry was about to leave when Buck asked, "Sir, I was wondering, could Abel take Lucy's room? Or even better still, the small one near the back door. I know it's tiny, but do you think he'd mind? It would give us a little more privacy."

Perry looked concerned; he didn't want Abel in the house. A thought occurred to him. "Buck, if we converted down under the verandah to an apartment, then you would even have more room; what do you think? It's also near the privy, without being too close. I'm not so sure about having Abel inside." Perry watched them consult.

Lucy gave a nod.

Perry added, "You may need room if children come, or should I say when they do."

Lucy blushed. "Sir? Wouldn't I have to leave?"

It was Perry's turn to be surprised. "I don't see why. We'll just get in some more help. You two are as good as family. Your rooms will be empty, so others can come, and you won't be totally useless, Lucy, except for a few weeks after the birth. If you still did the shopping and… well, Katy could work out those sorts of things when that situation arises." Perry grinned at the looks on both their faces. They had just become engaged, and he was already planning babies. "Don't get so preoccupied that you forget to move the coal, will you?" With that, he shook Buck's hand and kissed Lucy on her cheek, then left them.

As Buck had not let her go, he drew her back into his arms as soon as Perry disappeared. "Now, where was I when we were so rudely interrupted?" He chuckled and proceeded to resume his previous actions.

Lucy had no complaints at all.

They married five weeks later.

In that time, Perry had workers line and waterproof the underside of the verandah and turn it into a sitting room-cum-lounge room, and behind it, the area under the house he had converted into two bedrooms. They had a suite of rooms far better and bigger than they ever could have afforded. They still ate upstairs, but they were all good friends, so this was no hardship. If there were no visitors, everyone, including Abel, ate together in the dining room around the big table. This was easier for Betty as she didn't have to arrange two sittings and could get home earlier.

Lucy was thrilled with how her life had turned out. She never thought she'd ever be allowed to marry. To be able to stay with the only family she had ever known was a delight.

~

The proximity to the privy was needed far sooner than she expected. Within six months of their wedding, her frequent trips to the outdoor facilities inspired Katy to ask, "Lucy, dear, are you by any chance increasing?"

Lucy's blush, a nod, and then a giggle elicited a hug from Katy.

"You will need to go on light duties, dear, and no heavy lifting, and I'll arrange some extra help. With Davy now getting older, Nanny was complaining she wasn't needed anymore, so between us both, I think she will manage with the babies." Katy wondered if Lucy would pick up on the words she'd used.

She did. "Oh, ma'am, you too?" Lucy asked.

Katy nodded with a smile. "Yes, so it seems Nanny may have her hands very full after all. Just as well, Janey is here now. She will fit in her visits to the gaol somehow. I really will see if we can get more help, though. We'll start with a laundry maid. Janey is already doing the cleaning, and Betty is coping with the cooking well. How about that?" Katy just wanted everyone to be as happy as she was. She'd been feeling morning sick for some weeks and was surprised that she was still ill. She tried to think back to her last flow and worked out it would have been five months ago. She smiled to herself, then stopped short; if she was four months gone with-child, she'd been feeling flutters for a while, and her gowns were already getting tight; she stopped in her tracks, and a thought of twins flashed through her mind, but she quickly cast that idea aside. She didn't think she had twins in the family, nor did Perry. As they shared a great-grandfather, she knew that side of their family, but her mother may have had twins somewhere.

~

Buck and Lucy's little boy, Lindsay, was born on 1st June 1818. Perry and Katy's twins were born three weeks later, on 24th June. Colin and Joanna were small but healthy. Joanna made her appearance some thirty minutes after her brother; she was a massive surprise to everyone except Katy. She had felt kicks in strange places, but she was not much larger than when expecting Mia. Katy had put on more weight than she had with Jem, but she was in denial until the second baby arrived.

Nanny would have had her hands full with two babies, but three was far too much for her.

Buck had taken Davy into his growing class. Lou, now seven, had joined her siblings and excelled at reading and writing. Davy was four and would need careful attention as he distracted the older children.

Mia had already made some flashcards, and he thought these were a great game. He could pick lots of pictures from the words. Davy could already count to ten and could even put cut-out numbers in order.

Buck was impressed at Mia's game and thought it would be an excellent resource to use.

With the children now born, Perry could get back to planning. Whenever possible, Perry would inspect the local buildings with Lachlan. Both saw that there was much work needed.

Perry and Lachlan sat down one day and counted the edifices that Lachlan had on his lists. So far, over two hundred buildings had been either built or were under construction. Although some were only in the initial stages of planning. Lachlan used the two other architects, John Watts and Henry Kitchen, for smaller projects, but he used Francis Greenway's designs for most of the main projects. He also found that Francis had come with a recommendation from Governor Phillip.

Henry Kitchen designed and oversaw the construction of a new weir in Parramatta. John Watts designed the improvements made to Government House in Parramatta, with new wings built to either side of the main edifice. However, Lachlan discovered that Greenway knew his building material, stone, well, having been brought up in a family of stonemasons who worked in a quarry in Bristol. He was aware of the magnificence of structures that could be made using this material. The local stone was both strong and beautiful. Francis also preferred designs in the Georgian style.

Unfortunately, Francis's overbearing nature caused much ire to those he worked with. This first came to light when Greenway was asked to copy an existing plan. He wrote a reply to Lachlan stating, "*I will immediately copy the drawing Your Excellency requested me to do, notwithstanding it is rather painful to my mind as a professional man to copy a building that has no claim to classical proportion and character.*"

To appease him, he was then commissioned to design a lighthouse for South Head in Sydney. On completion of this, Greenway was given a Certificate of Freedom.

The new Parliament House in Sydney had already been completed, as had the Mint nearby. This had been needed when the colony had run out of coinage. Governor Macquarie purchased forty-thousand Spanish doubloons with Government finances, and he had the mint overstrike the coin and then punch a small hole from the centre. He called the two new coins the 'Holey dollar and Dump'. They were most of the currency now used in the colony.

Many towns were full of building teams. A small cottage called Cadman's Cottage was under construction in Sydney, along with the Kirkham Stables in Narellan. Other plans included a magnificent house out at Rouse Hill, a school for female orphans at Parramatta, new accommodations for convicts in Sydney and Brick Fields that they called the Carter Barracks, and new soldiers' barracks at both Hyde Park in Sydney which was now complete and Lancer Barracks in Parramatta which was moving into the construction stage. These were vital as the number of soldiers and convicts in the colony had outgrown the previous accommodation. Lachlan worked on other significant projects: a new courthouse, a church in Sydney, and a new courthouse in Windsor. Foundations for the new barracks both in Windsor and Parramatta were already being cleared, and footings laid. Stone for these projects had been ordered from the various quarries around town. As other buildings were already under construction, there was a backlog for the hewn stone blocks. Bricks were also in short supply as they were used for the less essential structures going up everywhere.

It was no use sending more convicts into the pits, as there was no room for them to work. It was hauled away for finishing as fast as the clay could be dug and stone cut. They were all working as fast as they could. Slowly the old wattle and daub huts and shacks vanished.

Another of Lachlan's projects was developing farmlands in and around Sydney, Parramatta, Windsor, Bathurst, Grose Farm, Longbottom, and Emu Plains. He placed emancipated convict Richard Fitzgerald in charge of the Emu Plains farm. The colony was proliferating, and food was desperately needed. The Emu Plains Agricultural establishment was a resounding success. The fertile plains soil grew whatever was planted. Soon it was supplying fruit and vegetables for consumption throughout the colony.

These farms also provided immediate accommodation for new male arrivals, and others were sent for the hard labour of those willing to defy the laws. The convicts were used to work the land. However, this influx of men caused a swathe of shanty cottages to be built by convicts working on the farms. They were made of wattle and daub or slab timber with shingle roofs. Many of the convicts sent to these farms had a level of unexpected freedom. Although supervised, they were allowed some free time after work each day. They were all supposed to work in their own small gardens, but many preferred to source grog from other locals.

Other convicts were set to collect oyster shells. These were crushed for lime. The jangle of the convicts' irons was heard across the water as they worked, so they called it Iron Cove. More convicts were set to cut grass for fodder, and others worked in new timber yards. The growing colony was a hive of activity.

~

Perry, Katy, and the entire White household kept their heads down, and life continued around them. Many more convicts had arrived in the colony by this time, including hundreds of female convicts.

Lachlan was nearly at his wit's end to know what to do with them. They still only had one room to house them above the men's gaol. Lachlan tried to hasten the building of a female prison, but it was a massive project, and no amount of wishing could make it progress faster. Lachlan even contemplated sending some to a farm, but there were absolutely no facilities for them. He also knew the abuse that they would receive.

~

By the time Perry's twins were walking, his staff had grown again. Two new young maids had been assigned to them; other maids had temporarily come but had moved on. These two girls had been sent to serve seven years apiece. Janey had found them cowering in the corner of the women's room in gaol. They were sisters caught pickpocketing. Janey had befriended them; they were added to the staff at her request. Beatrice and Clare Livingstone were young but good workers. They had six more sisters at home and had stolen to survive. Their oldest sister, Amanda, had been the only one to find work. All the other children were under ten and were hungry, so the girls had tried to find a way to get some food. To know they were now able to eat regularly and even had a bedroom to share with no fear of being molested, they blossomed. Clare proved to be a tremendous help to Nanny. She needed to be agile as she often chased after the three youngest children.

Perry found out their parent's direction and asked his father to collect the entire family and move them onto the castle estate. He was sure they would somehow be incorporated into the extended family with Duke Julian's children. Two others had been introduced to Perry and Katy: Bill and Molly Miller. Lachlan had introduced the young couple to Perry and explained their unusual story. He was in the process of constructing an Inn of the first quality on their behalf. They were to provide the top-grade accommodation that was so badly needed in town. It was to be known as the Rear Admiral Duncan Inn and was just down the street from Perry's house. This Inn was one more of Katy's suggestions.

Katy's idea of a new accommodation Inn in Parramatta was born from them having to stay at Government house when they arrived. The young couple Lachlan had chosen to run this venue were newlyweds Bill and Molly Miller. Molly's mother, Ellen, was to live with them and assist with running this new establishment. They were currently living in a rented house near Hyde Park in Sydney. Katy adored the young woman. All three had a fascinating background, having been staff at a big house in London. Then the young ones were accused of abuse by the employer's son, and when they arrived as convicts, they came with letters of recommendation from that same employer. It was a convoluted story, but they were now waiting for the new inn to be finished. Katy also really liked Molly's mother, Ellen. She reminded her a lot of her friend Mary.

Janey and Katy had put their heads together and suggested occupations for the female convicts. Spinning, weaving, and sewing were some of the ideas they had, but making the thin plaited straw for straw hats would be helpful too, as would felting. They tried using kangaroo fur alone but needed to add sheep fleece to make it feel together correctly.

When they mentioned the weaving to Lachlan, his ears pricked up. "They would be able to make fine fabric, seriously? Governor King had a few of them doing this in the old factory before a fire destroyed the room, but there is just no room in the tiny facility we now have."

Janey was surprised at his question. "Of course, why not? It's what most of us were brought up doing at home anyway. Spinning, weaving, and turning flax into linen were normal household chores for most of us as children. This would keep the women occupied and help keep them out of trouble." Janey and Katy had tried to buy some basic fabrics and found very little was available. Her friend Sarah had a store in Sydney, and sometimes Perry would bring her some yards of fabric.

Katy knew he'd not spent much time around women as he'd served as a soldier most of his life. "Lachlan, do you know that most women would also be able to sew? Maybe they could even make some clothing for use in the colony. You could sell that to offset the costs of running it."

Lachlan was stunned. "You really are serious, aren't you? What sorts of fabrics could they make? Previously they have only made rough fabrics for work uses."

Katy explained. "That all depends on the quality of looms you provide; the finer the thread, the better the fabric. The warp and weft of the weave are not the issue. They can only make fine fabrics if the looms are designed for such."

Perry was deep in thought as they talked. "Lachlan, I was thinking that not only spinning etcetera, but some jobs like washing and cleaning duties are needed for punishment. If women are put into third class, then oakum picking is a horrible thing to do. Removing the barnacles on the old ropes would be punishment in itself, but then they can remake the old ropes into oakum or other caulking. I know you plan to have the colony as self-sufficient as possible so let us start by putting the women to good use while they are awaiting assignment. We need both caulking and ropes, and lots of them. The men can then learn to splice and add the eyes in them."

Lachlan looked at his friends. "You three come up with some of the most amazing ideas. When Governor King first thought of a Female Gaol, he suggested some form of activity to keep them out of trouble, but to put them to good use would benefit everyone. The men are just been walking a useless treadmill, and it's unproductive." He fell silent for a while. "We'll need special fine thread looms then, won't we? Spinning wheels, wooden mallets for the flax and all manner of other things. I'll get the men started on making those. I'm sure someone here knows how to make looms. If not, I'll order some from England. I suppose I can order some crates of spun cotton spools. We don't grow it here, so I suppose even India can provide that. I will certainly order some woven cotton bolts so they can get started on making convicts shirts." Lachlan knew how hot the wool clothing they wore was. "The cotton shirts will need to be identifiable, so I shall order the fabric to have stripes. Blue, I think. I like blue."

"Fids too, Lachlan," Perry said.

"Fids? What the heck are those, Perry?" Lachlan looked as confused as the ladies.

Perry had spent a few hours talking to some sailors only the day before. "A fid is a long concave pointed thing used to push the twists of the rope apart so you can splice the eyes in ropes. They come in various sizes. If they are going to do ropes, they will need a set of fids. Even to undo them, they still need them." Perry explained the things he saw on board the ship on the way out. He saw many sailors splicing ropes and then binding the ends with thread. So, Perry had asked questions, not knowing how that knowledge would be used.

~

By 1820, the new Female Factory was nearing completion. Many bolts of blue and white, twin pin-striped cotton had arrived from India, and the convict women were all making shirts for the convict men. They were of a simple design but were cool and functional. Lachlan had set men to work making the required looms.

~

When Katy still had some eighteen months to serve, things changed. Mr Albert had agreed that she train some other convicts to do his bookwork. She was now teaching the women rather than doing it herself. Janey had sourced three semi-educated women from one of the batches of new arrivals. One young woman showed great potential; her name was Winifred Coates, and by the end of the first month, she moved into the small storeroom Katy had occupied and took over the bookwork for the Freemason's Inn. The other two were assigned to two of the other inns.

James Albert obviously approved of his new bookkeeper, as he married her less than six months later. She was a lovely gentle lady with a red disfigurement on her face. Winifred was everything Maybel was not. She delivered a son just nine months after their wedding, thus making his happiness complete.

Katy was now at a loose end.

Lachlan issued Katy a Ticket of Leave. The ticketing system allowed wives to be allocated to their husbands and serve out their time. Lachlan had changed this rule sometime earlier, but Perry insisted that Katy serve most of her time so it would not look like Lachlan was favouring them. Life remained much the same after her certificate was issued. Only now did the bookwork come to her if there were complicated issues.

Mr Albert even had the courtesy to thank her for her years of work. He still thought there was something fishy about who she was. He knew there was no way he would find out what or who she was after six years.

Katy asked Lachlan if the Livingstone sisters had to be reassigned to someone else when Perry went home or if, like Janey, they could return to England with them and serve out their time at the castle.

As Lachlan knew their stories, he sent instructions for their paperwork to be sent to him, and he assigned them to serve their remaining time with the Whites wherever they were to live and thus be allowed to return to England if they so wished. Lachlan knew the White's *home* was now at Cheatham Castle anyway, but that did not appear on the paperwork.

~

A new contingent of soldiers arrived early in 1820 and amongst them was someone whom Perry knew well. The man was unforgettable. At six foot two inches, and with his almost white blonde hair, the bluest of blue eyes and dimples, it made him stand out in any crowd. When a boy, he turned heads whenever he entered a room. His three brothers all looked similar. Surely there could not be two with the nickname that he was using. He was now a Major in the 48th battalion. It didn't take long before Perry cornered him and challenged him with who he really was. "Ned?"

The reply was a finger to his lips, a wink, and a grin. Major Ned Grace had also recognised him. When hunting for Katy, Perry had stayed with Ned's family only six years before. To now find Perry here shocked Ned.

For Ned to have command and attain the rank of Major at twenty was not unheard of, but this usually entailed buying a commission. Knowing who Ned's father was, Perry was not surprised to see such a young man as a Major. What did surprise him was the name he was using. It wasn't his own one.

The first time Ned realised Perry had recognised him, he subtly shook his head.

Perry nodded acknowledgement, but he was itching to know his story.

It took a few hours before Ned could get away. He had asked directions to Perry's place, and when he stood at his door, he took a deep breath before knocking.

Buck opened the door and saw a very young, red-coated soldier asking for Perry by his Christian name. Buck showed him into the sitting room and went to get Perry. Lucy was with-child again, so Buck stepped in as a quasi-butler when off-duty as a teacher. Lucy usually answered the door.

Ned was left kicking his heels for a few minutes before Perry appeared.

As Perry entered, he said, "Ned, so it really is you? What the hell are you doing out here and not using your own name?" Perry greeted him with a handshake, then a hug. "Feel like spilling the beans? Have a seat, boy."

Ned sat but was a little uncomfortable with being discovered. "Yes and no, Perry; it, of course, involves a woman." Ned looked a little embarrassed and Perry saw his nose screw up.

"But why the name change?" Perry asked.

"David's idea, I suppose. He told me to leave, so I did. Father doesn't know the dirty laundry, so I decided to keep it that way. I had a sponsor who overheard the break-up, and he paid for my commission. You might know him as he lives over near Lady Marianna Broome-Hall. He is James, Duke of Malvern?" Ned said.

"Break up? You've lost me," Perry said, somewhat confused.

Ned gave a colossal sigh realising that Perry had not heard of Elouise Wickham or his engagement to her. "Okay, here's the dirty laundry. But first, you are not to tell anyone I'm here or the name I'm under, do you promise?" Ned waited for Perry to reply.

"Yes, of course, Ned, but this is beginning to sound very... well, odd." Perry was getting worried. Ned had only been a boy, but he was a good listener. Of the four Lockley lads, Ned would have been the most honest and innocent of them all. Perry had poured his heart out to him years before.

Ned sighed. "Fine, well, the story goes, I had my first season in town. My friends Gerry, Robbie, Jimmy, and I, were all presented to the King at a Levée. Mother had dressed me up like 'little boy blue' as you can imagine. I was instantly a hit, being the son of a Duke. That year, a new 'incomparable' hit the social whirl. Her name was Elouise Wickham." He heard Perry gasp but continued. "Oh, Perry, she was so absolutely beautiful. Society cleared a path for me to court her, and soon we were engaged. It was only then that I discovered her beauty was only skin deep. Her ego was as vast as were her expectations. We had been engaged for only three weeks, and I quickly saw her for what she really was. I caught her in a compromising position at a ball. She laughed in my face. To put it bluntly, she is a wanton and a shrew!"

Ned got up and walked to the window. He stood looking out for a while before turning around and continuing. "Perry, I was trying to work out how to get out of the relationship when she found that I was only the Duke's second son, for she met David at the engagement party. He had come to town to watch Father speak in Parliament. It was then that the scales totally fell from my eyes. A week later, we were at another ball, and the shrew told me she had had a better offer and threw me over. Trust me, I was thrilled, but oh, it hurt when I found out she had her claws out for David as he would one day be a Duke. Unbeknownst to us, James, the Duke of Malvern, was outside having a cigarillo and overheard the entire conversation." Ned walked over to the settee and sat down again with his head in his hands. "That's when things got really ugly."

Perry sat listening without interrupting.

Ned met Perry's eyes and saw compassion. "Before the news had even been announced of our engagement being called off, she was throwing herself at David. He was bowled over, as you can imagine. I tried to warn him, and he thought it was sour grapes. I tried to tell him I was thrilled to be rid of her, but he didn't believe me. Perry, David told me to leave. So I did. I couldn't tell Father, he was ill at the time; but Mother had also seen through her, and they had already had a run-in. Mother was wonderful, of course, but you would not expect any less, as you know Mother. She also tried to talk to David. He wouldn't listen and went off in a huff. They should be married by now. Elouise will have her hands full trying to boss Mother around. No one does that, not even Father. Anyway, I went and spoke to the only other person who knew about how the wind blew, and that was Duke James." Ned sounded despondent. "I needed advice and impartial advice at that. I knew he would be honest with me. David had told me to leave the house, the town, and most of all, to leave them alone. As I still lived at the castle, I had nowhere to go. Duke James bought me a commission, and here I am, under the name of Major Edward Grace, instead of Lockley."

Perry had sat listening and then replied, "Cor, Ned, what a lucky escape you have had. I know Elouise Wickham; she's twice as bad as you have said. We grew up in a house near to the Wickham estate. Even when I lived in my tiny cottage, I heard of her behaviour. Numerous rumours were flying around about her nocturnal visits to the male staff quarters. They started when she was still a young girl. I only met her once when she was a teenager. Father had just inherited the Dukedom, and even then, she was a precocious child. I have a decade or more on her, at least. To say I was shocked by her behaviour is an understatement. You had a lucky escape."

Ned nodded in agreement but said, "It's not me that I feel sorry for Perry; it's David. I doubt any child they have will even be his, from what I've heard and even seen. So yes, the rumours were true. I knew she was even playing around while we were engaged. I tried to think of a way to clear out without being charged with breach of promise and disgracing my family. I couldn't do it to them, Perry. I was delighted when she cried off, truly, I was until she told me she would catch David instead. Duke James heard everything, and she knew that. Her shrieking cackling laugh tore through me. The fact that she had jilted me for my brother, she thought hilarious. She knew David would not believe me as she had already poisoned him against me." Ned ran his fingers through his fair locks. "So, I came here. I'm running away, Perry. But not *from* David, *for* him, for I am unable to face my older brother and see him cuckolded by the shrew and every other man she can entice into her bed."

Perry was horrified, and it showed on his face. "Oh, Ned! That's simply awful! I'm here if you need to talk to anyone. Sadly, we'll be leaving next year when Katy's term is up. However, in the meantime, I'd love to reconnect." Perry filled Ned in on the part of his own story that had occurred since Katy's conviction. Then talk turned to more bland subjects.

Perry asked Ned to stay for dinner, and he willingly agreed. Soldiers' rations were scant, and he was itching for a home-cooked meal rather than rations. Ned stayed for dinner that night. Perry could tell that there was more to be said but didn't push the young man.

As Ned was as close as family, he joined everyone at the dinner table. As usual, all the staff ate together in the dining room. Over dinner, another person caught his eye.

Surprised smiles were shyly exchanged.

Nanny Grimes recognised him in an instant. She greeted him with a quiet, "Hello, Master Neddie; I was wondering if you remember me?"

"I do, Nanny; I couldn't believe you were here. May we talk later?" Ned was frightened that she'd say his name.

Much to his relief, she nodded but remained silent. She had realised a mystery existed when he was introduced to them all.

Katy retired to feed the twins after the meal, leaving Perry and Ned to themselves.

Nanny joined them in the sitting room for a short while. They rose as she entered.

"Hello, Nanny Rhymes." He chuckled at his nickname for her. "I'm Ned Grace here, Nanny, not Ned Lockley, and certainly no titles, please. I missed you when you left, but you have come to a fabulous family." He hugged her, and after a few more reminiscences, she excused herself.

After their meeting in the sitting room, Nanny left with a smile on her face. She had been only a young woman when Ned was sent to school with his brothers. Nanny would keep his secret; she had adored her four blonde charges. However, she left Gracemere Castle to look after Mia.

Chapter 14 *Questions of Identity*

After Nanny left the sitting room, Ned stood and started pacing like a caged lion. He knew he could not keep in what was worrying him. "Perry, I'm in the dickens of a situation. It's one of the new convicts that has come out with me. I have to see him tomorrow, and I'm sort of stumped." Ned had a worried frown on his face.

Perry prompted him to continue. "How so, Ned?"

The look Ned gave Perry stunned him. "Perry, I have a feeling he could be a by-blow of Father's. There has only been one son for the last three generations until ours. He's the same age as my younger brother Paul, and as he's as alike as could be his twin, only Paul's twin of the same name died at birth. His name is Charles Lockley too, but Perry, I could have sworn Father never would do that. Seriously I would have staked my life on the fact that he remains faithful to Mother. They adore each other and always have. I don't know of any other Lockleys, though. He even has a similar accent, and he's educated too. Perry, what the hell do I do? He's a nice chap, and I must give him a Ticket of Leave tomorrow as he helped put down a mutiny on the way out. But how do I look him in the face and treat him like... well, like I don't know anything about him? I don't know if I can do it." Ned swung around to face Perry. "Perry, he could be my brother." Ned looked haunted.

Perry was also astounded. "Ned, I'd be stunned if that were the case. Your father would never cheat on your mother. I saw their affection when I stayed with you for those three months when I was looking for Katy. I'm sure of that as I am of myself and Katy. There must be another explanation; it must be just one of those freaks of nature. Have you ever asked him?"

Ned shook his head. "No, I have not allowed myself to be in a situation of friendly conversation with him. But I must face him tomorrow, and well, I'd like to befriend him if possible. For some reason, I'm drawn to him. I certainly need to find a placement for him. I'd like it close by, if possible, so I can get to know him."

An idea suddenly came to Perry. "Abel had said he had an offer of a position out on one of the farms along the Hawkesbury. How about here, Ned? So, I have a position in the stables from Wednesday if he knows anything about horses. I wasn't going to bother filling the position, as we rarely go anywhere, but Abel did the vegetable garden and fruit trees too. I got rid of the dairy cow, so he has little to do. There are quarters above the stables so that he will be quite well housed." Perry waited for his reaction. "It seems I have already employed other members of your staff from home."

Ned smiled, then nodded. "Father found Nanny another position when we were all sent to school at Christ's Hospital. However, I had no idea where she went." The look of joy on his face made Perry smile. "As to the position for Charles, are you sure? Could he come here? Oh, Perry, that would allow us both to get to know him. Charles and another convict Jack Turner were the informants of the mutiny on board. Jack has already lined up something down south at a place called Camden. I have no idea how he heard about it, but it's on Macarthur's farm."

Perry relaxed. This was going to be good. He could see what sort of man this Charles Lockley was. If Ned said he was nice, then he'd take him at his word. "Ned, send him straight down after he collects his paperwork. Better still, bring him. I'll get Abel to show him the ropes before he leaves on Wednesday. This will work out well for us all."

They sat discussing his search for Katy and filling in some gaps for each other. One thing led to another, and they found themselves talking about babies and Davy in particular. That conversation made Perry say, "If you happen to know of another female convict who needs a placement, our maid Lucy is in the family way with her second child. She's married to our tutor, Buck. So, I'll need a temporary replacement for her." Perry smiled at his young friend. "I named our son David because of something your mother said, Ned. She told me it meant 'beloved', so I suppose you can say he's named for one of your family, as is our house, by the way. *Glenmere* is half named for Gracemere Castle and half as a homage to Lachlan's Scottish roots."

Ned met his smile. "Of course, Perry. I'll keep my eyes open; I think there's an assignment tomorrow. I will have to head down to collect Charles and Jack anyway. So, I will see whom I can find for you. I want to watch how they run the proceedings. As a Major, I'm supposed to have a housekeeper anyway. I don't have much to do as I'm a neatness fanatic. There's really just washing, ironing, and a bit of cleaning; mayhap we can share a maid?"

Perry sat with his arms folded. They might have been tempted to have a port if he were at home, but he didn't even have any to offer Ned. "As to sharing a maid, that would be fine, Ned. She could stay here with us and add your laundry to ours; see who's available. I'm sure the good Lord will lead you to the right lady. I'm sure one will stand out, so trust Him to bring the right one." He sat looking into the dregs of his tea. The leaves swirled mesmerisingly. "Oh Ned, I forgot to say that here we're known as Perry and Katy White, so no titles for us either, okay? Our staff know who we are, as does Lachlan, Elizabeth, and Major Tom Turner. But all have been sworn to secrecy."

Ned nodded. He met his eyes at the mention of Perry's faith, "I would not have survived this far without His care." Ned pointed upwards. "My nightly prayers have been the only thing that has given me the strength to cope with… well, all this change. I've had to learn to do everything for myself. It's been a rude shock, Perry, but I'm surviving. I've gone from having a valet and a dresser, a bevy of maids and, well, everything, to none. Sometimes I have used God as a crutch, but He has not failed me even doing that. Like finding you here, at the earth's farthest end, just when I needed a friend. I feel I shall come here often if that is all right?"

Perry smiled. "Of course, Ned. Katy and I often had to rely on our Lord, especially in that horrible year when she was missing. If you need a person to pray with while we are here, let me know."

Ned's heart jumped with delight. "I'd love to, Perry; I miss my family prayer time. Mother especially would start each day with prayer, and I miss that." Ned stood as Katy came in.

The conversation for the evening changed after Katy joined them. Perry told her about their possible new staff member and that Abel had requested a transfer to a farm. Perry didn't mention Ned's suppositions of any relationship, nor did Perry reveal to her who Ned really was. He just said that he knew his family from home. He would leave that for Ned to tell her sometime later.

The other room above the stables was prepared for the new occupant. Lucy already had the spare inside room cleaned and the bed made, but she took up a fresh ewer of water and a towel. Katy had already mentioned that she would again be put on light duties for the next six months. However, she was still mobile and willing to work.

Janey was still visiting the gaol once a day. She made sure that all the women were supplied with lots of water and food. Matron knew Janey had the Governor's ear, and although she didn't like it, she had little ability to stop Janey. Knowing there was to be an assignment, Janey had visited the overcrowded gaol room. She checked that they had adequate water to wash in, even though few knew how to bathe.

Lachlan had allowed Janey free access to watch over the rest of the female convicts. She had become his eyes and ears in there and knew he could trust her reports. She noticed that this lot was noisy and rebellious, but one lady sat quietly and seemed to be a little different from the mob. She was reasonably clean and considerably neat. Somehow, this convict woman had even washed her hair, which shone like spun gold. She was just pulling it back from her face. Janey smiled at her; she would be a possible candidate for Lucy's replacement. She was about to find out her name when they were all called outside to appear for assignment. The door was flung open, and the Matron and a detachment of soldiers stood and waited for the women to file out. Janey gave a sigh and stood back, and let them all leave.

~

Out in the quadrangle at the gaol, in the same spot Katy had stood some years before, Sal McCarthy stood fearfully, uncertain of the future. She had managed to wash her face and even found water to wash her hair last night. In the sunlight, it shone as her head was uncovered. Her mob cap had been stolen overnight. She looked clean, which made her stand out from the rest of the convict women. As she walked, she flicked her eyes to look around her. She moved towards her designated position. Partway there, her gaze met another pair of eyes that were fixed on her. Unable to break the stare, she stopped walking. Her mouth dropped open. His hair was even lighter than hers, but it was his blue, blue eyes that were so magnetic. Sal gasped; he was so handsome. He stood tall, even though he was in prison garb. She realised she was staring. All the rest of the women were already standing in line so she hastened to her position at the end. She was now concentrating on what was happening before her, hoping she'd not missed some instructions. They stood waiting.

After some minutes, a soldier appeared in front of her. "You, McCarthy, follow me."

Sal had seen him go to the table, and the Matron had written something. The soldier told her to fall in behind him, and he walked off towards the handsome man she'd seen earlier. His black and yellow jacket was unbuttoned, and the blue and white striped shirt under it was clean. She had not even noticed he was with another convict and a soldier. Her gaze had not even registered them. As she approached, she was too frightened to look up; she just saw many boots. Where was she going? Who had claimed her?

The soldier who had told her to follow him glanced behind him sometimes to ensure she followed.

She tripped along the pavement behind the soldier as the other three walked some distance in front of them. They arrived at a small office-like cottage. Standing outside were the two convicts, one with light brown hair and the other was the handsome blonde man who had smiled at her. She gave a wan smile when their eyes met, but she kept walking.

The escorting soldier was now holding the door for her. He waited for her to enter, then said to the soldier waiting inside, "Here she is, sir; I've signed her out already. She's all yours now, Major." He saluted and left. As he spoke, the handsome blonde man came inside again, and the escorting soldier walked out and shut the door.

Sal now stood in the office with two strange men. The one at the desk stood and was about to say something. She didn't hear what he said as she reversed back towards the wall. She figured that they were going to rape her. Why else would they shut the door and leave someone outside on guard? Tears oozed from her eyes. She was so frightened. She had escaped the ignominy of this so far.

The soldier behind the desk walked to the hob of the small brazier. She watched as he poured three big mugs of tea. Did a rape usually start with a mug of tea? She hadn't had tea for months. Not since she was at home in London. As she reversed, she bumped into a chair and sank into it. Her legs could no longer support her weight.

The man at the desk spoke, "Sarah, um, no, Sal McCarthy, I have had you assigned to me as my official housekeeper. My name is Major Edward Grace." As he spoke, he handed her the tea.

Her hands shook so much as she took it that it sloshed on her already filthy gown; she placed it on the ground next to her. Tears blinded her vision, so no rape. She thought, what then?

"Sal, you are safe; we shall protect you; do you understand? No one will hurt you. You and Charles Lockley are both being sent to a family who will care for you. Do you understand?"

Sal nodded. Did she understand that she was not to be raped? That she could not go home? That she was still innocent? She managed to mutter, "Yes, sir, thank you, sir." The trickle of tears turned into rivers. She leaned forward and wept with her head in her hands. The rivers of tears became great hacking sobs. She was safe.

The handsome man, Charles, came and knelt beside her; she felt his hand on her shoulder, but it was comforting, not at all suggestive or threatening. She lifted her eyes to meet his.

"Sal, we shall make sure you are kept safe. Do you understand?" She couldn't remember his name, but she loved his friendly voice.

"Yes," she murmured. She had no idea how she ended up in Charles's arms, but they were so lovely and firm. She felt as safe as they promised she would be.

Major Grace allowed her time to regain some control. "Are you all right, Sal? Do you think you can hear what we have planned?"

Sal sniffed and hunted around for something to blow her nose on. The handsome man handed her a clean handkerchief that the Major held out to her. She blew her nose. "Thank you, sir. I'll wash it before I return it." She held it tight. Her fingers traced an E monogram on the corner.

Ned smiled, then related what he had planned for them both. They would be living with friends of his. The Major said the handsome man's name was Charles Lockley. He would be staying in the stables, and she would work for the Major and the family. As he kept saying she was now safe, she finally began to believe him. The words family, children, and safe eventually penetrated her brain. Charles had released her and was now sitting on the other side of the room.

The next hour or so was a blur. Sal found herself walking from the office, escorted by two of the most handsome men she'd ever seen. She had not even noticed the Major before, but they could have been brothers. She wondered if they were at least related. She had no idea where she was going, but they kept assuring her of her safety. As they arrived at a corner house, she gasped. This was one of the nicest places she had seen since her arrival. The two-story sandstone building was wrapped with a wide verandah, top and bottom.

Both she and Charles gasped. "We're assigned here?" Charles was as stunned as she was. "Thank you, Major. This is wonderful."

Ned looked a little embarrassed. "They are friends of mine, so please don't let me down. Sal, you shall be filling in for... no, I won't say, Mrs White will give you more details, but you will be here part-time and looking after my place too. Washing, repairs, cleaning, and such, but I leave things quite neat, so there shouldn't be much to do. I can't stay long, so I'll leave you both with Perry, um, Mr White, and he'll explain things." Perry and Katy met them as they waved farewell to Ned.

Sal was shown into a lovely room with a bed and wardrobe. A large string-tied parcel was sitting on the bed for her. Katy pulled the string for her as she showed Sal the room.

Katy had sorted through her gowns and chosen some of the ones that no longer fitted. They were better than any Sal had ever owned before. There were also some lengths of fabric.

Katy hoped that Sal could sew.

As Sal fingered the lovely fabric, she said she could sew well. The blue was precisely the same colour as Charles's eyes. She smiled that she would be working near him if not with him.

When the two newcomers had been introduced to Katy, they were told they were to be called Mr Perry and Mrs Katy. Katy explained that she was a convict but lived with her husband. She now had her Ticket of Leave, but she knew how Sal felt. "Sal, Major Ned asked me to arrange a schedule for you to clean his rooms. Lucy, our current maid, is having another baby and her husband is our children's tutor. Our twins are nearly the same age as their son. Lucy will still be doing what she can, but we are a reasonably easy household. Everyone pitches in and does what is needed."

Sal was stunned; this was not what she expected.

Charles was walked through his work by Perry, with Abel hovering nearby. Charles said, "Yes sir" and "No sir," quite a few times until Perry said, "Charles, enough of the 'sir' stuff every second breath, will you? 'Mr Perry' will suffice."

By the time they had seen the stables from end to end, Charles had a grin on his face from ear to ear. "I think I can handle this, Mr Perry."

Abel was packed and ready to leave already. Since he had received his Ticket of Leave, he had been itching to get to a farm. He was going the next day, so Charles started right away.

After Perry left them, Abel showed Charles the garden. This was something he knew all about as they had a large garden at home that his mother cared for. Without that food, they probably would have died. He wondered how they were coping now.

Sal met Janey and realised that she was the lady helping everyone at the gaol. Janey welcomed her warmly. She was as surprised to see the clean lady she had picked out now working with her.

Sal took some time to settle fully. However, by the end of the week, she had worked out how to fit both jobs into the daily schedule. Sal was also stunned to find that they were to eat with the family in the dining room most nights. Only when they had visitors did the staff eat in the kitchen. Worried she would make a mistake, she watched Katy use the cutlery and followed how she ate.

Over a meal at the end of the first week, Sal mentioned to Janey that she felt a little uncomfortable walking down to Major Ned's place alone. She had been jeered once or twice already. Before she knew it, with Perry's permission, Charles volunteered to walk down with her to Ned's rooms. He waited until she cleaned the room and then carried back any laundry that Major Ned needed to do.

Within ten days, Charles had asked Sal if he could court her. She willingly agreed. Their relationship developed quickly as they were together daily. Shortly after, Charles asked to marry her. He had not kissed her but wished to do so. However, he would not until they were at least engaged. She willingly said yes. She had fallen for Charles on the day they met. Even the Major's handsome face and pristine red uniform could not tempt her from her adoration of Charles.

Perry also gave his approval and then helped file the application for a marriage of convicts with Ned.

Ned had not been surprised. He explained to Perry how they had both seen her on that first day. He told Perry that Charles had requested that he rescue Sal.

The relationship between Ned and Charles was still ambiguous, but they had become friends. Perry had invited Buck and Charles to join him for morning prayers. Ned was able to come most mornings after daily muster, and the discussions that followed opened the door of friendship between the four men. Formality was left at the door.

~

Toward the end of February, Charles and Sal were married. Reverend Marsden called the Banns throughout the month and did the deed only three weeks later.

Perry and Ned were to be witnesses to their marriage. Ned had requested that they be allowed to marry on the last Monday of the month after the third call of Banns, as Ned was heading off to Emu Plains Prison farm. He had a few calls to make in the area and would not be back until the next week, but it could possibly extend.

Perry suggested Sal move into the rooms above the stables as they were more commodious. Sal thought she was in seventh heaven. She was still quite shy and not prepared to put herself forward. She was content to do the work that everyone else didn't get time to finish; then, she would help Charles with the vegetable garden.

Katy chuckled and said she was a workaholic.

Sal kept Ned's rooms perfectly, and his clothing was always immaculate; her sewing skills were employed by many in the household. Occasionally Ned was there when she was working. They would chat as she cleaned, generally about things like faith and prayer. She had interrupted Ned at morning prayers a few times, and she wondered what he was doing.

Ned explained about prayer and his beliefs. From then on, every chance Sal had, she asked more questions. Ned willingly and patiently answered her. One day he explained about her sins being totally washed away.

She shook her head as she had no idea what he meant. He explained that by believing in Jesus' death and resurrection, taking her sins and wiping them away, she was as innocent as a newborn babe. Conversation with Charles followed, and both realised that whatever these new friends had, they both wanted. Something called Eternal Life.

Ned had taken to eating Sunday luncheon with the family, where he could relax. However, only with Perry could he really be himself. He had asked that Katy not be told his real identity. When he returned from his Emu Plains trip, he finally let that cat out of the bag himself.

Ned arrived frustrated. He greeted both Perry and Katy and then followed them into the sitting room; when they were alone, he said, "Well, that trip was a blooming waste of time. The 'sir' this and 'sir' that is nearly as bad as the many my Lord's at home." He'd forgotten that Katy didn't know his real identity, and he spun around and faced her. He stood mouth open, unsure of what to say.

Perry saved the situation. "Ned, don't worry, Katy is also a Countess; remember, we know how to hide a title. She will say nothing, will you, dear?" Perry looked at his wife.

Katy walked to Ned and took his hand. "Ned, we already trust you with who we are, be assured that you can do the same. When I go home, as Lachlan has hinted to me that I will be able to do, do you think I will want others to find out where I've been or what I've been doing? A Lady in irons would not go down too well, but that's what I am." She stood looking him in the eye. "Ned, trust us; let us be here to support you now. Perry has told me nothing, and that's fine. But know this Ned, whatever you say to us stays in this room. We all have secrets; if the worst thing we hide is our titles, then so be it." With that, Katy sat down.

Ned looked from one face to the other; a smile spread across his face; he said, "Then, in that case, Perry, you have my permission to let Katy know what you think fit to tell her. I appreciate having your support, both of you, for I desperately need it. Be assured that if I can do anything to assist you; I will. Especially once you do get home."

Katy asked, "I gather Lachlan does not know of your exalted status either?"

Ned shook his head. "I really haven't met everyone yet, but there is one I have stayed away from intentionally, but I feel I may need to introduce myself to him under my new name soon before he spills the beans." He took a sly glance at Perry with a funny look on his face. He said as though explaining, "Harry Moffatt is from home; we were at school together."

Perry looked at Katy. "Moffatt, do you know him?"

"Not unless you mean the new lawyer fellow. I saw him at Government House once. Is that whom you mean?" Katy asked.

Ned nodded. "We share mutual friends from home. He can be trusted implicitly should you need him."

~

Buck and Lucy's daughter arrived in the middle of a freezing night in September. The brazier in the room kept everyone comfortable. When Lucy started labour, it was evident that things were not as simple as her last delivery.

Sal heard her scream and, donning her new woolly dressing gown Katy had given her; she went quickly to assist with the birth. At six months gone herself, she knew this was to be ahead of her. Sal had helped to deliver three babies on board the ship out. Here at least, she had hot water and everything required for a birth, and it was clean.

Nanny arrived soon after Sal and saw that she had everything under control. Sal, however, willingly handed the delivery over to Nanny.

Lucy laboured for three hours; then, the contractions stopped ten minutes apart. Lucy was exhausted, and her waters had not broken.

Nanny suggested a hot bath for her.

Buck was enlisted to bring buckets of hot water downstairs for her. While they prepared the bath, Nanny and Sal walked Lucy around the room.

Janey was in the kitchen, keeping the hot water coming and listening for the other children. The other two new maids were left asleep as they could look after the children tomorrow when everyone else was resting. Childbirth was not Janey's thing. She'd had to assist with a couple and nearly passed out each time. Janey knew Sal was happy to help Nanny. Janey was even delighted not to be too closely involved. No one had yet told Katy what was happening, but Janey was sure she would hear the commotion soon enough.

The hot bath came and went, and although Lucy's waters had now broken, the baby just would not come. Every time she lay down, everything stopped again. Lucy screamed in agony; it was that scream that woke Katy.

Katy pulled on her dressing gown and went down the back stairs through the freezing night to see if she could do anything.

Lucy was lying on the bed, writhing in agony.

"Mrs Katy, the only time things start moving is when she is walking around," Nanny said.

Katy looked at Sal, Nanny and then Buck, "Then that's what we'll do."

Buck looked puzzled, he didn't want to be there, but somehow, he knew Katy would keep him close.

Katy suggested, "On the ship out here, a few of us gave birth. Davy also wasn't moving either, and my friend Catherine and the doctor on board had me squatting to deliver him. I did the same for Jem's birth; it was much easier. I was wondering if you want to try something similar. And Lucy, I need you to open your mouth to breathe. Long deep breaths, not little shallow ones, and shout if you want to."

Lucy was just starting to have another contraction.

Nanny said, "Remember, breathe Lucy, in… out…."

Lucy was clutching at Buck, and she was obviously tiring. She was still taking short breaths. "I'll do anything; just get this darned baby out of me."

"Breathe deeply, Lucy," Sal said. She'd forgotten about that.

Lucy groaned as Buck stood her upright again. "Come on, my brave girl, we have a child to deliver. I shall be your strength." He sounded brave, but his knees were weak as jelly. His stomach was full of butterflies, but he supported her as she walked around the room, stopping frequently, one contraction hit after the other. The pains were now closer. Lucy was finally taking the long deep breaths.

Five minutes apart slipped into two, then less than a minute apart. One after the other hit and Lucy was exhausted.

Katy had shown Buck how she wished him to support Lucy. He was now sitting in the wooden dining chair he'd been asked to bring downstairs. Katy had Nanny place some clean towels on the floor. Lucy was standing between his legs, facing away from him. Katy hitched up Lucy's nightgown and then had her squat between Buck's legs. He wrapped his arms around under hers and locked his hands together; Lucy leaned her arms on his legs. Within minutes, Judith Catherine was lying in her mother's arms. Buck was still supporting his wife and was gazing over her shoulder at the tiny child. "Oh, my darling Luce, she's beautiful."

Both parents gazed lovingly at their daughter.

Katy and Nanny knew that she had yet to deliver the afterbirth. Sal hovered close by to take the child. The time came, and Sal took the baby as Nanny tied, then cut the cord.

Lucy was already bleeding heavily, and soon the gush of blood that followed the afterbirth made all three women gasp. This was not normal.

Katy and Nanny stood watching, unable to think of what to do.

Sal realised they needed to stop the bleeding and fast. She shoved the baby at Katy. As Lucy passed out, Sal said, "Buck, get her on the bed and hold her legs up. Nanny hold a towel on her private parts. Mrs Katy expose her breasts and put the baby on to suck. Get Lindsay, too and give him a feed. It's all that will save her now." Lucy was now unresponsive.

This, too, had happened on board, and one convict lady had been a midwife. She did this, and the mother lived.

Perry chose that time to come downstairs.

Sal barked orders to him and to everyone else. "Mr Perry, we need cold water from the well. As cold as possible, and lots of towels, actually, sir, see if there is ice on the birdbath."

Perry left and checked the birdbath. Sure enough, there was a thick chunk of ice on the water there. He broke off a big piece and took it straight in. His fingers were cold, but the ice was needed.

Sal wrapped the ice in a linen cloth and placed it on Lucy's stomach under her nightgown. Both children were suckling, and Nanny said the bleeding was slowing, but she was piling up the bloodied towels on the floor. She was smeared in the red ooze, as were her arms.

When Nanny had sat at Lucy's feet, Buck had lowered her legs and went to her head. He tried to pull a covering over her exposed chest. "Lucy, darling Luce, you need to fight." Buck was beside her stroking her forehead, and he bowed his head in prayer. Although he knew it was not usual for any men to be at a birth other than the doctor, he now was glad he was there.

Perry watched; he had helped Katy with Jem's birth. He knew what to expect, and this was not it. That had been a wondrous experience. Perry realised Lucy was in grave danger. He joined Buck with a hand on both Buck's and Lucy's shoulders and prayed aloud, "Dear Lord God, it is at times like this that we realise how weak we are. We are nothing without you, and we know that only you have the power over life and death. We lift Lucy to you and ask, no, we beseech you, to heal our sister Lucy. We surrender her to you." He released a great sigh, and although he did not know why he started singing quietly.

> *"Amazing grace! How sweet the sound*
> *That saved a wretch like me!*
> *I once was lost, but now am found.*
> *Was blind, but now I see."*

Katy joined him in the next verse; tears were streaming down her face. Lucy lay still and unresponsive. Each person was still busy doing what they needed to do to save her life. Soon most of the others joined in softly singing while still ministering to Lucy's needs.

It was surreal.

Nanny checked the bleeding and saw that the suckling was working. Sal heard her say, "Come on, babies, suck harder!"

Again, they sang.

'Twas grace that taught my heart to fear,
And grace my fears relieved.
How precious did that grace appear
The hour I first believed.

Sal was now the only one not singing; she didn't know the words. She stood with her hands on her own growing stomach listening to the beautiful lyrics of the hymn. She'd not been to church for worship and didn't know any hymns, but tears were streaming down her face; something had happened to her. She was at peace; she understood God's power and knew He was in control. Charles and Major Ned had been teaching her about prayer and forgiveness. After Perry's words, she knew God was listening.

Charles then arrived and was sent to get more ice from the birdbath. He passed it in but waited outside in case he was needed. It was cold, but he spent the time praying too.

Nanny was still putting towels soaked in the cold water on Lucy's stomach under her gown. Tears were trickling down her face as she did everything she could.

Perry and Buck called Charles inside, and all three laid hands-on Lucy, then sang another verse quietly.

Through many dangers, toils, and snares,
I have already come;
'Tis grace hath brought me safe thus far,
And grace will lead me home."

As they finished this verse, Lucy's eyes opened. A tear slid down her cheek. She saw Buck in tears at her side. "I heard; I came back, Terry, just hold me." She put her hand up to his cheek and wiped away a tear. "So tired, Terry." She closed her eyes again.

Buck sobbed; he carefully hugged all his family. Lindsay had fallen asleep, but Judith was still suckling. He lifted his eyes and met his boss's compassionate look. "Perry, I had no idea that love hurt like this." Buck saw Lucy's eyes had closed again, "You have to keep fighting, Luce. Don't leave us; we need you." Buck did not even realise he had dropped the Mr.

Nanny saw that Judith had stopped feeding. "Mr Perry, can you get the twins, please. The babies suckling helps stop the bleeding."

Perry left and went to get his own twins.

Sal and Katy put Lindsay and Judith in their cots.

Buck stayed beside Lucy. He had pulled the sheets over her, and although now covered, she was shivering.

Sal said to Buck, "You need to warm her up. Lie beside her and cuddle her."

Sal went to stoke the brazier.

Buck looked to Nanny, who said, "She's right, Buck; I'm pretty sure she's out of danger now, but she needs to be warm, or she'll go into shock. I think that's what the shaking is, shock."

Buck crawled under the blankets and drew Lucy into his arms. The sight of so much blood and the pile of soaked rags on the floor when he had looked up at Nanny made his own blood run cold. He buried his head in Lucy's neck, whispering his love for her. He had no idea how deep his feelings for her were until this moment. He knew he cared, but she had become his reason to *be*. When he thought she would die, he almost stopped breathing. His faith, too, had been tested. When Perry had started singing, it was as though his strength was being refilled.

Perry returned with the sleepy twins. Katy was still giving them comfort feeds, even though they were now over two years old, so hopefully, they would not realise that they were not at their mother's breast.

One by one, Katy and Sal placed the children on Lucy's breasts.

Perry had his back to her while they worked. All the while, he prayed. He could do no more. The thoughts going through his mind made him lift his eyes to Katy. She went to his side and slid her arms around him. He bent down and whispered to her, "What we do to you women to slake our lusts is just not fair, Katy." He drew her into his arms and waited.

She could hear him murmuring prayers as he held her close.

Charles held Sal too.

It seemed an eternity, but Nanny finally said quietly, "Her flow is nearing normal. She needs fluids now, lots of fluids, warmth, and rest. Buck, stay where you are."

Katy and Perry both left to bring something for her to drink. Sal and Buck now held the two-year-old twins while they sucked.

After a mug of tea each, Nanny sent everyone away but Buck. Katy and Perry returned their own twins to bed. Hopefully, neither would remember their nocturnal trip. Charles escorted Sal to their rooms. She was exhausted. Nanny stayed and watched.

By dawn, the crisis was over. Lucy was sleeping peacefully, with Buck still curled up to her. He, too, slept.

Nanny sat in an armchair near the brazier and dozed so she could be on hand if needed.

Janey, Beatrice, and Clare Livingstone were told that they had to keep the older children quiet and pick up whatever duties needed to be done today as everyone else was going to sleep in.

When Perry explained the situation, they all stepped up and did the required work.

Buck didn't move from beside Lucy all morning.

Sal came and relieved Nanny at about nine, and Janey came a few hours later. Lucy was given more tea and some chicken broth. Nanny had already helped Lucy feed Judith once at dawn, and Sal did the same at ten.

By evening Lucy was weak but on the road to recovery. As Sal and Nanny gave Lucy a wash, Perry took Buck upstairs. Perry took him into the sitting room and offered whatever support he needed. Buck was still in shock, "Thank you, Mr Perry; I could not believe what she went through. How can we do this to them? She has no word of complaint against me, just love." Only then did Buck crumble; he was so angry at himself. He wiped angry tears away.

Perry knew that feeling well; he placed a caring hand on his friend's shoulder. "Buck, firstly, drop the mister, will you? And secondly, this is what life is. It's all part of the fall in the Garden of Eden so long ago. A woman's punishment was that she would travail in pain and still desire her husband. It's the way of things, but Buck, our path back to Christ is where we are to aim. Sickness and pain are not part of God's plan but as a consequence of our sins. I have no idea what made me sing last night, but it just felt right. I knew we had to hand things over to God. I just knew things would be all right if we did."

Buck sniffed back tears. "If I lost her, Perry, I don't know what I'd do. Last night I thought to myself, 'I didn't know love hurt that much'. I always thought that love was something gentle and loving, but not the searing pain of prospective loss and the struggle to survive. I could hardly breathe when I thought she was going to die. When I saw how much blood she'd lost and that there was nothing I could do…."

Perry didn't know what to say, so he asked if they could pray together.

Buck nodded.

The two men sat together on the settee for some time with their heads bowed in prayer.

Chapter 15 Beginning of the End

Charles John Lockley junior made his appearance in the middle of a very

wet November at the end of 1820. He was born with comparable ease, and Lucy ministered to her now dear friend, Sal, through her labour pains.

As they had done for Lucy only weeks before, Nanny and Katy attended the birth too. Charles was on hand and held her as she also delivered the baby whilst squatting. Her labour had lasted only five hours before she held her adorable cherub in her arms. Her son had his father's big blue eyes, dimples, and a shock of white-blonde hair. It was love at first sight for everyone.

Little Charlie was adorable.

Sal bounced back quickly, and although she was given a month's leave, she was back on her feet doing light duties within weeks. She had seen some of the aboriginal women with babies tied to their backs, and she decided to try this. Although it was hot and humid, it was very comfortable.

The rain continued, and the river rose. Charles told Perry that the river was rushing so hard that the new weir had partially washed away. On hearing this, Perry had visited Government House to report to Lachlan and heard the horrifying news that the storm in Sydney had produced a lightning strike. Government House in Sydney had been struck by lightning. Thankfully no one had been injured; Katy's friend Emily had married some years ago and was no longer there. But the experience had frightened both Elizabeth and little Lachie. Lachlan added this to the long and growing list of works needing repair or replacement.

Charlie was an easy baby, and Nanny loved looking after both him and Judith. However, because of the small volume of staff, the lines between servant and master were now well and truly blurred. All the children were treated as equals. After Judith was born, Perry had found out how well Charles could both read and write. He took over teaching the older children while Buck took some time to be with Lucy. Charles admitted his education was basic as he'd often skipped school.

Charles had discovered that Sal was literate when they married, as she had signed her name rather than just putting a cross on the page.

Ned had been surprised that both had some education, but Sal's writing was elegant and well-formed. Charles' writing was not neat but what Ned later termed as strong.

The men's prayer times became routine, and the four men grew in friendship and faith. Ned even invited Charles to call him by his first name when alone. It took a while, but as Charles liked him, he complied.

In early December, Lachlan loaded his family and dignitaries up in various carriages and headed south. Lachlan had the pleasure of opening a new town. His words were personal, "In honour of my beloved Elspeth, the new town is named Campbell-town after her family." Prior to that, it had been called the district of Airds. The area was vital to the farming communities nearby. The school was currently a bark slab hut, but it would soon have a permanent building, a chapel, and a planned town.

The rains continued through December, even stranding the Macquaries at the Georges River on one trip. With so much rain, various diseases were rampant throughout the colony, and many died.

~

The long-awaited Female Factory was finally complete.

John Campbell announced in the newspapers that the Factory would take its first occupants on February 1, 1821. The officers took the remaining women from the old gaol to the new Female Factory at eight in the morning. Most of the other female convicts had already been assigned. The discovery that some forty women who already knew how to spin, weave, and sew were held back from assignment and put to work in the temporary facility at the old gaol. The women were to start work in the new Factory soon after arrival. The new facility would hopefully supply much-needed fabrics for use in the colony.

Neither Katy nor Janey was happy with the final design, but it was still far better than the previous single cramped room.

~

The arrival of more convict ships was a regular occurrence. Hundreds and hundreds of people had to be housed, fed, and guarded. Lachlan had had enough. His health was failing, and he could no longer keep up the pace. Towards the end of the month, Lachlan received notification that the powers that be in England had finally accepted his resignation. Until they heard England terminated his tenure, he had to keep this quiet. He had submitted the paperwork more than eighteen months before.

Midwinter, Lachlan called Perry and Katy to his office at Government House. As they sat down, he noticed the concern on their faces. Lachlan delightedly told Katy that she had now finished her time; then handed her an Absolute Pardon. He explained to them both that this would allow them to return home. Katy and Perry had hoped Lachlan would make this decision without prompting; neither was prepared to ask him outright.

Katy was profuse in her thanks and sat staring at it. While the men chatted, her mind returned to that morning when she found Mary in Perry's arms. She had trusted him, but having misread the situation prior to that morning, she had jumped to the wrong conclusion. That led to seven years of her being clapped in irons. Now she was holding her unconditional release; the Government gave few this privilege.

After a while, Perry realised Lachlan had something on his mind. It didn't take long before they heard a gentle knock at the door.

Lachlan jumped up as if shot and ushered in his wife. She sat next to Katy, smiled then gave Lachlan a subtle nod.

Lachlan looked from one friend to the other; then, he dropped his bombshell. Lachlan looked at his friends. "Perry, Katy, we too shall be leaving early next year. I won't go into the details, but I find I must return to London to defend myself against John Bigge's accursed accusations. Most of it has stemmed from my supposed mismanagement of Andrew Thompson's estate. He left me a quarter of the estate, which was not popular, and a swathe of instructions of how to use it. He was a friend; and I did what he asked. I suppose you know how that friendship came about?"

Perry shook his head.

Lachlan frowned. "Oh well, Macarthur started it in reality well before I arrived; it was over rum grain. Blooming, rum again! A sum of £34 10s was for grain, owed by Andrew to John Macarthur, but before he paid it, another flood hit and Macarthur blew the price out to ten times the amount. Governor Bligh threw the case out of court. He restored the figure to the original amount, thus making an enemy of Macarthur. We have now both stood against John Macarthur. And now they demand that I provide a receipt for the Spanish doubloons I purchased. Are they serious? I know I have done no wrong. I can stand before our Lord with a clear conscience." He took a deep breath. "I have therefore resigned. However, I was wondering if you'd like to return with us?"

Perry looked at Katy's stunned face; he felt the same. Lachlan's resignation had come out of the blue for them. Perry knew Lachlan had so much more he wanted to do; they had already been discussing building a new Government House on the hill in Sydney. Already the colony was vastly different from when he had arrived.

Katy met Perry's unvoiced question and nodded. Yes, it was time for them to go home.

"Good, then we travel together," Lachlan said. "I also have some information for you about Charles and Sal. I have decided that Charles will take over the running of the new Jolly Sailor Inn down near the wharf, and with it, he shall also oversee the Government Stores. Major Grace has recommended him for the role; what do you think?"

Perry was stunned but thrilled. "Um, I think it's great." Charles and Sal had become almost family. Since the horrible night when Lucy had nearly died, Buck and Charles had become close. Again, Perry looked at Katy; he saw shock on her face and was puzzled. She knew that Charles had joined Buck and him for prayers most mornings. Lucy and Sal had become almost like sisters; parting would be hard for them both.

Perry wondered what the arrangements were. "Are they to leave soon?"

Lachlan smiled at his question. He'd thought about that. "Err, sort of, but the changes won't fully happen until you leave. I have a suggestion. As Sal has only recently given birth, I gather she's on light duties?"

Katy nodded, but Perry saw the strange set of her face.

Lachlan continued. "And Perry, as you don't go out much, I can't imagine that Charles is all that busy?"

This time Perry shook his head.

So Lachlan continued, "Then, as the new Government Stores is open for set times in the morning and an hour in the afternoon, I suggest they stay with you until you leave. The building they will be moving into is small, to say the least, and it needs refurbishment, if not remodelling. I'll set that into motion." By now, even Lachlan could tell Katy had something to say. "Katy…?"

Katy looked at Perry rather than Lachlan and watched his expression as she said, "Sal is expecting again. She's due in about October. She thought she was just exhausted from Charlie's birth, but she's having another baby and is in shock. It was only when she felt the child move that she realised."

"She's expecting in October? That will mean the babies are only eleven months apart in age." Perry questioned; he was stunned.

Katy nodded. She knew this would hurt Elizabeth as her history of losing babies hurt so much. At least little Lachie was thriving.

Lachlan held his opinions but experienced a wave of jealousy. He said, "It seems she's strong and copes well with childbirth. Her condition won't matter in the scheme of things. However, I shall make sure that the building will fit a growing family. So, they will need three bedrooms, a taproom, a kitchen and dining room, a barn and a big stable as I plan the stable to be a public one.. I'll get a gang or two onto it straight away. Major Grace has offered to oversee the project. I gather there may be some connection there, but he won't say what it is. Charles Lockley is as like him as, well, they could well be brothers." The look he saw Perry give Katy made him wonder if they knew more than they were letting on.

"Sir, as you know, Ned is a family friend of mine from home, and he knows of no relationship; it is indeed a subject we have discussed. The resemblance between them is, as you say, certainly marked. They have become friends; both join us for morning prayers." Perry knew what Ned thought, but that was not for him to discuss. Maybe one day, they would discover the truth.

~

Over the following months, they made plans for the departure of the two families. However, a new face arrived on the scene; Edward John Lockley came late afternoon on October 16. It was Ned's twenty-second birthday.

Perry had insisted on having a birthday luncheon to celebrate Ned's special day. It was a Tuesday, and Ned had taken a day off. Everyone except Bill and Molly from the new Inn down the road joined in the celebration with an outdoor meal. The weather was fine, and the fellowship was enjoyable.

The luncheon was a help-yourself buffet from the kitchen. Lachlan was away, and Elizabeth was busy with official duties so neither was present. The informality meant no fetching or carrying up and down the back stairs. The children could all run through the growing orchard. The small children raided the small mulberry tree and returned purple but content.

Charles and Sal had disappeared mid-afternoon. It was some hours before anyone noticed they had not returned, and Charlie was still in Nanny's care. However, it was not until Nanny heard a scream that they all realised Sal was having the baby.

Soon only Ned, Perry, and Buck were left in the yard, with Janey, Beatrice and Clare keeping their eyes on all the children.

After a few more hours, Charles stuck his head over the verandah railing and invited the three men to come and welcome the newest Lockley.

The men entered, with Ned holding the door for them. Everyone was standing around the bed where Sal was sitting up with a massive grin on her face.

Charles said, "Hello Ned, I have a special gift for your birthday. Please meet Edward John Lockley. He's to be known as Eddie, though."

Ned was stunned. "You're naming him after me, Charles? Really? Edward John Lockley, eh? Nice, I like that." Ned's heart was beating a tattoo.

Charles took the new baby from Sal's arms and handed him to Ned.

As Ned took the swaddled child in his arms, unbeknownst to them, Edward John Charles Lockley was now holding his namesake in so many more ways than they knew. Ned was itching to tell them his real name but just couldn't. His eyes met those of Charles with a crinkled grin. It was like he was looking into the faces of his younger brothers.

Little Eddie opened his giant blue orbs and, looking into Ned's face, yawned, smiled, dimpled, and gave an enormous burp.

Ned chuckled. "Well, my little man, that sound wasn't very gentlemanly, but I'm sure you will grow into your exalted name." Ned had cuddled Charlie when he was born, but his heart went out to this tiny mite. It was probably as close as he would ever get to having one for himself; with that thought, he almost teared up. Ned presumed that this was the bonding feeling he had heard women speak of. Yes, he had bonded with this tiny scrap of humanity. He would do what he could for the lad, even educate him when the time came.

Ned met Perry's eyes across the room, and they grinned at each other. "Sorry, Perry, but this gift beats all. Charles, Sal, he's beautiful. Edward Lockley, eh? I do like the sound of that." He could hardly remove the smile from his face.

Perry was the only other one there who realised the name's significance. Perry watched the happiness on the young soldier's face as he gazed lovingly at the tiny babe.

Charles, too watched Ned's face. The smile Ned gave the babe made his otherwise hidden dimples pop. Charles gave a small gasp; they were identical to his own and the new baby's too. Few men had them. Charles wondered if Ned knew more about a relationship than he was telling him.

Ned had sought friendship with Charles, and Charles had been stunned. Ned reminded him of a gracious lady he'd seen just the once. His mother had later told him who she was. Duchess Susanna lived in a castle nearby and was admired by many; her beauty was such that it had moved his teenage heart. One day he'd name a daughter after her, especially if they had the same fair hair as their two sons. Their first daughter would be named after both their mothers, though.

Perry and Katy had stood near the door of the stable accommodation watching the amazing scene unfold. Perry could see the joy on Ned's face as Charles handed him the tiny child. He saw a look of absolute delight flood Ned's face.

Janey soon arrived with little Charlie in her arms. He had just realised that both his parents had not been seen for some time. Janey had been watching him and keeping him both safe and occupied. As he walked into the rooms above the stables, he saw his mother in bed. He held out his arms to her.

Sal took her eldest son and gave him a big cuddle before pointing out that he was now an older brother. She pointed out the baby Ned was holding. She wondered if Charlie understood what that meant.

It seemed he did.

He said, "Brover?" His eyes grew as big as saucers. Charlie looked to his father, whom he idolised.

"Yes, son, you are now my eldest son. It will be up to you to look after him, but he will be a best friend for you forever. You will have to help us care for him." Charles didn't expect Charlie to understand or remember the words.

Charlie, however, knew what he meant. The baby was his, and he had to care for him.

Ned remembered that conversation all his life. Charlie was as good as his word, for he never forgot. Ed was his charge, and Charlie did everything to look after him. Everything!

Eddie reciprocated as he grew too.

The boys grew as the months passed.

~

With Perry soon to leave, Ned and Charles found themselves more and more seeking out each other in friendship. Up at the Rear Admiral Duncan Inn, Bill Miller suggested they call into his private taproom for their meetings. As both were his friends, no one would think twice about either being there. In the past eighteen months, Ned and Charles had grown close. Perry's presence gave them an excuse to be together, but they found they often made time for private conversations. Bill's Inn gave them a place for that.

Charles never overstepped the invisible line of friendship he had drawn for himself. Ned found they could be on first-name terms when alone, but when in public, Charles fell half a pace behind, and he was called 'Major' with due deference.

Ned worked hard to get Charles's new house built, the inn extended, as well as stables and barn completed. He also added a cellar to their home. The new Government Stores building was just down the road from the inn. The construction crews had already completed the structure. They had already moved some of the contents from the old Government Stores shed. Ned had Charles working down there already. More stock was arriving daily from Sydney.

As Charles oversaw the building of their house, life moved on for the others. Perry had a buyer for Glenmere and he made various trips to Sydney to visit friends. With Katy now free, Perry took her to meet Sam and Annie Corbett in Glebe. He would miss his childhood friend. Katy had been let into their secret but also told that Annie didn't even know Sam's illustrious status. They both were, like Katy, emancipated convicts. Up until Katy received her Certificate of Freedom, she had not been able to meet them as they didn't leave Sydney, and Katy only did if Lachlan Macquarie took them to Government House in Sydney.

Sam swore Perry to secrecy about his identity, although she did, however, know the rest of his story, but not that his father was an Earl.

Sam had never told his wife, as his father's final words to him as he was arrested was that he would disinherit him. He presumed his father had carried through with that threat, so he saw no reason to tell her or their now teenage son, Danny, what he could have been and the amazing inheritance they could have had.

Katy had been itching to meet Annie and get to know her over the short time they had left. Neither Sam nor Annie wanted to step foot out of Glebe. Both had done their time not too far from Parramatta, and neither had any desire to return, so the four would only meet in Glebe at their house. If Katy could not join Perry, then Ned did often. Ned had confided in Perry why he kept an eye on Sam, so Ned visited Sam with Perry when he could.

~

Lachlan was busy finishing many of the projects that were still under construction. A few of the buildings he realised he would not seen finished. Although the new barracks in Windsor were more than half completed, Lachlan had concerns about its necessity. Initially, he had it erected as a convict's barracks, but the area and his new ticketing system already made it less than helpful. Two of the other projects nearing completion were the two Courthouses in Windsor and Sydney. He had so wished that his ideas for a new Government House had been one of the projects he had achieved. Still, he was sure some other Governor would be made so uncomfortable in the leaky house that they would do something about the dilapidated timber building. At least the draft plans were done.

His term of office would be final in November, but he would not leave for a few weeks so that he could enact the handover without fuss. He wanted his tenure to end smoothly; he wrote this in the final section of his speech. Lachlan sat at his desk and wrote,

"To have been instrumental in bringing about so favourable a change will ever be TO ME, a source of sincere delight; and it is not arrogating to myself any questionable merit to say, that I have used every exertion of body and mind, I was capable of, to attain this desirable and important object; and I think all persons will allow, that I have not consulted my own personal ease, or convenience, in the execution of the various and arduous duties attached to my Office; on the contrary, I feel that my health is greatly impaired by the constant and unremitting attention I have bestowed on the faithful, zealous, and conscientious discharge of my public duties."

"I am well aware that every man in public life must have enemies, and perhaps it would be unreasonable, IN ME, to expect to be exempted from the virulent attacks of party and disaffection...."

Lachlan wished that he had seen the completion of his many projects and made fewer enemies. He had expected opposition with his changes, but not really from those who gave it. London was even demanding a receipt for the Spanish doubloons he had purchased. He had tried to change the lives of both convicts and indigenous peoples but knew that only time would make them realise what his efforts were.

Lachlan sat writing, and then images of Elspeth interrupted his thoughts. At least they would leave with one child, but he thought of the eight miscarriages or stillbirths and the death of their dear daughter. His heart hurt as he thought to himself, "Katy and Sal seemed to have children easily. Lucy had had some problems and nearly died, but Elspeth couldn't even carry them that far." He still felt sad over the loss of their daughter; he missed her chuckles. A thought crossed his mind that mayhap it could have been his own illness prior to marriage that caused the problems. After some time, he shook his head to make the melancholy thoughts leave. He wished to finish his final speech endorsing his successor, so he wrote,

"... *I cannot conclude this Address, better than by offering to the Inhabitants of this Colony, my sincere congratulations on their good fortune, in having an Officer, of such distinguished Reputation and highly established Character, as SIR THOMAS BRISBANE, appointed to be their Governor; and although I will not allow that He can surpass his Predecessor, in zeal and inclination, I trust and hope, He will, in ability and talents, in promoting the prosperity and improvement of the Country, and the happiness and unanimity of its Inhabitants. In these sentiments and wishes, deeply engraved on my heart, I now bid you all — Farewell!"*

LACHLAN MACQUARIE

Lachlan placed down his pen. He re-read his speech and tweaked some words. Satisfied with what was on paper, he went to rejoin his family. He decided to let Perry and John Campbell read it before delivering it.

~

Perry had arranged to sell his house with nearly all its contents. Their return to England would still entail much luggage packing but no furniture. He knew he should have no say about who purchased the house; no, it was a home, their first real home, and both were sad for it to be sold. Glenmere was emotionally special. He arranged to delay settlement until they sailed; this was to be either January or February the following year.

Perry had begged Lachlan for Janey to be allowed to return with them as they had discussed. Lachlan transferred her term to Perry, then winked. He made the one condition was that she remain in their employ for the term of her natural life, as was her sentence. He grinned, then Lachlan added that Beatrice and Clare Livingstone were to join her for the final years of their service.

John Campbell recorded the change of venue for the three ladies to serve out their terms.

On this news, Janey was overjoyed. It meant that she would be again living with her mother and cousins. Janey was bouncing around like a two-year-old when Perry told her. Then only minutes later, she was sitting on the settee in tears, sobbing as though her heart would break.

Katy looked at Perry, and he shrugged.

Janey was crying with relief; she had been so afraid that she would be left behind.

In the years that she had been with Perry and Katy, they had included her in their Bible studies. All the staff had grown in faith. Of all of them, Betty was the only one to stay; she would be the cook for the new owner. This meant that she, too did not need to be reassigned.

Buck, Lucy, Nanny, Janey, Sal, and Charles met each morning with Perry and Katy before work. They would join hands around the dining room table and dedicate the day to the Lord.

Perry explained that they had to set an example of running a faithful household, which was the first requirement of each day. Sometimes they were interrupted by one of the children, but even the children learned to stay in their parents' or carers' arms and pray too. Often, they joined in with a childish prayer of adoration to both God and parents.

Chapter 16 The Departure

*I*n December 1821, the fanfare arranged for the welcome and handing over to Governor Brisbane was a joyous celebration. Lachlan had been planning this for some years. To have Perry and Buck with him on their return trip would be a delight. The first time he had submitted his resignation was now nearly five years before, and the reply from that was silence. Now he could finally leave. Lachlan had sighed with relief when he had eventually had his paperwork accepted. He had not let anyone, but Perry know how ill he was now feeling. Elizabeth kept asking him, but he kept replying, "I probably could be better, but I'll survive." Perry had become far more than a friend; he had also become a confidante.

The departure of the *Surrey* was due the first week in February. Perry finalised the sale of the property. The luggage procession from Parramatta was long. The Macquaries had fully moved out to Parramatta months before, as Governor Brisbane and his wife now lived at the leaky Government House in Sydney.

This was one building Lachlan was unable to replace. He had not rated it highly on his requirements list, as the building at Parramatta was perfectly adequate for a Government abode. They were to leave Parramatta for the last time towards the end of January.

~

After the official welcome of Governor Thomas Brisbane, Lachlan had a few trips to do to tie up his Governorship. The first was a trip to Bathurst, and then, a few days after Christmas, Lachlan attended the congress of the Aborigines in Parramatta in the marketplace. Over three hundred and forty attended, including Perry and Ned. Lachlan made sure that all his friends were able to come. Even Bill, Molly, Charles and Sal were included in the number but not in the official party. Elizabeth had Lachie beside her. Katy had the four older children with her, and Sal had her two little boys.

Lachlan had great compassion for these poor inoffensive people. He encouraged the town's children to play with them occasionally.

Sal Lockley went one further by allowing one-year-old Charlie to play with the aboriginal children along the waterfront. They were dark-skinned versions of her own adorable children. They were dimpled and charming. Sal encouraged them to come for the food she always carried with her.

Charlie and Eddie had curly blonde fair hair with big blue eyes; the aboriginal children had black curly hair with delicious chocolate eyes. Charlie was sitting with a little boy with deep dimples, as did both Lockley boys. Bill's wife, Molly had only weeks to go before she delivered their first child. All the children loved hard-boiled eggs, and Sal always had some of them with her on her riverside walks. She would hand them out to the many reaching fingers.

Lachlan took this opportunity to introduce several tribal leaders to the new Governor. He also introduced Thomas Brisbane to the children at the Female Orphanage.

Some eight weeks after the arrival of the Brisbanes, the vice-regal families had swapped residences. The Brisbanes were now in situ at Parramatta and Lachlan and his family in Sydney; this meant many early starts from Sydney to collect Thomas Brisbane for various tours. They covered the area from the north to Windsor and Campbelltown in the South. Usually, they would leave after breakfast at Parramatta Government House, then head in whatever direction was required. Thus, January was fully occupied with many trips saying farewell and showing the new Governor the area. Lachlan had not been awarded this courtesy on his arrival and realised its importance.

Towards the end of January, the Macquaries had arranged to stay with Perry in Parramatta for the night. The Whites luggage was to be moved to Sydney a few days later, and this would be a double celebration for not only was it farewell to Ned and Charles, but it was also Lachlan's sixtieth birthday a few days later. There was an official function on the day, but he wished to share the celebration with friends.

Lachlan still did not know the precise details of the strange friendship of the two men, but to share faith and fellowship with them was enough. He knew Perry was an Earl, he had figured that Ned knew that too, but the connection between Ned and Charles puzzled him. Buck, it seemed, was a ring in, but his faith was strong. Bill Miller was another with strong faith and was pleased to see that he was included in the circle of friends. Lachlan just knew they were good men and non-judgemental ones at that. That was a rare gift.

Ned, Buck, and Charles always gave Lachlan due deference and never overstepped the bounds of propriety but noticed that the others were all on first-name terms even when not in private.

Lachlan knew them to be convict and master, servant, and soldier. They were an extraordinary combination, but was this not his plan to break down boundaries for the colony? In these four, his dream had become a reality. Bill's inclusion had added to the strange friendship.

Elizabeth, Katy, Sal, Molly, and Janey were also four women from vastly different walks of life. Yet the same applied to them. Sal seemed to be the odd one out, yet she was the ringleader to some degree. Of them all, Sal's leadership skills motivated the others to do more than they felt necessary. Sal had compassion oozing from her, and many a beaten wife or abused woman would be found a bed or a corner in a storeroom.

Perry had sold most of his furniture with the house. Some of the books he gave to Bill as he had mentioned his love of reading. The children and the staff packed what they would need for last week in Sydney. When they were ready to leave, everything was put in storage until the ship was ready to load.

The table was to be one of the last things removed from the house. Perry, Buck, and Charles emptied the Glenmere stable rooms of all the furniture for Charles and Sal's new house and inn. Perry would also send not only the dining room table and chairs but also a large sideboard, which they had not included in the sale. He had been going to leave it but realised Charles could fit it into the large dining room.

Ned had been thrilled when he discovered that the western red cedar dining room table would be given to Charles.

Charles had asked Perry what was to happen to the handcrafted extension table. It had been the one item Perry had to purchase when he had bought the house. For Charles to want it was wonderful. It had been around this table the men sat and prayed; the family sat and eaten here, and many stories had been told and retold.

Perry gifted them joyfully and told them the furniture was a belated wedding gift plus Ned would still get the use of it too. The faith of all the men had grown.

Charles and Ned were going to be left with Bill Miller to continue their prayers. Hopefully, many more would join the others in the years to come. Charles had already asked Ned if he would continue to come for Sunday meals at the new Inn. Ned had been delighted to accept the invitation. Ned, Charles and Bill had drawn even closer since the news that Lachlan, Perry and Buck were leaving.

Perry found it hard to say goodbye to Ned. Perry had later said on the day Eddie was born. "This boy is named after you, Ned. Colin only got Edward as a middle name." Perry had named his third son Colin Edward after Katy's father and Ned.

Young Davy was bouncing off the walls with excitement. He had just discovered they were going home to a ducal-crenellated castle. Jem had finally told him all about their home and what it looked like, even to drawing a picture of it. Thankfully little Colin had not discovered this information yet. Perry somehow kept Davy from discharging the description to everyone.

Sadly, the lease on the cottages had expired at the end of the last year, and each had since been sold. Sal had requested that she continue assisting the abused women by sharing their quarters. They opened their extra rooms to those in need. Perry had purchased more beds, and many had been assisted over the years.

Knowing their secret work, Lachlan had a hidden room of sorts built under the inn for these women to use. It was a little better than a storeroom, but it would suffice. It had two double bunks built into it. Sal wanted to have a safe place for these ladies. Bill and Molly Miller's Inn had some rooms that women and children could use, but they were so often full that the new beds were desperately required.

The White family farewells to Charles and Sal were hard.

Katy may well be nearly twenty years older than Sal, but it was like saying goodbye to a little sister. Perry felt the same about Charles.

Their farewell to Ned was to be delayed a little, for he was coming with them to Sydney for a few days. He would stay at the barracks in town until the Macquaries sailed. He was part of the security detachment of the 48th battalion, and also he wanted to catch up with Sam and Danny. Tom Turner and he had got into the habit of seeing them regularly.

Once in Sydney, Perry moved his extended family into the rooms at the King's Arms Hotel close to the docks. The farewell to Ned, Charles, Sal, and the boys was sad. Perry promised to write. There were many hugs and tears.

Charles and Sal had been moved into their new inn a few days before Lachlan's birthday party, but they still had to carry the table, chairs, and sideboard down the street.

Ned arranged a contingent of soldiers to do the deed, and soon the lovely dining suite was in situ at the inn. The new dining room ran the width of the building; although strange, the main entry was directly into this room. Odd for a house, but for an inn, this was ideal. The family rooms were all out of the way of the public and were, therefore, private. There was a public privy off to the side of the inn; this meant that patrons did not have to share facilities with their family. Sal kept this public facility immaculate. Charles had whitewashed the inside of the small slab-built shed, and the door only covered the neck to knee, so plenty of light entered.

~

The only visit Perry planned to make in Sydney was to Sam. They had arranged to meet at one of Sam's building sites, as Sam had a drawing to do and needed to sketch the floor plan. He would then work out what the finished house would look like. It was a new project he had taken on to help with finances for Annie. Sam knew the drawing would only take about thirty minutes to sketch; he would finish the work at home. Sam told his son Danny that he was going down to the Bond Store and would catch him at home.

Perry watched as Danny grinned and punched the air in glee. "Happy lad, isn't he?" Perry exclaimed.

Sam chuckled. "Oh yes, but he's been itching to see his girl, and he won't have to hurry home now. He's walking out with his boss's daughter Vanessa."

Perry looked surprised. "You haven't told him either, have you?" Perry's question needed no explanation for Sam.

Sam shook his head. "What use would that be? Do I then say, sorry, son, you have lost all your privileges because of me? You have no status in society because I'm a convict? You can't use my title to better your life because my father disowned me? No, Perry, he knows nothing, and neither does Annie. We will make our lives here and be totally content. I have more love and friendship here as an emancipated convict than I ever had at home. Why would I ever go back, Perry? You know how unhappy I was."

Perry was full of compassion for this man. He knew both his loving parents awaited his return; his home had always been happy. Even when he left there some sixteen years before, his parents understood and still supported his decisions. Even here, his father sent an allowance regularly. Sam had nothing from his father other than neglect. He had been sent out for theft because he needed food and money for travel from university. As they were both peers' sons, Perry had been horrified when Sam had told him his story. Now, Perry felt guilty that he had never followed Sam up all those years before.

Major Tom Turner visited Government House to say his farewells to Lachlan and Perry. Again, he never overstepped the bounds of propriety. He paid due deference to the Governor, but Tom and Perry had also become friends over the years. On this last visit, Lachlan had been called away, and Tom revealed to Perry the reason he befriended Sam. "Perry, the Duke of Malvern has Ned Grace watching over Sam and Danny, and I've been asked to watch over Annie by someone else. Shall I just say I was told why, as my mother was a maid to Mr Sam's mama? Perry, I have more than suspicions or even rumours. I heard the story when very young from Mother. There were rumours and a whisper of the truth, but nothing was ever proven or admitted." He didn't say anything but made the action of swapping hands.

"Changelings?" Perry gasped.

"No, sir, more like a cuckoo," Tom said, blushing.

"Ohhh!" Perry found this one word to make sense. Perry knew both families from school; he suddenly realised Sam was the image of the Duke of Malvern, and Annie was far more like Sam's supposed father, the Earl of Meldon. He sat absolutely gobsmacked, knowing the houses were next door to each other.

"Neither knows, sir; I shouldn't either but for the fact that Mother had to be let into the situation. The Earl is aware of them both and asked me to keep an eye on her for him. They will never hear it from me, though, sir. It's not my story to tell."

"You probably should not have told me, Tom," Perry said.

"Possibly not, sir, and I would not have done so if I had not trusted you. However, you see, sir, I have just heard Mr Nigel, Sam's older brother is dead. I can't let him know that I know, but sir, he's now the Viscount, and he will have to return home to West Sussex sometime to sort it out. Mr Perry, sir, he's going to need a friend. One who knows him and what he's been through."

This made sense to Perry; yes, he would stand beside his old school friend. "Thank you, Tom; what about Annie?" If Tom knew Sam's story, he surely would know Annie's, too as he was watching her.

Tom shook his head. "I know it all, but it's not necessary to that part of Sam's story. It's for Sam and Annie to tell if they indeed know themselves." Tom wanted to relate everything he knew but realised that he could not. An idea occurred to him. "Mr Perry, your cousin, Lady Mari, would be a good person for you to befriend on your return." He lifted his eyebrows in such a way that Perry knew where he would first head when he returned home, and that was to West Sussex, then Kent. After that, he'd take his family the one hundred and fifty miles home. Jem, at twelve, was already being adequately tutored by Buck.

Davy would sit in on his lessons and absorb everything his brother was taught. Davy patiently showed his little brother how to hold a pencil and draw. Colin, at three and a half, was beginning to scribble.

Colin looked at his brother with admiration.

Perry overheard Davy explaining to Colin what reading was. "Col, you know the ABC's and the sounds they make?"

Perry saw Colin nod vigorously. "Yes," said the small boy.

"Well, to make words, you put those sounds together, and they make words." Davy sounded out, "C, A, T, is cat. Now you try Col."

Davy pointed to a D an O and a G.

Colin sounded out each letter, then the penny dropped, "Doggie, I read dog. Like Uncle Sam's doggie 'Rip'." Colin had only met the ragged mongrel once, but he was taken with the strange but gentle beast. He looked part wolfhound, part scarecrow. He had once followed his father home after he'd been to visit. He had padded along behind the carriage, and Perry had had to take him home.

Davy was thrilled. "Yes, you have just read your first word. Now you do that with other letters, and that's called 'reading'. Reading means you no longer have to wait for other people to tell you stories, but you can read them yourself. When you get good, you can read them to others like Joanna. You know how Twinny loves stories." Davy chuckled at using Colin's pet name for his twin sister. He expected an explosion, and he wasn't disappointed.

"She's my Twinny, not yours," burst Colin.

"Okay, okay, but you know what I mean," Davy teased him.

Colin was taken to class with Jem and Davy from then on. Every day he learned new words and had realised that the pencil could be used to copy the letters. He could write his name by four and even attempted writing Joanna's name.

With the Macquaries departure now imminent, the following article appeared in the Sydney Gazette announcing the proposed plans for the retiring Governor's departure. The paper was read in the far-flung houses of the colony. Many planned to make the trip to bid farewell to their hero.

Major General Lachlan Macquarie, the retiring Governor, was adored by all but those in power. He helped the underdogs and educated as many as he could and he set a precedent for following Governors. Some achieved something close to his results, but no one anywhere near the popularity of this man.

Ned and Tom were leading the official send-off, and Ned had the honour of escorting them aboard.

GOVERNMENT AND GENERAL ORDERS.

Head Quarters, Sydney.

Thursday, the 31st of January 1821

MAJOR GENERAL MACQUARIE, late CAPTAIN GENERAL and Governor in CHIEF of this Territory, having signified His Intention of embarking for England on board the Ship Surrey, on Thursday the 7th of February, at Eleven o'clock in the Forenoon.

Colonel ERSKINE, C. B. will be pleased to parade the 48th Regiment, on occasion, for the purpose of paying the usual Honours to the late Governor, on His Departure. The 48th Regiment will march to the Government Wharf and will form a Line from thence to the Government House; the late Governor in CHIEF to be received with presented Arms, Officers saluting, Band and Drums playing "God save the King!"

A Salute of Nineteen Guns will be fired from Dawes Battery on the Major General's quitting the Shore. The Government Artificers and Labourers will be excused from work on that day, from Breakfast Time.

By Command of His Excellency

Major General Sir Thomas Brisbane, K. C. B.

JOHN OVENS, Major of Brigade.

Sadly, the weather set in, and the farewell plans were postponed. The sailing date was delayed for more than a week due to extremely inclement weather. On the 12th of February 1822, the ship *Surrey* sat at anchor in Watsons Bay. This, however, was a blessing for Lachlan, for the 31st of January was his actual birthday, and it meant he could spend it ashore with friends.

On return to Government House, Lachlan found Perry sitting in the library drinking a mug of tea. Lachlan sank into a winged armchair and relaxed. "Perry, I have had a wonderful day. I never thought a birthday at my age could be, well, fun. But I have enjoyed today. It's a nice end to our time here. I think I shall even record today for posterity." Later that night, Lachlan sat and wrote in his diary,

"Thursday 31 Jany 1822! This being the anniversary of my birthday (when I complete my Sixtieth year), my dear Mrs M. gave a Breakfast to a few select Friends at Elizabeth-Town, the Native Village where we have established the Sydney Tribe. The Revd. Mr. Cowper, Mrs. & Miss Cowper, Mr. J.T. Campbell, Major Antill, Dr. Stevenson, and Mrs. M. Lachn and myself made the party. We also treated forty-two natives to breakfast and tobacco.

The Cowper Family, Major & Mrs. Antill, Mr. Campbell, Dr. Wentworth, Dr. Stephenson, Major Ovens, Lieut. Marshal, and ourselves, made up our Dinner Party.

A large party of the Emancipated Colonists assembled at Sydney this day and gave a dinner in honour of my birthday."

Lachlan had promised never to make any record of Perry and Katy's existence in the colony, but the last sentence was intended to cover them all.

Captain Raine was happy with the cargo he had been able to acquire. Over the past weeks, vast quantities of tanned hides, whale and seal oil, sealskins, wool, and coconut oil were loaded into the convicts' quarters. That whole level of the ship would have otherwise been empty. It settled the level of the craft to a line that he considered safe. He knew of other captains who overloaded the return cargoes. Captain Raine also knew he had to balance casters in the hold, or their speed and safety would suffer. Too little in the lower decks was also a danger.

When the now-loaded ship was finally brought closer to Sydney Cove to be boarded, it anchored a short distance off Dawes Point; the ship sat and waited for its special passengers.

By soon after dawn the next morning, the throng of well-wishers was already thick. There was hardly any room on the dock for Perry and his family to move. They boarded early, hoping to miss any scrutiny from the public. Sam came and saw them on board, then left for work.

Perry wanted the festivities to focus on the Macquaries, not the other passengers. They had been rowed out to the *Surrey* early. There they were assisted with the difficult task of gracefully climbing from a moving rowboat to the deck of a sailing ship. Once on board, Perry introduced his family and staff to the captain and ship's surgeon.

The captain showed them to their cabins.

A few hours later, they stood at the railings on deck where Perry and Katy watched the official carriages leave Government House. They proceeded at walking pace towards the quay through the seething mass of humanity, and they arrived on the stroke of noon. The entire route was lined with the red-coated soldiers standing at attention in honour of their departing Governor.

The enormous crowd of people fell in behind as the carriage passed.

Behind the soldiers, who were standing shoulder to shoulder, were many tearful souls; they were emancipists and convicts who were all losing their hero. They were the ordinary people who had been given a chance at a new life; Macquarie gave them a fair hearing. They were the lowest of the low, given a chance to be someone; he returned their respect and dignity. They were his people.

Voices were heard shouting this poem in unison.

"Macquarie was the prince of men!
Australia's pride and joy!
We ne'er shall see his like again.
Bring back the old viceroy!"

Lachlan sat silently. He was both happy and sad to be leaving. He wished these ordinary persons had stood up for him vocally when John Bigge questioned many of them for his report. Lachlan had enough of the bickering and political mud throwing by his peers, not to mention the free settlers that were causing strife. Lachlan thought many of these people did not realise that he was going home to fight for his reputation. He had fought for them and now had to go and defend his decisions. The report John Bigge had filed in London had landed him in hot water, yet it was those same actions that had changed the colony for the better.

He frequently waved, as did Elizabeth and little Lachie as they drove. Lachlan's heart was heavy. He was looking forward to settling into their cabins. They saw a flotilla of assorted watercraft waiting to escort them to their ship. On arrival at the wharf, there were so many there that they realised that solace would be some time away.

Elizabeth admired the flags, bunting, and streamers adorning every possible solid surface. Their son was in awe at the colourful sight. At nearly seven, it was hard to get him to stay seated. He was almost bouncing around the carriage, wanting to see everything.

Their luxurious vehicle finally arrived at Sydney Cove foreshore. As the door opened, the cacophony of cheers that greeted them was deafening. Soon, they turned to face the applause; the crowds fell silent. Many were crying, watching their benefactor leave them. The group was now standing in sincere respect.

Once on the jetty, they were loaded onto a government barge, festooned with more decorations, and slowly moved through the flotilla of garland-strewn watercraft that was almost blocking the path of departure.

As the barge drew closer to the ship, they could hear the chant of "God save the King; God save the King," repeatedly shouted across the water. The pipes and drums were playing, and the guns at Dawes Point started booming.

The harsh discord of sounds was jarring on the ears and almost deafening.

Little Lachie had jumped at the explosion of the first cannon shot, then clung to both his parents. Eighteen more booms followed, and by the time the first few had sounded, the young boy was enjoying the noise.

Governor Brisbane, Major Tom Turner, Ned, Captain Antill, and faithful Sergeant Whalan, also from the 48th, joined them on the barge, as well as Lachlan's personal attendants.

Charlie Whalan, the sergeant's son, insisted on staying with his friend. He and young Lachie had become best friends and were sad to part.

~

Reluctantly, Ned and Tom had to return to duty, but not before Ned left the Macquaries and sought out Perry and Katy. They took their farewells in the privacy of the White's main cabin. It was cramped as they had not finished unpacking, but no other space was out of the prying eyes of anyone.

Katy took the opportunity to see the children, leaving Ned and Perry alone to discuss the future.

Ned asked Perry what he'd do on his return home, "Are you going south to Kent by any chance, Perry? Could you do me a favour or two first?"

"Sure, Ned. Do you want me to visit Gracemere and report in?" Perry had so enjoyed having someone like Ned to talk to while here.

"Yes, please, but only tell them I'm here and safe. They know I'm in New South Wales but do not know the name I'm under or exactly where I am." Ned looked almost anxious. He handed Perry a letter to his parents.

Perry knew he was, in essence, hiding. "I promise, Ned, but I shall let your father know that if absolutely needed, I will tell him where you are. Would you write to me and let me know how you are going?"

Ned nodded. He was almost unable to say his farewells; such was the lump in his throat. As Major and an upstanding one at that, he was still a twenty-two-year-old lad who was all but alone on the other side of the world. At least Charles would be with him. After a minute or so, he asked, "Perry, what about you? What will you do when you return home?"

Perry and Katy had spent months discussing this exact problem. Neither wanted to enter society. They knew they would have to go to London sometime for the children's sake eventually, but they would put that off as long as possible.

Perry took a breath and voiced his reply to Ned. "We have plans Ned, ones that will probably be unpopular, but we feel that with our backgrounds, well, it's how we can help." He drew a deep breath before saying, "We are going to help others with physical and emotional scars." He expected Ned to be surprised, but the look he saw was of joy. "God will have to open the doors, but He's good at doing that."

The smile on Ned's face told Perry that their decision was a good one. "Wonderful news, Perry; I knew you would put your wounds to good use. I have already been able to see God's hand at work here. With Katy by your side, you will be able to reach out to many people in personal isolation."

Perry nodded; yes, he was pleased that Ned liked their idea. "Ned, you said two favours; what else?"

Ned unbuttoned his red coat and drew out a second letter. "It's about Sam, can you deliver this letter for me? I don't want it getting into the wrong hands. When you meet the recipient, you will know why I'm sending it." Ned handed Perry a sealed envelope.

Perry looked at the elegant script; he read, "His Grace, Duke of Malvern." Perry's eyes flew to Ned's. "He's Sam's father, isn't he? Tom said something, but I must admit I didn't believe it was true. However, Sam looks nothing like Nigel or the Earl, but he's the image of the Duke. That's why you befriended him, isn't it?"

Ned nodded again. "Yes, the Duke knows why I'm here as I told you before, but I'm watching over Sam for him. Other than you, the Duke and my friend Jimmy Westaweller are the only ones who know the name I enlisted under. I didn't even tell Gerry or Robbie, but please let my mother know if I'm ever needed."

Perry took Ned's missives and tucked them into his Bible next to their bed. "We're going to see Lady Mari in West Sussex anyway, so it will be no trouble to go next door and see the Duke. He always seemed like a nice chap."

Ned's smile reassured Perry. "He is, Perry, and someone you can trust for sage advice should you ever need it. He was only about twenty when Sam was born. He didn't marry until Sam's mother, Anne, died." Ned sat thinking about how much to tell Perry. "You know the Duke has never even properly met Sam. He only knew about him and what he was doing through a groom, but he'd go and watch him play sport at school. That's the closest he'd allow himself to get."

Perry knew the story well. "Yes, I know; he would often be sitting near my father. It's how we got to know him. He said he was there as a sponsor of the school. He was on the school board back then." Perry sat back, thinking of their school days with Sam. Now it made sense that the Duke always placed himself near the White's. The two boys were friends, so Sam would come to the Whites picnic after the game. Sam's father, The Earl, never came. The Duke was often there with his wife and small son, Jonathan. The Duke had even become friends with his own father, Percy, ostensibly so he could be close to his son. A slow smile spread across Perry's face. "I'll enjoy this visit, Ned, and I promise I'll not say anything unless he does, but I can fill in more of Sam's story for him and Sam's time here than even you can. I have spent quite a bit of time with him over my years here."

"I know, Tom told me." Ned reluctantly took his leave. He was sad that his only link with home was leaving.

Tom left with Ned. Both stood to attention, and then the long boat carrying them departed.

Lachlan smiled as the official party were farewelled.

Sir Thomas Brisbane took a final salute, shook Lachlan's hand, and thanked him. He then disembarked while Lachlan stood watching. He was deeply moved by the fond farewell of so many onshore. All were still cheering. They had all stood for hours in the February sun for this occasion. None wished to leave.

Lachlan checked his watch, it had been two hours since their arrival at the quay, and the crowd had been there since just after dawn. The captain also noticed and suggested that they move out of sight of the quay. They could be towed to Watson's Bay until the wind changed.

Lachlan nodded his agreement.

Thank goodness Perry and Katy would be travelling with them. His nephew, Horace Macquarie, had been acting as an aide with Major Antill for most of his tenure. However, he had needed to make a trip to Van Diemen's Land in early January. Thankfully Horace had made it back from Hobart in time, arriving only two days before their proposed departure. Horace may not have made the connection if the ship had been on time. Now they could travel home together.

~

Governor Lachlan Macquarie had arrived in Sydney in the wake of the Rum Rebellion. He was the replacement Governor for Bligh, and he was anxious for reform. The same people who caused that rebellion were now responsible for seeing him leave.

Thanks to Elizabeth, Lachlan had experienced an epiphany before remarrying, rediscovering his faith after the death of his beloved first wife. He clung to that now. He knew what the temptations of the flesh were, having fallen into them himself, and tried hard to make this colony great despite its obnoxious start. The colony was certainly different from his arrival. When he arrived, the old buildings were derelict and almost collapsing. Many were merely wattle and daub shacks with rotting shingle or bark roofs. Few buildings were permanent structures. So much for it looking like Albion; he had read that had been Governor Phillip's dream.

Lachlan took on those people who caused the injustices in the area and challenged them, and although still often overruled, he cleaned up the penal colony pulling the unruly towns into order. He closed pubs and built churches. He encouraged everyone, black or white, to learn to read and write. He could not force them, but now it was their choice rather than never having the opportunity. He tried as hard as he could, and yet the carpet was still ripped from under his feet. Rather than be proud of his achievements, he was almost crushed. The negativity received from John Bigge and his report almost suffocated him. He could look back on his achievements, at least with pride, at the over two hundred and fifty of his building projects he saw completed in the years just past. Perry's discovery of Francis Greenway and Joseph Lycett was a joy. Joseph had already had a few incidents and served some extra time but had come good. His paintings would serve as a permanent record.

Elizabeth was watching his face as his emotions showed clearly to her. Soon the departing dignitaries walked away.

They turned and gave a final wave, and Lachlan and Elizabeth walked indoors to their cabin. As the door shut behind them, he drew Elizabeth into his arms. "Twelve years, my love; we have given twelve years to this place, and I still feel stabbed in the back." He didn't kiss her but just held her close. They both knew they had to reappear on deck shortly, but for a few minutes, they were alone. Neither had even looked around them. It was no use, as even if they hated the cabin, they couldn't change their accommodations, but their first glimpses showed an adequate space. They had some five months ahead of them to settle into the small suite of cabins, so it was no use complaining. After some minutes of relishing the time alone, they drew apart.

Elizabeth cupped his beloved face in her hands, "We have to reappear, you know; we have to put on our false smiles and say our final farewells." Elizabeth knew it was their duty; then, when the ship sailed, they could relax.

They had not long parted when they heard a gentle knock at the door. When Lachlan answered it, Captain Raine was standing there and welcomed them on board. He informed them that they would depart from their mooring in thirty minutes and that Major Henry Antill and Sergeant Whalan, with his two sons, James and Charlie, were still on board with Lachie.

Lachlan nodded and thanked him. They plastered their faux smiles back on their faces and went to find Perry, Katy, and Horace. Few other guests were on board travelling with Perry's staff, which was going to be a delight. Little Lachie was with his friend, Charlie Whalan. His own nanny had taken him on board as soon as they had arrived. However, the child loved the White's nanny and Janey too. He was as comfortable with them as he was with his own parents. Charlie, though, was young Lachie's best friend. Every moment they could spend together was precious. It was unlikely they would meet again, and both knew it.

Lachlan thought over the persons travelling with them; Major Taylor and his son, Lachlan's nephew, Lieut. H. Macquarie ADC; their personal servants and cousins, George, and Mary Jarvis, who were expecting a child, John and Nancy Moore; Ann James and her child; Martin Lawlor, a servant; and finally, James White, a convict with an absolute pardon and no relation to Perry; this man was the assistant cook. He was returning home to his wife and family in England. Other servants, including Major Taylor, were employed to look after the stock; William Walker, a poulterer, cared for the birds; Nathaniel Scott was his personal groom; and finally, William Buckle, a servant to Major Taylor. Then there was Perry's family and a couple of steerage passengers.

The Macquaries reappeared on deck at two o'clock as a final rousing cheer rose from the shore; the ship weighed anchor and was slowly towed down the harbour. The going was slow as the winds were against them.

Hopefully, they would be in Watson's Bay by sunset, but they were at least out of sight of the crowds. The captain informed Lachlan that they would drop anchor in Watson's Bay and await a wind change.

When they had arrived twelve years before, they had waited three days as they were becalmed inside the heads. Now the same thing occurred. They saw it as a God incident. It allowed them to settle. So, although the ship left Dawes Point, it did not yet put out to sea. Katy knew that Sarah's house overlooked this bay and wondered if she could see them. At least there, they could be away from the sight of the thousands onshore.

The first person they all wanted to meet was the doctor on board. He seemed like a nice enough person; everyone hoped they would not need his services. Captain Raine had introduced them to Doctor Ramsay.

For two days, they waited. Having time to settle into things on board in the calm of the bay was nice. Having to ride a pitching sea and unpack would have been uncomfortable. Sergeant Whalan had brought a large cut of meat on board as his farewell gift. The galley was emitting delicious smells of roasting beef; the aroma drew all to the dining rooms well before the meal. All, including the Macquaries, wished to meet the others on board. They knew they would spend much time with these people with months ahead of them, and they all settled down to the long weeks.

Captain Antill took Charlie and young Lachie onshore for a romp. Perry planned to do the same for his children, knowing it would be months before they were once again on dry land. They all arrived back for the evening meal.

With them arrived Judge Advocate Wylde had come to say his personal farewells. He stayed the night with them on board. Sergeant Whalan and his youngest son Charlie stayed for their last night too.

The next morning most were up at dawn; the winds had turned. Charlie and young Lachie took their final farewells and parted with tears. Judge Wilde left with Sergeant Whalan and Charlie as soon as breakfast was done and they were taken ashore. The anchor was up by eight, and the ship was heading towards the heads. At nine, they sat between the massive headlands for the final time.

The wind filled the sails and the ship jolted as the billowing white sheets on the masts carried them eastwards. As the ship headed out to sea, it was as though the giant headlands had closed the harbour door.

All stood at the railings and watched the remarkable bay fade into the distance. It would be the last time most of the passengers saw the view. By four o'clock, the lighthouse had faded into the distance.

Chapter 17 The Way Home

*K*aty had been locked in a hellish dungeon similar to the lower decks of this ship. She wished to take Perry to the convict deck to show him the sort of quarters that she had to experience on her trip out. At least this ship wouldn't have the stench of foul smells she had to endure. They did the tour below decks while in the still waters in Watsons Bay.

Lachlan accompanied them, wishing to see the convict situations without the smell for himself. The captain led the way to the lowest decks. Lachlan stood clutching Elizabeth's hand, and next to them, Perry stood with his arm around Katy. Katy had told them to cover one eye for a minute or so before heading below deck. When they reached the darkness, they realised why the strange request. They could see with the eye they had covered as their eyes had acclimatised to the darkness.

Elizabeth was seeing the sight for the first time; she could not believe what she saw; the cramped wooden bunks were horrific; the pallet beds were just slabs of timber. No one was able to stand to their full height except Katy. Although now filled with cargo, they could still smell the remaining odour from the last October passage.

Katy then described the stench of excrement, vomit, and unwashed bodies. She then elucidated the nocturnal visits of the sailors and soldiers and the general context of the women's treatment.

The graphic picture she painted left the two men gasping. Elizabeth held her knuckles to her mouth in horror. None had truly understood the appalling conditions the poor convicts had inflicted upon them, nor the abuse that the women endured.

Even the captain was horrified; he was not usually permitted to know the conditions of the prisoners. They came under the surgeon and soldiers' authority. He had insisted on keeping the hatches open when the weather was good. He was determined to be more caring in future.

Lachlan was pleased he'd had Katy's council as well as Janey's to assist the plight of the other convicts. Hopefully, their lives would have improved somewhat. Although the captain had stood waiting for them at the door, he heard what she said. He was amazed that this beautiful woman had been a convict. Hopefully, he would be able to find out her story over the time on board.

After they toured the below decks, Lachlan wanted to check on his livestock whilst he was there.

Perry had heard that they were taking some unusual animals back with them but was amazed at what he saw.

Elizabeth had enough of the lower decks, so returned to their cabin.

Lachlan gave a deep chuckle as he spieled off the stock on board. "There were seven kangaroos, but one died yesterday after a beating by his companion. We also have six emus, seven black swans, four Cape Barren geese, one Narang emu, two white cockatoos, two bronze-wing pigeons, four wonga-wonga pigeons and several parrots and Lowry lorikeets belonging to young Lachie. I would have brought more, but with the other livestock I have, I thought I had to draw the line somewhere." They stood looking at the various cedar cages and penned animals. Most of the gun deck had been converted into a menagerie.

Perry was amazed. He had wanted to bring his horse but gave him to Charles. He knew Bobs would have a good life with them and he had access to much better bred ones at home. He exclaimed, "Cor, Lachlan, what else did you bring?"

"Do you really want to know?" Lachlan asked, grinning.

Katy answered, "Of course, I'm now intrigued."

Lachlan started reeling off the animals that were below decks. "Well, there's my horse, Sultan, I couldn't leave him, nor our cow, Fortune, she's a great milker, and we need milk on the trip home. Our three goats and forty-two sheep for the farm will save me starting from scratch. We have pigs, twenty-one turkeys, forty-seven geese, sixty ducks and one hundred fowls. But some of these are to eat while on board."

The captain was still within earshot, and he added, "Sirs, ma'am, we also have provisions and fresh meat on the hoof for five months at sea, as well as water for the same. We have little need to stop for replenishing unless something catastrophic occurs. We also have corn, bran, and hay in plenty for all the livestock."

"Sheesh, Lachlan, are you going to start a zoo or similar?" Perry said.

Lachlan answered with a bit of a chuckle. "Some of the menagerie belongs to our lad; I did not wish to upset him more than necessary. Some are for me, and some as gifts, including to His Majesty. Perry, I have brought plants and seeds too; come and see." Lachlan turned to the captain. "Captain, please lead on; I have not seen them myself. These animals look comfortable enough. I do hope they survive."

The captain led them to a cabin at the other end of the deck from their own. The first one was an array of very large tubs, two containing Norfolk Island pine trees, two more tubs containing gigantic lilies, and many more botanic specimens and strange flowering plants that Perry had never seen before. The pine trees were not small ones. In five months, they would probably be touching the ceiling. "The rest are in the cabin next door, sir," the captain said. He left the door open and walked to the adjoining room. More small plants stood inside, but the rest of the room had a myriad of assorted labelled cartons.

Lachlan nodded a thank you. "Ahh, wonderful, captain. These are mostly seeds, Perry. This will do nicely, thank you." Thus content, they returned to the upper deck.

Buck intended to occupy all the children by continuing their lessons, the girls included, as they needed education and didn't have a governess. Janey, Lucy, and Nanny also had brought fabric to teach them all to sew.

The Macquaries and the Whites group were content to socialise little with any others on board. The nine children, plus Major Taylor's son, were all good friends and content in their small group.

At fourteen, Mia was like a mother hen with all the little girls, Lou, Jo, as well as Buck and Lucy's two-year-old daughter, Judy, trailing her every move. Buck had the boys in tow, Jem, Davy, Colin, Lachie, and his four-year-old son, Lindsay; teaching them would be interesting as there was only weeks between the two youngest boys. Mia's flashcards were beginning to wear out. Buck had kept them and replaced them as each child learned their letters using this method.

There were only three other female passengers on board, so the small group of ladies settled themselves to sewing.

At Katy's suggestion, Nanny Grimes had purchased a massive box of fabrics from the Bond Store at the docks. Nanny had included all the buttons, thread, and notions needed to make gowns, shorts, shirts and even some huckaback to teach the children some basic sewing skills. They had both blunt and sharp needles for the various tasks. Depending on the winds, they should arrive in England in July or thereabouts but that was five long months away.

A squall blew in, but the winds were favourable, hastening the passage southwards. By the end of February, they had rounded the tip of New Zealand and were battening down for a strong gale that had blown in. Sadly, another kangaroo died from injuries, as did nine sheep, but the other animals fared well.

~

Six weeks after leaving Sydney, young Lachie turned eight. They celebrated the event with fireworks and a party. There were calls of "Land ho" by just on dusk from the crows-nest. Cape Horn was within sight. Sadly because of the continuing gale, a landing was not attempted.

~

March slipped into April.

Since the death of the largest emu some two weeks before, the care of the animals became paramount. As the children grew bored and were getting restless, a trip to the animals to feed them and checking their welfare turned into a few hours.

One morning, the children were filing out of the gun deck after feeding the animals when they all heard a scream. Lachie had gone ahead to play with his parrots on deck before following his friends; sadly, the ship pitched at the wrong time, and he fell from the top of one of their cages. As the ship tilted, he slid across the deck and became jammed under one of the longboats. A trail of blood marked his path. The screaming child sounded the warning of a catastrophe.

Mia and Lucy were in attendance quickly and took him to his parents and the doctor for treatment. A few stitches, and Lachie was up walking but now bemoaning the lack of activities he was allowed to do alone.

Thankfully the rough seas soon abated, they they were becalmed, the ship sat with its sails luffing in the light breeze. The two-day lull gave Lachie time to heal. All willingly danced attendance on the injured child.

Perry and Katy were enjoying the calm seas. Their cabin was much smaller than the Macquarie's one, so they spent much of it outside.

Finally, a stiff breeze arrived and took the little ship northwards. Sadly, it didn't last long. The vessel became still again. The children played chasing on deck and enjoyed the stillness of the sea.

For five days, they sat waiting for a breath of breeze. Everything broken had been repaired, so the captain suggested some dancing to break the monotony. However, even that grew stale.

A sailor sighted a sail on the morning of the fifth day. There was now a slight breeze, but the sails were only luffing. They didn't know how long it would take to draw alongside the ship, but many took time writing letters, just in case it was heading to Sydney. By four o'clock, the brig had drawn close. Information was passed across the decks, but no letters. The vessel was Portuguese and not heading to Sydney. They suggested pulling into St. Salvador Harbour, where the ships waited for a change of wind. As the captain had told Lachlan they were running low on water, they decided a break in the trip would benefit everyone.

After a few days, a call of "Land Ho" came again from the crows-nest, and soon they were pulling into the St. Salvador Harbour. Everyone was very wobbly when they first stepped ashore. The senior cook ordered fresh fruit and vegetables, and everyone relaxed and took time to wander around the town. Lachlan took the opportunity to purchase some more animals. He added a few parrots and a marmoset monkey to the menagerie. It was a week before they were on their way.

The ship's assistant cook was a convict and was not supposed to have gone ashore. He became terribly drunk on the illicit spirits sold in town. Following this, he came down with an illness and some ten days after they left port, the doctor reported the cook's sudden and unexpected death.

~

Eleven days later, they crossed the equator; it was May 22nd. They celebrated with a Neptune party for those crossing the equator for the first time. Sadly, this was only the children on board, although Katy had been below decks on her last voyage. They nevertheless had a feast, and the adults enjoyed generous rations of rum.

They sailed northward for the next three weeks before tacking to the northeast. They were dodging the shoals and reefs that ate ships with glee. Captain Raine carefully steered around them all. Once cleared of this area, they had some clear sailing. Three weeks passed before the next event occurred. Heading further north, they crossed the Tropic of Cancer. A week later, the ship was surrounded by a pod of whales, much to the children's joy.

Katy stood under Perry's arm. She had never seen beasts this large either. For an hour, the gigantic aquatic animals stayed within sight. One inquisitive fellow that was almost the length of the small vessel decided to come up for a closer view. He surfaced and rolled, so his eye could take in the movement on deck. Then with a spurt out of his head, he submerged and came up on the other side of the ship. He rolled half onto his side to see the watercraft. This time as he blew, the spout of water caught the breeze and liberally doused all the watchers. The adults heard squeals of mixed horror and delight as the children scattered. The whale sank as quietly as it appeared.

That was the last breath of wind felt for the rest of the day, as sadly, the breeze fell quiet at the change of tide. Becalmed once again, they decided to fish. Fishing lines were produced, and the flapping of fresh fish was soon heard on deck. An occasional sail was seen from the crows-nest throughout the day, but they, too were becalmed. The sea's current was all that moved the ship, and sometimes that was backwards.

~

Mid-June, Perry noted it was four months since they left Sydney. Weeks earlier, Mary Jarvis had given birth safely, with Katy assisting in the delivery. The time had flown by, though sailing days were becoming few and far between. Often, they were becalmed on every alternate day. Although the trip was smooth, the loss of time was frustrating. Lachlan emerged one day from the animals with a dead swan in his arm. Four days later, it was one of his precious Cape Barren geese.

Days more passed, and a ship by the name of *William Miles* caught up to them. The captain telegraphed across the ships with flags to learn they were a free trader heading for London but from Calcutta. At least now the wind was light, and as the ships were of similar weight, they stayed close by for over a week. By the end of the month, the *Surrey* pulled ahead as they neared the beginning of the English Channel.

A five-knot breeze was enough to move the lighter *Surrey* a little further ahead and make for London. The light breeze picked up throughout the day and was directly behind them. All sails were hoisted, and the little ship almost flew across the smooth seas.

Ghostly distant headlands changed quickly as the passengers watched the land formations pass by. They retired to bed, knowing it would still be about a week more until they reached London. The captain had explained that winds normally dropped in the Thames River, and they would have to move upstream with the in-going tide. He called this going with the flow.

England's eastern shores appeared on the horizon. They continued past the Isle of Wight. The captain woke Lachlan at two in the morning to say they were passing the shallows and were safely by an area known as *the Lizard*. This apparently was a well-known landmark, but Lachlan nodded and wearily climbed back into bed. However, he was up again at dawn, as were more of the family group. At noon, a pilot, Henry Griggs came on board at Dover to steer them into the docks that were still a few days away. The ship sailed past Deal, Hythe, Ramsgate, Margate, then the pilot called for the anchor to be lowered at Nore. The light had failed, and they could not navigate at night in the river.

At five the following morning, the noise of weighing anchor was heard. There was a scurry to dress. The children were so excited that it was hard to contain them. The flood tide carried them up the Thames River to anchor off Lee in Kent. The queue of ships before them would mean a delay. It would be at least a week before the ship could officially dock, but that did not mean the men had to stay on board until that occurred.

Lachlan knew he had to arrange accommodation for his family yet. Perry had hoped they would stay with them, but Lachlan was impatient. He tried to wait, but the wind was such that they stayed at anchor until the tide changed.

By ten that night, they had only progressed as far as Woolwich. Again, the wind and tide beat them, so they anchored until the next day. The wind stayed as a headwind until noon the next day when the flood tide carried them up the river a few more miles.

July was approaching fast.

They anchored at Deptford for two days, where Lachlan arranged for transport to shore and decided to hunt for an apartment for his family and retinue. Perry stayed on board to watch over everyone.

Perry asked Lachlan to inform Cheatham House in Piccadilly that they would be arriving. He also said that the Macquaries would be welcome to make their home with them for as long as required. However, Lachlan refused Perry's kind offer.

On his return from London, Lachlan said he had delivered Perry's message and also that he had found lodgings at five shillings a week, and the abode was delightful. In the few days since they had arrived, the Macquaries were swept up in a swathe of appointments. Knowing how spacious Cheatham House was, Perry was somewhat disappointed. However, they said their farewells and wondered if they would meet again.

By the last Friday in June, Elizabeth was in a fluster. They were dining with His Royal Highness, the Duke of York, at the United Service Club, and she had nothing suitable to wear. Lachlan was officially welcomed back even though the ship was still to berth. He knew he had yet to meet with Lord Bathurst, and that appointment was for three days hence.

Young Lachie was still safe on board with Perry and Katy.

Sadly, Perry now had to use his title. It would soon become officially known that the Earl and Countess of Collingsford were currently in residence in London. No one knew where they had come from, and that's how they liked it. They had arrived with one day's notice and found the household was seriously understaffed, although the building was in good condition. Perry sent word through to his father and asked him if he could hire some more staff. They had decided to make London their home base for the summer. How long they would stay would depend on the outcome of finding Elizabeth Fry.

~

On the morning of the last day of June, Perry and Katy welcomed their morning visitors at the commodious palace-like building in London that they now called home. The ship had berthed the day before, and the children and staff finally were unloaded. Elizabeth and Lachie stayed with them for the day while Lachlan presented his report to Lord Bathurst. Elizabeth was in awe when she saw the amazing edifice of the spacious house in London. The building was brick, but its front seemed to be many, many windows; all were glazed in small squares, set in white frames. There were two rows of chimneys with smaller windows peeking over the roofline on the top. "Oh, Lachlan, now I understand Jem's comment about the small size of Government House in Sydney."

Lachlan replied, "Elspeth, my dear, remember that this is only the London house; I dare say the Cheatham Seat in Warwickshire will be vast. It's referred to as a palace, you know. I was asking a friend about it. Perry's father also mentioned its vast size when I met him. Perry said the land alone is over one thousand acres. It is apparently a Jacobean Palace that rivals Hatfield House in Hertfordshire. Jem wasn't wrong; he said something about over one hundred and fifty rooms and a crenellated old section." Lachlan was now ready to get out. "He meant bedrooms, you know. Goodness knows how many actual rooms a place like that would have," he said as he handed Elizabeth out of the carriage. He then leaned in and lifted Lachie down. "Davy awaits you, son, off you go."

Lachie was out and inside as Davy bounced on the spot in

anticipation of his best friend's arrival. The two lads were gone before the Macquaries reached the top of the stairs.

Lachlan was not looking forward to the meeting with Lord Bathurst. When he met Perry, he asked if Buck could join them and pray before the meeting. Elizabeth and Katy came too. Katy slipped her hand into Perry's and gave it a loving squeeze. Lachlan left soon afterwards for his meeting. The colossal size of the house astounded Lachie. Until now, he had always lived in a bigger house than his friend. Lachie's nose was a little out of joint.

On Lachlan's return, he was not forthcoming about how the meeting went. Perry saw that his lips were grey and he was worried about him. Before he collected Elizabeth and Lachie and returned to their lodgings, he mentioned to Perry that he had another meeting tomorrow with the Marquess of Londonderry.

"Londonderry? Do I know him?" Perry asked.

"You may know him as Lord Castlereagh or even Robert Stewart. I am not looking forward to that. Perry, I must front up tomorrow to him. Lord Bathurst said he's not been well. Pray for me, will you?" With that one short conversation, Lachlan departed.

Perry and Katy made no plans except to stay in London and support Lachlan and Elizabeth where they could. While they waited, they set about finding Elizabeth Fry. Katy wondered if she had continued to work with the convict women. She knew where she lived, and the day of Lachlan's meeting with the Marquess of Londonderry, they went calling.

On arrival at Betsy's house, they were welcomed by her brother, Joseph, who was just leaving. Betsy was not officially receiving them; however, she welcomed them warmly. The reason for her withdrawal was apparent. Betsy was obviously expecting a child. Katy knew she had other children but was surprised to find her in such an advanced condition as she knew her to be forty-two as she was three years older than herself. When Betsy saw who it was, she was up and in her arms as fast as she could move. "Katy, oh Katy, you're home." Perry stood watching both weeping ladies with a silly grin on his face.

While still hugging Katy, Betsy said to Perry, "So you found her all right?"

Perry nodded. "Thanks to you, Mrs Fry, and a lot of prayers. Once in Sydney, I went to see the Governor, who called in the ledgers. I found what name she was using as she'd changed it again, then it was just a matter of getting to her."

Finally, Betsy released her friend. "I'm so pleased, Perry. And Katy, you are a naughty girl; I told you that you should have trusted him." She looked at her friend. "Well, my dear, now you are back; what are your plans?" She rubbed her stomach. "This certainly was not one of my plans. It's number eleven, you know."

"Eleven, oh, Betsy, however, do you cope?" Katy asked as they seated themselves.

Betsy's eyes twinkled with mischief. "Kitty helps, and so do the others, but I suppose you can say that being, um, in the family way again has been good in one way. For me being out of action has meant that others have stepped up to assist." Betsy smiled, half-embarrassed. "I have been busy with politics, Katy and have the ear of some who know my work. We are working towards a Bill we are calling the Gaols Act. It should be ready by mid-next year."

"Oh, who, Betsy?" Katy asked, wondering if she knew any of them. She doubted she would.

"Probably none you would know unless you have met my friend Ann Dumaresq; she and a few others have been wonderful. Her daughter Eliza worked with us until her marriage; she's now in Mauritius with her husband. He's acting Governor and a General, you know," Betsy smiled as she spoke. "Lord Castlereagh and others have also added their tuppence-worth to the Bill too. He spoke very well at the Congress of Vienna, and so I asked him for his opinion on the reform."

Perry was astounded that the very person whom Lachlan was meeting with should be mentioned by Betsy.

Katy frowned as though she was trying to remember something. "I remember meeting Lieutenant Colonel John Dumaresq and his wife at my come-out ball in 1804. I remember they were supposed to have a few children, but I don't remember meeting any of them. They must have been small."

"That's them; Eliza was the fourth of six children. John died when she was about six, and it was about then that Ann came to help me with our work. She may have even been one of the women who came with me when I visited you in 1814. Eliza was normally in our wake by then, so she may have come too." Betsy rubbed her stomach again. "Eliza and Ralph had a little boy last year named Frederick. Ann is full of their news," Betsy chuckled.

Over the next half hour, Perry sat listening to the work Betsy was now doing. All the while, his mind was working overtime. If Betsy and her female philanthropy friends could assist the convict women, what was stopping him from helping those people too? The burned, the scarred, the incapacitated, indeed, these people had some skills to do some work. Once they saw his face, he knew that they would see compassion, not charity. He knew how it felt when people stared at him or cringed when they looked at his melted face. There was a lull in the conversation between the two women. Perry voiced a question that he could no longer contain. "Mrs Fry, may I ask if you come across disfigured persons often? Ones whom society shuns?"

"Call me Elizabeth or even Betsy would be better, please, Perry, as there are way too many Elizabeths around. Perry, as to the injured folks, I have no means of helping them. Do you have an idea?"

Perry swallowed, "I do actually, Betsy, we both do." His eyes sparkled as he spoke, but he was also anxious. He said while looking at Katy. "We need staff, and I know that many won't like working for a man with half a face. If we employed staff with similar injuries, I'm sure, well, I suppose they would accept that sort of assistance."

Betsy sat with her jaw dropped, stunned at what she heard. Unbeknownst to them, she'd been praying for some door to open to a few men she had met that were able-bodied but horrendously scarred and hideously burnt. She had no more places to fill in her friend's houses. At least none who would employ them. This was a true answer to prayer. "You would do that, truly?"

Perry nodded. "We need staff, lots of them. Father wrote back and said we are to employ whomever we wished. The only ones we don't need are the housekeeper, butler, gardener, and cook. There is only a skeleton staff as my father never comes to town. We could use, say, thirty inside and more outside staff whom we can train and then replace with more. Could you find that many?"

Betsy was so excited. "Perry, I could find ten times that many with the click of my fingers. Just send me the list of the jobs you need."

Chapter 18 Scarred and Weary

On returning home from Betsy Fry's house, Perry and Katy set into action plans for new staff to be employed. Perry interviewed his butler and housekeeper and asked what jobs needed filling.

With a glance between each other, they embarked on listing some of the many roles they wished could be filled. Housemaids, under housemaids, laundry maids, scullery maids, houseboy or boys, coachmen, carriage footmen, grooms and even a stable boy or two. Each alternated with functions needed from a selection of footmen and ladies' maids for Katy and the children. Valets for Perry and the boys, housemaids, and an under-tutor to assist Buck, a junior governess to assist Janey, who had been promoted to full-time governess as this lifted her status to eat with the family at most meals. When required, Lucy's position was elevated to Katy's personal dresser and companion-cum-Janey's assistant. The rest of the household had discovered the family connection. As Buck's wife, she also joined the family for meals. Perry kept suggesting more and more roles. By the time the list was sent to Betsy Fry, it was quite extensive.

Within two days, Perry and Katy were busy interviewing a line of people with much more horrific scars than Perry. They employed each one they interviewed, knowing they would never get another offer from anyone. Knowing that money was not a problem, they took on some thirty groundsmen and stable hands, five of whom they kept in London and the rest they sent to straight to Cheatham Castle. They had three inside men to assist the butler, but the men were not trained footmen yet. Some boys expressed an interest in kitchen work as kitchen hands. All were single-leg amputees and could not walk far but still had full use of their upper bodies. Perry set some other scarred ones to do maintenance; still, there were more that Betsy Fry had yet to send. He wrote to his father and asked if they needed more groundsmen. When he explained the situation, Percy replied, "Send them all." And so, the Duke of Cheatham gained new staff. Some were in training, and those who weren't skilled would now be taught. The idea was that they could be placed in other houses once trained. Word of mouth amongst the Duke's friends, full qualifications and a fabulous reference would open doors otherwise closed to them.

Three days after Lachlan's meeting with the Marquess of Londonderry, he visited Perry. Katy took Elizabeth to the sitting room, and the men retired to Perry's study. Lachlan paced the room, obviously at odds with his feelings. "Perry, have you ever met someone where things just aren't, um, well, right?"

Perry didn't quite know how to answer, so just asked him to elaborate, "How so, Lachlan?"

"Here I was, so fearful at meeting this man, but it seems we agree on so much. However, he seems to have got the backs up of many. I admit he seemed somewhat concerned that we were being scrutinised and kept checking the door. He told me he was being watched and was so anxious about nearly everything and every noise." Lachlan, who had been looking out the window, turned and said to Perry, "He's, well, to put it bluntly, somewhat disturbed. He was unable to think straight and was easily distracted. You are the only one I can ever say that to." Lachlan looked positively worried, but he continued. "He's to plead my case, but I'm not sure if he's going to help or hinder, Perry. Is it treason to speak so against a Marquess?"

Perry was still unable to say much but commiserated with his friend. He'd not met the man but knew that Lachlan would not have made it up. He told Lachlan about their visit to Betsy Fry's house and how she fitted into Katy's story. As he spoke, he tugged at the bell pull, and a footman came in. "Lachlan, would you like tea or something stronger?" Knowing Lachlan never drank when at their place, he was just being polite with the offer.

"Just tea, please, Perry," Lachlan answered distractedly. He turned when the door opened. His eyes widened on the entry of the footman.

"Tea tray, please Cyril." Perry said politely, then asked, "How are you settling in?"

"Wonderfully well, thank you, Your Lordship," Cyril replied.

"Sir will do fine, Cyril," Perry chuckled.

As the door closed Lachlan spoke softly. "Seems we all have new roles to get used to, eh?" Lachlan didn't say anything about the man's injuries.

"He's new. We hired over fifty injured and scarred staff yesterday. Oh, Lachlan, if I thought my wounds were bad, you should see some of these poor souls. We couldn't turn any away. For some reason, I expected them to be all men. However, some of the poor girls who have had live coals thrown in their faces or clothes have caught alight. We both found it hard not to weep at their misfortunes. One glance at my face, and they knew they had found a sanctuary." Perry thought back to the raw emotions that many of them showed. He could empathise with them. "We hired all of them, Lachlan, and Betsy Fry said she had more. We sent twenty-five to Father, and there are other estates he owns, and more will filter through to them once they are trained."

His friend lay back and folded his arms. "So, your work here has started." It wasn't a question, more of an explanation to himself. Lachlan now wondered what to do. They chatted for some time before the tea tray came in. They fell silent until the door closed behind Cyril and the departing maid. She also had burn marks on her otherwise pretty face.

"It seems so, Lachlan." Perry would love the company, and it was the least he could do as they had often stayed with them in Australia. "Can I not persuade you to come and stay at least until you return to Scotland? Elizabeth mentioned to Katy that you wish to leave soon."

Lachlan stood with a frown on his face, intently looking into Perry's. Eventually, he replied, "We may, Perry, we just may." He sounded distracted. "I find that the rented rooms are not as commodious as Government House. And add that to the fact that Lachie misses Davy, and my lady love, Elspeth, misses your good lady. I must say I didn't think you would have room at first, so if I may accept that would be wonderful. Hector and the Jarvis's have already gone home, as have some of the other staff and family, but may we also bring the rest of the retinue?"

Perry chuckled. "Um, Lachlan, we have ample room for the entire Parliament if you so wish. Bring them all. We have so many new staff you can get your retinue to assist in their training." He gave a sigh of relief. "Now, when are you planning to flee the city? Not too soon, I hope?"

The tension left Lachlan's shoulders; now he could relax. "The season finishes mid-August as usual, so we'll stay until then or soon after, so that's about six weeks away. Are you sure, Perry?"

In the middle of July, Betsy Fry introduced Perry and Katy to some of her philanthropic friends as well as to her brother Joseph, whom they had briefly met. Sarah Trimmer, Hannah More, and Ann Dumaresq were invited for morning tea at Betsy's house. They had all to yet meet Betsy's husband. He was a banker and worked long hours. Katy and Ann hit it off straight away. Ann was twelve years older than Katy but much of an age with Perry. Betsy had filled Ann in years ago about Katy and her story of what she thought was unrequited love. Katy's situation inspired Betsy to encourage her friends to become involved. Ann could not wait to meet her and subtly took her aside and told her that she knew her background. Katy was delighted. One of the things she feared was that her background was known and she would be shunned.

Ann's advice to her was, "Ignore them, my dear. One day you will be a Duchess, and they will come crawling to you and lick up the crumbs you cast them. Stand proud and instigate a haughty look. My friend Susanna Lockley does this. She, too, is a Duchess. She has 'the look' down pat." Ann saw Katy start at the name. "Do you know her, Katy?"

Katy shook her head and looked around before she answered. "No, I don't, but I know her son, Edward. Perry knows them all well. He stayed with them when looking for me."

"Ahh, well, then Perry will know what I mean. She is aptly known as the Duchess of Gracemere. Behind her back, she is called Duchess Grace, but don't dare tell her, will you? I quake when I meet His Grace. Duke Charles is the epitome of the aristocratic Duke. He's some twenty years older than his wife, but he is putty in her very capable Scottish hands. Oh, Katy, as a couple, they are, well, awe-inspiring. They have a true and active faith that they put into action, and they don't tell anyone what they do. I haven't met the boys, but she often talks of one called Neddie. I'm guessing that's your Edward, as she said he was in the antipodes somewhere."

Katy nodded, knowing that she'd promised Ned they would not let on where he was nor what name he was under. Now she knew why he'd taken the name of Grace. She smiled to herself.

Ann and Katy returned to the conversation, and Betsy outlined the plans for the Gaol Reform. Perry had been talking to Betsy's brother, Joseph Gurney.

Ann waited until all her friends were sitting and listening. She sat still and remained with her hand sitting cupped in her lap. Eventually, everyone realised she wanted to say something. "I have some news for you all. The Home Secretary, Sir Robert Peel, has decided to back our Bill, and we now have a date." She took a deep breath, "On July 10th next year, it will be presented. Joseph and I met with him, and he's keen to do what he can to get this passed."

Joseph had told Perry about the gaol situation. He'd caught glimpses of some of the regional gaols, but when Joseph told him about Newgate prison, Perry gasped. "They keep the men and women together? Seriously? What about the women getting abused?" Perry saw Joseph nod. "Are you kidding?"

"Sadly, I'm not Perry," Joseph said.

"Why, that's appalling!" Perry gasped.

"It's worse than that; there are male warders who are free with their lusts. The women have no say, Perry. It's why we must do something. I think of Katy every time I talk to someone about this. Thank goodness she was held on the hulks instead of the gaol. It's the lesser of the two evils, believe me. At least there she was safe. I paid the guards to leave her alone."

The stunned look on Perry's face showed Joseph that he had no idea. "You did that for her? For me too? How can I ever thank you?" Perry asked.

"Easily Perry, by throwing your weight and title behind this Bill." Joseph continued explaining the meaning of what this Bill entailed. "Perry, this Bill is not just the segregation of genders, but there are other conditions. Regular visits by clergy and payment of gaolers' salaries rather than by the prisoners themselves. We have also added the introduction of female warders for the women prisoners and the prohibition of irons and manacles. It will also lift the death penalty from one hundred and thirty crimes. All I can say is that's a start. It's nowhere near enough, but we had to start somewhere. Stopping the molestations was our number one thing."

"Were there that many?" Perry had blanched. Katy had been in there. He'd prayed for her each night, but he'd not discovered her whereabouts. If it had not been for Betsy's letter, he might never have found her.

Joseph nodded. "Hence Katy was our inspiration to do something."

"How did you get into this, Joseph? What was the starting point, Katy said you were involved with Justin, Mary's cousin, but how?" Perry wanted details. Any information he could glean would help.

Joseph sat back in his chair and explained. "Our parents were members of the Society of Friends; they were wealthy and into wool. There were also family banks and other money connections. Mother died in childbirth when Betsy was twelve, and as one of the oldest girls in the family, she helped raise us. That went on for some six years, not that she stopped then, but with our father's permission, she became involved in charity work. She started by cooking more food and feeding some poor local folk. Then she decided to help educate people. She even set up a Sunday School in our house after church. She met her husband, another Joseph by the way, just before 1800, and they married the next year." He paused and looked at Perry to see if he was interested.

Perry nodded and said, "Go on, then what?"

Joseph continued, "Well, just before Katy was arrested, Betsy was told of a mutual friend, Stephen Grellet, who had visited Newgate Prison and he was so appalled that he told Betsy all about it. She decided to see for herself and visited. I should not have let her go, but I'm glad she did in the long run. Perry, I went soon afterwards. On that visit, she found over three hundred women and children in two wards and two cell blocks. The poor women had no option but to sleep on the floor. They had to wash, cook, sleep, and, well, you can imagine the rest. But facilities were virtually non-existent. As you can imagine, Betsy could not leave well alone, and she returned with clothes and food. She asked around, and soon, a small group of ten others started stirring up interest. They built a school, and change began." Joseph kept talking. "By 1817, the improvements were making a difference. It was too late for Katy, but you can see where she fitted in. When Betsy saw Katy in Newgate, it was her first visit there."

This stunned Perry; Katy had done much the same thing in Parramatta. He looked up and met Joseph's eyes. "Joseph, we will do everything we can, absolutely everything. We have been doing similar in Parramatta, very similar actually. We found conditions there were nearly as bad as here. Only even more cramped with even fewer facilities."

Joseph's grin spoke volumes, "So far, our work is very localised. It doesn't cover more than just Newgate. We need to reach further, much further."

Perry gave a lop-sided grin, "As I said, we're in. Betsy has already sent us a bevy of new staff. Father has taken most of them in. I have made only one stipulation, other than a disfigurement, that they all must conform to house rules. If they are not prepared to do that, they can look elsewhere for help. House rules are no alcohol, respect, especially the women, and be prepared to learn to read and write. Father started a school years ago, and all our staff are educated to some degree. So far, all are willing."

"Excellent, excellent!" Joseph got up and walked around the room. "Perry, in 1819, Betsy and I did a tour of gaols; I even printed the findings in a booklet called, 'Prisons in Scotland and the north of England'. Some like Durham's old gaol, are not too bad, but it was the exception rather than the rule. The prisoners are allowed 4s 6d per week and have to supply their needs from that, but they are bored silly. They and every other prisoner need an occupation. Glasgow gaol was the best of the lot and it even had cells they called dandy cells where the occupant could weave in the privacy of their own room."

By the time the group departed, the group had expanded by two. Perry was in an excellent financial position, and having a title would add to the power of the punch his support would give. Even his horrific injuries could be a blessing for the project. It was this Katy and Perry sat discussing on their carriage ride home. "Perry, can you see God's hand on this? He's even using your scars. Neither of us saw that did we?"

Perry sat stroking her hand. He had gotten somewhat used to being stared at but didn't like the prospect of having to speak in public. He had been very good at debating, but that had been decades ago. "I'll do it, Katy, but I'll not like being gazed upon. However, if that can assist in easing the condition, then it's worth a try."

Katy leaned into his shoulder. "Thank you, Perry. It's funny how things have worked out, you know. Because of me, she didn't just do a few visits, and because of her, I wanted to do the same in Parramatta."

Both fell silent, thinking of the conditions suffered in the prisons. Katy had been in a few, one in Kent, then Newgate, the hulks on the Thames River, *The Wanstead* and finally the Female gaol in Parramatta. She knew of the horrors of which they discussed. Sometimes if she closed her eyes, she could feel she was back there again. She jumped as the carriage hit a bump.

Perry noticed, and he felt her hand tighten on his. "Are you sure you wish to be involved, Katy? We can pull out." Perry put a protective arm around her shoulders and drew her close.

"I'm sure, Perry, I am in a unique position to supply accurate information. I don't have to be front and centre, not like you, Betsy, or even

Joseph, but I need to do this. I can think of a few times in the Bible that tell us to do just this. So yes, we will do this, Perry. I think of when Jesus told us to do exactly this. *'I was naked, and ye clothed me: I was sick, and ye visited me: I was in prison, and ye came unto me.'* In Matthew 25 verse 36. But there are others too. Matthew 10 verse 42 is another. *'And whosoever shall give to drink unto one of these little ones a cup of cold water only in the name of a disciple, verily I say unto you; he shall in no wise lose his reward'.* Perry, we are in a very unique situation."

He was unable to answer fully as they pulled up at the entry of their house. He squeezed her hand quickly and said, "I concur."

The ambiguity of his comment meant nothing to the footman or any others listening. But for Katy, it spoke volumes.

The next day the Macquarie's entourage arrived with all the luggage at nine in the morning. The children welcomed their long-lost friend with glee; Lachie was settled into the room next door to Davy. The room was more extensive than his parent's suite in the apartment they had just left. Lachie walked in and froze. There was a man in the room with only one leg. He was leaning on a walking stick and had obviously just done the last of the room preparation.

"I'm sorry, Master Davy, I was just leaving." Andrew Wilson was one of the new staff.

"It's fine, Andrew; thanks for fixing up Master Lachie's room for him. I'm sure it's perfect now." Davy stood aside so Andrew could leave.

Lachie stood in silence, watching the strange occurrences. When the door was closed, Lachie said, "Did you see his face? The scars are a bit like your papa's, Davy, but what happened to his leg?"

Davy hopped up onto his bed. "It was something called the Battle of Waterloo. Andrew told me it was seven years ago. He got injured in the war, Lachie, and you will see plenty of others here like him and some of the new maids. Not that they fought in a war, but they are injured. Try not to stare."

Davy was only four months older than Lachie, but his world experiences had vastly differed from the younger boy who had always lived in the lap of luxury.

Lachie lay back on the colossal feather bed. "I want to stay here forever, Davy. I like London, not that I've seen much, but there is so much going on all the time. It's fun."

The two boys lay daydreaming on the huge bed and talking about what they had left behind. Both decided that London would be fun to come back to when grown up.

Lachie sounded sad as he said, "Papa says we are going to live in Scotland. We're going home there in August. Davy, I don't want to leave. Mama said it's cold and often windy and covered in snow. I don't like cold. I like it hot like it was in Parramatta." Lachie told Davy more about Scotland. Davy didn't like the sound of it either.

After some time, Davy said, "Nuff of this, Lachie, come with me."

He hopped off the bed and held open the door. "You have to come up to the toy room!"

It had needed a spring clean on his last visit. It was only now they had the staff to clean the enormous attic room and all the toys it contained so the children could finally use it.

The two boys spent the rest of the day in absolute bliss with every toy they could dream about. Even with Mia, Jem, Lou, Col, Jo, Lindsay and Judy, there was so much room that none competed for the same toy. The boys played with the soldiers and the war board. The girls were occupied with various dolls and a tremendous dolls house; Jo was sitting on a rocking horse with a maid pushing her. The only sound was laughter.

Chapter 19 Season's End

*L*achlan was sitting in the library with a newspaper open on his lap. "Perry, did you see that the poet Percy Shelley died last week?"

Perry nodded, and they chatted about some of the poems he'd written.

Lachlan fell back to reading. "Oh, listen to this, Perry. This Rosetta Stone that was found some time ago is supposed to be the key to understanding the Egyptian hieroglyphs. This story is mostly about the Englishman, Thomas Young, who says he's deciphered a few pictures in an oval. He's calling them a cartouche. There's a Frenchman called Jean-François Champollion, who's also claiming he's close." Without waiting for a comment, Lachlan fell back to reading. When he had finished the article, he offered the paper to Perry.

Perry had read the paper that morning. "I read it this morning thanks, Lachlan. I like all the history of Egypt; I didn't know you did too. I found more about it in our library this morning."

Without looking up Lachlan said, "I hope Young beats the Frenchman to the discovery though. Let me know if you hear any more of this." Lachlan folded his newspaper and set it aside.

Having listened to his small talk for the last half hour, Perry knew he wanted to say more. "Lachlan, what's bothering you?"

Lachlan swallowed. "I have to take the family home soon, Perry. I need to get them settled before I come back to London. The animals are already at home and Lachie is anxious about them. It's about that I need to talk to you. I must wait until I hear when 'the powers that be' want me back for questioning about John Bigge's report. Lord Castlereagh has said he wants to see me again, but not when."

Perry knew all that and wondered if that was bothering him, "Lachlan, be assured you know that your room here is always available, even if we are not here. We need to keep the staff busy."

Lachlan smiled, thinking back to their first meeting in Sydney. "Thanks, Perry, that will solve a big problem, but by the time they write to me at home, then I come back, it could take months. So, I could arrive without much notice." Lachlan had been worried about where he would stay as his finances were not as viable as he thought until he got home and sorted things out. On the Isle of Mull, things were far less expensive compared to London. With a deep sigh of relief, Lachlan replied, "I accept your kind offer unconditionally."

Thus sorted, Lachlan made plans for the return home to Scotland.

Lachie didn't want to go. He now realised that their Scottish home was in the middle of nowhere in the wild islands of Scotland and he'd not get to see his friends again for a long time; even his animals did not entice him.

After much investigation, Lachlan booked their passage on a ship to take his family home. This mode of transport was by far the quickest and most convenient. The last part of the journey would have to be by sea to Mull anyway, so it was better to go all the way.

Lachie begged his father to for him to stay. "Papa, can I stay with Davy, and you go home with Mama? You said you will be returning; I'll go back then."

Lachlan looked at his son. He hated tearing him away from his friends again, but he needed to see them settled at Gruline on the family farm. "No, son, but I'll think about allowing you to return with me later."

Lachie knew that was the final decision, and it was no use pestering his father any further. He said his farewells to his friends.

~

The final weeks of the Season meant some official engagements for both families. Perry and Katy had not entered society in the usual way, but as Earl of Collingsford, he had certain obligations to fulfil in the House of Lords. He also knew that the sooner he got the initial viewings of his face over and done with, the sooner he could hide again. He had promised Betsy that he would support the Gaol Reform Bill and needed to see Sir Robert Peel about it.

Perry also needed to fill Sir Robert in on what Bill Miller was doing in Parramatta. Bill had asked Perry to fill Sir Robert in on what he and Molly were up to. Sadly they were unable to stay to find out if their first child was a boy or a girl. However, he could report they were happily married, and, when they departed they were expecting their first child.

Sir Robert had occasional letters from Bill but was pleased to hear things were well settled.

Lachlan was supportive of the new Bill and had made suggestions for some tweaks to the reform, so they invited Sir Robert to their house. This venue meant that both Katy, Lachlan, and Elizabeth could sit in.

Betsy Fry was supposed to be housebound by her condition, but she decided to attend the White's townhouse as she was only seven months along. The other invited person was Ann Dumaresq, who arrived with Betsy.

The first week of August, the seven sat discussing how they could use Perry and Katy to further the Bill. Sir Robert had already met with Betsy and Ann, but now they had Perry on their side. He was still drafting the Bill's final wording and decided to read them what he had written and see if this was what they wanted.

They spent the morning discussing some of the finer points, and Sir Robert added notes to his speech. Ensuring that Perry was in London for the vote was vital. Perry had already planned for them to return from Cheatham Castle for the Season the following year to continue the work Betsy had asked of them.

Sir Robert was happy with the notes and changes and asked if they could meet again next week before Perry and Lachlan departed. They arranged to meet again on August 12th at nine o'clock. It was to be held again at Perry's house as it was central for them all. Sir Robert wanted Lachlan there as he was familiar with the legal terminology required for official submission. When they parted, all but Betsy were making preparation for their departures from London at the end of the season.

Perry had to plan for the new Cheatham household. Many of the new staff would be directed to Cheatham Castle.

~

Lachlan had decided to delay his departure for another week and found a berth on a ship heading north the last week of August. They would have been in London for a little over seven weeks by the time they were to depart. He hoped the house in Scotland was in good order, but they needed to return before the snow arrived.

After the meeting, Katy was also making plans. There was one person she needed to see before they went north to Warwickshire. She wished to visit Mary. She needed to apologise in person, and she wanted to hug her as she said sorry.

Perry also wanted to take Katy south and introduce her to the Duke and Duchess of Gracemere, Ned's parents, and pass along his messages and letter. Then he wished to see The Duke of Malvern in West Sussex and he had arranged to stay with his cousin, Lady Mari Broome-Hall while there. Major Tom had intrigued him with his suggestion about the possibility of a round-about link with Sam and Annie. It would be an interesting visit. It was years since he'd seen either of these people and with some back knowledge, this meeting would be interesting.

All these visits would take some weeks, and then they would head northward for the winter.

Mia and Jem were looking forward to seeing the Castle again. Lou was too young to remember it, and the youngest children had never been there. It would become their home. Perry would one day have to take over the running of the estate and inherit the title, so he needed to learn how to do that.

However, the meeting on the 12th in London did not go as planned.

Betsy and Ann arrived on time and sat in the sitting room waiting with Lachlan, Elizabeth, Perry, and Katy but there was no sign of Sir Robert. The six sat discussing their ideas for over an hour.

Perry was wondering if he should send a footman with a note when a carriage finally pulled up at their house.

Sir Robert's carriage stopped to let him alight. Instead of the usual energetic arrival, Sir Robert nearly dragged himself inside. He entered with apologies for his tardiness but said no more, for as he arrived, so did the footman with the tea tray.

Ignoring everyone, Sir Robert walked to the French windows and stood looking out. When the door had closed behind the footman, he turned and spoke to the six listeners.

Perry noticed a greyness around his lips and his furrowed brow as he turned. When he spoke to the group, Sir Robert did not look well. "I must apologise, but I have just come from Lord Castlereagh's rooms. I regret to inform you all that he took his life this morning. There have been concerns about his health for some months. His valet has been removing all means of harm for some time, but sadly he overlooked a tiny knife."

All listening gasped.

Sir Robert quickly sank into a nearby armchair as though deflated.

Lachlan and Elizabeth both looked at Perry. The three had previously had a long conversation wondering if Lord Castlereagh was in his right mind.

After clearing his throat, Lachlan said, "I met him a few weeks ago, Sir Robert. I wondered back then if he was well." His careful wording was the politest way of saying that he wondered about his sanity, but he left that unsaid.

Sir Robert, however, was more forthcoming about his mental health. He released a long breath and then said, "There is a strong case for him being declared not of sound mind and therefore being allowed a Christian funeral. He's been showing signs of, um, well, being slightly unhinged for some time. Even the King said something to him not so long ago."

With the events of the morning, their meeting was very brief. All were reeling with the sad news and wondered what would occur now with Lachlan's case. They each knew they must write letters of condolence to Lady Castlereagh.

Perry was later informed that Sir Robert had been correct.

With the diagnosis of illness, Lord Castlereagh had been buried with all the church blessings due to his mental health; this was a great relief to many.

Lachlan's future, however, had been thrown into chaos. He had learned that his case had been deferred for two years. However, on receipt of this news, relief showed on Lachlan's face. He took Perry aside soon afterwards and said, "After we have been home and unpacked, I might take the family away for the winter, Perry. I'll see how things stand at home before making plans. Elspeth said she was not looking forward to a cold winter, so I'll take her away. I don't know how she will cope in the future. Mull is not the warmest place on earth, but it's home for us both. Young Lachlan has never even seen what will become his primary dwelling place and inheritance. A major concern for me is that there are few friends for him there."

They departed with promises to keep in contact. Lachlan packed up his family and left for Scotland.

Perry, Katy, and their entourage planned their trip south to Mary's place in Kent.

Justin had come to London and visited Betsy Fry. While there, he discovered his good friend's return.

Perry asked him to deliver a note to Mary, questioning if they could come and visit. Since their return nearly three months ago, they had not sent word to her of their return. Perry knew they should have done so, but Katy wanted to delay the stay as long as they could. She was still embarrassed by her lack of trust in them both.

That night as they lay cocooned in bed, Katy said, "Perry, when Justin arrived today, everything came flooding back. All the uncertainty and guilt. I know I was wrong, but my brain seems stuck in the past." She couldn't face him to say the words. She was pleased that he could not see her expression. "I love Mary, but…." She still could not voice her words.

Perry gently rolled her onto her back. "Sweetheart, I wondered if this would happen." He leaned down and softly kissed her sweet lips. "My darling love, I want you to feel my cheek."

Katy reached up and stroked the puckered skin. Her continued treatment over the years had meant the scarring was no longer red and weeping. It was even soft to her touch. She met the smiling honey-gold eyes gazing down at her.

He continued, "Do you really think I would have travelled halfway across the world chasing you if I didn't care? Even when we were at Mary's house and everything was well and settled between us all, did I brave the world, the snickering, and the nasty comments? No, my darling, I still hid. You are my world. If no one else existed but you, I would still be content. When I said so long ago that you took my heart with you, I meant it." With those few words, he bent and gently nuzzled his lips over hers again.

Rather than deepen his kiss, she pulled away, then buried her head into his shoulder and murmured, "I'm so sorry, Perry. I should have trusted you both. I should have stayed and fought for you; I should have believed. I'm so scared that I now must face her. She was my best friend, and I'm not sure she will forgive me."

Perry's fingers lovingly caressed her cheek. As he gently moved a lock of hair from her eyes, he said, "She will, my sweet, just as I did. And I mean 'did' and not 'have.' Past tense, as in not current. It is not only forgiven, but forgotten too, until you keep bringing it up again. Look at the wonderful new friends we have. And because of everything that happened, we now have a purpose in life. Betsy Fry may not have done a second visit to any gaol, but for you, and the women in Australia had a champion in you. Molly Miller certainly benefited; Janey would have been tied to a life of horror over there, as would the Livingstone girls, not to mention their family; and now, even though Janey will still have to serve her term, she is with us and happy. Buck found Lucy, and Nanny found Ned. Who would ever have believed that she was the Nanny at Gracemere? Father must have known, yet he never said anything to me. Oh, Katy, I can see God's hand in every step of the way. Can't you?" He was still caressing her cheek lovingly. "And, sweetheart, then there is our friendship with Lachlan and Elizabeth. Through that alone, many have lives changed."

Her big blue eyes met his, both now hooded with passion. "Yes," she replied meekly. As she still had her hand on his cheek, she slid it into his thick, rich locks and pulled his head down to hers.

Perry set about correcting her melancholy attitude.

She willingly let him, returning his affections wholeheartedly. This conversation was not the first time that issue had come up in past years. However, Perry hoped this would be the last.

~

Mary had sent a short welcoming note, expecting them to stay with her. She mentioned that she had a surprise for them. Katy had never contacted Mary in all the years they had been away. Perry's father had informed Mary that Katy was found, and then there was silence.

When Justin had arrived back from London with news of their wish to visit, Mary was delighted. Mary could have written a long letter, but she wasn't sure it would be well received.

Consequently, both women were on tenterhooks with their meeting.

Perry's recent words finally made Katy realise that he loved her no matter what happened. On leaving London, they planned to stay with Mary for up to a week if things went well. If not they would go to Blackberry House nearby, then travel to see Ned's parents after they left her house. From Kent they would travel a day west and meet up with their cousin, Lady Mari, in West Sussex. There Perry would report to Duke James before heading back to Warwickshire for winter.

The trip to Aylesford from London would take all day with the children. Normally, a carriage could do the distance in a few hours. However, with the considerable entourage and eight children, stops were frequent.

~

By the mid September, only the enlarged skeleton staff remained in London. Most of the staff had been sent on to the castle to await them.

By four o'clock, Perry's carriages were turning into the familiar driveway of Mary's place. As usual, it was immaculate. Little had changed from when they lived there with Mary. The wheels crunched over the newly raked gravel, taking the carriages to the front door. The porticoed entrance was soon occupied by people waving. As they drove closer, a man appeared and stood beside Mary in a very possessive manner.

Katy gasped. "Perry, look. Who's that?"

Perry was intrigued. "I have no idea, but he's obviously far more than just a friend." He saw the man slide his hand around Mary's waist and draw her close.

Their carriage slowed, and Katy too, saw the man's hand on Mary's waist. She gasped again, then giggled. By the time they had opened the door, Katy had her giggles under control. She fell into Mary's arms as soon as she was out. Soon both ladies were laughing like the schoolgirls they had once been. Mary ushered her guests inside before introducing the handsome man still standing so close to her. His eyes almost oozed with lust for Mary. His gaze barely left her.

Nanny whisked the children upstairs; she wished to renew her acquaintance with all of her old friends. Buck and his family followed.

Perry, Katy, Mary, and the man were finally alone. Mary stood and went to the man's side as the door shut. "Katy, Perry, I'd like to introduce my husband, Donald Spencer."

Perry recovered his shock quicker than Katy, who sat stunned, then her smile spread to her eyes. "I really should have trusted you, shouldn't I?" Katy looked at the three others in the room. She started chuckling again. Soon the others joined in. All three had been as nervous as she had been. Katy's giggle had broken the ice.

Mary held Donald's hand. "Katy, we have more news. We have a daughter; we named her…." Mary looked at Perry, then Katy. "…We named her Catherine Louisa; she's 'Caty' with a 'C' for short, though."

After an hour of catching up and clearing the air, they decided to visit the extensive nursery and meet each other's children. Nanny and Lucy had carried the little ones, but Mia led the way. She was fourteen; she remembered the house as it had many happy memories. She had only been six when she left, but the rooms were all still familiar.

~

The week sped by, and by the time they were due to leave, they had extracted a promise from Mary and Donald to visit with Colm and Caty.

They had been surprised to find Donald had no title or fancy background. He was a returned soldier whom Justin had assisted. He had needed some moral support which Justin provided, but Mary needed a friend. In him she found what she desired. A loving husband and a wonderful support. Her first marriage had only lasted eight short weeks.

Donald would be her support from now onwards. He had a severe injury on his torso that had since healed. But he had been unable to do much work for some years. Mary had needed a new butler; Donald had volunteered to fill the position until she found a suitable person. Mary had fallen in love with the handsome soldier. He too had grown exceedingly fond of his new employer but hardly dared to presume anything. The relationship grew surprisingly quickly, and they married less than six months after they met. Donald was everything Mary needed. Mary and Colm supplied the loving support that Donald craved. Having no home of his own, he was content to be the father figure Colm needed. When Mary fell with-child only months after they married, both were in seventh heaven. Mary had never fallen again, but neither of them were worried. They had a boy and a girl and were happy, deliriously happy. Both Perry and Katy found it a delight to be with them. Even after some years of marriage, they were like a newlywed couple.

One colossal revelation had been that Justin and Mary had traced their older siblings. Her half-sister Narelle was dead, but Ellen had remarried and come from Parramatta for a visit with her new husband, a doctor. It did not take long for Katy to work out that this Ellen was Molly Miller's mother from the Rear Admiral Duncan Inn in Parramatta. It was another cog in God's puzzle.

Katy bade a tearful farewell to her dear friend. They were both looking forward to December in Warwickshire. Mary and Donald were coming for Christmas and staying until the snow cleared.

The next stop was Princhester House to see Lady Jane and John Princhester for a quick visit. From there, they were heading to Gracemere Castle for a few days.

Jane greeted them, and after they had tea and caught up on the passing years, the family departed to their next destination.

Perry had warned the children not to mention any people they had met in Australia, especially Uncle Ned. They all agreed, but Perry was still concerned they would let out Ned's name.

Katy was worried too, "However, how are we going to stop them from spilling the beans about Ned?"

Perry smiled, "Easy, they will not appear unless requested. I have told them they must not say a word about Uncle Ned, and they promised. Out of sight, out of mind. Duke Charles is about the same age as my father, possibly a bit younger, but not much. However, my darling love, we will be staying at Gracemere Castle so keeping eight small children out of his way, will not be hard."

She looked puzzled.

Perry had seen the toy room. "Just wait until you see their nursery and you will know what I mean."

They decided to spend only three days at the castle instead of the planned week. The Duchess realised they had been sworn to stay silent about more of Ned's details. However, Katy did say that he was both safe and happy, and he sent his love to his parents and brothers. Katy also told his mother that he had many good friends there. With Ned's permission, she told the Duchess about the sort of work he did and how happy he was that he'd been able to shrug off the titles, duties and responsibilities of being a Duke's son and live a normal life. There he was, just Ned.

Perry passed her the short letter Ned had entrusted to him.

Before they arrived, Perry had told Katy the entire Elouise Wickham saga, and of her, Katy spoke at length with the Duchess. David and Elouise were living in London, and she rarely saw them.

Duchess Suze admitted to Katy that Ned had had a lucky escape. David was not happy, that much she knew. From being the obedient oldest son with great responsibility, David now rarely came home.

While Perry was with Duke Charles, Katy sat in the Duchess's sunny sitting room and poured out their hearts over the sadness of love triangles.

The Duchess confided to Katy that she had also been victim of one. Not that she had ever returned the man's affections, but his obsession with her had forced a wedge between a family that should have been friends. Suze's eyes dropped to the large diamond ring that had worn a groove in her finger. Charles had given it to her when she was just eighteen. She was as crazy in love with him now as she had been back then. That had been twenty-six years ago and she and not regretted a day of it. They had four healthy sons, plus one had died soon after birth and she remembered her beautiful stillborn daughter.

Katy watched her in silence. At forty-four the Duchess was at the height of her beauty. Katy thought that rather than Duchess Grace, she should be Her Grace, Grace. Ned had chosen his name well.

The graceful dame was deep in reflection. A smile hovered around her lips and she brushed away a single tear. Suze fell silent and sat looking out the window, deep in thought. She did not tell Katy that Elouise had fallen with-child early in their marriage and lost it. Suze knew that horrible feeling, she and Charles had talked over the loss of their twin son, but she had coped with the death of their daughter all alone.

Charles had not known what to say. After she lost the child, David and Elouise had drifted apart. Yes, they shared the house in London, but they were rarely seen at the same functions. They lived in separate worlds. No, Suze could not reveal that to anyone, including her beloved husband. Thankfully, Elouise had not conceived again; if she had, from what she had heard of her daughter-in-law, Suze doubted any child would be David's offspring. She could not tell that to anyone. Her heart hurt, and she couldn't fix it. She knew that to compensate, David had thrown himself into Parliament to occupy his time.

It left him little time to do much else. David had only once mentioned his wife to his mother. He said that he wished he had listened to Neddie. Now they had no way to contact him, and it was too late to say sorry anyway. Suze had a wave of pain shoot across her face.

Katy watched with concern. "Your Grace? Are you all right?" Katy had said a few things to her and saw Suze was sitting mute and staring out the window.

Duchess Suze turned to Katy with a beatific smile on her almost perfect face. Her voice still had a soft Scottish lilt as she replied, "Katy dear, I was wishing Neddie was here, not over there, but while that shrew he escaped from is still around, that won't happen. I can never tell Charles what she's doing, but Katy, Neddie, will need to come home one day and step into David's shoes. Paul and Douglas don't want a thing to do with the place. Both want to go into law, and they have my blessing. I have no desire to lose either of them to war." Suze took a deep breath. "At least they both have their heads screwed on straight. Do you know the problems Elouise has created?"

Katy nodded.

Suze continued. "I hope they choose better than a pretty face. Time will tell. It's a pity your Mia is so young."

Katy was stunned; Mia had hardly been around the Duchess. "She turns fifteen soon; how old is Douglas? He can't be much older, can he?" Katy asked.

Suze looked up excitedly. "She's fifteen when?"

Katy smiled. "April, ma'am." She planted the seed and wondered if it germinated. She could imagine nothing better than seeing her daughter marry into Ned's family. She could do no more, but she wanted Mia and Douglas to meet before they left. At fourteen, she was lovely. She had gone through the gawky pimply stage early, and her skin had cleared to an English rose, and her puppy fat had gone as she shot up. Mia was now a graceful young lady and grew more beautiful daily.

"Fifteen, eh? Douglas won't be ready to settle down for a few years, but Paul is only a year older. Let's introduce them at dinner and see if she likes either of them." Suze smiled; the twinkle in her eye had dispelled the melancholy feelings she had recently experienced. "It will be fun watching the three of them. At this age, they are somewhat competitive. She is rather lovely. They should be here for dinner tonight." She chuckled. "I must admit I can't wait until they see her." Suze thought of the child's glorious long dark golden ringlets and honest blue eyes that looked out from a heart-shaped face. Her lips were always smiling. Yes, she liked this girl, and her younger sister Louisa, too, who was destined even to outshine her sister. Sadly that girl was only eleven. Still, Law took quite some time to complete. There was a possibility that both boys could fall for the two girls.

Dinner would be fascinating.

Katy informed Mia of the two extra dinner guests, and she suggested that Mia get to know them. Katy smiled, when their time came, these two glorious gems of girls would take London by storm.

Mia's young heart quickened as soon as Paul walked in. Her eyes grew as big as saucers when she heard that Uncle Ned's younger brothers wished to meet her. Katy wondered if it was too soon to tell her why. However, being so understanding, she quickly saw she needed no explanation.

Perry sat watching Mia through the meal. She sat laughing with Douglas, but Paul was the recipient of her shy glances and blushes throughout the dinner. Whether he was aware of it or not, Perry didn't know, but he felt sorry for Douglas.

Katy and Suze each caught a shy smile given to Paul by Mia. It was far too soon for any other relationship to be formalised, but they would encourage him to spend time with the family over the holidays. He was at Oxford University, and Warwickshire was much closer than Kent. Close enough for weekend visits should they wish to come. Perry issued the first invitation after dinner.

Paul's eyes lit up, and with little encouragement, they planned a visit for the Easter break. Douglas, thankfully, didn't seem interested in her as he'd spent the evening chatting with Louisa.

The parting from Gracemere was bittersweet.

Perry was thrilled that the children did not let on about Ned, but to know that Mia was getting to an age when they had to start thinking about her marriage made him sad. She may not be his blood daughter, but she was undoubtedly his heart child. If she had to think of marriage, then she could do no better than Ned's brother. Time would certainly tell.

The family departed for West Sussex;

~

Perry's carriage and the team of four matched white horses drew up at the Broome-Hall Manor. Behind it was a train of slightly less comfortable vehicles, some laden with luggage. Two more passenger carriages followed with the children spread evenly throughout the vehicles.

They stayed at Broome-Hall Manor with Lady Mari's nephew, Sir Timothy Broome-Hall and his family.

Perry had not seen his cousin since shortly before the fire some twenty-five years before.

As a widow his cousin had moved into a grace and favour cottage on the edge of the estate after her husband died many years before. She had come along to the Manor house to greet the family.

Their entourage's welcome was very warm, and Sir Timothy suggested that they make Broome-Hall Manor their base while visiting the area.

Sir Timothy had recently returned from an overseas trip and was once more ensconced at Broome-Hall Manor. He had taken over the title when his uncle had died years before. He was vastly surprised to see Lady Mari out of her cottage. He knew she rarely moved from the boundary of the small premises.

Sir Timothy's two older sons, Robbie and Tim were slightly older than Mia. Katy gave Perry a nudge, he could see that Mia had instantly forgotten Paul. Tim had now caught Mia's eye. And to top it off, they were distantly related. Admittedly only by marriage, Tim, or TC as the family called him, was only three years older than Mia. At eighteen, his dark hair and blue eyes, accompanied by his tall, good looks, were the young girl's delight. He set her heart a flutter all over again.

That night, while Perry lay cuddling Katy before sleeping, he asked her about Mia and her fluctuating adorations.

Katy replied, "Sweetheart, a young girl's heart can be given in a grand passion many times. She can be in love with him one moment and hate him the next. It can be something as silly as how he holds his cutlery, picks his teeth in public, or that she may see him smile at her sister. Or it may be that she sees someone more interesting. Mia liked Paul well enough, but Tim is more her own age, even though Paul is only twenty-two, and of course, there is a relationship between Tim and Mia of sorts."

"Oh, then what shall we do when Paul visits at Easter?" Perry was now somewhat concerned.

Katy gave him a long kiss before answering. "We shall leave them in God's hands. Our job as parents is to keep her from those who are not suitable. Then place those who are suitable in her path. Hopefully, she will choose one of them. However, at fourteen, her passions will be engaged and disengaged frequently." She reached up for Perry again for another long, drawn-out kiss before saying, "Darling, I saw Louisa's face when she saw Paul. Did you not notice how silent she became when he was in the room? She likes him, and there are only three years between the girls. Paul will have years ahead of him to study at university before he is ready to settle down. Lou is nearly twelve and very mature for her age. Girls marry from fifteen, you know, although I would not wish that on any lass."

Perry's hand started stroking her thigh. He had other things on his mind now other than their two daughters. "Are we really talking about marriage for our twelve-year-old daughter?" he chuckled. "I have a better idea to discuss, and it does have something to do with children in a very roundabout way." He trailed kisses all over her face and then claimed her lips, leaving her in no doubt about what those ideas were.

She willingly consented.

~

Perry had messages to deliver from Ned. Ones that Ned could not put in writing. Perry acquiesced, knowing that he wished to see Duke James for his friend.

After a week with them at the family Manor House, Perry made his excuses and departed to the Duke's estate next door. He merely said he had a message to deliver personally. She seemed interested in his friends in Sydney and, in particular, asked him if he knew of any others from their area.

Perry was not going to tell her of Ned but thought that telling her of his school friend Sam would not hurt. Tom had hinted she knew more than he expected. He related their friendship and that of his delightful wife, Annie.

Lady Mari's eyes lit up.

Seeing her interest, he elaborated; Perry spoke of Annie in glowing terms and described her baking skills. Her smile made Perry give his cousin a questioning look. It made him wonder even more when he saw the portrait of Mari soon after their wedding. It could well have been Annie. He said nothing but, "Oh." Finally, the pieces were falling into place, and Tom's story was probably true. There was a strong possibility that Annie was not the abandoned orphan she thought she was.

Malvern Hall sat nestled in a valley and didn't become visible until they turned into the long driveway. The road between the various estates was gracefully sweeping through an ancient avenue of yew trees, but Perry could see the tower of Sam's palatial house, Meldon Hall, from the top of the rise before descending to the Hall. He smiled, now guessing the secret of Sam's parentage. He had not yet been to Meldon Hall and he had no reason to go. Sam was not on good terms with his so-called father, the Earl, and he had told Perry that his father had disinherited him. He was itching to tell him that he knew why, but Ned had sworn him to secrecy. Before he left Sydney, Tom Turner found that Perry knew more than he was letting on. The smile and a very subtle nod he had given Perry, confirmed Ned's story. But Tom was watching Annie more than Sam. Tom said always ensured he spent time with her on every visit. Having seen Lady Mari's portrait, he wondered if there was not more to her story too. Perry had watched his cousin with a knowing eye. He wondered who Annie's father was. It certainly was not the Duke; could it be The Earl, Sam's supposed father? He presumed he'd never know.

Perry met the Duke's wife, Lady Adelaide, and the children. The daughter, Grace, who had come for a visit that morning, and his son, Jonathan, whom he called Nathan. He was as like Sam as two brothers could have been. Danny, however, was his younger image, to the point that Perry was startled when they met.

Soon after this, the Duke said he needed to stretch his legs and asked Perry to accompany him. The time with Duke James passed with a long walk outdoors where Perry could fill the Duke in on Sam's welfare. Duke James had noted Perry's gasp and had not needed to question him as to why.

Perry had said, "My Lord, Sam's son, Daniel, could well be a younger version of Lord Nathan, so alike are they. Sam, too is similar, but I imagine much like you when you were young. I know the Earl, having met him before. There is no resemblance."

The Duke smiled and gave a not-so-subtle nod. "I do wish I could meet him just once as my son. I have wanted to acknowledge him all his life, but the Earl was making his life hard enough as it was. I was away when he was convicted, or I would have done something. I still don't know the full story."

The Duke asked Perry to spare him no detail of Sam's life. Sadly, Sam had not confided much to Perry about his years as a convict. So, Perry was not able to reveal much about that; however, he was happily married, and Perry told Duke James that their life in Sydney was one of stability and happiness. Perry told him about Danny and his building work. Then mentioned that he was courting his boss's daughter.

The Duke was stunned, "Sam's a builder? Is he in construction himself? Well, I never!" Duke James pumped Perry for everything he knew about his son and grandson, which sadly was little.

In the last years, Danny was often at work when Perry met with Sam. He explained that Vanessa was a pretty lass but what Perry referred to as a silly girl. Perry thought that she giggled a lot and seemed a little too touchy with Danny. He wondered if their relationship had not progressed further than it should have done. Neither Sam nor Annie obviously minded; however, he did not relate that to the Duke.

Their time drew to a close, and they made their farewells. Perry had to return to his family and take them home to Cheatham Castle.

Chapter 20 The Long Way Home

*T*he one-hundred-and-thirty-mile trip to Warwickshire took a few days.

They decided to stay at staging inns en route rather than arrange accommodation at various acquaintances' houses.

As the middle of October approached, the train of carriages rolled into the newly macadamed surfaced driveway. Usually, the crunch of the carriage wheels on the gravel driveway would alert the footmen to the arrival of visitors. However, Percy and Meg were on the doorstep awaiting them, and behind them, a bevy of staff stood at attention.

The gatekeeper had sent a groom cross country to inform the castle of their arrival.

Jem was the first to speak. He hopped down from the front carriage and was in his grandfather's arms. "Grandpa, I missed you so much." Jem was at that wonderful age where he was a fully grown boy that was not quite a man. His voice had broken but sounded more like it had cracked.

Perry smiled at the sounds.

Katy greeted her mother-in-law with a big hug. "Hello, Aunt Meg." Katy opened her mouth to speak but saw Meg's sign.

Meg put her fingers on her lips and turned to walk inside. Apologies and explanations would come but here was neither the time nor the place; they would do that privately.

Once inside, Perry introduced the younger children to their grandparents, and Percy congratulated Buck and Lucy on their growing brood. He knew about their union and was thrilled.

Lucy had not long told Katy that she was expecting again. After Judith's tricky birth, this was concerning news to them all. Hopefully, there will not be any complications this time.

Perry and Katy settled into their appointed suites and joined Meg and Percy in the private sitting room for a catch-up. The staff took all the rest of the children into the nursery. Katy knew from her previous visits that they would not see them again unless they went up there. This room had every toy imaginable, and the children were delighted. Mia would watch over the little ones. It was more extensive than even Gracemere Castle, which was vast.

As they entered, Percy moved the newspaper he had been reading. "You might be interested to read this later on, son," he said to Perry, "The Frenchman, Jean-François Champollion, has done it. He has beaten Thomas Young to translate the entire Rosetta Stone and transcribed the Egyptian hieroglyphs." Percy handed his son the paper as he had read it twice already. He knew his son loved Egyptology as much as he did. One of the things that had been in the castle when Percy inherited it was an Egyptian room. Both his sons had become obsessed with what they found. Some of the items in the collection had a carving or engravings with strange writings inscribed on them. One had an oval cartouche with a line under it, similar to what Champollion had mentioned.

Perry took the paper to read later; it was something he would certainly want to investigate.

Meg looked at Katy and patted the settee next to her. "Sit next to me, my dear, so we can chat." Meg had a look of love on her face; she reached out her hand to Katy. That one caring act was Katy's tipping point. Katy had expected a grilling or at least some chastisement from her cousins, but the unadulterated and totally unconditional love and acceptance had her weeping in Meg's arms.

Perry sat on the arm of the couch, comforting her, his full attention now focused on his wife.

Percy watched his son's apparent devotion.

After Katy had recovered a little, Perry said, "Mama, Katy and I had a long talk about the entire experience. We know that even though *how* she got there was, well, um, unconventional, *why* she went has turned out to be a blessing."

Katy was now sitting up and leaning into Perry as he sat on the settee's arm. Meg still held her hand.

Perry continued, "I know you will have heard of Elizabeth, or as she prefers, Betsy Fry's work with the women in the gaols in London. What you don't know is that she saw Katy on her very first visit. Because of what Katy told her, Betsy and her philanthropy friends started working to assist the women incarcerated in the various hell holes around the country. I'm sure you've heard of what she's now doing?"

Both Meg and Percy affirmed that they had.

Perry gave a single nod of acknowledgement and continued. "Anyway, because of that visit and what Betsy brought her, that inspired Katy to help in Parramatta, albeit differently. So much so that Lachlan Macquarie built a new Female Prison. It opened last year, and although far from ideal, it is much better than what they had."

Meg and Percy sat stunned. "Betsy visited you in London? Really?" Meg asked, surprised as she was known as a Quaker.

"Yes, Aunt Meg, it was Betsy who gave me the only possessions I had for Davy, and she even brought me one of her own warm shawls as I had all my luggage stolen. Not that I had taken much." Katy felt a gentle squeeze of her shoulder as a sign of assurance from Perry.

He nodded for her to continue.

She did. "Betsy came again to the hulk I had been moved onto, and then for a final time when I boarded the ship. Oh, Aunt Meg, it was comforting for me to know at least one person knew where I was." Katy blew her nose delicately before continuing. "I made her swear that she would not tell Perry until I sailed." She glanced at Perry, wondering if she should say more.

Perry knew what she was feeling. "Tell them, love, they will want to help us," Perry said with assurance as he stroked her neck with his thumb as she spoke.

She tilted her head to acknowledge his comforting action. "Uncle Percy, Aunt Meg, we are still helping them. The *we* includes Sir Robert Peel, Betsy and her brother Joseph, and us. We hope to present a Bill in Parliament next year." Katy swallowed; she had no idea how they would react to what they were going to do.

Yet, her comment started a conversation that went on for some time. Rather than meet with opposition, they were met with unconditional support. Percy decided to also throw his weight behind this Bill and the other changes Sir Robert proposed.

Perry had given his father a copy of the draft Bill during their conversation, and Percy read it while they spoke.

"I like it, I really do," Percy said when he finished the document. "But you know it's not going to change much. The death penalty has needed revision for many years, and no one has been brave enough to say anything. So, yes, I'll certainly throw my weight behind this." Percy mused aloud and said, "Sir Robert Peel, eh? Well, I never!"

Meg wanted afternoon tea; she asked Perry to tug the bell pull.

The butler answered the summons and brought the mail.

Lachlan had written.

Perry read the letter while they waited for tea. He related that Lachlan's return home had been a vast letdown, as their house and lands had fallen into significant disrepair and were not habitable for a harsh winter in Scotland. He had already mentioned to Perry his idea of taking a break in Italy, and this was now his plan. By the time they received this missive, Lachlan would have already set builders to do the repairs but packed up his family and staff. They would be now en route to the warmer climes in Italy.

As he read the rest of Lachlan's letter, Perry realised that they would now draw apart from each other. Their friendship had served a purpose to assist the convicts in Parramatta. The experience gained, however, would feed into the new Bill.

Percy walked to the window. He stood pondering his words. He slowly turned and looked at his son before saying, "From the time you told me what happened, son, I wondered how all this was part of God's plan. You may wonder how God gets the glory in anything. As you know, when I inherited the title, I had no idea what was ahead of me. No one had told me what Julian had been up to. You can trust me; it's been a nightmare sorting what I can. Perry, you know about the school and the staff and that sort of thing. Well, I have now sorted that out as much as I can. Any more offspring of his will be assisted when discovered. I was looking for another project when your letter arrived, asking if you could send some wounded men who needed employment." He glanced at the three dear people sitting and listening to him. Katy leaned into Perry again. She hoped he would fully support Perry's plans.

Percy smiled at them and continued. "Dear ones, my heart soared. It was as though God was revealing his reasons for your injuries, Perry, and your actions, Katy, my dear. I have grieved over these years about what happened. I was your father, Perry, but I could not shield you from the hurt and pain you were going through. As a parent, you now know what I mean, but all you wanted to do was hide back then. I understood, but I hurt too, as did your mother. You not only shut down but shut us out; however, as I said, we understood." He turned his eyes to Katy. "Now, my dear girl, we get to you. You lost your papa, Colin, on the day of the fire, which devoured Perry's life as well. While you mourned your father's loss, you grieved too for Perry, for even then, I knew what you felt for him. He was so ill that we decided not to say anything; no one even noticed there was no funeral for him. Quite honestly, we did not expect him to survive. Even then, your feelings for him were strong."

Katy reached up and took Perry's hand in her free one.

Percy watched the loving gesture, then continued. "However, we will move on some years. Katy, your mama, Catherine, then died after you came to live with us. Perry was gone, and you were our light. A reason for living, if you will. We hoped you would marry Jeramy, but it was not to be. Then you met and married Jeramy's friend Phil Harrington. I thought everything was settled when you were expecting your first child." He took a deep breath. "But, then you lost your son at birth, and less than eighteen months later, Phil died. Of course, we lost Jeramy that terrible day too."

He swallowed, thinking back to the difficulties of that time. Percy turned from their gaze and walked to the window. His hands were clasped but his thumbs were flicking against each other.

A place Meg had often seen him stand.

With a deep sigh, he said, "Through it all, I'm yelling loudly at God, shouting 'Why God? Why us? What did we do to deserve all this?' It was a Job moment for me, like in the Bible. It was all so unfair. I still do not understand why all this had to happen." He looked at Meg, who nodded for him to continue.

Percy acknowledged her action with a nod of his own, then did just that. "When Jeramy died, I nearly gave up. Perry, your mother will tell you how close I was to throwing in everything and running away. With Perry gone, Katy, I was battling with more than what to do about all the poor girls Julian had abused. More than once, I lost my temper with him. I would go down to the crypt and shout at him."

Percy relived the horror of the lurid discoveries he had made about his predecessor. Now and then, the emotions got the better of him, and he blew his nose.

Perry and Katy were also deep in their own thoughts.

"Thankfully, Perry, you had given me Justin's contact details, so I knew you were near Aylesford, but I knew you were not in our old home. However, I did not look for you as I knew you did not want that. Your mother knows that you returning one day was the only straw I was grasping onto. Now, back to you, Katy. I expected you to come here if your second child was a girl. We are your closest family; this was your home, so I presumed you would come here. When I heard that Eustace was now the Earl, I wondered where you were. I was sad you had not turned to us." He blew his nose again. "Then I had word from Mary via Justin that you had vanished. That was another blow. I thought you had gone somewhere else. I came south to visit Mary, and as you know, we searched everywhere around Buckland Manor in Great Buckland. I stayed with Charles and Susanna Lockley at Gracemere and searched the entire area around Aylesford. You had vanished."

Katy looked up at Perry.

Meg lovingly squeezed Katy's hand. Percy saw and smiled again. "Then Justin let me know you had been found, safe and well, but you can imagine the surprise we had when he said that you had been with Perry the entire time. Then Justin told us that he arranged for you two to marry and that Bishop James had already done the deed. I'm not too proud to admit that I wept like a baby, with the greatest relief you could imagine."

Meg was nodding. "I was too, my dears." She caressed Katy's hand. "But you know much of this."

Percy came to Meg's side and perched on the other arm of the settee. "To find you two married was an answer to prayer from us both. We already knew about the baby girl, of course. Then, Katy, my dear, you blessed us with not just yourself, but with Jem, then Lou and now the other children too. We look forward to getting to know all our grandchildren. Well, that is all a bit of blather. I'm trying to say that, looking back, I can see our Lord's hand on every step. Of course, there are many, many things that I wish I could have stopped occurring, Perry, your burns and, Katy, your papa's death, Phil and Jeramy's deaths too, and everything you have both gone through as well. However, that is not changeable, so from what you told me, our work is just starting with these poor people. I have already placed the thirty poor souls you sent me recently, plus the family of girls from London you asked me to assist some years ago. I believe they are sisters to the young lasses who work with you, are they not?"

Perry nodded.

"The Livingstone family live in a cottage attached to the dairy, where they now all now work; they love it. Do you know they make the best cheeses?" Percy looked at his son's face; he saw him grin. "Of the others, the injured men are all in training for various other roles. They will get references and move on when or if they wish. Their move here has already made a difference to them. Now you tell me we have more work in this field. We await them with glee." Percy looked down at Meg and stroked her cheek as lovingly as his son had been doing to Katy. "We are ready to start where and when we are needed, aren't we, love? We can absorb many, many more hurting souls."

Perry was thrilled. "Father, as you know, we found someone over in Parramatta, another one of Julian's offspring, as I wrote you. You mentioned the Livingstones and Janey is here with us but did you ever find her mother?"

Percy's eyes lit up, but he didn't need to answer.

At that moment, Janey came in with the three youngest children. Mia, Jem and Lou were hard on her heels, with an older lady following.

Janey's grin told the story. "Mr Perry, Katy, his Lordship found my Mama. May I introduce you to her?"

Percy and Meg welcomed Jennifer Brien when she had arrived some years ago. She had been at a loose end, as she was a governess with no children to look after. Now she was in her element. It had initially been hard for her to return to Cheatham Castle, but she had now overcome her anxiety.

Meg loved having a woman her own age as a companion. Jennifer had become just that. "Jennifer, I think you will have your hands full now," Meg said. "I believe Lucy and Buck have a few more to add to this brood." The smile on Meg's face made Katy chuckle.

"Yes, ma'am, and of course." Jennifer turned to Katy. "I still work at the school, too," Jennifer said.

Perry thought that life here was going to be so very different from what he expected.

Percy's smiling eyes glinted as he met his beloved wife's grin. The family was together again.

~

Their first Christmas at home brought snow. The season was vastly different from the scorching summers in Parramatta, where the daily temperature was rarely below 100° Fahrenheit. It was now bitterly cold outside. Snow and the cold were something that the younger children had never seen before, and it took some acclimatisation from all the returning travellers.

The children had learned to adore their grandparents. Jem was often found shadowing his grandfather, inundating him with questions.

The castle was too far from town for the local villagers to come carolling, but the staff decided to stand in the grand foyer on the staircase and sing. The joyous sounds echoed through the rooms, and soon all the children joined in. The twins, Colin and Joanna, were wide-eyed. They sang too while sitting on the floor, watching the events unfolding before them.

Buck and Lucy's two older children joined the six others. Their grandfather watched all the young people with a big smile. This season was the first Christmas they could share with the children. Meg clasped Percy's hand. She too was grinning. Finally, they were a complete family.

Lucy stood cradling their new baby, who had been born only two weeks before. Archibald Peregrin had entered the world with little fuss. Archie was very like his big brother, Lindsay.

Buck stood with his hand on the small of Lucy's back. His father, Daniel, was still Castle Manager and warmly welcomed his new daughter-in-law and grandchildren. Perry treated them as friends rather than staff, still insisting on first-name terms. For them to enjoy the blessings of everything the Castle had to offer was a pure delight.

Percy had refused to continue some of the traditional Christmas traditions. There was to be no Yule Log and no Wassailing unless he could trace a tradition to have some Christian reason; he did not do it. However, the family assisted the staff in preparing a feast in the great hall. Christmas food was brought up from the kitchens and placed on the sideboards in the great banquet hall. All the inside and outdoor staff ate at the great table with the family. From the new scarred stable hands to the Duke, they shared the joy and mutual acceptance of a united and welcoming Christmas.

Perry insisted on having Katy near to him. They sat holding hands under the table. Meg, sitting opposite them, saw the many smiles of adoration. Neither could wipe the grins from their faces; They were home, safe and happy, and best of all, there was no stuffy protocol.

The week before Christmas, Katy and Meg had noticed that Perry and Percy often walked to an ordinarily empty barn. On leaving, they locked it behind them. Not even the ladies were permitted entry.

On Christmas Day, the entire castle staff were called together after luncheon and told to follow the two men in the barn. Once there, each received a specially chosen gift. Some were gifted books; some a puppy or a coop of chickens; a sty of piglets or similar. There was not a single length of red flannel to be seen. This had been the traditional Christmas gift for decades from the previous Duke. Everyone, male or female, had received the same. In past years Percy had given each a book, but with Perry's arrival, the two had decided to give each something they would like and find helpful. Both men wished to get to know their people. So, this year, they started a new tradition.

~

The New Year arrived, and so did more snow. The children had never had a snowball fight, nor had they seen a snowman, let alone build one. They had all become familiar with rugging-up to play outdoors, something they had never had to do before at Christmastime.

Sadly, the snow melted quickly, and the roads turned to mush; the household could get into the village, but not much further. Visiting was limited to the area surrounding the castle.

~

Winter passed, and Easter drew close. Paul would be arriving for the Easter break from university; however, others had written and asked if they may also come. Sir Timothy's three sons, Robbie, Tim and Adam Styles, Lady Mari's great nephews, were also coming to stay for the break. At twenty-one, eighteen and sixteen, the three young men were there at Lady Mari's suggestion.

Fifteen-year-old Mia was both concerned and excited. She liked all four young men and hoped one would show more particular interest in her than the others. She knew all of them, except Robbie, had yet to finish university, so none were in a hurry to marry. She had time to make her choice.

The week before Easter, the young men arrived together. When they discovered they were heading to Cheatham Castle, they decided to travel with Robbie, who had come to collect his brothers. He had done a second season in London the year before and had not enjoyed it. He vowed and declared never to return. Even though he was a Baronet's son, this was almost social suicide, but his refusal was absolute. He still sat in on Parliamentary sessions from the gallery but took no part in the social whirl of gaiety enjoyed by so many. Robbie showed no partiality for any particular girl either. He would sit watching his brothers but would rarely participate.

Robbie saw things; he watched his brother Tim's interest in Mia. He also noted a distinct interest that Paul had in Louisa. She may only be young; however, she was mature, and Paul was in no hurry to marry.

One evening after dinner, Katy noticed Robbie staring at her and wondered why. He was standing at the big French doors. Katy subtly made her way across the room; she was concerned about him. He looked so sad but had so far refused Perry's questioning to reveal why. Katy knew that both Perry and Percy had tried to draw him out but to no avail. She thought she would try. His eyes had followed her progress across the room.

On his arrival, he hoped to have a chance to talk to Katy but decided to leave it to the Lord to make an opening. It seemed that tonight would be it.

Katy arrived at his side, and after her greeting, he saw compassion on her face. "Robbie, you worry me. I can see something is sitting on your heart."

Robbie nodded. "Nothing dire, my lady."

"Call me Katy, please, Robbie; we are cousins," Katy said.

Robbie glanced at her; a micro frown flashed across his brow. He wondered how to phrase what he had to say. He looked at her and saw empathy in her returning glance; suddenly, he blurted out, "Katy, on my first season in London, I fell in love. Only no one introduced us, so I do not know her name. I went to every function afterwards, and I never saw her again. The next year I also attended every ball, soirée, and outing imaginable with just one intent, and that was to find her. But there was no hint of her."

The story pulled at Katy's heartstrings. "Oh, Robbie, truly? No sign of her at all?"

Robbie shook his head, "None at all; I have hunted high and low." He released a long sigh. "I shall keep looking, but I'll not return to London as I now know she is not there. Jimmy has asked me for a visit, but they have a girls' school at the house, so I shall avoid that."

Katy nodded; this made sense. She gently touched his arm to show her compassion for his hurt. "Let us know if we can assist in any way."

Robbie smiled, at least his mouth did, but it didn't reach his eyes. "Just knowing someone knows and believes me is a help, Katy. My brothers and friends all tease me. But I'll find her, Katy, I will, if I have to door knock every single house in England."

Katy knew his heartsore feeling. Nothing could help him other than prayer. She offered him the solace of an ear to listen should he wish to avail himself of it.

Robbie assured her that he certainly would let her know should the need arise. In the meantime, he would keep looking for his lost love. "Keep praying, Katy, for only with God's help will I find her. That I know."

Perry came and joined their conversation; Robbie turned its direction. Robbie showed interest in assisting Perry with sourcing more wounded men and scarred soldiers. Perry was keen for his help and willingly accepted, then told him of the Prisons' Bill up for presentation in July.

Robbie's eyes lit up. This reform was just the sort of thing he needed to distract him.

~

Sadly, after an enjoyable two weeks, their visit ended, and Robbie took the three younger men back to university. He assured Perry that he would meet them in London to present the Bill in July.

By June, the majority of Society returned to London as did the Whites. Percy and Meg intended to help where they could but would arrive the week the Bill would be presented in early July.

Sir Robert, Betsy, and her brother, Joseph, knew they had to tweak the wording of the Bill; it covered too much. Therefore, Sir Robert decided to split the Bill. He suggested that the first part be a Transportation Act. This part would cover how convicts were transferred around the country before being transported. One of the most considerable effects of the change in law was that prisoners were now held in the ship's hulks, moored in the Thames River, Portsmouth, and other areas in the Empire rather than overcrowding the cells. This had already been trialled, as Katy could attest. Some female prisoners were still transported in open wagons rather than closed carriages.

Katy gave the feedback that compared to the horrific cells the hulks, as bad as they were, were still better than the cells.

Moving the prisoners to the hulks cleaned up many of the gaols. The condition of the wrecks was far from ideal; however, it was a start. Most were for male prisoners, but one was for females. This Bill also covered the removal of five smaller Acts, and one of these was the removal of the Death Penalty for over one hundred minor crimes.

On July 4th, the first Bill passed. The gallery in Parliament was full of family and friends. Meg sat holding Katy's hand as they watched their husbands below.

Sir Robert's impassioned speech moved the listeners, and some changed their vote on the day. As he stood, he looked up at the gallery; he saw Katy leaning forward and giving him the thumbs up, and then she lifted her hands in silent applause.

Perry watched from his seat. Next week it would be his turn to present a speech. He intended to speak first-hand about the convicts' treatment. He knew that if he didn't choose his words wisely, they would both be ostracised forever. However, he knew he had to reveal Katy's background to some degree to strengthen the argument. Somehow, he had to do it without mentioning her name; he hoped that would be unnecessary. But the years they spent in the colony under assumed names would now prove vital. Thankfully Katy had used a false name twice during her imprisonment in England. She was virtually untraceable, and Perry discovered that for himself.

~

The following week the House of Lords gallery was again crowded with family and onlookers. This time, Katy sat next to Betsy Fry, her husband, Joseph. Her brother, Joseph Gurney and Meg, sat close by and watched. The Frys and Gurneys were not allowed to speak in the Parliament as they were Quakers; they had to sit and listen from the gallery. Sir Robert was to present part two of the Bill. Perry and Percy were in their seats below; Percy in the front, and Perry was hidden in the corner at the back. Sir Robert had timed the vote to be just after Perry's speech.

Percy had already spoken to the Bill; Perry was last to speak before they voted. Until today, he had remained hidden at the back of the room, coming in last and leaving first. He sat with the good side of his face to anyone passing him. They had attended no social functions, and few had met them. Today Perry's cloak of anonymity was to be cast off once and for all. As he walked to his place to deliver his speech, silence hung in the room. No one even shifted in their seats as he lifted his head and swivelled around so everyone should see his horrific scars. He stood in a shaft of sunlight filtering through the windows from above. His melted face was now clearly visible, as though a spotlight had highlighted it.

Gasps were audible from everywhere around the room.

Perry lifted his eyes to the gallery before he spoke and saw Katy blow him a kiss. A smile appeared on his distorted face, then he began his speech. His rich, resonant voice echoed off the walls. His words sank in. Perry, a man with such horrific injuries, spoke of the injustices he had personally witnessed. He spoke of the Emu Plains Prison farm and its success in dealing with the many unexpected convicts. He told of his time in Sydney and Parramatta and his connection with Lachlan Macquarie. He spoke of his assistance with the prison reform in the colony and the need for much more. His words were impassioned and graphic; his descriptions of the work Lachlan had achieved and what still needed doing.

Until his speech, no one had thought about what the Government in New South Wales had to cope with when an unexpected shipload of convicts arrived without warning. With food already scarce and accommodation minimal, another three hundred men or women would arrive and need immediate care. Sometimes one or two ships full of convicts arrive in the space of days or weeks. Often many were ill or malnourished. After Perry's speech, none were ignorant of what they were inflicting on the infant colony. Perry described the female gaols in graphic detail. Then he related Betsy Fry's visits with her brother and their discovery of the horrific conditions of the gaols in London and around the countryside. Betsy knew he was speaking of Katy's own experiences and clung tightly to her hand as Perry's speech continued.

Perry paused and looked around the room; he drew his words to a close but wished to push home the need for reform. "I hear you ask; how do I know these things?" He looked at the members sitting close to him. "I know them because one I hold dear was one of them. Through my experience," he stroked his cheek, "I can assist those whom I do not know. I have visited the prisons, seen the squalor, brought them food and clothing to cover their nakedness. These souls are no less human than we are ourselves. Due to poverty, not evil or malice, many have found themselves in this situation." The sun had moved as he was talking, so he moved back into the shaft of sunlight. His melted face was again evident for all to see. He turned so none could miss his wounds. "I have visible wounds from a fire. They have them too; only theirs are invisible but just as deep. Cruel words hurt me as much as they. I empathise with them and know their pain. So, they opened up to me. We need to do what our Lord Jesus said to do: *'Love thy neighbour as thy self.'* Perry said, "I do not just mean the attractive people and the ones who don't smell. Jesus meant everyone." Perry then quoted from the book of Matthew to them. *"Verily I say unto you, inasmuch as ye have done it unto one of the least of these my brethren, ye have done it unto me'.* This passage is from Matthew, chapter 25, verse 40. But a few verses before that Matthew wrote this, in verse 35 and 36, *'For I was hungry, and ye gave me meat: I was thirsty, and ye gave me drink: I was a stranger, and ye took me in: Naked, and ye clothed me: I was sick, and ye visited me: I was in prison, and ye came unto me'."*

There were more gasps than when he had revealed his face. They were each convicted due to their lack of action.

He thought that now was the time to bring that in too. He put his hand to his cheek and said, "When this happened to me many years ago, I thought my life was at an end. For years I hid. I was scared to show my melted and scarred face as it made others fearful and uncomfortable. My beloved wife taught me not to fear the scorn of those who saw. Yet even from this, I have found God's hand of blessing, for I can relate to the maimed soldiers, sailors, and men with similar wounds. As I said before, my scars are visible, but many scars are deep within. My visible scars broke through their barriers. As I said, many in our gaols are there because of poverty and hunger, not because they have a wicked streak. When I spoke to those in Parramatta Gaol, I found they were in dire circumstances prior to committing any crime. This Bill will not address *that* matter, but we must do something for the care of these people once incarcerated. I ask that you listen again to Sir Robert's words and vote to pass this law." Perry hoped that his few words would make some rethink their refusal to pass the Bill. Time would tell. He returned to his seat at the back. As he sat, those around him reached over and started shaking hands. However, the gallery erupted in applause.

Katy had noticed many taking notes and later discovered they were reporters.

The speaker called for order.

They voted and then waited.

The Bill passed.

Chapter 21 The Way Forward

*T*he two new Bills brought some changes, but not enough. After the transfer of many more prisoners to the hulks, gaols emptied somewhat, but the conditions were still horrific. The derelict ships were leaky, and conditions were not much better, although the inmates did have more room to move around. Betsy Fry and Joseph Gurney continued to visit both the prisons and the hulks with many of their supporters. Conditions improved for the women. They were no longer under the control and abuse of male warders; the female prisons also separated them from the male prisoners. They could at least sleep without fear of rape.

Perry and Katy visited when they could.

~

1823 faded into 1824.

The news was announced that Ralph Darling was to take over from Governor Brisbane. It was barely three years since Lachlan had left. Perry and Katy had made a quick trip to London at the end of January to see Ann Dumaresq's daughter, Eliza, and her husband, Ralph, off to Australia. Betsy Fry had let Eliza know that Katy and Perry were good friends of Lachlan and Elizabeth Macquarie. They wished to have many of their questions answered before stepping into the unknown. Eliza had first heard about Katy from her mother and requested to meet before departure. For over a week, Katy and Eliza Darling met each day for some hours while Ralph and Perry sat in the office holding a similar discussion.

Katy took the opportunity to tell Eliza of the reforms the Macquaries had been working on when they resigned. She also let her know of some of the other things Lachlan had wanted to do but had not had the time. Katy had a journal with her that she had kept while in Parramatta. The book was of great assistance to the Darlings.

By the time the Darlings sailed in February, they knew what Lachlan had been trying to achieve. Sadly, they didn't have time to go to Scotland and talk to him. Katy however, knew where Eliza should start, and that was with education. By supplying teachers, it would give the convicts a way forward. She explained the lack of conditions in the gaol when she was there and how Lachlan had built a new Female Factory. Hopefully, the building facilities would still be in good condition; though there was more room in the new gaol, overcrowding was still a temptation. Short term, the women could manage, at least until an assignment. The problem now was the abuse of women once assigned. There had been no vetting of the men requiring women. This situation still worried Katy, and she voiced this concern to Eliza. Katy also explained about the lack of water in gaol. Lachlan had a well added while constructing the new Factory, and the weir on the river made access to drinking water plentiful. The river water was suitable for washing but needed boiling to drink. However, a flood shortly before they left had ruined the weir, and Katy wasn't sure if the government had repaired it yet. That needed checking.

Perry and Katy stayed in London until Ralph and Eliza Darling sailed for Sydney. In the carriage on return from Woolwich, Perry reached again for Katy and drew her to him. "More doors have opened through you, my darling one. We shall never know how many will have a better life but for your incarceration."

Katy snuggled up too Perry. "I have learnt to trust, Perry. I trust both you and God. Many times have I seen His hand at work. I came to no harm, and for that again, I thank Him. But through what I experienced, we can now understand the trials and trauma of others. Hopefully, Eliza and Ralph can continue Lachlan and Elizabeth's work. I'm sure God has already gone before them. Did you get to tell them that they can trust Ned and Tom?"

Perry kissed the top of her head. "I did, actually but didn't let on Ned's secret. I told them there were two soldiers they could trust and one, in particular, to hold at arm's length. I didn't tell you of him, but I banned one man from our home. His name was Simmons, and he made me shiver. Oh, sweetheart, the rumours I heard about him and his *penchant* for little boys. Ned warned me about him, so he was banned from coming near us, and I hope Charles can keep his two little boys safe."

"Oh no!" Katy exclaimed. Katy felt Perry shiver just thinking of him. "Bill and Molly have a little boy, too; remember, young Timmy."

Perry continued. "Ned keeps Simmons on guard duty outside his office. Simmons thinks it a privilege, but it's so the brute can't hurt any children in town. All his men know and are happy for him to be kept under Ned's watchful eye."

Perry and the family celebrated Easter at the castle again.

With Mia now sixteen, her emotions were more pronounced. She had confided her admiration for Tim Styles and hoped Robbie would again bring his young brothers for Easter.

They did, and by the time they left, Tim had approached Perry to ask permission to walk out with Mia.

Perry gave conditional approval, as Mia had turned sixteen last birthday. Perry said that the standard rules applied, "Tim, you are never to be alone with her, and walking out did not mean more. No kissing or touching other than her on his arm. She still had to be presented, so she was not allowed any official attachment until after that had occurred." Perry found it hard to believe that his little girl was getting ready for marriage.

Tim would come each break from university, usually accompanied by Paul and Adam. The three young men would happily spend time with all the Castle children. All the visitors were young enough to kick a ball on the lawn. Jem, Davy, Colin, and Buck's two boys, Lindsay and Archie, made two teams. The girls stood as umpires. If it were raining, they would sit around the piano singing or find other inside activities. There were many other adventures to be found in an old building, and they all often went investigating the original part of the Castle, which was hundreds of years old.

Buck discovered a room in the magnificent old edifice that he could not wait to show Perry. It was one that was sure to excite all the young ones. Buck was convinced that the old castle would have had some sort of stage at some time. With Percy's permission, he went looking in the predominantly unused old castle. He wanted a location for the children to perform shows. He pushed on many doors until he found an ancient oak portal. The heavy wooden door creaked open and revealed a teacher's dream, a sunken theatrette. Many decades before, someone had built a stage. It had armchair seating under drop cloths for over twenty people and red velvet draw curtain. He dared not enter without Percy's permission but went directly to show him.

Both Perry and Percy could see his excitement, and they followed willingly. They discovered a full puppet theatre and even the half-high marionette stage in the back room. There were more boxes behind the backdrop, and all were in good condition. An old case still stored there contained over thirty puppets. This room became a favourite rainy day room for all the young people.

Perry's only condition was that unless they were practising for a show, or the weather was inclement, they had to spend as much time as possible outdoors. Tim, or TC as he was regularly called because he was often confused with his father, and Mia were never left alone, nor did they seek to flout Perry's rules. Tim had another year at university, then an internship in law, and then he had to find a job. Mia still needed to be presented at Court.

Meg had explained to them all that Mia must be unattached before that occurred. So, although the family knew of the relationship, it had to stay in the family only.

Louisa sighed; she wished she could grow older much faster then Paul could ask permission to court her properly. He whispered to her that he would wait. Her dimpled cheeks and glowing smile warmed his heart. She would outshine her older half-sister, but she was far more than just a very pretty face.

~

After Easter, Lachlan had notified Perry that he would be returning to London to petition the 'powers that be' for his pension. Lachlan still had to answer to John Bigge's accusations. Neither of which had made him happy. Lachlan had said he had found rooms in St James and would not trouble Perry for accommodation. Elizabeth and Lachie were still in Scotland.

Katy was sad that she would not get to see them. The family knew that Betsy Fry needed some assistance in the gaols and on the hulks, and they were soon involved heavily with that work. Perry also wished to scour the streets for more needy persons, so they moved back to London.

Lachlan had already appeared at three meetings before Perry arrived with his family. Perry voiced his concern about his health when they met. Lachlan hesitantly admitted, "I must say, I've felt much better. I'm hot and cold and feeling decidedly ill. I have put it down to nerves, Perry." Lachlan didn't let on to Elizabeth how ill he felt before he had left her. Perry arranged to see him in his rooms the next day. Lachlan looked worse but told Perry that he was feeling better. He expected to be in town for some four months at least.

~

By July, Betsy, Perry, and Katy had visited every prison and lock-up in London. Perry had also gone with Joseph Gurney to most of the hulks anchored in the bay down at Portsmouth. They did everything they could to assist the plight of the prisoners. The two men also willingly told every one of the convicts about their faith. Perry had some Bibles with him and handed them out to at least one per vessel or prison cell. Few could read, and those who could had learned at a Sunday School. All were keen to receive the small books.

Perry managed to catch Lachlan in early June. Both had been out of town and busy most days. When Perry finally caught up with Lachlan, Perry called a physician immediately. Lachlan was nearly unable to stand and was in great pain. Not only did he call a doctor, but he also sent urgent word to Elizabeth in Scotland. Perry sent money to cover a return trip and asked her not to delay her passage.

Elizabeth arrived as soon as she possibly could and assisted in nursing Lachlan. His illness had now spread to his bowel, and he was also fighting a bladder infection. Things for Lachlan did not look good. Days passed, and his condition did not improve.

Lachie was sent to stay at Cheatham House with Davy. The boys had grown apart in the intervening two years. However, at eleven, the toy room still had enough distractions to let them enjoy their time together. Katy, Buck, and Nanny packed around him and tried to protect him from hurt. Sadly, everyone's ministrations were not enough.

Lachlan Macquarie died on July 1, 1824.

Elizabeth was absolutely shattered but rallied herself to make arrangements for his interment. She insisted that Lachlan's body was returned to Mull and buried on his beloved island.

Perry and Katy accompanied Elizabeth and Lachie on the return trip to Scotland. Buck and Lucy remained with the children. Lachlan was buried on the Estate at Gruline, on the Isle of Mull in Scotland in August 1824.

Before leaving for Scotland, Perry had written to Ralph and Eliza Darling in Sydney telling them about Lachlan's demise. Perry later heard that they had held a memorial service in Sydney soon after the news arrived.

In Scotland, Reverend David Bell of Fifeshire was of great support to Elizabeth, Lachie, and the extended family in the area. Lachlan had just completed their house, but the farm was still in great need of management. Money was tight, Perry did what he could, but Elizabeth was determined to carry on. It may take some years, but she wanted to have a special grave marker made and said she would erect something special one day.

~

On return from Scotland, Perry and Katy returned home. The children were already at the castle. They did not want to go to London but continued with Perry's new work on the estate. News of Queen Charlotte's death shocked everyone; sadly this also meant that the court presentations were now left to the Regent. With his reputation preceding him, none were in any hurry to introduce a beautiful girl to him and his court.

Perry voiced his concerns to Tim, and they agreed that as he had finished university, his year internship was due to end in 1825. Perry put plans for Mia to be presented at Court on hold for another year. Mia and Tim were in no hurry, so they made plans that 1826 to be her presentation year. They could announce their engagement very soon afterwards. Perry also arranged they would remove from London days after the presentation and return to a new estate that Perry had purchased. It was the small farm of fifty acres that Perry had grown up on. It was a tiny private valley, bounded by three friend's large estates. Mary and Donald were to the north; Robbie's best friend Jimmy was on the southern boundary; his father, Horace Westaweller, Viscount Pittford, had sold Perry the land. The third estate was Princhester Court, next to Jimmy. Sir Phillip Princhester had lived here with his wife, Jane, and young son John.

Lady Jane had almost gone into seclusion since Sir Phillip's death. Perry knew John must be about twenty now, if not a bit older.

Blackberry House became home for Perry and Katy. It was only a day away from London and close enough to return to town if Betsy or Joseph needed them. Percy had the castle in order, and for the time being, the family wanted to enjoy the last years of their children's childhood together. With no social responsibilities but close to family and friends, they set to enjoy their final year before the responsibilities of adulthood intervened. Tim was a regular visitor. Robbie was busy helping his father on their estate or was off continuing his search.

Lady Mari was still in her lovely thatched, grace and favour cottage on the edge of the Broome-Hall Estate. However, her maid Sarah had recently died, and Sarah's daughter had stepped into that role. She was content in the small house with just her maid and a gardener. Sir Timothy sent food down regularly and made sure she never required anything, but she now rarely had visitors. In the time since Perry had last called in, she seemed to have shrunk into a saddened state.

The family returned to the castle in Warwickshire for Christmas. All were to stay until they returned to London for the beginning of the season at Easter. After being presented at Court, debutantes were allowed to partake in all the exclusive social diversions of high society; attending parties, balls, horse races, and being eligible for marriage. With no Queen, court Presentations were now a small affair. The coveted item now was a voucher for the Almacks Ball. Sir Robert Peel had offered to secure them for her; Lady Castlereagh would supply them.

Once Katy had presented Mia, Tim could have two dances with her. Tim made sure he was seen in deep discussions with Perry as Mia danced with someone else; both pairs of eyes followed her around the dance floor. Mia's eyes would often seek out Tim's.

Soon after Mia's presentation, Perry announced their engagement. They had then all been able to retire from society. Soon after this festive occasion, a financial calamity hit England. Perry still hated the looks and sniggers the unfeeling and cruel aristocracy gave him. He would hate to know what society would do if they discovered Katy's convict status. Thankfully, Tim already knew her entire story; he didn't care.

His father, Sir Timothy, had been out to Sydney a few times for his diplomatic work. He would courier messages for the Governor and return with a diplomatic bag. Inheriting the Barony did not mean the trips around the seas had stopped. Sir Timothy had confided to Perry that he also visited Sam and Annie on his last trip. On his previous trip some years before he had needed to let Sam know that his brother Nigel was dead. Robbie stepped up and ran the estate with his mother, Lady Sophia. Mia and Tim married in a quiet family wedding as, during the financial crash, lavish weddings were not possible.

The charity work in London was also in strife. A financial crash had occurred and severely damaged the Fry family fortunes. Percy and Perry stepped up and helped where they could, but many prisoners missed the care ministry. They had responsibilities in the country and could not stay to do the work in town. Ann Dumaresq and her friends fundraised even harder and assisted more, but the visits suffered due to a lack of funds.

Chapter 22 Helpers and Losses

*J*n 1827 many businesses closed, and banks galore shut their doors. By the following year, sadly, Betsy Fry's husband's business was one of the banks affected. Fry's Bank closed its doors. Another of Betsy's brothers, John, gave her an allowance to continue her work, but sadly it could not save the family banking business. Her husband had to return to being a tea merchant. This venture was risky and meant time away from home. Betsy had little spare time with ten children to care for at home. However, she now called on her helpers more often.

Towards the end of 1828, Perry made a quick trip to London and met with Sir Robert Peel. Protected in Warwickshire, he heard the horrifying stories of financial collapse from Sir Robert. Rumours abounded of Jimmy's father, Sir Horace Pittford. He was now supposedly in gaol for embezzlement of government funds, and Amelia, his daughter, had been arrested for theft. However, no one could confirm either of these stories. Jimmy's mother had vanished, and all the staff had disappeared from Pittford Manor. Perry had visited on his return, but the front door was locked, and not a soul was in view. The front gate was hanging from one hinge. The grass was long, and the driveway was overgrown. Jimmy was not home, or if he was, he wasn't answering his door. Perry thought the state of the Manor certainly looked as though the rumour was true. It was abandoned.

Only one week later, Robbie planned a surprise birthday visit to Jimmy. However, he didn't stay long at Pittford Manor before heading to Blackberry House. This second visit was not his original plan, but things don't always go to plan. Robbie had brought a birthday picnic luncheon as a present for Jimmy. He and Robbie had done this often as boys to celebrate the auspicious day. They would often go fishing or on some adventure. This trip, Robbie had brought a hamper of gourmet foods with him. Hams, roast chicken, pâté, hard-boiled eggs, cucumber sandwiches and champagne to wash it down. All were Jimmy's favourite things. There would be a considerable amount left over, but that was part of the gift. They sat in the middle of the immaculate kitchen garden and ate their picnic. After enjoying their feast, Jimmy asked Robbie inside. Jimmy said the family were all away, so they would not be disturbed. Robbie had not seen a soul so far, but he had noticed the butler leaving as he arrived. He had recognised him and waved. Robbie had seen the front gardens were overgrown, but Jimmy explained that it would be restored when the staff returned.

Robbie knew that Jimmy's parents usually ran a girls' school in one wing of the ancient Manor House. It was one of the reasons he had not come more often. Lots of little squealing girls were not his 'thing'. They viewed the now empty schoolroom, and he saw it was somewhat dusty. Jimmy said it was holiday time; therefore, all of the staff were absent.

They arrived in the long gallery; and Robbie froze. His dream girl was on Jimmy's wall. Both men stood gazing at the beautiful girl's portrait. Jimmy said, "This was painted just before Milla's debut, Robbie; she had grown into a beautiful woman. We only went to one ball, her come-out ball, before we had to return home."

"It's Milla? That's your sister? Jimmy, you said *had*. What happened to her? Did she die?" Robbie's heart was in his mouth; that would make so much sense why he could not find her.

Jimmy wondered how to tell Robbie where she was. He was nearly choking with anxiety. Jimmy ended up blurting it all out. "Milla was arrested for theft last year and was transported to Sydney." Jimmy wiped away tears that now streamed down his face. "I did what I could, Rob, but I couldn't save her. I have written, but I have not heard back. I don't know where she is, other than she was sent to New South Wales." Jim reached out and stroked the beautiful face on the painting.

Feeling winded, Robbie felt as though Jim had kicked him. He knew he should stay and console his friend, but he needed to escape. Robbie made his excuses soon after and left; he couldn't leave fast enough. He was reeling at the revelations Jimmy had made. He needed to get to Katy as soon as he could. Rumour and stories had abounded; reports of embezzlement, of thefts and arrests, but he had not heard any names. Jimmy still had not mentioned his parents, but Robbie only really cared about Amelia. He needed to see Katy; he needed her advice. His mind was racing as he travelled the short distance to Katy.

Robbie arrived unannounced on the doorstep of Blackberry House and asked for Katy. He was shown into the sitting room and stood at the window, waiting for her.

Katy entered and saw Robbie's stance and knew something significant had happened. He was leaning on the windowsill with his head drooped. He stood and turned as she entered. Without waiting for Katy to ask, Robbie turned, "I found out who she is Katy." He almost collapsed in the armchair behind him. He looked haunted and distraught. He rubbed his hand over his face in anguish.

"You found your mystery lady? Where?" Katy sat in another chair nearby. All this time, she had prayed for this nameless lady and that Robbie would find her one day. He should be joyful.

Robbie nodded. "I needed to talk to you, for I believe that you are one of the few who will understand." Robbie proceeded to pour out his heart. "Katy, I went to Jimmy Westaweller's place and saw her portrait in the long gallery at his house. It is his sister, Amelia, or Milla as I called her as a child." He stopped and took a deep breath. He bit his lip and glanced at Katy. "Katy, she was sent as a convict to Australia. She was accused of theft by some Duke and was transported last year." His eyes misted. He wiped the unshed tears away angrily. "All this time, she was all but under my nose, and I kept refusing Jimmy's invitations to come and stay so that I could look for my mystery lady. Every blooming moment I was away, I could have been with her. I could have saved her." He jumped up and stalked around the room. "How stupid am I? It was at her come-out ball that we met. Of course, I knew her as a child, but as Milla, a nine-year-old girl, following us and covered in mud, so different to Amelia, with her hair up and looking so very beautiful, as a nineteen-year-old. It had been some ten years since I saw her, and she looked so vastly different that I did not recognise her, but now I think back and realise it was definitely her." He was raking his fingers through his hair and almost pulling out his dark wavy locks. They were now in disarray. His anxiety was evident. "Oh, Katy, her familiarity must be why she drew me." He let out a howl. "Oh, dear Lord, what am I to do? Katy, can I go out there? Can I marry her there? Can I get her reassigned to me? I would do anything to be with her. What am I to do?" He repeated with a catch in his voice. He spun around to face Katy. "I will wait for her because I love her."

Katy knew what he was feeling but from the other side of the irons. "Robbie, come and sit down; tell me everything; what did Jimmy tell you?"

Robbie's heart hurt. "He said he has not had a reply to his letter yet."

Katy continued. "Did he give any hint of her situation?"

He shook his head. "Only that she was shipped to Sydney in New South Wales."

Katy nodded, thinking for a while, then said, "Rob, offer to be a liaison for him, through me, if necessary, but somehow become involved. Even tell him your discovery, for he already knows you are looking for someone." Something suddenly occurred to her. "Robbie, Ned is there, and Jimmy knows the name he is using. We know that because Ned told us. Get Ned and Jimmy to contact each other. Perry will give him the address. We can't tell you, as we promised Ned we would keep it secret. But you know he's in New South Wales, just not what name he's using."

Robbie frowned. "Is he in a position to help?"

Katy grinned while nodding and said, "Yes, absolutely he is." She knew he would move heaven and earth to do what he could to help his friend Jimmy's little sister. She smiled at another thought, there was also Eliza Darling, but she would not mention that to Robbie. Katy would write immediately to Eliza; she would get Perry to tell Jimmy Ned's address and make him write immediately. Rob now knew Jimmy was hiding in an empty house.

Robbie was not permitted to write to Amelia as they had no relationship. However, he could write to Ned and give it to Katy to post. Katy took Robbie along to Perry's office and left him writing his letter to Ned.

~

Katy, Robbie, and Jimmy sent their letters, but many months passed before Jimmy received back news. His initial letter had taken some eighteen months to make its way into Amelia's hands. He had addressed it to Amelia Westaweller, but she was using the name of West, so it sat unclaimed until Ned went hunting for it. It was mid-1830 before any reply came.

For some reason, Jimmy had asked that Amelia and Ned send mail to Robbie. They thought it strange, but that was his business, so they didn't ask why. Maybe he just wanted the company. Jimmy planned to meet Robbie halfway to collect his letters.

When Robbie next met Katy, he had discovered that Amelia had been assigned soon after she arrived in Parramatta. Katy had told him about what that meant and what she had gone through herself. Amelia's letter said she was now living in the Hawkesbury River area. Jimmy had not wanted Robbie to read Amelia's letter, but he snatched her screed from him. Jimmy was dry retching as he read the graphic things his little sister had gone through. Amelia's letter laid her life bare. She revealed the horrors of her existence. They could see tear-stained and smudged ink on the page as she wrote. The filthy man who claimed her, had raped her frequently and she had conceived a child soon afterwards. She described this man in full and so descriptive were her words, they could almost smell him. Both men sobbed as they read her long letter. However, by the time she wrote her reply to Jimmy, this evil man was dead, and she was living with a lovely family. She told them that she now had a beautiful daughter named Esther. Ned had found her and was sending care packages. He had received Jimmy's letter. Hopefully, things would turn out well for her.

Almost monthly Jimmy rode to meet Robbie halfway. Robbie gave him Amelia's newsy letters. None were as horrible as the first one and now Amelia was to be transferred to Sydney.

Katy received a letter from Eliza Darling. Thanks to Ned, he had transferred Amelia into Eliza's keeping as a nanny. Eliza promised Katy to keep Amelia safe. Katy sent an urgent letter to both Jimmy and Robbie; both came as fast as they could. She outlined what Eliza had said. She also said that Amelia's daughter was adorable. Her name was Esther, but Amelia called her Essie.

~

With mail taking so long to go back and forward, the following letter brought news that Eliza and Ralph were coming home. Eliza was expecting another child and would probably give birth on board the ship.

That was interesting news enough, but Perry chuckled to find that they were travelling with the Earl of Meldon, his wife, son, and grandchildren. Perry read the letter twice before the information sank in; he roared with laughter. "Katy, that's Sam!" He chuckled as he read more. "I heard Sam's father died some time ago, and Major Tom and Robbie told me of the passing of Sam's brother, Nigel. Sam, Annie, and Danny are coming home with the children. Sam's title of Earl must have caused some ripples of discontent over there. Sam would hate that." He read on. "I'm not sure if Sam would have to kowtow to the Governor or vice versa. I doubt Ralph would allow that to continue if Sam tried it." Perry smiled; he had kept his word and never mentioned that he knew who Sam really was. With five months or so on-board Perry was sure that Ralph would find out everything if he didn't already know about his title, also about Sam's story and conviction without asking questions. Ralph had the uncanny knack of extracting confidences.

That night in the privacy of their bedroom, Perry said to Katy, "Sweetheart, we will have some visiting to do next year. I feel there is some mystery behind the Darling's hasty return, also that Sam needs to face Duke James." He trailed his fingers down her cheeks as he spoke. He loved looking at her beautiful face. She may now be greying and have some wrinkles, but her face grew more beautiful as she aged. Both had their minds on their friends and the anguish they now had to face on their return. He drew her into his arms, and they eventually settled down to rest, but Perry's mind returned to Sam.

Perry had not been in the area during the visit of Danny and his wife Vanessa in 1829, but through Sir Timothy, he had heard that they had met with Duke James and then had a clash with the minister who had accused Sam of theft. Danny had won that round. He thought then that the word would seep out about a possible blood relationship between the Duke and Danny, but he had heard nothing. He was also intrigued there was no mention of Danny bringing his wife on this trip. There was also no mention of Danny's wife in Eliza's letter. As Perry lay cuddling Katy, they wondered if Sam knew the state of his inherited estate. Sir Timothy told Perry that Charles Garney, Sam's cousin, had retired or fired most of the old staff and now administered the property in Sam's absence. His cousin used his own staff and had employed his manager's son to get Meldon Hall into some semblance of order. Perry remembered Charles from school too as they had been in the same year. Charles had been one of the few people who also knew of Sam's home life.

Perry smiled to himself when he thought of the vast estate Sam had now inherited. He hoped that Sam would come on board with the assistance programme inspired by Betsy Fry. There was so much they could do if he did. Sir Timothy had told Perry the size of Sam's estate was even more impressive than Cheatham Castle, and it was now in essence, void of a workforce.

However, it would almost be a blank slate.

~

Being firmly stuck in Warwickshire, the next news they heard, Sam and Annie were home; they had arrived with the Darlings. Like Lachlan, Ralph too was facing an enquiry. It was some months before the Whites could visit. Eliza had brought letters from Amelia and posted them in London. Robbie wrote to Katy and told her that Amelia was now with a new family, the Landons, from Eliza Darling's church in Sydney. From Sydney they were assisting with work at the Female Factory in Parramatta. Katy chuckled as this was just what she was doing when there, only she was living in Parramatta.

In mid-July 1833, they were finally able to visit Sam.

Although, Perry had written welcoming Sam home soon after they arrived. It took some weeks, but they received an invitation to come. Perry couldn't pack fast enough. On arrival at Meldon Hall, there were two people they didn't expect to see. One was Duke James and on his arm was their cousin, Lady Mari Broome-Hall. The octogenarians looked decidedly comfortable with each other too. Sam was no longer the convict emancipated builder but the tall upright Earl of Meldon.

Sam's welcome to his friends was warm and genuine. "Come in, and we shall untangle mysteries of our lives for you. T'is true, Perry, you will love this." The revelations that followed were remarkable.

Once in the privacy of the vast sitting room, Sam greeted Perry with a hug. The school friends now reunited; confidences followed. Perry met the Duke's eye, and Lord James, as he was now known, smiled, raised one eyebrow, and nodded.

The revelation of the parentage of both Sam and Annie was a shock for Katy. Perry, however, sat with a smile on his face. He had wondered about Annie. Lady Mari's wedding portrait had made him first think about a possible connection between them. Annie's father was still a mystery, though. That missing jigsaw bit fell into place when Lord James said that Danny and his son would be the rightful bloodline of the title as Earl of Meldon. Major Tom had been right all along. He had said, "Cuckoos in the nest and such." The previous Earl was Annie's biological father and Lady Mari her mother. Perry and Katy were both stunned.

Lady Mari said that she now lived with Sam and Annie with her maid, Betsy White, who was her half-sister. Duke Julian had abused her maid Sarah, and Betsy had been the result. Sarah had since died, and Betsy now looked after Lady Mari as her companion.

Perry sat watching Danny's face; his new wife Georgina sat next to him. The revelation that his first wife, Vanessa, had died soon after giving birth to their son and heir had been a shock to them both; that Danny had since remarried Robbie's sister was a bigger one.

Sam's incredulous home was only a few minutes away from Robbie's parents' residences, Broome-Hall Manor. While they were there, Perry took his family for a visit to the Manor, not that they needed to see Robbie, as his sister was now married to Danny, and he visited daily, but Katy wanted to see Robbie alone. Neither Sam nor Annie knew anything about Amelia. Soon they would have to know.

Robbie greeted them with a happy face. "Katy, another letter has arrived. She's alive and happy. I'm just back from meeting Jimmy. She's living with a wonderful family in Sydney, and she's well. Her time is nearly finished, and Ned has already started arranging her return. He has suggested that she come to Sam and Annie, what do you think? Ralph Darling left instructions that she is to get an Absolute Pardon so she can come home." He punched the air with glee. "Ned wrote to Jimmy too. Some women recently kidnapped her in the Female Factory, but even this has turned into a positive. It has opened more doors for her to assist more with this Factory place." Robbie was almost bouncing; his wait was nearly over. She would be coming back home. His face shone with happiness.

~

On the family's return to the Castle in Warwickshire, Lucy was the first to notice interest between two of the young ones and told Judith she had to get Davy out of her mind. He was above her station.

Katy now was watching Davy and Judith; she could see a relationship developing and was delighted. She had never agreed with separating people by class. She took Lucy aside and said, "Lucy, we are all God's people and if He sees fit to make us in His image, then who are we to separate them?" Katy could not be happier.

Sam wrote to Perry, informing him about some exciting news. Lord James and Lady Mari had married secretly and now were both living at Meldon Hall with Sam and Annie. Both wished to participate more in the rehabilitation of the new arrivals. Both were eighty-three, but they hid their ages well. Katy had wondered about a closer relationship when she saw them earlier that year.

More abandoned illegitimate peers' children arrived at Meldon Hall and Lady Mari, Lord James, Sam, and Annie incorporated them into their family and a new school started in the great north wing of the palace-like building. With their history, this was the project Sam had decided to focus on. These innocent children were adopted into Sam's family and treated the same as his own grandchildren, as they were all equal by birth.

With Perry as his inspiration, Sam also now employed nearly one hundred of the worst affected soldiers, sailors, and patients who were considered unemployable. He paid to retrain them and also educated them. Part of the work was that each participant must be willing to learn to read and to obey house rules. That included church attendance. Due to the previous Earl's penny-pinching ways, the Estate was flush with funds. Sam intended to use this in a way that would irritate his so-called father.

Soon after Sam had arrived, he had the long-awaited run-in with the minister who had accused him of theft. The man was sacked on the spot, and the Parish became vacant. Mary's half-brother, Justin, had been visiting another much younger half-brother at the theological college when Sam came looking for a new minister. Justin introduced them. Hugh wondered if he would ever get a placement with his background. Justin had just finished telling him to have faith.

Sam sat Hugh down and questioned him. Before he realised what was happening, Hugh Williams had poured out his entire life story to Sam. Sam employed him on the spot. Reverend Hugh Williams was young, vibrant, and faithful. Being the illegitimate son of an Earl himself, he had the most amazing rapport with the children at Meldon Hall. The scarred warriors and workmen were greeted with compassion but not pity. Sam and Hugh worked hand in glove and met the emotional needs of these people. One of the first things they had to establish was to work out what each worker *could* do rather than what they *couldn't* do.

~

In 1835, just one week after Jem and Cate's wedding, Lord Percival, 14th Duke of Cheatham, died. Life for Perry and Katy changed drastically. Meg was grief-stricken, as was Perry. For Katy, she had lost her foster father. They all went into deep mourning, shunning the world. Duke Percy's passing almost crushed the family. Perry went from being an Earl with little to do to a Duke with an immense estate to run. He had certainly been doing a lot for his father, but now the mantle of responsibility fell squarely on his shoulders.

Perry could no longer fight against the role now thrust upon him. As the 15th Duke of Cheatham, he had responsibilities, ones he had resisted since his birthday in 1798 when his father had inherited the title. On his father's death and his own succession as Duke, Jem would become the 13th Earl and the inherited responsibilities it entailed. He thought it interesting that Jem was also twenty-six and Cate was nineteen. Yet, both were prepared for the challenge ahead of them.

The night of the funeral, Perry was lying in bed with his arms behind his head. He couldn't sleep. Katy's even breathing was comforting. He was sixty-three and knew that his position as Duke should open more doors for them for their work. Sam had already asked for more staff for his property. Trying to do this from a distance was difficult. They knew they had a year of mourning before any appearance in London, but that didn't mean they could not go to Blackberry House for a few weeks, if not longer. Buck was now manager of the castle and had things running smoothly; his father, Daniel, although retired, was still on the estate for consultation. Jem was available, as was Davy. He was happy to leave the castle in their hands. The children all wished to stay at home, but Perry and Katy would take a break. They could do some private visits from Blackberry House, the first of which would be to Sam. With that thought, he settled down to sleep. He carefully drew his sleeping wife into his arms, and with her now cocooned against him, he closed his eyes.

~

Amelia had returned earlier that year and moved in with Sam and Annie as Robbie had hoped.

Of Jimmy, there was still no sign. He had come to welcome Amelia home, then vanished again. Robbie didn't press him for information.

John Princhester, next door, also seemed to be almost a recluse. Perry had met him a few times, mostly at church. When he visited his home, John, or Jack as he preferred to be called now, nearly always had his sleeves rolled up and was tinkering with something outside. Jack loved the farm work. There seemed to be few visitors, except tradesmen and deliveries. Princhester Court was his world.

Mary and Donald were travelling overseas as Colm had recently married and was settling into the Milesdowne Court with his new wife. Mary had wanted to see something of the world. Donald had been to Italy, and he wished to show her the beautiful country. Mary had rarely left the estate since her return from her first marriage, so she went willingly.

In October, Perry and Katy arrived for a short visit to Sam. They unloaded their luggage into their room. Sam informed them that they were to head directly to their daughter as Mia was expecting them for dinner. Within the hour, they departed for Tim and Mia's house in Billingshurst. Mia and Tim had married some years before in a quiet family service.

On arrival, Robbie was waiting for them. He was thrilled to tell them that he was hopefully about to announce his engagement to Amelia. He had proposed the day before and was awaiting her decision. He had finally revealed to Sam that he had met her at her debut ball. Amelia had remembered him and had thought about him often. She also did not know his name. Robbie was killing time before he had to head over to Sam's house for dinner with his parents. Her response was encouraging, but she would not commit to him until she heard from her parents. Robbie wondered what to do.

Katy and Perry had discussed this problem at length. Perry took Robbie outside, and they mulled over the situation. Eventually, Perry turned and looked Robbie in the eye. "Take her home to see Jimmy and challenge him" Perry then added, "Don't tell him you're coming; just go. I have been a few times, and Rob, the place is now very neglected. Lad, I am wondering if the financial crisis hit them."

Robbie was shocked. Why hadn't Jimmy said anything? He knew his father had been accused of embezzling; maybe that was the reason. Mayhap he was ashamed. Rob just nodded, too stunned for words.

While Perry was with Rob, Katy and Mia had a chance to chat privately. Mia was expecting another child. She had greeted her mother with a big hug, and the child kicked Katy as she did so. Katy chuckled and then looked her hard in the face. "Are you happy, darling girl? Really happy?"

Mia's reply was a nod and a giggle. "Mama, Timmy is wonderful. He's everything I dreamed I would find in a husband, as he's just like Papa."

Katy sighed with relief. "Good, because sometimes marriage does not quite meet one's expectations."

Mia sighed with delight. "My marriage is, Mama. Timmy is the best father too. Like Papa, he plays with the children and is what he terms 'hands-on' father."

Robbie left soon after their arrival.

Katy enjoyed every moment they had with them. The children were all well-behaved and charming. They stayed with Mia for dinner before returning to Sam's place with the promise of further visits while they were in the area.

On return to Meldon Hall after dinner, they found a celebration in progress. Lord James and Lady Mari were there too. Robbie and Amelia had announced their engagement about an hour earlier. It seemed like the entire household was in the enormous sitting room toasting the happy couple. Essie was to have a Papa, and she was delighted.

Robbie took Perry aside and explained that he had taken his advice. Sir Timothy and his wife Sophie, Amelia, and he were leaving the next day to see Jimmy. Depending on what they found, well, they would see exactly what they would find. He was determined that nothing would stop him from marrying Amelia. Hopefully, Jimmy would reveal everything to his sister.

~

Amelia and Robbie were married in November, just four weeks after their engagement. Perry and Katy were still with Sam, so they stayed for the wedding. Perry's suspicions were correct, the financial crash had hit hard, and Jimmy had locked himself away; he was at his wit's end. Their unexpected visit a few weeks before the wedding found him almost starving. Jim had returned with them and stayed until after the wedding.

Perry used the time they were away to talk to Sam and Lord James. Once he explained the work of placing unemployable men who simply had disfigurements, all the doors opened. Sam had already taken some, but his focus was on abandoned children who were illegitimate of peers. Sam had not understood the vast need of assisting such men.

The Darlings had come up from Brighton for the wedding. Sir Ralph sat in on their conversation. They had lived with Sam and Annie for nearly a year and knew of all the twisted relationships. Ralph also saw there was a hole in their project. There was a massive need to aide street women, unmarried mothers, and the like, they all needed assistance too.

Soon, Sam, Perry, and Sir Timothy had the system working brilliantly. Month by month more and more completed their training, and were given references, then sent to new positions around the country. However, Betsy Fry's group sent Sam more than a regular supply of sick and needy people. From a dribble, it turned into a flood. They now desperately needed somewhere for the permanently disfigured to live. Sam's place was now overcrowded, and he needed to concentrate on the new staff and rescues. There were too many who could not face the world. Four terribly scarred stable hands were the catalyst for that. They prayed that the Lord would provide such a venue. When Jimmy arrived before the wedding, Perry turned and looked at him. He was gaunt and stick thin.

Jimmy said, "Yes, I finally admit I need help." But it was said with a sulky attitude.

Sam was thankful for that, as, behind his back, Sam had already sent a team to Jimmy's place to get things started. A clean-up team were to mend the perimeter fencing and do the immediate repairs, and they had also been asked to have every form of accommodation prepared. Sam wanted a complete inventory done of the estate and would send supplies for repairs and food.

Jim had accepted with bad grace until one day; Amelia sorted him out. Soon wagon loads of workers were on the road to Jimmy's Pittford Manor. Thatchers, builders, carpenters, harvesters, gardeners, and every other sort of work that Jimmy had said needed attention. He had the raw materials on hand; he just needed the hands to do the work. These people were previously prostitutes, street workers, sailors, soldiers, and the downtrodden and outcast. Yet each now had specific skills and were prepared to work for their keep: cooks, cleaners, carpenters, builders, and farm hands. Sir Timothy and Perry supplied funds, and Sam supplied food.

After a short honeymoon, Robbie and Amelia were returning to live with Jimmy until he was back on his feet. All the workers were now pulling together. The threads between the various families pulled tighter. Soon all the households were working as a well-oiled machine.

Ann Dumaresq and Betsy Fry's friends sourced needy people from throughout England. Sam's palatial house became the initial venue for healing, sorting, assessing, and the first stage of training. From there, Jimmy got the able-bodied, scarred ones to work on his farm. Perry's Warwickshire Castle was a training and education venue for those who lived in the north.

It was now all hands on deck at Jimmy's Manor House. It took six months to get it back on its feet to the point that food was being produced. Financially it would take years to re-establish a functioning money-making farm. However, they didn't need it to make money yet. They just needed Pittford Manor to train staff and educate them too. It would eventually come good, but in the meantime, Jimmy was now throwing himself into the rehabilitation of both his property and his new people. One displaced man had been an Estate Manager. He took over that office and soon had the farmland in profit.

Word soon spread and soon trained staff were requested from the Domestic Bureau in London. All were sent with references and the assurance that positions would be found for them back on one of the other properties should their new job be untenable. Sam wrote excellent references for every one of them. Each with their new qualifications and skills listed. Education was the key. Perry and Sir Timothy did the same when required. Those sent to Jimmy's place were so appreciative. These were the poorest of the poor. The folk had all been living in the slums and streets in London and other towns. Jimmy supplied them with accommodation, food, and a lovely place to work in lieu of payment until the farm started being productive again. Jimmy then promised he would give them back pay. Considering the lives they had left behind, none complained.

Sam and Sir Timothy kept their ears open for ways to help. Through Perry, they heard of some almost free stock that was unsaleable. They had been walked from Wales and were nearly dead on their feet. Much to the horror of Jimmy, the stock was driven in through the front gates of Pittford Manor. He stood gasping at the decrepit animals. The cattle were the first to arrive. It was a mixed herd with a smattering of dairy cows amongst them; they were followed by sheep, horses, and a wagon with some penned goats and numerous cages of poultry. Amelia and Rob stood next to Jimmy, watching the living skeletal procession pass them. Perry arrived from next door to watch Tim's reaction.

Sam and Sir Timothy had ridden in before the cattle and waited next to them. Perry had heard of their imminent arrival and ridden over to take a look. Jimmy started to argue with Sam when Sam turned to him and explained the deal.

"Sick animals need care, the staff need to learn." Sam would retain ownership of the majority of the stock, but any of the ones born to them would become Jimmy's. Jimmy was about to object again when Amelia turned on him and told him to bite his tongue. He did.

Sam chuckled at her comment and then replied, "Jim, these beasts are the most decrepit, sorry bunch of air-suckers I have ever seen." It was a term he had picked up from his convict days in Parramatta's outskirts.

Perry chuckled. Sir Timothy had never heard the term before, but he immediately knew what it meant. The phrase had Sir Timothy in stitches. It was very apt. The stock was skin and bone, and they were hardly worth the air they breathed. They were all surprised that so many had survived the walk from the Smithfield Markets in London. Sam and Sir Timothy had left soon afterwards. Perry had wished they could stay, but knew he had to return to his mother, who was still in Warwickshire with Jem and Cate. The new project had begun, and Perry had his own work to do.

With Jimmy's care and nutritious grasses, the stock grew fat and were soon healthy and breeding. Their experiment was working.

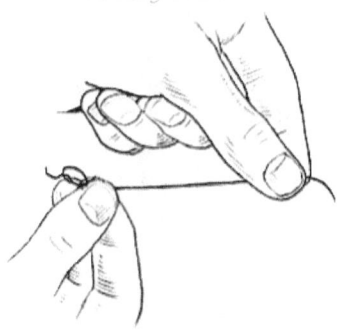

Chapter 23 Drawing Threads Together

*S*oon after they returned to the castle, things changed.

His Majesty the King died, and eighteen-year-old Princess Victoria took the throne. When the teenage girl was informed that she was to be the next monarch, her words were reportedly, "I will be good." These words resounded throughout the Empire. Soon she was leading her country from strength to strength. Many wondered how she would cope. She did far more than just manage; she thrived.

~

After some two years on the throne Queen Victoria announced her engagement to Prince Albert. Court procedures altered drastically. No longer were lax morals allowed, and rules were tightened.

Meg, Perry, and Katy wholeheartedly agreed with these changes.

~

Although many communications went back and forwards between all the houses, it wasn't until 1843 that Perry and Katy were able to take an extended break again. The word that Ned had returned home brought them down to Kent. He had arrived with his new wife in August of the year before. Christina had delivered their twins shortly after arrival. Ned now had a son and heir and a daughter, and Perry could not wait to see him again. Stuck in Warwickshire, no one had told Perry that Ned's father, Charles, Duke of Gracemere, had died some years before. It must have occurred soon after Louisa and Paul's wedding. Perry also had not heard that Ned's brother, David, had taken over the Dukedom or that he had been killed in a riding accident only two years later. Perry knew that David had no children. So, Ned became the 10th Duke of Gracemere.

Some years before, Perry had the misfortune to again meet David's wife, Elouise, in London on his required visits to the House of Lords. Some of the functions Perry and Katy attended, like the opening of Parliament, David had attended too. Perry had not had much of a chance to catch up with him. However, Elouise wheedled her way into most social functions. She was universally disliked and totally mistrusted.

Katy avoided her as much as possible, as did most of her friends. Elouise's claim to fame was that she held her age well and was still beautiful, though in an evil sort of way. She certainly did not look forty. She could easily pass for ten years younger. After that one meeting, Katy said, "Perry, when I see her, I wish to wash my hands and face after speaking to her." Katy shivered as she spoke. "I feel dirty, tainted. I've not known anyone like this before."

Perry was not one to say nasty things about people, but in this, he heartily agreed. "She is making David's life hell, you know." He had met him recently at Parliament. He was one of the few whom Perry sat with for a session. Perry had asked how she was, and David had shrugged. Perry had always really liked the family, so he would go out of his way to talk with David when they were at the same function.

David had seen the error of his ways; he had merely said to Perry, "I should have listened to Ned you know." He did not elaborate, he had no need to. He looked haunted. David knew he had ruined his own life by not listening to his brother. Up until Elouise intervened, they had always been close. When Ned had tried to warn him, David told him to leave them alone, preferably somewhere else other than Gracemere. Ned had, he had enlisted and fled to Sydney. David died in a riding accident less than twelve months after the conversation with Perry in London. Perry also did not hear that Elouise had returned to Gracemere Castle in Kent for her year of mourning, but she stayed for two years.

Two years later, when news arrived that Ned was returning with his wife, Elouise fled. No one knew where she had gone to, nor did they ask. All were just glad she had vanished. Perry heard she had appeared in London and then disappeared again. Again, no one knew where she had gone.

Dowager Duchess Susanna lived in the Castle Dower House with Frederick Jamison, the old castle butler; her secretary, Colin Fraser; and her maid. They were the few staff she had taken with her beside some outdoor gardeners and a cook. She had employed new footmen and maids.

Jimmy told Perry that Gracemere Castle was another blank slate for staff requirements. Paul and Louisa, who had married quietly just after Jem and Cate, set to work to keep the place in order as best they could. They had been in Europe when David died. Douglas had turned to his mother and Colin Fraser to keep things running until they returned. Paul then managed to hire some temporary staff to get the grounds immaculate once more, but he left the inside well alone. As to planting crops or starting breeding programmes, he had no idea what to do. Once Elouise had gone, Frederick Jamison stepped back into his role as butler at the castle. He oversaw the hiring of some of Sam's trainees. By the time Ned arrived, there were only some twenty staff in a castle that could house over two-hundred employees. Therefore, Ned was brought into the unique trainee programme soon after his arrival.

~

When Perry turned seventy, he announced to everyone that he and Katy were going to semi-retire. Jem was to take over the running of Cheatham Castle, and Perry would be on call to assist. He and Jem had discussed this at length, and Jem was delighted. At thirty-five, he would take the reins. Jem's son, Peregrin Colin Jeramy, was seven and known to all as Pippin. He had his father's dark locks and honey-gold eyes. He was the first potential Duke that had been born on the estate for four generations. Pippin was already showing compassion and great promise.

Perry and Katy's move back into Blackberry House was a huge relief to them both. Perry still hated the limelight; this way, he could oversee Jem's work on the estate from a distance but free himself up to help with their pet project of assisting the unwanted, as he had begun to call them. Most of this work now occurred in West Sussex or Kent, so Warwickshire was too far away. Cheatham Castle still was a training school, but Jem had that in hand. Mia and Tim were close to Sir Timothy and Lady Mari. Paul and Louisa lived on the Gracemere Estate in one of the grace and favour cottages. Louisa and Davy both had quiet weddings not long after Percy died.

Decades before, Judith had been allowed to marry Davy, much to the surprise of Buck and Lucy. They married in the chapel in Cheatham Castle, and a month later, Louisa and Paul married in the chapel at Gracemere. Most of the extended families knew that both couples had been courting for years. Because Percy had recently died, they only made it immediate family. Perry only placed the announcement of the marriages in the paper after the ceremonies had taken place.

Buck was now working for Jem as the Estate Manager and Davy was learning the role. Davy was now working with his older brother as co-Estate Manager and one day would take over. Buck had expanded the role so there was enough work to keep them both fully occupied. Jem and Davy had added to the volume of children currently attending the estate school. Soon, nine more of the castle children would attend classes with more following as they grew. Colin was now fully qualified as a doctor and had started a clinic in one of the unused grace and favour cottages. He had not yet found his marital match, but he was in no hurry.

Years before, Louisa and Paul had married in the chapel at Gracemere Castle. Duke Charles was ill but well enough to be pushed into the service in a wheeled chair. All the immediate family but Ned had been there. However, Ned had sent his warm regards and congratulations in a private letter to Perry. Perry had told him of the potential union sometime before; Ned was delighted. Now years later, Paul and Lou had three small sons. Ned's youngest brother, Douglas, had now married one of the senior partner's daughters, and they also had three boys.

Jimmy Westaweller's farm was now viable and self-sustaining. The one property that remained an enigma was Princhester Court. Although the grounds were always immaculate, the front gates at the Princhester estate remained chained and padlocked. Jack, however, had vanished. No one knew where he was; rumours abounded that he had married, although there was no sign of either he or his wife. Someone was living at Princhester Court as food was still delivered. The doctor mentioned that he had been summonsed once or twice but refused to elaborate. All he said was that it was on Jack's instructions. The gatekeeper refused entrance to all visitors but the doctor; he made no exceptions. That was a mystery for another day.

Perry and Katy still made visits to London. Other philanthropy groups had come on board with assistance. The pressure of responsibility had shifted. Perry's primary purpose was now fundraising. He had only to appear in public, and the compassion he garnered brought the pounds and guineas flowing in. He thought how ironic his wounds inspired people's compassion and understanding just because he was a Duke. Yet without his voice speaking for the unloved, they willingly walked or drove past similarly wounded people on the streets with barely a second glance.

In the past thirty years, London changed. Even more since Her Majesty, Queen Victoria had become monarch. Soon after ascending the throne, the young Queen demanded an audience with Perry and Katy when she heard what they were doing. Surprisingly she threw her support behind the reforms but could not say much publicly. However, she gave him her blessing to continue. She offered him all sorts of accolades, including the Order of the Garter. Perry refused them but thanked her politely. He was not doing this for earthly glory, and he wanted no recognition. He suggested that mayhap she could support Elizabeth Fry's work publicly. Her Majesty smiled at his suggestions but refrained from replying. However, she handed him a rolled document and told him to read it. Perry was stunned to find that despite his protests and refusal, he was bestowed the title Marquess of Oxhill. Her Majesty's letter explained that in days of old, the Title of Marquess was trusted to defend and fortify against potentially hostile neighbours.

With a glint in her eyes, the young Queen said, "We believe your son is now entitled to use this new title."

Jem was to start using the new title immediately, and Pippin would become the Earl. Perry and Katy still tried to keep a low profile unless it was to fundraise or talk at a function for Betsy Fry's group. Betsy's *Society of Friends* now numbered some twenty-thousand members. Many wanted reform for the prisoners, but few knew how to go about it. The task was daunting. Betsy had enlisted an army of peers and politicians to follow her cause, but as the finances dried up due to the economic crisis, so did the effectiveness of the work. Perry's conversation with the young Queen stayed with him. He would appeal to her for assistance again, even if it were behind the scenes. He realised that she might not be able to do anything publicly, but a word here or there would see the work continue.

On one trip south, Meg moved to Blackberry House with them. She had been with them for over eighteen months before becoming unsettled. She said she wanted to move back to the castle. They packed her up and took her back. However, the relocation did not work out as she expected. Meg's memories of the building had obviously romanticised the castle in her mind. She was cold and, therefore, miserable. She was there for less than six months before she wished to move back with Perry and Katy into her suite at Blackberry House. On her return, Meg realised that what she missed was Percy. His presence had warmed any room. They all missed him. At nearly ninety-one, Meg was entitled to change her mind as often as she wished. They were all delighted to still have her with them. She settled down and celebrated her ninety-second birthday surrounded by family.

Weeks after her return, Meg had a fall and broke her ankle. It meant that someone had to be always with her. It was usually Katy, but she didn't mind. It was wonderful to make time to sit and chat during a busy day. Meg could still tat or knit, and as she did, she retold many stories of the boys' childhood. They laughed about many of the boys' adventures. Then Meg told Katy about her feelings of loss when Perry left after the fire.

Their conversation gave Katy a totally different perspective on Perry's burns. One she could not have understood before she became a mother herself. Katy had not thought of that side of the injury. She sat holding Meg's hand, then felt it go limp. Thinking she had fallen asleep, she left her and went to order a tea tray. It was getting cool outside, and Katy needed help moving Meg indoors. She returned less than ten minutes later and saw that Meg was still in the same position. She bent and felt her hand, and noticed that it was warm, so she was all right, just asleep. She sat beside her and waited for the staff to arrive to assisted Meg into her room. Katy was enjoying the quiet of the afternoon when Meg started making strange noises. Her arm dropped to her side, and her head fell sideways. Katy was on her feet in a moment and calling for help. Meg's gaze fixed on Katy's face. She had a panicked look, but she could make no sound.

Perry came and was about to pick her up when Katy stopped him, knowing he was no longer as young and fit as he once had been. Instead, a young footman picked Meg up and gently carried her into her room. Perry followed, questioning Katy as they walked.

Katy could only think of one explanation. "I think she has had an apoplectic attack, Perry. We were sitting and talking, then she fell asleep. I left her to collect something, and when I returned, she was as I left her. Then she made a funny noise, and her hand dropped." Katy saw the grief etched on his face.

Meg lingered for nearly six weeks. When she died on October 12th, Perry, Katy, and every single grandchild and great-grandchild were nearby. Perry and Katy were holding her hands when she fell asleep for the last time. Perry watched his mother fade away. Although it was expected, her passing was still a significant loss. Towards the end, Meg died peacefully. Perry watched her in her slumber and waited for another breath, Meg took a breath and exhaled, but the following one did not come; she had breathed her last.

Doctor Gerry Winslow-Smyth, another of Ned's friends, attended the sick room for the week before and was there as she died. He had arrived a few days before from Gracemere Castle, where he lived with his family. He ran a Medical Clinic from the back of Gracemere Castle. The clinic was in the process of moving to one of the houses, so Gerry took a few days to stay close to Perry for Meg's expected passing. Gerry's profession had inspired one of Louisa and Paul's sons to train as a doctor rather than a Lawyer in the family firm. The young man had done his first year at medical school already. Perry was still surprised at how fast those years had passed. His grandson and Gerry alternated shifts. He was permitted to leave college and attend to his grandmother's bedside. However, when she died, it was Gerry who pronounced her death. A strange peace descended on the house, and although each were sad at her end; they knew the Lord had called her to a better place. They had spoken of Heaven often in the years since Percy had died. They each believed in the everlasting life that Jesus promised. None doubted that, but the passing was nonetheless sad, and her absence hurt.

Perry turned and gathered Katy into his arms, both weeping over their loss. The children and grandchildren had each said their goodbyes. They promised Meg she would be buried in the family crypt next to her beloved Percy. Knowing her demise was imminent, everything was in readiness to transport her body to Warwickshire. However, Reverend Hector James, Ned's old minister, held a full service in Gracemere Castle Chapel while all the family were together. Having done the service already, meant Meg would be laid beside her beloved Percy as soon as the carriage arrived in Warwickshire. Louisa and Paul were going to travel home with Perry and Katy.

Early the following day, just before they left, a message arrived from Betsy Fry's brother, Joseph Gurney. Betsy had died at precisely the same time as Meg. Both extraordinary ladies were now gone.

Perry sent an apology note back to both Joseph's, explaining their own loss and why they could not come to her funeral.

It was a great sadness for both families.

Betsy Fry had also had a stroke but passed quickly. She had been only sixty-five. The work she started would outlive her. Betsy would not be overlooked in death as she had been in life. Her passing meant more would now pick up the baton she held out to them and keep the work forging ahead.

Chapter 24 Perspective

*P*erry drew Katy aside after the short committal service in Warwickshire.

The family crypt had always depressed him. Inside this building lay all their loved ones; Katy's parents, Perry's parents, and of course, Jeramy, in this cold, dark hole.

When they arrived, Buck opened the crypt portal. As the door swung open, the dusty smell of death floated in the air. They saw motes of decomposition floating in a shaft of sunlight that lit the doorway. Everyone hung back until the air cleared. Perry clung tightly to Katy's hand, almost crushing it. Their children were all now grown, and some were grandparents themselves. All were as silent as the crypt occupants.

The minister's resonant voice prayed the final prayers over Meg's body. Six chosen pallbearers, of which Perry and Jem were two, carried Meg in to join her beloved husband for their eternal rest.

Buck once again swung the old oak door shut.

The clunk of the bolt going home hit Perry hard. He finally wept.

Once the short service was over, the family, except for Perry and Katy, returned to the house with the minister.

Perry drew Katy away from the departing group. They walked towards the folly on the top of the hill overlooking the castle. The joyous voices of their great-grandchildren sounded over the valley. Perry just wanted to be alone with his beloved Katy.

As they approached the exquisite Grecian folly, built by some long-ago ancestor, Katy asked, "I don't suppose you remember us playing here when I was a child Perry, but I fell over, and you helped me up, then carried me home as I had hurt my ankle."

Perry smiled; he remembered that day well. "I remember; I realised how pretty you were that day, but you were only twelve. Father had come to visit, and we found you here with your family. Duke Julian was bedridden, but he had summonsed us all for some reason. We knew nothing about his history back then. He took another two years or so to die."

Katy shivered. "Thankfully, none of us knew." She paused for a short time, then looked up at him lovingly. "Perry, that was the day I fell in love with you. I clung to you as you carried me, and I wished you would take the long way back." Katy walked into his arms and leaned her cheek against his shoulder.

Perry stood holding her, gently stroking her back. He chuckled. "I can't even lift you now, darling one. Getting old is not good; my back hurts, as do my feet, and even my poor knobbly old hands can't grasp things as they used to." He flexed his fingers. "My eyes are tired too. They focus enough to see your sweet and cherished face, my beloved." He quickly kissed her before adding, "But, my love, that doesn't mean my desire has died."

They moved through the pillars and sat on the marble bench seat overlooking the valley; they could see the house in the distance and their gig tied up to the crypt hitching rail. At least they didn't have to walk the three miles home.

Perry settled himself and drew her under his arm. "There are days like this when I need you near me. When you left me and fled to Sydney, Katy, I felt dead inside, even worse than I do today. I felt crushed by your rejection of me. I may be a Duke now, but I am no more than an insecure little boy at heart, my dear."

Katy's guilt spread through her again. "Perry, I've said I'm sorry so often."

Perry took a deep breath. "No, no, sweetheart, that's not what I mean. I look back on it now and see that God has used us because of what happened. Father pointed that out to us soon after our return and many times since. My darling, I would have been happy to sit at home with you and our children and live with Mary. Living in seclusion in Aylesford looking after her farm for her, but that is not what God wanted us to do, my sweet." His free hand stroked hers with his thumb. "Katy, you know there was absolutely nothing between Mary and me, and there never was, but because you walked in on that hug, it triggered an entirely different life for us all."

Katy looked up at him and smiled. She had loved their life in Australia. It was warm and much more friendly than society here in England. She, too, acknowledged that they learnt a lot in a short time. They were both more like the convicts in their attitude than the stuffy peers with whom they now had to mingle.

Perry was gazing at the beautiful vista in front of them. He continued, "I had begun to think about my all too comfortable life, even then. I acknowledge that it was stagnant. I was happy for you and Mary to see my wounds, also Justin and the staff. But that was as far as my comfort zone expanded. Even when Mother and Father came to stay, I just wanted to hide. Then you left me. Katy, I was ready to tear the world apart to find you. It was to young Ned that I poured out my heart. To find him in Parramatta was again God's blessing. He was only a boy of sixteen when I stayed with them back then, but he was… well, Katy, he listened with compassion. There is something about that man that is, well, he's just godly. To know him is to want to confide in him. I'm so glad he's now found his angel of a wife, just like I did."

Katy nodded against his shoulder but remained quiet. She also loved Christina; and their blonde-headed children were adorable. They had just had a third child, a second son, William, to be known as Liam.

Perry gently lay his unscarred cheek on her silky hair. "Katy, our time in Parramatta made me grow in confidence. I suppose you can say it was a kick up the *derriere* I needed. Finally, I felt like my scars did not define me. Yes, I know you had told me that often, but seeing how others bore such pain and agony, I suddenly realised that my scars were truly only skin deep. Over there, I was like so many others that I no longer stood out. I saw the scarred backs from floggings, the maimed, lame, and emotionally wounded. The scourges had shredded the backs of far too many of the poor wretches. I finally saw past my scars; my vanity was such that I thought a handsome face defined me. You know what I looked like before these, my love. However, I saw that I could reach out to others because of my own wounds. I could relate to the traumatised convicts as no others could. I blended in, and they saw themselves reflected in me." He drew a deep breath and sat thinking for a while. "Finally, I was handing things over to God; I'd never done that before." He lifted Katy's chin and kissed her lightly before continuing. "I had clung to hurt and anger at God. I could see no point in anything. Then you came into my life."

Katy heard a break in his voice. His memories of those lonely years still hurt. "My darling, the work we did with Lachlan and Elizabeth has changed many lives, including mine. Yes, I know transportation to Sydney has now ceased, but our work made a vast difference for those who went. I was informed that over twenty-four thousand women were transported to various Factories and gaols in the colony. I believe over five thousand went through the Female Factory that Lachlan built in Parramatta. Goodness knows how many men were sent. Then through our help before Ralph and Eliza went, we know they continued that work. We told them Lachlan's plans that he had always wanted to see completed. Do you know that Sir Thomas Brisbane commented that Lachlan would not recognise the place now, should he ever have returned? I felt like saying to him, and there is no way Sir Thomas would recognise the town if he had seen what Lachlan had found on his arrival. Lachlan was just starting the building program when we arrived. Do you remember the horrific state of most of the buildings? He had replaced many already by the time we arrived."

She shook her head. "I didn't see much, Perry; I was in shock when we were unloaded. It was so hot, and Davy was tiny. I remember doing everything I could to drink enough, but I was worried he would die as I had so little milk for him. I only have vague recollections of what Sydney looked like, but what I saw didn't inspire me with confidence. It smelt and I remembered lots of shacks and tents."

Perry looked down at her with sadness in his eyes. "I forgot that, sweetheart." He gave her a quick peck on her lips again. "Amelia told me she continued what we were doing once she was assigned to the Darlings. Do you know that your friend Sarah's daughter, Hetty Walker, took more of the abused girls after we left? Some thirty went through her care refuge. Janey has kept in contact with her. Anyway, after the Darlings left, Amelia went to Sadie Landon, and Phoebe King, the minister's wife, and they set out to find more ways to assist the female convicts. The Benevolent Society took over much of the works."

Perry and Katy had spent days with Amelia and Robbie since she returned. Her story was both gruelling and amazing.

Katy and Annie had taken Amelia aside and let her open up to everything that had happened in Australia. They were the only two who could fully understand the conviction process, even though they were all innocent of true crime. Then there was the trauma of assignment. The total vulnerability and lack of control one had over one's life. The three women each knew of the abuse suffered by so many other female convicts. Amelia had been the only one of the three to experience such degradation.

Amelia, also told them both of the unsavoury warders who continued the rapes in the Female Factory; the poor women were demoted to third grade, and put on bread and water rations for a week or more if they complained, or if they even reported the abuse. Neither Annie nor Katy had experienced such violation that Amelia had gone through at the hands of the man who had claimed her. They wept with her as she recounted the multiple violent attacks and brutality in her life with the man she later found had not just claimed her but had also married her. She could never have escaped. It had been a blessing when he had been killed after only a few months. It was only that Essie was legitimate that Amelia could hold her head up in society. Amelia would never tell her daughter about her father. When the time came for her to enter society, Essie would have a clear conscience. Only Ned and Amelia knew the horrific nature of Cyrus Black.

Amelia would always have scars on her heart. Robbie knew everything and walked with her through healing tears and hurts. She had no confessions she had to make to him and no explanations, for he knew it all. Katy knew there would be many talks between the three of them in the coming years. Duchess Christina joined in on some discussion about her life in the colony. Though, as she had never been a convict, for some time, they kept their sordid details from her until she confided in them that her first husband had been a deep drinker and was often violent. She had suffered abuse at his hands. She had never been able to tell anyone until now. Now she could voice her anguish and found support. Ned didn't even know as she could not bear to tell him. Katy had promised she would not say anything, even to Perry. She never had, although she wondered if he already knew.

Now Perry sat silently; he was deep in thought. After a few pensive minutes, Perry spoke. "When we came back, I fully intended heading directly here, to Cheatham Castle, and I wished to bury myself again. But somehow, we became drawn into Betsy Fry's work, and it just seemed like it was an extension of what we were doing in Parramatta. We stayed in London and threw ourselves into it. I felt like we had found our purpose. Then the work and needs just kept growing." He fell to thinking again. They saw that in the distance, the family had reached the castle and they had all had gone inside

He released a deep sigh. "When we met Sir Robert Peel, I still don't know what I was thinking when I said *yes* to speaking in Parliament. But I did it, Katy, I knew you were listening and praying for me too, but my heart was in my mouth. I felt as though I was stripped bare. I did it, not just for you, but for us and the work God had given us to do. He gave me both the strength and the words."

Katy was sitting on his unburned side. She turned, lifted both hands and cupped his cheeks; she looked him in the face. "Perry, I have no physical scars, and my emotional ones are mostly from my own lack of faith. But at night, I dream of what others went through, and somehow, I escaped it all. No, I didn't escape; God protected me from it all. Amelia's experience was absolutely horrific. I'll never understand why God did not spare Amelia and her friends, but I was kept shielded. Her strength is astounding. God did surround her with some of the most amazing people after her first husband died. But why did God shield me and not her? The soldiers abused my closest friends on board, but they spared me. It was as though I was invisible to them. I had a few inconvenient days in the gaol in Parramatta, but nothing lasting occurred. Then Mr Albert took me to work in a nice clean office, and I was given work I loved. Perry, you never knew Mrs Albert, but she was a real tartar; yet she never hurt me. I only ever got a tongue-lashing. She died at the beginning of the week you came; and life at the inn was peaceful for that last week. Then you came and took me away." She was still gazing at his face. "Perry, I love you! I always have and I always will. I didn't trust you for a time, but I trusted God. He turned my lack of faith in you and Mary into so much good for others." She moved and wrapped her arms around him before saying, "So many things just went skewed, and I read things the wrong way. However, I felt protected from the moment I left home on that fateful day. I knew I was where I was supposed to be at each stage, but I had no idea why. Although my heart was crushed, my spirit grew strong. I had already drawn three other girls to me. Then Betsy Fry walked into the cell; I tried hard to hide from her. I did not know it was her very first visit there, but how important that visit was to become to so many others. When she returned, the warders gave us some private time together, and she heard first-hand the needs of the women. The need for the separation of the genders of prisoners, the lack of food and facilities and those conditions were something she would not have known about for years had it not been for me being in there. God used me, Perry. He used my unbelief in you to help others." She settled back under his arm, but now he wrapped both arms around her, holding her close.

There were times Perry just needed to hold Katy tightly; this situation was one of them. Silent tears slid unchecked down his cheeks. Katy felt a few as they dripped onto her head. They sat in the beautiful columned folly, relishing the solitude; they enjoyed the togetherness that a long and loving marriage brought. They each had known the other side of life, the cruelty, the horrors that one man could do to another, the hurtful comments, and the ugly side of life. It gave them a unique perspective on their existence. They had each other, and their children followed in the path set for them.

Neither Perry nor Katy had protected their children from the seamier side of convict life. Many discussions had occurred explaining the consequences of bad decisions that others had made. Their children saw for themselves how a little assistance could change the lives of the most woe-begotten humans, to live again with dignity and purpose. Their best friends, and even spouses were servants' children. Buck was still amazed that Perry treated him as a brother. Davy had married Judith, and she was now The Honourable Mrs Judith White. Perry had said to Buck that they were brothers in Christ, and if it was good enough for God that they were friends, then society be blown. They were friends, good friends. Judith and her family were welcomed as social equals. Buck and Lucy were introduced as friends and part of the extended family. A foundling and a tutor's daughter were now part of the nobility with a title in their family. Lucy was called 'Aunt' by all the children in the castle; Buck was just known as Buck to all but Lucy.

Perry and Katy wanted their children to know that their titled positions could make a difference in others' lives. They were to put their faith into action as Betsy Fry had.

Betsy had faced many challenges, not because of her gender, which was the least of her problems, but because she was a Quaker. She was segregated from society because of her faith. She and her family were almost shunned from acceptance because of her beliefs. Yet it was she who had brought about change for the downtrodden while others sat and let the atrocities pass unnoticed.

When Betsy had first spoken with Justin after a charity meeting, he suggested visiting the prisons. Due to his own illegitimacy, he understood the ostracism of society. He had introduced Katy to Betsy soon after his first visit to her. The aide had now gone full circle.

Perry and Katy taught their children that they were all to be judged by what they did with their faith. They explained that if they followed what Jesus taught, they couldn't go wrong. Yet, it wasn't through the works, but through how they treated their fellow humans. Sadly, greed often got in the way.

Katy had been one of the oppressed for a short time, as had Annie, Sam, and Amelia. They were all now pulling together. Ned, as the youngest of the group, had taken up the baton and would continue the work when they had gone.

When Ned returned from Australia, he discovered that Charles Lockley was his legitimate third cousin. Unknown to them all, Charles included; he was the 3rd Earl of Coxheath. The two friends shared a Great-Grandfather in the 6th Duke of Gracemere.

This knowledge brought him into the story too. Charles and Sal continued the prison work in Parramatta, living in Ned and Christina's old cottages where Perry and Katy had first lived. Charles was still the keeper of Government Stores, but Charlie now lived at the Jolly Sailor Inn with his wife, Bill and Molly's daughter Gracie, beside him.

Ned's last letter from Charles contained news that the new Governor had asked Charles to become the Viceroy for the Parramatta and Western District area. He had accepted, and he had handed the Inn to Charlie and he and Sal had moved into Christina's cottage.

It was another circle completed and another link made. Christina's cottage was the western cottage where Perry and Katy had first lived.

Perry found it hard to believe that Charles and Sal's two little boys were now in their twenties and both were married. Their eldest son, Charlie, had married Gracie Miller in 1841. Eddie married Jenna Turner a year later.

Jenna's papa, Jack, had been Charles's friend who received an early Ticket of Leave on the day Charles met Sal. He had moved to Camden and later to Emu Plains. It had been their family who had rescued Amelia on the day Cyrus had died. Jack Turner had married Martha, one of the girls sent to Hetty Walker's place on the Hawkesbury River. Another circle of the link was completed.

Jenna, Eddie's wife, had presented him with twins only weeks before Ned and Christina's twins were born. Only the good Lord knew where their lives would lead them. Perry hoped they would visit England one day. Hopefully, he would still be alive when that occurred, but he doubted it.

He sighed, and Perry's thoughts returned to the present. They had just buried his mother, who had been his rock. A smile slowly crept onto his lips. Yes, his mother *had* been his mainstay when he was young; but Katy was his strength. She had been so for a long, long time, nearly thirty eight years, in fact. She had restored his faith and kept him strong. Katy had pulled him out of his long melancholy and certainly out of his comfort zone. Katy had become the mother of the children that he never thought he would have.

Perry moved a little and, with tear-filled eyes, looked down at her beautiful, softly wrinkled face and quietly said, "Katy, you know I'm sad Mother has gone, but she and Father had a wonderful life together, and they were happy. But sweetheart, I have just realised that it was not her I have been relying on for the past three-plus decades; it's you. Well, you and God. Yes, I know I'm a little slow sometimes, but…." He released her so he could give her a long and loving kiss. Cupping her adored face, he said, "My beloved sweetheart, you may well have been a lady in irons long ago, but to me, you are my strength, my Iron Lady."

Katy slid her arms around his neck and drew his teary face down for a loving kiss. "Perry, my wonderful husband, your love was all I ever wanted."

If you want to find out more about Ned Grace
and why he was in the colony under an assumed name-
Read "The Lockelys of Parramatta"

Characters

Earl **Phillip Harrington** d Feb 1808 - shooting accident Earl of Leatherbrooke
M 1805 Catherine (**Katy**) White b 1770 (convicted as Kate Harrison 1813-1821)
    #1 boy still born b 1806
    #2 Mary (**Mia**) Phillipa b April 1808 at Harrington Hall,
        m **Tim** Styles, many children, Son of Sir Tim & Sophie Broome-Hall
m2 Peregrin (**Perry**) White 1808 -Katy's 3rd cousin (Earl of Collingsford)
    #1 Jeramy (**Jem**) Peregrin b 1809
        m1835 Catherine (**Caty**) Louisa Spencer b 1816 (Mary and Donald's daug)
    #2 Louisa Jane (**Lou**) b 1811 m **Paul** Lockley
    #3 David (**Davy**) Jacob James (**JJ**) b 25 Dec 1813 m Judith
    #4 Colin (**Col**) 24 June 1818 twin
    #5 Joanna (**Jo**) Catherine 24 June 1818 twin (**Twinny**)
Eustace Harrington - Phillip's brother Harrington Hall became Earl.

Percival (**Percy**) **White** - b 1750 cous. to Katy
    14th **Duke of Cheatham** (Perry's father) **Cheatham Castle** d 1835
m Margaret (**Meg**) Hamilton b 1753 d 1845
    #1 Peregrin (**Perry**) b 1772 d 1854 aged 82 (fire 1798) m **Katy** 1808
        (Blackberry House in Aylesford - Between Jimmy and Mary)
    #2 **Jeramy** b 1774 (d Feb 1808 - shooting accident with Phil)
Lady Marianne (**Mari**) Broome-Hall b 1752 nee White d 1898
    daug Duke **Julian of** Cheatham (See 'Dancing to her Own Tune')

George Miles m 1807 Milesdowne Court,
    Next to Princhester Court, Aylesford 6.2 miles from Chatham
M1 1807 - **Mary** Louise Williams (Lady Mary) Daug of Earl Weedhame
    #1 Malcolm (**Colm**) b March 1808
M2 1815 **Donald Spencer**
    #1 Catherine (**Caty**) Louisa b 1816
    m Jeramy (**Jem) White** became 15th Duke of Cheatham

Rev **Justin** Williams, half-brother to Mary. Father was an Earl Weedhame
Hugh Williams - another half-brother b 1810 (minister for Ned 1840s)
Nanny Grimes (Nanny Rhymes - as Ned called her)
Terrence Buckridge - Jem's tutor (**Buck**) (father Daniel- Estate Manager)
M 1816 Maid **Lucy** - no surname
    #1 **Lindsay** b June 1817
    #2 Judith (**Judy**) Catherine b Sept 1820
    #3 Archibald (**Archie**) Peregrin b Dec 1822
Janey Brien - b 1769 nice convict lady at gaol. later housemaid for Perry and Katy & their 3rd cousin Governess. (illig. daug of Duke Julian)
Abel Jones - convict stable hand and coachman (honey gold hair - grey eyes)
Betty Corby- Cook for Whites in Parramatta
Beatrice and **Clare** Livingstone -new maids
James Albert Innkeeper, Freemasons Inn (Mason's Inn),
and finally, the Woolpack Inn. It is still in existence.
    m2 - **Maybel** - died Jan 1814
    m3 **Winifred** Coates - convict and 3rd wife
(see Once a Jolly Swagman- Lockleys of Parramatta series)
Sir **Phillip** Princhester b 1770 d 1808 - carriage accident
M **Jane** Buckingham)
    John (Jack) b 1798 d 7 April 1880
    m 1842 **Elouise** Lockley, née Wickham
Unlikely Convict Ladies series:-
Bk #1 Sam and Annie's story (see Dancing to her Own Tune)

Bk #2 Robbie and Amelia's story - (see Amelia's Tears)
Lockleys of Parramatta Series:-
Bks #1-4 Charles & Sal Lockley:
6 children; **Charlie; Eddie,** Liza, Anna, Wills & Luke

Duke, **Charles** Lockley, 8th Duke of Gracemere
M Susanna (**Suze**) Bland, Dowager Duchess d Nov 1856 - Gracemere House,
London, Gracemere Castle in Kent
    1 **David** m 1820 **Elouise** Wickham
    2 **Major Edward 'Ned' Grace** b 16.10.1798 - Parramatta
    Edward John Charles Lockley of Gracemere) at Maidstone 48th Batt.
    M Dec 25 1841 **Christina 'Tina'** Meadows, née Hunt b 25.12.1808
    (daughter of Edmund & Catherine Earl of Riverdell at Tunbridge Wells
            Twins, 1Charles (Chip) & 2 Sarah; 3 William (Liam)
    3 **Paul** b 1900 m **Louisa White** - 3 boys
    4 **Charles** (twin- died at birth) b 1900
    5 **Douglas** m unnamed lady (daug of snr partner in law firm), 3 boys
    6 still born daughter

Real People
Lachlan, Elizabeth (Elspeth) and Lachlan (Lachie) Jnr Macquarie
(Italics are extracts from his own personal diaries)
John Thomas Campbell - Lachlan's Secretary & Elspeth's cousin
John Watts - Adie
Hector Macquarie - Aide and Lachlan's nephew.
James Larra, owner of the Freemason's Inn, later Woolpack Inn
Richard Fitzgerald - in charge of Emu Plains Prison Farm
Rev Samuel Marsden
Simeon Lord - Emancipist & Magistrate
Andrew Thompson - Emancipist & Magistrate d 1810
Francis Greenway, Henry Kitchen & John Watts Architects who arrived on
convict ship General Hewitt
Joseph Lycett (Artist)a forger who arrived on convict ship General Hewitt
John Bigge & his report
Major General Sir Thomas Brisbane
Sir Ralph and Eliza Darling
Ann Dumaresq (Eliza Darling's mother)
Elizabeth (Betsy) Fry nee **Gurney,** (husband also **Joseph Fry**)
Joseph Gurney, Betsy's brother,
Sir Robert Peel & others incl Lord Castlereagh
Queen Victoria & Prince Albert

Bibliography

James Larra
owned the Mason's Inn, later Freemasons Inn and finally, the Freemason's Inn, which is still in existence as the Woolpack Inn.

Francis Greenway
arrived onto *General Hewitt* in Feb 1814 - the same ship I have Perry coming on. Two other architects were also on that ship, Henry Kitchen, a convict and John Watts, a soldier. The Artist Joseph Lycett was also convicted of forgery and was also n that ship. Francis Greenway did not build the 3 cottages in Phillip Street (they were built later), nor the house I have used for Glenmere (a fictitious house). He was a convict, sent out for forgery, and later became the most amazing architect. Francis and artist Joseph Lycett both arrived in 1814 on the *General Hewitt* as convicts. Both were sentenced to fourteen years for forgery. Francis was an architect. Lachlan Macquarie discovered both their skills and put them to work, utilising their talents.

The Benevolent Society
https://en.wikipedia.org/wiki/Benevolent_Society

Edward Smith Hall Benevolent Society
https://en.wikipedia.org/wiki/Edward_Smith_Hall

Female Factory Parramatta - Feb 1821- 1840s
https://en.wikipedia.org/wiki/Parramatta_Female_Factory#In_popular_culture

Appin Massacre - Lachlan's diary entry
https://australian.museum/learn/first-nations/unsettled/fighting-wars/appin-massacre/?gclid=Cj0KCQiA5OuNBhCRARIsACgaiqVuAgk_Sa6qXUzi0b3Jo4A63D2hffw6xNWHNatk8n_ov1rf35PD7A8aAtUBEALw_wcB

Elizabeth's carriage accident
https://michellescotttucker.com/2016/08/20/mrs-macquarie-and-the-tragic-accident/

Blue Mountains Trip 1815
Original held in the Mitchell Library, Sydney. [ML Ref: A779]
https://www.smh.com.au/entertainment/lachlan-macquarie-the-father-of-australia-20140905-10cvez.html - extract

Convict Activities
https://www.freesettlerorfelon.com/commissioners_of_enquiry.htm#26

Lachlan Macquarie
https://adb.anu.edu.au/biography/macquarie-lachlan-2419
https://michellescotttucker.com/2016/03/18/the-journals-of-lachlan-and-elizabeth-macquarie/

Macquarie's final address
https://www.mq.edu.au/macquarie-archive/lema/1821/1821farewell.html

Departure of the Macquarie's - diary extracts
https://www.mq.edu.au/macquarie-archive/lema/1822/1822jan.html

Pets for little Lachlan
https://www.mq.edu.au/macquarie-archive/lema/1820/1820oct.html

Andrew Thompson
https://adb.anu.edu.au/biography/thompson-andrew-2728

Elizabeth Fry
https://www.britannica.com/biography/Elizabeth-Fry

Notes

Main Buildings built in Lachlan Macquarie's time

NSW Parliament House, Macquarie Street, Sydney (1814)

The Mint Museum, Macquarie Street, Sydney (1814)

Cadmans Cottage, George Street, Sydney (1816; Francis Greenway?)

Kirkham Stables, Kirkham Lane, Narellan (1816)

Rouse Hill House, Windsor Rd, Rouse Hill (1818)

Former Female Orphans School, Rydalmere Ho
spital, Rydalmere (1818)

Hyde Park Barracks, Macquarie St, Sydney (1819; Francis Greenway)

NSW Supreme Court Building, Elizabeth Street, Sydney (1819; Francis Greenway)

Juniper Hall, 250 Oxford Street, Paddington (1820 - 22)

St James Church, 179 King Street, Sydney (1822; Francis Greenway)

Windsor Courthouse, Court Street, Windsor (1822; Francis Greenway)

Summary of Other Buildings and Structures in the Sydney Region from the Macquarie Era

1816-46 - Windmill Hill House Ruin, Wilton Road Appin. 1812 - Northampton Dale, Brooks Point Road, Appin

1818 - Bonnyrigg Homestead, Brown Road, Bonnyrigg Built as the male schoolmaster's residence for the Female Orphan School. A rare surviving example of Colonial Georgian architecture Remnants of the Female Orphan School date from 1806 include fruit trees and a grape vine.

1816 - Warbys Barn and Stables, 14 - 20 Queen Street, Campbelltown

1811 - Hadley Park, RMB 113 Castlereagh Road, Castlereagh

1810-17 - Glenfield farm house, Leacocks Lane, Casula

1821 - Clarendon Servants Quarters, 96 Dight Street, Clarendon

1812, 1825(?) - The Round House, Cobbitty

1819 - Brush Farm, Marsden Road, Eastwood

1811 - Rose Cottage, Australiana Village, Ebeneezer

1812(?) - Myrtle Bank, 1 Tizanna Road, Ebeneezer

1817 - Ebeneezer Uniting Church Schoolhouse, Ebeneezer

1817 - The Schoolmasters Residence, Corromandel Road, Ebeneezer

1815 - Galvins Cottage, Macarthur Road, Elderslie

1820 - Rose Farm House, 17 - 19 Honour Street, Ermington

1820 - Eschol Park House, Eschol Park Road, Eschol Park

1818 - Horsley Park, The Horsley Drive

1820, 1825-26 - Denham Court & Chapel, Campbelltown Road, Ingleburn

1812 - Portland Head Farm, off Portland Head Road, Koromandel

1810 - Collingwood, 12 Birkdale Crescent, Liverpool

1818-20 - Anglican Church of St Luke, Liverpool

1819 - Clydesdale, Richmond Road, Marsden Park

1819 - Belgenny, Elizabeth Macarthur Avenue, Camden

1811-20 - Coxs Cottage, St. Thomas Road, Mulgoa
1816 - Kirkham Stables, Kirkham Lane, Narellan
1818 - Harrington Park, 499 Camden Valley Way, Narellan
1814, 1820s - Clare House, 4 Clare Street, Oakville
1810, 1825 - Exeter Farm, Meurants Lane, Parklea
1821 - Brislington, Cnr George & Mardsden Sts, Parramatta
1813-18 - Female Orphan School, James Ruse Drive, Parramatta
1810s - St Patricks Cemetery, Cnr Church St & Pennant Hills Rd, Parramatta
1817(?) - Old Manse Farm, Punt Road, Pitt Town
1813, 1816 - Mulgrave Place, 104-106 Bathurst Street, Pitt Town
1806 - Mountain View, Inalls Lane, Richmond
1815-17 - Bowman Cottage, Richmond
1807 onwards - Cumberland Place Steps, Cumberland Street, The Rocks
1813-18 - Rouse Hill House, Windsor Road, Rouse Hill
1815 - National Trust Centre, Observatory Hill Sydney
1820 - Stoneleigh, Cnr Castle Hill Road and Pennant Hills Road, West Pennant Hills
1810s - Rose Cottage, Buttsworth Lane, Wilberforce
An excellent example of a Macquarie era farmhouse
1814 - Macquarie School, Macquarie Street, Wilberforce
1814-16 - Toll House, Bridge Street, Windsor
1815 - Macquarie Arms Hotel, Thompson Square, Windsor
1817 - St Matthews Anglican Church, Greenway Crescent, Windsor
1820-22 - Hawkesbury District Hospital, 95 Macquarie Street, Windsor
1820-21 - Court House, Court Street, Windsor

FROM
http://www.visitsydneyaustralia.com.au/history-7-macquarie.html

If you loved this book, these are similar.
(All Stand-alone stories)

A First Fleet Convict Story 1788
A First Fleet story with the descriptions taken directly from the Journal of Doctor Author Bowes Smith who was the doctor on board the Lady Penrhyn.

Gentle Annie Soames
Her dreams lead to unexpected outcomes. An Australian First Fleet story.

Annie Soames is a girl beloved by the community but not afraid to voice her desires. That leads to trouble, illicit love, and a world turned upside down.

Oliver Quilpie, the recently married Marquess, discovers his arranged union is not to his taste; he is drawn to his wife's companion. Unfortunately, he is unable to keep his hands off her. For revenge, Annie mimics his every move while riding but is dressed as a highwayman. However, she had now fallen in love with him. This action finally leads to her arrest and transportation to a faraway land.

After some years, Oliver's wife dies, and his thoughts turn to Annie. He seeks to find her, but she has vanished. He is horrified to discover she was transported to New South Wales as a convict on the *Lady Penrhyn*. He follows with a shipload of supplies on the *Kitty*. Will Annie want to see him?

ISBN 9780645441574   ISBN ebook 9781923097063
July 2024

The Hunter to Macquarie Collection 1795-1822

When Upon Life's Billows
Sydney 1795-1821 - Governor John Hunter

Captain John Hunter was born to a life at sea. The wind blows where no man knows, and John is caught up in the tempest. Although wrecking his ship, the *HMS Sirius*, in 1790, he became the second Governor of the rough and filthy penal settlement of New South Wales. He always seems to be in the wrong place at the wrong time, trusting the wrong people.

Helena Rosedale is not a typical female convict. She fights tooth and nail to stop the men from abusing her. She gains the name of Helena the Hellcat.

Crispin Milroy is alone in the world and one of the new Governor's security detail. Can he win the fair lady's heart? Life in 1795 in Sydney Cove is raw at best. Food is scarce, and disease often ravages the settlement. Life throws everything except death at these three, yet somehow, they survive. Why does John trust this young couple when others betray him?

What trials must Helena and Crispin endure to make their new lives in this raw town bearable? How can John ease their path?

ISBN: 9780645783339   ebook ISBN: 9780645783346
Coming 2025

Saddler's Song
London 1790s to Parramatta 1840s

George Ellis is a tanner's son living on the outskirts of London. When disease takes his family. Alone and hurting, he seeks to find a new life for himself. Hearing from a friend about the possibility of setting up a business in New South Wales, he sells up and leaves all he knows. His beloved violin is his most valuable item, and his talent for making beautiful music is hidden from all but a few.

Ben Parker is a saddler, like George; he is also alone in the world. Ben also sells up to move to the new colony. The two young men meet and combine their skills to start afresh in a new world. During the journey out, George's skill as a violinist is revealed. On arrival, they find accommodation with a family with many lovely daughters. Two of these girls steal their hearts, but how will the business survive in an animal-starved land where access to leather is limited? What is the saddler's song?

ISBN : 9780645783353   eISBN: 9780645783360
Coming 2025

Tuppence to Pass
London 1800s to Parramatta 1820s - Governor Lachlan Macquarie

Josh Callan is a London lad who makes the best of the life that has been dealt to him. Stealing from the man who killed his father gives the family a change of direction. Josh is arrested, but the judge belittles him, saying he's not worth tuppence. He is transported to the penal colony of Sydney as a convict just as **Governor Macquarie's** term starts. He proves his worth and falls on his feet, becoming the Governor's groom and confidante.

Life in the Colonial town opens opportunities they could never have dreamed about in England, but can Josh find his niche?

Where will this strange friendship take Josh and his family?

ISBN : 9781923097070   eISBN: 9781923097087
Coming 2025

His Majesty's Pageboy
London to Emu Plains, Australia, in the 1800s

Jack Turner was born into a life of pomp and privilege that was not rightfully his. He was brought to the royal court for his own protection. By the age of ten, he was King George the Third's pageboy and known as Lord John. For years, Jack roils against the immorality of society and the shallowness of people; then, he meets an unspoiled young girl amongst the mire of humanity whose purity stands out. He is unable to pursue her before his life hits a wall.

Martha Alexander is the daughter of a wealthy shipping merchant. She has been presented to London's second tier of society, where she meets the young man of her dreams. She is expected to marry well, and Lord John sets her heart fluttering. However, her father's drinking shatters her future. He was made to sign all his possessions away while drunk, unknowingly including his daughter. Refusing a forced marriage changes her life. How do these two end up as convicts in Australia?

Paperback ISBN 9781923097308   eISBN 978192309792

Coming 2026

Far From the Whispering Sheoaks
Set in Australia in the 1820s

Fanny Little was in the wrong place doing something she thought was legal. Her actions see her arrested, tried and banished. She is assigned from the female prison to ex-soldier Gordon McKenzie and soon finds herself in a despicable and humiliating situation of being sold in the public marketplace.

Phil Bentley is a man running from his jealous uncle, and he finds solace in a secluded farm half a world away. With the community on their side, can Phil save Fanny from Gordon's vile abuse? Why is their relationship destined to court controversy? And who is Jas? Why does Gordon wish to harm the child? Will they ever escape the shadows that are chasing them?

Paperback ISBN 9781923097315   eISBN9781923097322

Coming 2026

Bound Down in Iron Chains
Set in Australia in the 1820s

Howard Marlow was a studious and honest London bookkeeper. He is asked to help a friend's brother, who he finds himself arrested, convicted and transported. Who are the men involved in the Cato Conspiracy? How does he become involved with some of the worst criminals in the penal colony of New South Wales?

Naomi Buckingham is a convict maid assigned to a man who has no respect for women. Rather than used as a cleaner as she expects, her duties include warming his bed. She wants to escape his oppressive household but has no one to turn to but his new accountant. Can she trust him? Howard is assigned to a retired soldier and gets tricked into using his skills to keep a double set of books and therefore, avoid paying the extra taxes on his boss's illicit rum profits. Being new to the colony, he doesn't know who he can trust.

Naomi turns to him after she overhears a violent altercation between them. Can he use his brains to save them both?

Coming 2026

Unlikely Convict Ladies Trilogy 1792-1840s
Dancing to her Own Tune
Co-authored by Sheila Hunter and Sara Powter
Sydney 1790s to England 1830s

Annie White is released after serving seven years as a convict in Sydney. She gets a visitor who, with his help, she can start a baking business. She is then asked to assist another sick man, **Sam** Corbett. Annie nurses him back to health, and a relationship develops. They settle into a life together, barely making ends meet; she realises she's expecting a child. Sam has his past laid bare and must adjust to the revelations. They both must face their accusers and find that the answers to their questions are not what they thought. Their life experiences seem to cling to them, and unable to shake them off, they end up back in England. They must face their ghosts and discover they are not who they think they are. How can they turn their anger and spite into love and forgiveness? The Dance of Life goes on.

ISBN 9780645110715   ISBN9780645110722

Long-listed in the Historical Fiction Company Competition 2022

Amelia's Tears
Parramatta 1828 – England 1840s

Amelia Westaweller awaits her assignment in the Parramatta Female Prison. Forced to leave the relative safety of gaol, she is assigned and now faces her worst nightmare. A foul man claims her and makes her life a living hell. Then, her world goes black. A glimmer of hope arises when she hears from her brother, Jim, who has enlisted a friend to help her. She writes to Jim, pouring out her heart and telling him of the horrors of her new life. He encourages her to stay firm in her faith. All she can do is pray. When Major **Ned** Grace, her brother's friend, enters her life in Parramatta, he starts to ease her path. Things have changed, as now she has a child in tow. How can Amelia forge a new life for herself? What man could want her with her background and a child at her side? Who is the gentleman who turns her tears of sadness into tears of great joy?

ISBN: 9780645110739   eISBN: 978-0-6451107-4-6 Hard Cover ISBN 979-842061-7953
https://amazon.com/dp/0645110736   https://amazon.com/dp/B09SS855BR

A Lady in Irons
England 1800s - Parramatta 1808+

Katy Harrington is mourning the death of her husband after he died in a shooting accident. Barely coping, she awaits the birth of their child. If it's a girl, she must hand the family home to her husband's brother. The day after giving birth to a daughter, she and her daughter are left on the side of a road. She collapses and is found by someone she thought had died in a fire ten years before. **Perry White**, badly scarred himself, nurses her back to health. They marry and move in with her widowed friend, Mary.

After some years, she discovers her husband and friend in each other's arms. Now living in a love triangle, she flees. Grasping the only straw available, she intentionally gets arrested and is sent to a colony far away. By doing this, her marriage can be annulled.

What happens in the Colony is different from what she expects. Governor Macquarie comes to her rescue, but what of Perry and her children?

ISBN: 9780645110784   eISBN:9780645441505
https://amazon.com/dp/0645110787   https://amazon.com/dp/B0BCWSXB9Z

The Convict Birthstain Collection 1830-1840s

NO MORE, MY *Love*
Hunter Valley, NSW 1820s

Jess Elkin is distraught when tragedy ravages her family. She becomes the victim of a carriage accident and is nursed back to health by the driver, **Marcus Ryan**. Marcus was not expecting to fall in love. Yet, when Jess's fortunes suddenly turn for the worse, Marcus must decide how far he will go to pursue her. As time passes in Newcastle, Australia, Marcus must take a business trip and is taken by pirates. Jess is left wondering if he will keep his promise to return to her... Will she ever see him alive again?

ISBN: 9780645441536   eISBN 9780645441581
Long-listed in the Historical Fiction Company Competition 2023
https://amazon.com/dp/0645441538   https://amazon.com/dp/B0BSBH143Q

The Vine Weaver
Hawkesbury River area 1820s+
New Beginnings and Old Threats

In the 1820s, Australia, **Joel and Hetty Walker** live on a secluded farm on the Hawkesbury River, which becomes a healing haven for the protection of young convict women. A series of events brings **Fran Rea** to Hetty's attention, and she is taken to the farm. Fran and Hetty develop a cottage industry under the compassionate eye of farmhand **Hector Macdougal;** Hector's loving words change lives. It is to him that Fran turns when threatened.

The vines now must draw them close to survive the future revelations, and of those, there are many.

ISBN: 9780645441512   eISBN 9780645441529
Long-listed in the Historical Fiction Company Competition 2023
https://amazon.com/dp/0645441511   https://amazon.com/dp/B0C6Z552Y2
The story continues in Scotch at The Rocks...

Scotch at The Rocks

Glasgow, Scotland, early 1800s to The Rocks, Sydney 1830s

Orphaned children Brodie Stewart and Heather Anderson live on Glasgow's streets. Although hungry, somehow they survive and keep out of trouble. Heather finds a job and looks to be settled; things go pear-shaped for them both. Eventually, they marry by declaration, yet even that gets messed up, and they are both arrested soon after they make their vow. In 1838, they were transported to Sydney as convicts. Heather arrives within weeks of Brodie, and they are assigned close to each other. They are now living on the docklands in Sydney, called The Rocks. They now have to forge a new life halfway across the world from their homeland.

Adventures abound, and Brodie gets press-ganged. While he's away, Heather's life changes and soon, she's officially selling Scotch Whisky at a shop in The Rocks.

You can take a Scot out of Scotland, but where did the Scotch come from?

ISBN 9780645441550 ebook 9781923097001 Large Print 9781923097254

Waiting at the Sliprails

The Bathurst Road 1830s

A Convict's Tale

Bea Dawes's term of conviction nears an end, and she has few options other than marriage to a stranger or going on the street.

Jack Barnes, the hired drover, wants a wife. Bea accepts his offer; then, she discovers that he could be gone for months, leaving her alone with **Billy and Netty**, part of the tribe of an Aboriginal tribe who live on his secluded farm. Bea learns to love her husband and also this wonderful aboriginal couple.

Drought ravages the farm, and Jack must hit the long paddock with the flock. In his absence, a visitor arrives, threatening to destroy everything she has worked so hard for. Can Bea touch her heart? Can she cope? Will the drought ever end? And when will Jack return?

ISBN: 9780645441543   eISBN: 9781923097032

August 2023

Convict Shadows of the Past

Two Jennifers, two hundred years apart

Eight year old, **Jenny** Kellow learns of her convict family history and discovers that she was named after a convict from nearly two hundred years ago. Her grandfather's stories inspire her to dig deeper into her ancestors' convict past. From her grandfather, she hears stories of bushrangers, convicts, and life in the infant colony of Parramatta. She sets about retracing the footsteps of her convict great-great-great-grandmother to honour her. Jenny's search starts with microfiche back in the 60s, and she learns about the small tin mining town in Cornwall and the production of a cheese that sets London afire. She discovers her ancestor, **Jennifer Kellow**, has brought these cheese-making skills to Parramatta, where she taught others her craft. Echoes of the past can still be heard if you know where to listen.

Who was the first Jennifer, and what does she have to do with cheese? Why is she so elusive? Did Jenny's ancestor, Jennifer, ever see those two small crosses carved into the bricks of the Female Factory? Would Jenny ever find out her ancestor's story?

ISBN: 9780645783315   ISBN ebook 9780645783322

A NaNoWriMo 2022 book winner

January 2024

In Defence of Her Honour

London 1800s to Parramatta 1819

Bill Miller had been raised and educated with the sons of the family. The youngest, Bert, had been his best friend. However, jealousy intervenes when Bill's excellent schoolwork curtails their friendship. He wins a scholarship and enters Oxford University. When Bill's father, the old butler, dies unexpectedly, Bert insists that Bill take over the position, but it's more to oppress him. Bert's jealousy grows and festers. Now looking for a way to rid themselves of their new butler, a ruckus ensues, and Bill is arrested for assaulting Bert. The housekeeper and her daughter, **Molly Ross,** vouch for him, but it's too late; Bill has been arrested and sentenced to be transported. With Bill gone, Molly now needs to defend herself from Bert. After hitting him with a pan, she is arrested and sent to Sydney. Bill and Molly arrive with letters of introduction and compensation from Bert's father. Soon, they will be running the best inn in Parramatta with an endorsement from the governor.

ISBN 9780645441567   ISBN ebook 9781923097049

April 2024

I can't stop Tomorrow
Irish Famine 1840s to Avoca Beach, Australia

Escaping bigotry and prejudice in Ireland, the **O'Shane** family lives on a secluded farm on the west coast of Ireland. The potato blight soon decimates their farm. It's always darkest before dawn, and the two remaining girls cling to the hope of a new life. With the kindness of strangers, the eldest girls, **Clare** and **Kerry O'Shane**, head to their cousin, Sal Lockley, in Parramatta, Australia. A new, wonderful life awaits them both. **Shéamus Connor** is the annoying teenage boy who reluctantly draws Clare's affection. However, living in a convict town means ruffians abound.

John Moore is an angry and troubled Irishman, content to live alone on another secluded farm until he discovers Clare and two other lads need rescuing.

Can John protect her from the pain inflicted by an evil world?

Can Shéamus find his lost love who had fled?

ISBN: 9780645441598   ISBN ebook 9781923097056

October 2024

Madeline's Boy
England 1830s to New South Wales 1840

All is not straightforward when money and a title are involved.

Madeline Brougham is asked to care for her best friend's orphaned son when his life is in danger. **Christopher Downes** is the pawn between a greedy, unscrupulous uncle and his inheritance. Maddie must do everything she can to keep him safe, including moving halfway around the globe to take Chip to his guardian, Major Humphrey Downes, in the Australian Corps in Sydney. Humphrey's best friend, another soldier, **Major Tim Hinds**, meets Maddie, and with the support of these two men, a chase around the colony ensues. Will Maddie and Tim be able to find happiness together?

Can the three adults keep Chip safe until he's old enough to claim his inheritance?

ISBN: 9780645783308   ISBN ebook 9781923097094

Dec 2024

Jam or Marmalade for Tea

England 1820s to New South Wales 1825 (Governor Brisbane Era)

Martha Hamilton is the eldest of four orphans struggling to survive on their own. Caught stealing, she is tried, convicted, and transported to New South Wales. With her family gone, she becomes despondent. Life holds no meaning for her, and The ocean waves look inviting.

Captain Guy Manning is a frustrated and injured redcoat soldier returning to Sydney to take up a new assignment. He notices Martha trying to jump overboard and rescues her. How do two cats bring them together?

A convict ship is no place for romance, and she's far too young anyway, isn't she?

Can Guy save her and forge a life together for them? What connections does he have to try and save her siblings? Why is marmalade important for their future?

Paperback ISBN 9781923097933   eISBN9781923097285

A NaNoWriMo 2023 book winner

October 2025

A 100-year, six-part Australian Colonial series

The Lockleys of Parramatta 1800-1900

Hands upon the Anvil

A blacksmith's life and love are more than work

Parramatta 1830s

Eddie Lockley's parents were transported for their crimes. Can a steadfast lad rise above his origins and guide others to succeed in a land of opportunity?
Ten-year-old Eddie longs to help his mum and dad. Living in a convict town with his family, the keen youngster has been working with the local blacksmith since his sixth birthday. But when a lieutenant doesn't stop abusing his older brother, the young boy yearns for the day when he can stand up and end the torment. Though he's thrilled when his mentor offers to send him off to learn his letters, Eddie fears he won't be around to watch his sibling's back. But as he takes on the biggest adventure of his life, the brave believer soon discovers God is looking out for everyone he loves. Does this young man in the making have what it takes to change everything for the better?
ISBN 9780994578235 Ebook ISBN 978-0-9945782-5-9 Hardcover 9798496177368
Released 2021
https://amazon.com/dp/0994578237 https://amazon.com/dp/B08TB51L19

Out Where The Brolgas Dance

Gold is found, and so is love

Parramatta 1840s

How can a question change so many people?

It's the 1840s, and discoveries across the Blue Mountains continue. Major Mitchell's new road is complete, and towns are planned and being built. Abundant land is available for those who want it.
William "Wills" Lockley, 18, has laid a solid foundation for a respectable career as a blacksmith, but the Lockley lust for adventure flows deeply within his veins. He dreads the monotony of work at the blacksmith's forge and yearns for adventure in a new frontier. Wills meets six Englishmen (*Coping with what is now known as PTSD*) who have the means to make his dreams come true. What they discover changes the Colony and their lives forever. Gold fever ensues. In the West, Wills has to deal with an uncertain romance. Does she even want him?
ISBN 9780994578242 Ebook ISBN 978-0-9945782-6-6 Hardcover ISBN 9798755445504
LP ISBN 9781923097155
Released 2021
https://amazon.com/dp/0994578245   https://amazon.com/dp/B08T6NS3XX

Diamonds in the Dirt

Diamonds, love and money… but there is much more to life.

Parramatta 1850s

Luke Lockley, the youngest Lockley son, has completed University, and his life has no direction. No job, no money, and no love. Desperately alone, he prays for guidance. How can Luke trust that God has a plan for him if he can't even find a job? He does the only thing he can … he prays. Within a week, life has changed … oh, how it has changed as his brother Wills turns up with a suggestion. Would Luke be interested in joining the expedition with John Evans? **Reverend William Clarke** needs assistance on a Government Mineral Survey. The challenge, adventure and finds are life-changing for many. However, it gives Luke meaning, purpose and direction. The condition of his heart problems also takes a turn. Can he walk away?
ISBN:9780994578273 Ebook ISBN: 978-0-9945782-8-0 Hard cover ISBN 979-8788011141
Released 2022
https://amazon.com/dp/099457827X   https://amazon.com/dp/B09NH1MLXZ

The Earl's Shadow

Who or what is the 'shadow'? How does it affect so many?

Parramatta 1860s

Charles Lockley is the Earl of Coxheath. He spent his youth as a convict in Parramatta and had no idea he was an Earl. He had minimal education and few social skills. His eldest son, **Charlie,** is no different.

Now faced with his own mortality, Charles has to work out how to live the remainder of his life after a near-death experience. He is called to step way out of his comfort zone in London. His action will change the world for many. The echoes from the past still haunt Charlie. London is calling the family, and they can't postpone the trip. How does the Cobb and Co. coach driver **Jim Leslie** fit in? And precisely what is *'The Earl's Shadow'* that he speaks about? What happens if the 'Shadow' is gone?

ISBN: 9780645110708 Ebook ISBN 978-0-9945782-9-7

Released June 2022

https://amazon.com/dp/0645110701   https://amazon.com/dp/B0B158SKSK

Once a Jolly Swagman

An old black Billy Can contain the secrets of an incredible life

An Australian Historical Novel

Set in 1870s Parramatta and Kent, UK

Rick Lockley, battling his family's expectations, runs away to find himself. **Jack**, a jolly swagman, takes him under his care. Even after years together, Rick knows little about the old man.

On his death, Jack leaves Rick his precious billy can; the contents reveal Jack's identity. Stunned, Rick must travel to England to finalise Jack's wishes. There, he uncovers Jack's life of love, betrayal and a link to his own family. Rick also discovers there is much more to learn about this enigmatic man.

ISBN 9780645110753   Ebook ISBN 978-0-6451107-6-0

Released Sept 2022

https://amazon.com/dp/0645110752   https://amazon.com/dp/B0B5JN1WCV

Jonty's Journey

Gems, Love, Artists and a Golden Lion

Australia and South Africa 1880-1902

Sydney Jeweller Jonty Evans' passion for gems takes him to Africa at a volatile time. He finds the diamonds he wants and is given a lion cub. Jonty is all but kidnapped. His experiences in the Transvaal plunge him into questioning everything he knows of life. Soon, nightmares haunt him. (Now known as PTSD.)

On return home, he nearly messes up his love life with **Lottie** before it even starts, and he struggles to settle. Lottie's father, **Luke** Lockley from Parramatta, takes him in hand and points him to someone who can help.

Jonty is then recalled to Africa as a liaison and reconnects with his lion, Chimbu, when he saves the life of his security detail. His life journey introduces him to the most amazing Heidelberg artists, politicians, poets, rebels, and the scapegoat soldier Harry Breaker Morant. Can Jonty bury the past and regain the peace he's lost?

ISBN 9780645110777 HC ISBN 9781923097124   Ebook ISBN: 978-0-6451107-9-1

Released Feb 2023

https://amazon.com/dp/0645110779   https://amazon.com/dp/B0BLJ7ND1Q

Australian Colonial Trilogy 1840s
By Sheila Hunter
Co-Winner of 1999 NSW Senior Citizen of the Year, In the Year of the Senior Citizen

Mattie
Coming of Age in Convict Australia

Twelve-year-old London street urchin **Mattie Paul** is convicted of petty theft and sentenced to seven years of transportation to the penal colony of Port Jackson, NSW. Peg, another female convict, takes Mattie under her wing and gives her a chance to make something of her life by teaching her to read. Mattie seizes every opportunity that comes her way. Though life is not particularly kind to her, she battles through earning her freedom, marrying and becoming a mother in her homeland. On this journey, she encounters bushrangers, is widowed, and becomes an entrepreneur in the Bathurst goldfields. She mixes with escaped convicts, but her spirit is indomitable, and she becomes a pillar and much-loved treasure of her adopted community. Mattie may be a fictional character, but her experiences are only too real and invest us in immersing ourselves in the lives of those remarkable women who helped to make Australia what it is today. *(Mattie's story continues in The Lockleys of Parramatta - bk 2+)*
ISBN 9781503252370 & ebook AISN BOOTTEDBTO
(The story continues in The Earl's Shadow & Once a Jolly Swagman)
Released 2015
https://amazon.com/dp/150325237X   https://amazon.com/dp/B00TTEDBT0

Ricky
A boy in Colonial Australia

Ricky English and his mother immigrated from England to join his father in the new Colony of Sydney. Upon arrival, there was no sign of his father. Ricky's mum uses the tiny amount of money they brought to get lodgings in a run-down building. Things go from bad to worse when his mother dies; he is thrown out of the rooms, and the caretakers confiscate all their possessions.
Ricky lives on the streets of Sydney Town as a street waif. Ricky finds safe places to sleep and befriends freed convicts who can help him survive. One day, he encounters a lost child and helps reunite her with her family. These people try to help him, but he insists on doing things his way because of his stubbornness. However, he has found a mentor and confidante. The story follows him through his life. He survives and turns his life around, helping others along the way. **(The Story continues in Jonty's Journey)**
Paperback ISBN 9780994578211   Kindle ASIN: B00MLYN6IG
Released 2014
https://amazon.com/dp/1500770574   https://amazon.com/dp/B00MLYN6IG

The Heather to The Hawkesbury
Four Scottish families brave a new life in a strange land.

Mary Macdonald and husband **Murd** and family; her brother **Fergus** MacKenzie; sister-in-law **Caro** MacLeod; cousin **Alex** Fraser and all their families who have had to emigrate from the Isle of Skye during the "Clearances."
The story follows the four families from Scotland on the ship out to the NSW colony in the 1850s. Mary does not cope with the changes and losses that occur in the first months in the colony. The other women in the family rely on her, and she nearly crumbles. The families struggle together through accidents, losses, trials, floods, and hard work and forge a strong bond with their new country. Trials, tribulations and triumphs see the four families make a firm mark in their new homeland. The immigrants from Scotland helped make Australia what it is today.
ISBN 978994578228   ebook AISN B01A21JYWQ   Large Print ISBN1533473641
Available on Amazon/Kindle & Large Print
Released 2016
https://amazon.com/dp/1503251438   https://amazon.com/dp/B01A21JYWQ

Sara's Author Bio

Sheila Hunter and Sara Powter were a passionate mother-and-daughter team of amateur genealogists. While working together on their family tree, Sheila and Sara made many captivating discoveries. The greatest of these was finding four convicts, and these four had very different perspectives. They were sent to Australia from 1792 to 1814 during the height of Convict transportation. Before her *passing* in 2002, Sheila adapted some of these histories into enchanting stories, her Australian Colonial Trilogy. Sara later had these published. A fourth she left unfinished, and this inspired her to finish it. However, before she did, **The Lockleys of Parramatta** were created. The first two in the series were completed before she completed '**Dancing to Her Own Tune**' for her mother. (*Sheila wrote the first 30k words*)

Vividly living through the Colonial Era, these books delve further into the theme of overcoming adversity in Colonial Australia and how it developed, the demise of the Convict system and the discovery of mineral wealth.

Sara intricately weaves accurate archival data and a charming narrative to create a series of tales of faith, love, loss, and redemption.

And so, two hundred years after her family arrived in Australia, Sara continues the Australian Colonial stories started in **Lockleys of Parramatta,** followed by the **Unlikely Convict Ladies** Trilogy. **The Hunter to Macquarie Collection** and **The Convict Birthstain Collection** are all stand-alone novels. More Historical Fiction books are to follow… as they are already in the editors' queue.

See Sara's web page to keep up to date with more stories.
With an online store available for a signed copy of Sara's books.
www.sarapowter.com.au   (*Australian Postage only*)

Amazon Aus QR

Feel free to email me at
saragpowter@gmail.com
(*Australian Postage only*)

Feel free to email me at
saragpowter@gmail.com

BOOK BUB https://partners.bookbub.com/authors/6273615/edit

FACEBOOK https://www.facebook.com/profile.php?id=100063887262514

FREE Newsletter signup
https://preview.mailerlite.io/preview/41388/
sites/77987646202184961/wCAAcK

www.ingramcontent.com/pod-product-compliance
Lightning Source LLC
Chambersburg PA
CBHW031028260626
47153CB00016B/697